SNAKES AND LADDERS

A LIZZY BALLARD THRILLER

MATTY DALRYMPLE

WILLIAM KINGSFIELD PUBLISHERS

With love to my rock star, Wade Walton,
and with gratitude to my fellow authors at Table 25 for your
support and friendship.

Lizzy Ballard struggled to move. Forward or backward —it didn't matter which, as long as she could unwedge her body from the tiny space. The edge of the metal window frame, where it had caught on the back of her pants, kept her from slipping back into the basement room. The concrete wall outside, which had already scraped the skin from her bare shoulders, kept her from pulling herself up and into the freedom of the wide-open outdoors that beckoned only a few feet away. She could hear the rasp of breath in her throat and the pounding of blood in her ears. She could sense panic pushing its way to the surface, like the rattle of china in a cupboard as the first tremors of an earthquake strike.

She had to calm herself, had to breathe. *Breathe out the bad energy, breathe in the good.* She stifled the incipient bubble of a hysterical giggle.

She inhaled, bracing herself for the pain of her spine pressing against the unyielding metal window frame, then tried to relax into the exhale, which provided a moment of relief. If she could push every atom of air from her lungs, would it give her the room she needed to push herself free? Or would she merely wedge herself more inextricably, squeezed so tight that her lungs could no longer draw in air? Would she suffocate with the cool, sweet air of the Pennsylvania night right above her?

She drew in as deep a breath as she could manage, hoping to store up oxygen for the exhale to follow, but the breath caught in her throat. Because being trapped in this metal and concrete box was evidently not her biggest problem. Because she could smell smoke.

The house was on fire.

Two Months Earlier

Lizzy lay on her yoga mat, arms outstretched, palms up. The lights of the studio were dimmed for the closing exercise, the thrum of New Age music almost drowning out the hum of passing cars.

"Breathe out the bad energy ... breathe in the good," intoned the instructor, Donna. "Focus on and control your breath."

Control—that was why Lizzy was here. Because with control came the possibility of a normal life. A life filled with all the things that any other seventeen-year-old would take for granted, not the isolation and guilt she knew.

She had almost lulled herself into that contemplative state where control seemed within reach when a loud bang from outside shattered her peace. She flinched, her arm knocking over the water bottle sitting on the mat beside her. A dribble of water began to form a small pool on the blond wood floor of the studio.

She righted the bottle and snatched up her sweatshirt,

which she had removed when the effort of the poses had warmed her up, and mopped at the spill. Others in the class cracked their eyes open to see what the commotion was.

Donna knelt beside her. "Don't get your sweatshirt wet," she said softly as she wiped up the small puddle with a towel.

"Sorry about that," Lizzy whispered.

"No problem. Just try to get back into the exercise. Try to relax." She bent toward Lizzy and said, too low for the other students to hear, "It was just a car backfiring."

Lizzy nodded, feeling simultaneously foolish and grateful. She lay back on her mat and resumed her breathing. Breathing out the bad energy. Breathing in the good energy. It had to work one of these times.

A normal life was all she wanted. But what stood between her and a normal life were Louise Mortensen and her enforcer, George Millard. Louise and George were the reasons Lizzy and her godfather, Owen McNally, were hiding out in Arizona. The death of Louise's husband, Gerard Bonnay, was the reason Louise and George were on their trail.

At the end of the class, Lizzy hurried to roll up her mat and pull on her shoes, but Donna managed to catch her at the door.

"Are you okay, Elizabeth? That's the second time I've seen you jump like that at a loud noise."

Lizzy nodded. "Sure. Just got startled."

"How one reacts on the mat is how one reacts in life," said Donna. "Is it something you'd like to talk about?"

"No, thanks. Really nothing to talk about."

The last student stepped out the door, and they were alone. Donna sat down on the bench under which the students stored their shoes during class and, with a gesture of her hand, invited Lizzy to sit down next to her.

Lizzy sat.

Donna smoothed the silky harem pants that were part of her usual class garb. "Do you feel like you're getting what you want out of the classes?" she asked.

"Yes. I really enjoy them."

Donna waited a beat, then asked, "And what is it that you're hoping to get out of them?"

"More control over my life."

Donna nodded and folded her hands. She was quiet for a moment, then said, "Yoga isn't really about control."

"But what about controlling the breathing? Isn't that supposed to help us control other things in our lives as well?"

"Yoga is less about control and more about being able to weather difficulty. We meditate to navigate the suffering that is an inevitable part of our lives. Concentrating on our breathing helps us with that meditation."

A tiny tinge of anger crept into Lizzy's voice. "If I could have more control, I'd have less difficulty to weather. And there wouldn't be so much suffering, in my life or anyone else's."

Donna smiled kindly at her. "That's a big responsibility for one young woman to take on."

"Yeah. Well." Lizzy fiddled with the strap of her rolled yoga mat. "I don't mean to be disrespectful, but if that's all yoga is— just recognizing that our lives are going to suck and we need to deal with it—it's a little ... disappointing."

Donna nodded. "That's not all there is to yoga. It's also about being aware of what triggers us and causes us to suffer so we can heal, make different decisions, and move forward. We learn about ourselves during meditation so we can apply those learnings to other parts of our lives."

"Yes, that's exactly what I'm looking for," said Lizzy, her voice now animated. "Understanding what my triggers are, and then finding ways to control—. Okay, maybe not control, but to deal with them. To make the outcome different."

Donna put her hand on Lizzy's arm. "Maybe to find a place where the intrusions of the outside world—like a car back-firing—don't seem like more than they are."

"Yeah. Maybe." Lizzy stood and slung the strap of the mat across her shoulder. "Sorry again about the water."

"No need to apologize. See you on Monday?"

"Yup, I'll be here."

"I'm glad. I think the practice will bring you benefits that you can't necessarily foresee now."

Lizzy nodded to Donna, then stepped out of the studio into the stunning Sedona afternoon, the January sky an electric blue over the red rock buttes that surrounded the town. She unlocked her bike from the rack and turned it toward the house where she and Uncle Owen were staying.

She could never tell Donna that in the moment they rang out, those sounds weren't backfires, but pistol shots. And that the long-sleeved, back-covering tops she wore to class were to hide the scars those shots had left behind.

3

Louise Mortensen smiled politely at the woman serving dinner. "Gracias, Juana. La cena se ve deliciosa."

Juana smiled. "Gracias, Doctor Mortensen." She placed a plate in front of the young man who sat opposite Louise.

"Gracias, Juana," he said. "Se ve maravilloso como siempre." When he had learned that Louise knew Spanish, he had memorized a few phrases to use with Juana at dinner.

Juana bobbed her head. "Gracias, Señor Pieda."

Mitchell Pieda saw what he frequently did when he scanned Juana's thoughts: a low-grade resentment of his insertion into the household and a grudging curiosity about the reason for his extended stay. All this set against a semi-permanent backdrop of sadness at the death of Louise's husband, Gerard Bonnay, the previous month. Tonight it was overlaid by a concern about the success of the dessert she was preparing. He pinged her thoughts again. Lemon meringue pie.

Juana nodded to both of them and disappeared down the short hallway leading to the kitchen.

Louise lifted her wine glass to Mitchell. "Cheers."

Mitchell lifted his glass in return and took a sip. "This is very good," he said. With Louise's permission, he had been spending some time in the wine cellar in the basement of the Pocopson, Pennsylvania, home. Armed with a huge reference book he had found in Gerard's library, he had begun to develop an oenophile's expertise. He prided himself on the fact that he could have held a reasonably informed conversation with a sommelier at any fine restaurant in Philadelphia at an age when most of his peers were still making runs to the beer store for cases or kegs.

Tonight he had picked out an '82 Mouton.

Louise picked up the bottle and looked at the label. "This was a favorite," she said, setting the bottle down. "Nicely chosen, Mitchell."

They ate in silence for a few minutes, Mitchell trying not to wolf down the filet, asparagus, and parmesan-topped potatoes.

Louise picked at her meal and eventually pushed it away. "I have to tell Juana not to serve so much red meat."

Mitchell reluctantly put down his fork.

Louise took a deep breath. "The lawyers just notified me that the Pennsylvania attorney general, Russell Brashear, is launching an investigation of Vivantem."

Mitchell sat forward. "What?"

"Two of the Vivantem mothers became friends—evidently they struck up a conversation in the waiting room when they were at the office for their fertility treatments, which I didn't foresee. Both of the children died—one in September and one in October—and autopsies were performed. Both had experienced cerebral hemorrhages."

"They gave *themselves* strokes?" asked Mitchell, aghast.

"Apparently. Not a result that has appeared in any other

cohort. Although I had made a slight adjustment to the treatment for those two women."

"How old were the children?"

"Not quite a year old." She folded her hands on the table. "At first, the police suspected child abuse, but there were no other indications—no signs of external injuries. Unfortunately for us, one of the women was a friend of a friend of Brashear, and she brought their stories to him. Now he wants to see the records of all the Vivantem clients so he can see if there are any other anomalies." The knuckles of her folded hands whitened. "They were planning to announce the investigation right after Christmas, but when Elizabeth Ballard murdered Gerard, they postponed the announcement until now. Evidently," she added tightly, "a month is a sufficient amount of time to wait to show your respect for the dead."

After a pause, Mitchell said, "Are you still ... experimenting on the children?"

"Strictly speaking, we're not experimenting on the children at all, we're experimenting on the mothers. But to answer your underlying question—no. Once Gerard and I knew about you and Ballard, I suspended my experiments. I've been reviewing the data to try to see what was different about the treatments received by each of your mothers from the other patients. And what was different between you and Ballard that resulted in different abilities."

"Have you found anything?"

"No." She sighed. "The results from subject to subject are so inconsistent that it makes the investigation challenging." She looked toward the tall dining room windows, which were framed by gauzy silk curtains. The glass was opaque with the darkness beyond, but during the day it would have revealed a stretch of lawn, lightly covered by a recent snowfall, with a distant view of a Chester County horse farm.

She was silent for some time. A person's silence was usually not much of an impediment to Mitchell Pieda learning what they were thinking, but Louise was an exception. He tried to open his mind to hers, but hers was as opaque as the window, the scenes beyond her mental boundary hidden from his view. He didn't sense it was an intentional blocking, but rather her natural state—not like the inhabitants of a castle pulling up the drawbridge, but like an island with no bridge at all.

Finally he broke the silence. "If you started the experiments again, which would you try for—telepathy or the ability to cause strokes?"

"Based on your own situation, we might not have to choose one or the other. You can read minds *and* you took care of the man who bullied you at work."

Mitchell thought back to Brett Ludlow, his boss at his first job out of college. Mitchell had at first thought Brett would serve as a mentor and a model for his own path up the ranks of the company, but when Mitchell had dared to question Brett during a sales presentation, Ludlow had called him a piece of shit and orchestrated a department-wide shunning of Mitchell. A week later, Ludlow was dead of a stroke.

"But that took days," said Mitchell. "Days of me spending hours and hours with him. I can't just walk up to someone and do what—" He stopped.

"What Ballard did to Gerard?" asked Louise.

"Yes." After a moment, he added, "And to Lucia Hazlitt."

Louise gave a single nod. "She has great power, there's no doubt of that. But she's unsophisticated in her use of it. She wields her ability like a sledgehammer. What we want is more like a scalpel."

"A sledgehammer may not be very sophisticated, but it—" He stopped again.

"It gets the job done, one might say," Louise finished bitterly.

Mitchell nodded.

She looked toward the window again and took a deep breath, then continued in her usual brisk manner. "It may get the job done, but it leaves a mess. And messy is what we don't want."

Mitchell sighed and looked down at his plate. "A sledge-hammer on one end of the spectrum, and a toy mallet on the other."

"Don't denigrate your ability, Mitchell," she said. "Ballard has shown no evidence, as far as we know, of the ability to read minds, and I believe there are ways to increase your ability to affect others' brains physically."

"How?"

She sat forward. "I can give you something that will magnify the effect and, I believe, enhance your ability to apply it effectively. A performance-enhancing drug, one might say."

"Sounds like an athlete on steroids," said Mitchell.

"Yes. Exactly like that."

He hesitated. "I've read about what steroids do to the people who take them."

Louise waved her hand. "That's when a person takes them over an extended period of time—you would only need to take the drug for the specific times when you wanted to apply your ability. And I'm still refining the drug—we won't test it out until I know it's safe."

Mitchell nodded. "Of course."

Louise took a sip of wine. "The immediate concern is Brashear's investigation."

"What are we going to do?"

She put her glass down. "If this drug works as I anticipate it will, *you* can take care of the attorney general, Mitchell. The basis of his investigation will sound so ludicrous to his colleagues and to the public that I'm surprised he's taken it on. If we eliminate him, I believe the investigation will be dropped."

Mitchell shifted uncomfortably. "What about Elizabeth Ballard?" he asked. "And Owen McNally?"

"George is taking care of that," she said.

"Do we even know where they are?"

"George will find out." Louise dabbed the corners of her mouth with her napkin and pushed back her chair. "I'm going to be in my study, looking through the records. Please stay, though, and finish your dinner. I'm sure Juana has a wonderful dessert prepared."

Only if she's figured out how to keep the meringue from collapsing, thought Mitchell sourly as Louise left the room.

4

Lizzy and her godfather, Owen McNally, were headed up 89A on a day trip to explore Flagstaff when Owen noticed the restaurant on their left.

"That looks nice," he said.

"Uncle Owen, we just left home!" protested Lizzy.

"I'm too hungry to wait until Flagstaff," he replied sheepishly.

She rolled her eyes.

The place turned out to be a combination restaurant and market. They placed their orders at the counter—sandwiches for both of them, plus soup for Owen—then retired to the outdoor dining area behind the building with gourmet sodas and chips to wait for their food to be delivered. Owen eyed the metal chairs with distrust—he was a huge man, with a height that was almost, but not quite, commensurate with his girth. He lowered himself onto one of the chairs with his customary caution, but it exhibited no signs of distress and he relaxed a bit.

Over the back of each chair hung a colorful woven blanket, and Lizzy wrapped hers around her shoulders against the slight chill of the January air and of the shadow cast by the towering red rock cliffs that rose immediately behind the restaurant.

Owen's phone pinged, and he glanced at it. "Andy," he said. He read the message, then rolled his eyes. "He's just taunting me about the Coyotes. Evidently while we're in Arizona, the Coyotes are my adoptive hockey team, and he's laying claim to the Flyers, who won in overtime last night."

He held the phone out so Lizzy could read the message.

Yo bro even your width couldn't have blocked that last shot into the net

Lizzy laughed. "He never cuts you a break, does he?"

Owen tapped out a response, still smiling, and a moment later the phone pinged with another message. His smile faded as he read it. He tapped out a brief response and slipped the phone into his pocket.

"Is everything okay?" Lizzy asked.

"Oh, yes—you know ..." He glanced around, then said jovially, "Ah, here's our food."

The dreadlocked staffer delivered their lunches, and Owen busied himself extracting the utensils from the rolled napkin and popping open his bag of chips.

Lizzy opened her own bag of chips. "So, is everything okay with Andy?" she asked again.

"Oh, yes. He says he's keeping an eye out, and he hasn't seen anyone who looks like your description of George Millard, or anyone else doing anything that seems suspicious."

"Maybe Mr. Millard disguised himself."

"It's possible. I keep reminding Andy to be careful."

Lizzy gazed speculatively into her bag of chips. "He doesn't really seem like the careful type."

"He can take care of himself," said Owen, but his voice held a hint of brotherly concern.

"How about Ruby?" asked Lizzy.

"Andy's checking in with her periodically. He says she hasn't seen anything suspicious either, and unlike Andy, she would recognize Millard if she saw him. I think that if anyone could see through a disguise, it would be Ruby DiMano."

Lizzy smiled. "Yeah, I agree."

They ate in companionable silence for a few minutes, then Lizzy said, "We should go back to Pennsylvania to check on them."

"I don't think there's much checking we could do there that we couldn't do equally well from here," replied Owen, although he didn't sound entirely convinced.

"They could come here."

"I have asked them about that. Andy ... has some things he needs to take care of in Philly, and Ruby says she needs to be there to help her sister care for her brother-in-law."

Lizzy put down her sandwich and heaved a sigh.

Owen put down his own sandwich. "It's all going to work out okay."

"I wish I could do something."

"We'll come up with a plan."

"When?"

"Soon."

Lizzy returned her attention half-heartedly to her sandwich.

After lunch, they wandered to the building next door, which housed a jewelry store.

"Can we go in?" Lizzy asked.

"Sure."

Lizzy wandered along the glass-topped display cases while Owen checked out a selection of Indian pottery in an alcove off the main room. She stopped at one of the displays and gazed down at the offerings.

"May I show you something?" asked a woman who had appeared behind the counter.

"Can I see that?" Lizzy asked, pointing.

It was a bear-shaped pendant, the body of the bear divided vertically into three parts—the back section lapis, the middle section onyx, the front section turquoise. The woman put the pendant on a square of black velvet.

"It's really pretty," said Lizzy.

"It's a Zuni bear."

Lizzy picked up the pendant. The bear was such a pleasing shape, the inlay so smooth that she could run her hand over it and not feel where the lapis changed to onyx changed to turquoise.

"They say that the Zuni bear changes passion into wisdom," said the woman.

"That's neat."

"And helps you forgive yourself for past mistakes."

Lizzy's fingers froze. After a moment, she asked in a small voice, "Really?"

"That's what they say," said the woman cheerfully. "Would you like to try it on?"

Lizzy turned the pendant over and glanced at the small hand-printed price tag. "Uh—no, thanks. I don't have enough money with me."

"What have you got there?" she heard Owen ask at her shoulder.

She turned the pendant back over and held it out to him. He bent to peer at it.

"That's lovely work," he said.

"Yes," said the woman behind the counter. "One of our local artists."

"And did I hear you say it has a special meaning? A special power?"

"Yes, they say it helps the person who wears it forgive themselves for past mistakes."

Owen took the pendant in his hand and turned it under the light.

"Yes, I think this is just the thing for my friend to have," he said. "We'll take this."

Considering the off-the-grid existence the Ballard girl had lived in Pennsylvania, George Millard wasn't surprised that she was pretty much a nonentity in the sources he had access to. However, he figured it would be harder for someone like McNally, with a more sizable presence, both physically and professionally, to disappear completely. If possible, he wanted to find them without resorting to online searches in order to reduce the chance that anything that might happen to them could be traced back to him and then to Louise Mortensen. The old-fashioned way would be cleaner, and he always prided himself on being clean.

On a rainy early February afternoon, Millard stepped into the administrative office of the Neurobiology Department at Philadelphia's William Penn University, carrying an envelope with Owen McNally's name on it. Inside was a copy of *Psychology Today* that he had picked up at a bookstore.

A young woman looked up from her computer. "Can I help you?"

"Yes, I have a package for Dr. McNally, but his office is locked."

"Dr. McNally's on leave at the moment, can it wait until he gets back?"

"How long will that be?"

"I'm not sure. He's teaching a class in the fall semester, so he has to be back by then. If he needs to get it sooner than that, I could mail it to him."

"I don't want to put you out. If you could give me his address, I can mail it."

"I'm sorry, we can't give that information out, but it's no problem—I forward mail to him all the time. He gets a ton of journals."

"That would be great." He handed her the envelope. "Do you think you could send it out today?"

"Sure, no problem."

"Great, I really appreciate your help."

After wishing the young woman a good day, Millard went down the hall to an alcove from which he could watch the hallway. He had to wait only about an hour before another woman—this one younger than the woman in the office and sporting a scattering of pimples across her chin—appeared from the elevator, pushing a cart containing a few small packages and envelopes. She stopped in front of the door to the Neurobiology office, sorted through the contents of the cart's top rack, picked up a few items, and disappeared into the office. She appeared a moment later with Millard's envelope, which she put on the cart's lower rack. She trundled the cart down the hallway and repeated the process at the next office. When she got to the end of the hall, she turned the cart around and retraced her steps to the elevator.

When Millard heard the bing of the arriving elevator, he

stepped out of the alcove and jogged down the hall
toward her.

"Miss, can you hold up a minute?" he called as she pushed
the cart into the elevator.

Her head popped out of the elevator door. "Me?"

Millard stepped into the elevator. "Sorry, I think I put the
wrong address on the package for Dr. McNally." He waved a
piece of paper on which he had written McNally's name and a
made-up address. He pointed at the bottom rack. "I think it's
that envelope."

The door slid closed and the elevator waited for one of the
occupants to press a button.

"Uh, sure." The girl pulled out the envelope. Millard took
it from her before she could object, and glanced between the
address the woman in the office had put on the package and
the slip in his hand.

"Oh, good, it is the right address." He handed the envelope
back to her. "Sorry to have bothered you. Going down one?"

"All the way down. I'm done for the day."

He pressed the button for the first floor and smiled at her.
"Me too."

M illard drove from Penn to the Vivantem offices in Center City and took the elevator to the research facilities and Mortensen's lab. During business hours, the floor where clients were seen—one floor above the labs—was as busy as ever, despite the absence of its ever-photogenic founder, Gerard Bonnay. In fact, in the weeks after Bonnay's death of a massive stroke, the waiting room had been filled with bouquets of flowers sent by grateful couples who owed their offspring to Vivantem's intervention. There was more than one Vivantem baby named after Gerard, although none, as far as Millard knew, named after Louise. Millard figured that there wouldn't be any more flowers, and a lot fewer clients, if word of the attorney general's investigation got out.

He wasn't interested in having the AG, or anyone else, upset the gravy train. Tracking down Elizabeth Ballard and her fat godfather, Owen McNally, was one step in ensuring that didn't happen. He didn't need Brashear, digging for dirt among the Vivantem children, to stumble upon Ballard and start poking into her past. And, he thought with a wry smile,

Brashear didn't need that either, because things could turn out badly for anyone who upset Lizzy Ballard.

Lizzy Ballard took an axe and gave her mother forty whacks. Not so much whacks, thought Millard, as a death of a thousand cuts. And she hadn't given her father forty-one—Millard himself had taken care of that.

George Millard had worked for Louise Mortensen for almost fifteen years. His first job for her had been to discourage a colleague who was exhibiting an inconvenient interest in her research. Millard had discouraged—no muss, no fuss—and other jobs had followed. He had done work for Gerard Bonnay as well, and didn't have any major complaints. Both Mortensen and Bonnay tended to let him decide how to handle a job without much meddling; treated him, if not as an equal, at least with respect; and paid him well for his services. But if one of them had had to fall victim to Ballard, he was glad it had been Bonnay. He didn't miss the man's tendency to say "we" when he really meant "you"—*We'll have to take care of this situation.* And the guy's manner was so smooth that it sometimes seemed more like slipperiness—you never knew where you stood with him. He'd take Mortensen's bluntness any day.

He had never worked for them exclusively—there were always people who wanted to pay under the table to have dicey situations taken care of—but as he banked his payments from Mortensen and Bonnay, he could be more choosy about the work he did, and more and more of it was for them. And the payments enabled him to indulge in his one interest outside his work and Philadelphia sports: fly fishing. He had traveled to the best fishing spots in North America: the San Juan, the Bighorn, the Alagnak, Five Rivers, the Colorado, the Blue. Always catch-and-release—there was no need to keep those gorgeous fish once you had fought it out with them.

A couple of years ago he had bought a piece of land in Montana, near Dillon—paid cash—and in another year or two, he'd have enough in the bank to build his dream house on it. Then he'd retire, and he wasn't even fifty. Until then, he had almost as much incentive to keep the AG's office away from Vivantem as Mortensen did.

He stepped out of the elevator and keyed in the passcode that provided access to the research facility. Unlike the area where the on-the-books work of the fertility clinic was done, the area that housed Mortensen's private lab had always been quiet, but it was quieter than ever these days. Since Mortensen and Bonnay had found out about Lizzy Ballard and Mitchell Pieda's Vivantem-bred skills, Mortensen had reassigned the few assistants who had helped her with her personal research back to the clinic staff. No doubt she didn't want anyone else with access to her personal research files getting curious about what might be behind the attorney general's investigation.

The files themselves were also getting cleaned up. Since Louise had learned of the AG's interest in Vivantem, Millard had been hauling boxes of papers from Vivantem to the house in Pocopson, where he was scanning and then destroying the paper copies. Most of the content was Greek to him, but he understood enough to know that she couldn't have anyone else looking at those records—there was plenty to feed not only an AG investigation, but also the ire of any medical ethics board that saw the contents.

Quite a backlog had built up—she had been conducting her clandestine research since her late twenties, thirty years before, and she wasn't willing to lose a single note or test result—and he wasn't going to make progress on it until he got through these other jobs she was giving him.

Reaching the door to Mortensen's lab, he looked through the glass pane and saw her, as he often did, peering through the eyepiece of a microscope, taking notes on a pad of paper. He was struck by the fact that she didn't hunch over the microscope, but rather tilted toward it, her back straight as a ruler. It had to take some muscles to do that hour after hour.

He pressed another passcode into the keypad by the door, gave a courtesy knock, and entered.

She leaned back from the microscope. "Anything?"

"They're in Sedona," he said. "At least McNally is, and I've got to believe Ballard's with him."

"Sedona?"

"It's in Arizona—"

"I know where it is, I'm just wondering how on earth they ended up there. And why."

"It's as good a place as any to hide out, and you couldn't get much further from Philly without going all the way to the left coast."

"You have an address?"

"I have a PO box, but the town is pretty small and it shouldn't be hard to find him once I'm there. And he must have settled down, at least temporarily, if he got a box."

"What are they doing there?"

"Trying to figure out their next move, is my guess."

Louise gazed at the notepad next to the microscope for a few moments, then tore off the top sheet and dropped it into a shredder next to the table. The machine whirred briefly, then fell silent.

"What do you suppose their next move will be?"

Millard shrugged. "I didn't get a sense that McNally had told anyone at Penn he wouldn't be back, and I found out he's supposed to teach a class in the fall. Maybe they figure if they stay off the radar long enough, we'll lose interest."

Louise smiled mirthlessly. "I'm not in the habit of losing interest once my interest has been piqued."

"Yeah," said Millard, "I know that about you."

She shot him a look, which Millard returned with a bland gaze.

She sighed. "I need you here until Brashear's taken care of," she said, "and I don't know how long it will take before I can get Mitchell ready. If Ballard and McNally are settled down in Sedona, it makes things easier, and I think we can assume that they are as interested in staying out of the public eye as we are. After all, she is a murderer."

7

Despite her concern about what might be happening back in Pennsylvania, Lizzy couldn't deny the attractions of Sedona—not least the fantastically gorgeous hiking trails: Courthouse Butte, Boynton Canyon, Thread-the-Needle. Some trails were too far from the house where she and Uncle Owen were staying to reach on her bike, so she had to rely on him to drive her.

Today he was tied up on a conference call with another Penn professor to discuss a class they would be co-teaching in the fall, so she decided on a pleasant alternative that was within walking distance of the house: the Sugarloaf Trail, whose attractions included a glorious view of Coffeepot Rock.

The day was cool, with the temperature falling and rising as ranks of gray clouds hid and revealed the sun. It was odd to walk on a trail that looked so wild in places, but in others provided vistas not only of the desolate red rocks, but also of a valley filled with tidy neighborhoods of small houses and tiny shopping centers peopled by even tinier shoppers. Occasionally the hoot of a car horn or a chorus of dog barks—quickly triggered but less quickly quieted—drifted up to her on the trail.

She was looking down on such a view, idly trying to identify the Sedona streets with which she was quickly becoming familiar, when a loud snort startled her out of her reverie. She looked up to see two javelinas on the trail in front of her, one larger and one smaller. A mother and baby? Lizzy knew better than to disturb a mother and baby in the wild. The animals seemed unconcerned with her presence, gazing at her with placid eyes, then turning to root among the prickly pear. But even at twenty paces, Lizzy could see the sharp teeth protruding from the larger one's jaw. She couldn't remember anything in her hiking books about whether javelinas were dangerous, but it seemed smart to step off the trail to give them some room.

Stepping off the trail was hardly a hardship since, as was the case in many sections of the Sugarloaf Trail, the small bushes growing throughout the area were separated by convenient widths of red dirt. Oftentimes the only noticeable difference between on- and off-trail was the wire-enclosed stone cairns that marked the official route. She passed the snuffling javelinas at what seemed a safe distance, then turned to join up again with the trail.

In a few minutes, the path that she thought was the trail dead-ended at a line of wooden privacy fences, on the other side of which were the back yards of the homes that backed onto the trail area. As she stood with her hands on her hips, contemplating her options, the sun passed behind a cloud and the temperature dropped a degree or two.

Irritated, she retraced her steps and cast about for a bit, but could see no sign of the trail. She looked up, trying to judge if the weather was going to hold out. If it was, she'd keep looking for the trail without the help of technology. If not, she'd check the map on her phone, which she had discovered on previous hikes displayed trails as well as roads.

The sun made what looked like one last appearance ahead of solid ranks of clouds, and she stepped into the shade of a short, bushy tree to better see the screen. At that moment, a bike rounded the curve where the path skirted the tree, headed right for her.

"What the hell—" exclaimed the rider, as Lizzy jumped back to avoid being run down. Her arms pinwheeling, she fell back into a patch of thorny bushes. She heard the skid of bike tires on the path, and then the whoosh of expelled air as the biker hit the ground.

She tried to get up, but thorns snagged her clothes and skin. "Ouch!" she said, trying ineffectually to free herself. She looked toward the biker. "Are you okay?"

The biker had climbed to his feet. His pants were torn and a trickle of blood was beginning to seep from an ugly scrape on his forearm. "What the hell were you doing?" he sputtered.

"What was *I* doing? You almost ran into me!"

"You picked a hell of a place to decide to stand on a busy trail!"

"You're blaming me for standing on a hiking trail?" said Lizzy, her voice rising. She glanced around. "And it's not busy —you're the first person I've seen in at least ten minutes!"

"You teenagers, always on your phones, always texting," said the biker.

"I wasn't texting, I was looking at the trail map!"

"That's a five thousand dollar bike! If you think I'm going to let some smart-ass girl—"

But she didn't hear the rest of what he was saying, because she sensed the dreaded flush rising from her neck to her cheeks, suffusing her whole body with the heat of anger. In a panic, she tried to remember the yoga classes—*breathe out the bad energy breathe in the good energy breathe out the bad breathe in the good breathe breathe*—but the anger had the upper hand.

She had to get away. She started to thrash, not caring that the thorns were tearing her skin as well as her clothes. She tried to concentrate on the pain, thinking perhaps it would distract her from her anger at the biker, but then the thought that he was the person responsible for the pain intruded.

The biker's rant was cut short.

Lizzy stopped thrashing, watching round-eyed as he clamped his hands to his temples.

"Goddammit," he rasped.

"Go away," she said in a hoarse whisper.

He looked at her, his eyes squinted in pain. "What?"

"Go away or I'll scream and say you attacked me," she said, her voice louder with her rising panic.

"You'll do what?" he said, incredulous. "But—"

She sucked in a lungful of air. "Run away!" she yelled. "Do it now!"

The biker snatched his bike off the ground, mounted it, and retreated rapidly down the trail, fighting a wobble caused by the bent front tire.

Lizzy watched until he disappeared around the curve in the trail, then wrenched her arms out of the grip of the thorns and clamped her hands over her ears, her head between her bent knees. But she couldn't block out the sound that was tormenting her—it was the sounds of her mother's fear-riddled voice from a decade earlier: *Lizzy, run away and hit your pillow! Do it now!*

Eventually she became aware of the cold shock of rain-drops. She lifted her eyes. The clouds had darkened, the sky lowering so that it looked like it rested on top of the mesas. She looked around frantically for the phone, which she had dropped when she fell, and spotted it under the bush. She snatched it up and pushed it into her jacket pocket just as the rain morphed from droplets to a steady stream and the dusty ground began to turn slick.

She began the painstaking process of extracting her torso and legs from the bush, tears mixing with the rainwater that now dripped down her face.

She had almost freed herself when she heard a grunt from a dozen feet away. When she looked up, her eyes were even with those of the two javelinas, their hairy faces registering surprise, then caution. The larger one shuffled between the smaller one and Lizzy and gave a menacing snort. A mother for sure. A mother ready to protect her child.

Lizzy froze. A half minute ticked by, then a minute, and finally the larger javelina turned away and led the smaller one into the brush.

Lizzy scrambled out of the bush, turned in the opposite direction, and ran.

She didn't know where the trail was, and didn't want to take her phone out in the drenching rain. She looked for the landmarks that had only recently begun to become familiar to her, but nothing looked familiar in the dim light of the rainstorm.

Suddenly, in one of those transitions from seeming wilderness to settled suburbia that seemed common to trails near the city limits, she found herself on a road of carefully rolled black gravel, the tiled roofs of million dollar homes just visible beyond gates and walls.

She looked up and down the road, but couldn't orient herself. She got out her phone and, shielding it as best she could from the rain, pulled up the GPS. She was a mile and a half from home. More like two thousand miles, she thought with a twist in her stomach.

She thought briefly of calling Uncle Owen to come get her,

but she didn't want to spend even a short ride in the car with him, having to explain, or to hide, what had happened.

She jammed the phone back in her pocket and started down the road, the rain sending its cold fingers down the neck of her shirt. The sounds of water rushing in the gutters and the slap of her feet on the wet pavement filled her ears, but the sound in her mind drowned these out: the sound of her mother's final scream as seven-year-old Lizzy—grumpy with a cold and angry over a puppy she couldn't have—had squeezed her mother's brain. All because her mother had been doing what she could to protect her child.

Lizzy closed her fingers around the Zuni bear pendant and trudged on.

8

M illard glanced in the rearview mirror, to where Louise and Mitchell sat in the back seat. He had driven them to Philadelphia, and now they were parked on Race Street, near Logan Square. At this time of night, most of the main attractions in the area—The Academy of Natural Sciences, The Franklin Institute, The Barnes Foundation—were closed or deserted, and the only people on the streets were occasional well-dressed couples hurrying to one of the area's upscale hotels or restaurants, or vague shapes hugging the shadows as the homeless made their way toward the square.

"Do you remember what you did when you took care of the man who bullied you at work?" Louise asked Mitchell. "What force you exerted?"

"Yes."

Louise waited a beat, then said, "Can you describe it? It might help you focus your efforts for the test."

Mitchell snapped off a loose thread from the sleeve of his coat. Finally, he spoke. "Have you ever heard of peine forte et dure?"

Louise thought for a moment. "Strong and harsh punishment?"

"Yes. It was a punishment they used hundreds of years ago if someone was accused of a crime and refused to plead guilty or not guilty. They would pile stones on them until they pled or they died."

Louise shifted in her seat. "How do you know that? And how does that relate to what you did to the person who bullied you?"

"After Brett Ludlow died, I looked up 'crushing death' and that's what I found. That's what it felt like. It was like piling one stone on top of another, hour after hour, day after day, until he died."

Louise's eyes flicked to Millard's in the rearview mirror, then returned to Mitchell. "That man treated you disrespectfully," she said.

Mitchell rolled the detached thread between his thumb and finger. "I know."

Louise reached out and patted him awkwardly on the arm. "You just need to do that same thing again, except the effect is going to be magnified many times."

"Isn't there someone you'd like me to take care of who has actually wronged you in some way?" he asked for the second time since they had left Pocopson.

"That's sweet of you, Mitchell," she said briskly, "but if too many people who are standing against Vivantem start suffering unexplained strokes, especially after some of the things that the attorney general has let slip about his investigation, it will make things worse, not better."

Mitchell looked out the window.

"What is it?" asked Louise, an edge of annoyance creeping into her voice.

Mitchell turned to her. "I don't like the idea of trying it out on some innocent person."

"They're homeless."

"I know. But still."

Now Louise turned her gaze to the window. After a moment, she turned back and said, "You can pick whoever you want. If it makes you feel better, pick one you think is dangerous. One you think the world will be better off without."

Mitchell was silent.

"George will go with you." She glanced in the rearview mirror. "Won't you, George?"

"Sure," said Millard.

Her briskness returned as her new plan solidified. "It would only be dangerous if the person you chose had a gun, and that's extremely unlikely. You don't think I'd send you out there if it were really dangerous, do you? I'm counting on you to help me protect what Gerard created, to keep meddlers like Russell Brashear away from the company Gerard spent his life building. You don't have anything to worry about—once I give you the injection, you'll see. But you'll have George backing you up, just in case."

Mitchell's eventual reply was grudging. "Okay."

"Excellent," she said as she pulled a small case out of the bag at her feet. She unzipped the case and removed a syringe, which she filled from a glass vial. "George scouted the area yesterday. George, where did you say Mitchell would find the homeless men?"

"Either in the square itself," said Millard, "or on the steps of the Basilica."

Louise turned to Mitchell with the loaded syringe. "If you can just bare your upper arm ..."

Mitchell pulled his arm out of his sweater and shirt.

Louise gave him the injection. "I estimate it will take about five minutes for the drug to take full effect," she said as Mitchell got his clothes straightened and shrugged into his coat. "And it won't last more than about fifteen minutes, so don't take too long to locate your subject. When it's done, we'll rendezvous back here. If the parked car seems to be attracting undue attention, I'll drive around the block until you get back."

Mitchell nodded, climbed out of the car, and headed toward Logan Square.

Millard and Louise got out of the car as well.

"Just want me to keep an eye on him from a distance?" Millard asked.

"Yes. Try to keep him from coming to any harm. I'm relying on him to extract us from this situation with the attorney general."

Millard nodded and began to turn away, then turned back at Louise's voice.

"But if things go awry, remember that the most important thing is to make sure that they can't trace him back to us. I'd hate to lose him, but if things do go wrong, make sure he can't tell any tales."

9

M itchell walked toward Logan Square, his head down. He pushed his hands deep into the pockets of his coat, both against the biting cold of the February night and to hide their trembling. He resisted the impulse to look around for Millard, trying to convince himself he could do this by himself—he didn't like the idea of Louise thinking he needed a babysitter. His heart was beating fast, but whether from the drug or from the circumstances, he couldn't tell.

He crossed 18th Street and the Benjamin Franklin Parkway, relatively quiet at this time of night, then took one of the spoke-like paths toward the fountain in the middle of the square.

On one of the benches facing the fountain sat a lone figure, its arm around a knapsack at its side. Glancing nervously around for any witnesses, Mitchell walked toward the figure, which pulled its knapsack closer as Mitchell approached. As if someone who slept outside in February could have anything worth protecting.

But as Mitchell neared the bench, he saw by the glow from

the streetlights that it was not a knapsack next to the man, but a dog, a brown and white pit bull poking its head out of the top of a tattered sleeping bag. The man's eyes narrowed as he watched Mitchell approach, and he tightened his hold on the dog. The dog, also watching Mitchell, curled its lip back from its teeth and issued a low growl.

Mitchell adjusted his direction slightly and passed the man and the dog, wondering as he did so whether this enhanced power that Louise's drug was supposed to provide would work on the dog if the man decided to send it after Mitchell. Both dog and man stayed on the bench.

He turned onto the next path, the crunch of the gravel under his shoes unnervingly loud, and followed it back toward the outer walkway.

He could hear voices raised in debate, then came upon the debaters—two destitute-looking men standing face-to-face, one emphasizing his point with a finger poked into the other's chest. When Mitchell appeared from the path, they redirected their irritation from each other toward him, and again he turned away. Not only did he not want to get in the middle of an altercation in progress, but the walkway where they stood ran right next to the Parkway, and he needed privacy for the test.

How much time had gone by since Louise had injected him? He looked at his watch. The hands and numbers seemed impossibly small, as if he were looking the wrong way through a telescope, but he knew he was running out of time to complete the test. He glanced around for Millard—trying to see into the shadows cast by the trees dotted through the park —but could see no one other than the two men, who had returned to their dispute.

He recrossed the Parkway and stepped into the small Sister Cities Park on the east side of the square. Its meandering paths and somewhat more closely planted trees gave it a more secluded feel than the Circle, but as far as he could see it was uninhabited by possible targets.

Across 18th Street stood the Basilica. Although his near vision was distorted, his distance vision seemed unusually clear—he could see several figures huddled at the bases of the four massive columns that marched across the front of the building. His heart was beating harder now, and he didn't think it was all nerves. He felt a flush, as if a slow fire had been lit in his gut. The Basilica was where the test would take place.

He waited for a couple of cars to pass, jogged across the street, and stopped on the sidewalk at the base of the Basilica steps.

"Cop?" one of the shapes muttered.

"Nah, just some guy," another replied.

"Get out of here," came the tremulous cry from an invisible source deep in the shadows of the portico.

"Yeah, run home to mommy," said a fourth, this voice raspy and slurred.

"I have as much right to be here as you do," said Mitchell loudly, hoping his voice would be steady. "More right, I'd say."

"Oh, yeah?" replied the man. "And why's that?"

"I have a job. I pay taxes. I don't lie around like an animal, waiting for hand-outs."

The man rose and advanced a step toward Mitchell. "Animals, are we? And why would a fancy boy like you bother talking to the likes of us? Hoping to talk us into getting a job and paying taxes?" His voice dripped with contempt. "Or maybe you came to look at us like we're in the zoo?" he asked, advancing another step.

He was big, made bigger by the layers of clothes he wore. It was impossible to tell if he had a weapon.

"Going to the zoo like a little schoolboy," the man sneered. "Like a mama's boy."

Mitchell involuntarily glanced behind him, looking for Millard.

"Looking for your mama to help you?" the man trilled, then his voice dropped to a growl. "Don't make me come down there and teach you a lesson."

Mitchell turned back to him and squared his shoulders. "Teach me a lesson?" Mitchell's voice was strained, but now it wasn't from fear. That heat in his gut was spreading. It had reached his head, and it was all he could do to keep from closing the space between him and this piece of trash.

"'Teach me a lesson?'" the man fluted in an unsteady falsetto. "I'm going to teach you a lesson just for the fun of it."

Mitchell reached out mentally to probe the man's thoughts, but rather than the images he was used to perceiving when people weren't intentionally blocking him, he encountered only a confusion of swirling colors—muddy browns and grays, like a river in flood churning over farmland. His inability to read the man's thoughts momentarily unnerved him, but that building internal heat overcame his hesitance.

Mitchell turned to his left and began walking, waiting for —hoping for—the sound of the man's steps behind him.

"Let him go," Mitchell heard the querulous voice call.

"Mind your own business," snarled the man.

Mitchell heard the footfalls behind him.

A few yards away, the Basilica's facade stepped back beyond a concrete-paved courtyard separated from the side-walk by a black metal fence. A light in the adjoining parking lot flickered on and off, creating a strobe of light and darkness. He stepped through the fence's gate, planning to pass through the courtyard and into the parking lot to get further away from the street, but the metal fence ran along the side of the court-yard as well, blocking his way.

He turned back to the gate, his hands balled at his sides.

In a moment, the man ambled around the corner, obviously knowing his prey was trapped. "Well, look at that," he said. "Looks like someone wandered into a cage all on his own. Who's the zoo animal now?" The man held something in his hand, and Mitchell saw light glint off metal.

Mitchell tried again to probe the man's thoughts, but this time could not perceive even the swirl of colors he had seen earlier. They were overridden by the fiery red swirling of his own mind. If the force he had used on Brett Ludlow had been a slow stone-by-stone crush, the power now building in Mitchell's brain felt more like a pneumatic press waiting to be triggered.

The man stepped through the gate, and Mitchell retreated toward the darkest part of the courtyard.

The man followed him with a rough chuckle. "You're not the smartest mama's boy, are you?"

The pressure—the power—in Mitchell's head was becoming unbearable.

The man was only a few feet from Mitchell when the parking lot light flickered off.

Mitchell released the force.

The man's head jerked back as if he had been hit by a bullet—the grainy images of the Zapruder film swam into Mitchell's mind—and the man dropped to the ground face down, a knife clattering out of his hand onto the concrete.

Mitchell advanced on the inert form, the taunt of *mama's boy* clanging in his head. He placed his foot on the man's shoulder and pushed. There was no reaction. Face down, it looked less like a man and more like a mound of dirty, discarded clothing. Mitchell pushed again, harder, and this time the body rolled over.

The man's eyes—yellow-tinged and rheumy—stared sightlessly. The mouth hung open to reveal teeth clogged with decaying food. *Mama's boy*? This thing was barely human. Mitchell pulled his foot back and kicked. The head snapped to the side, a senseless piece of meat.

But there was still the trash on the steps of the Basilica, and Mitchell Pieda had the means to clean it up.

He took a step toward the gate, but suddenly the brutal brightness that had lit his vision began to darken to gray. He staggered to the fence and steadied himself with a trembling hand. He could hear a squabble break out on the steps of the Basilica, like irritable pigeons fighting over a crust of bread, then quiet.

He heard steps approaching and staggered back into the shadows of the courtyard. A moment ago he had felt invincible—had been invincible—but now he could barely stand. If those men from the Basilica steps were coming to get him, he had no strength left to defend himself.

"Mitchell?" he heard from the sidewalk. "It's George. I'm going to get you out of here, okay?"

"Okay."

Millard stepped into the courtyard. He bent over the body and placed his fingers on the man's neck for a moment. Then he straightened and crossed to Mitchell. "Can you walk?"

"I think so," said Mitchell, but he stumbled as he pushed himself away from the fence.

Millard took his arm, looped it over his shoulders, and led him—hauled him, if Mitchell were truthful with himself—out of the courtyard. They turned right, away from the Basilica steps, and once they had cleared the fence, turned right again, into the parking lot.

"Hold on to my shoulder for a minute," said Millard.

Mitchell did his best to grip Millard's shoulder.

With his free hand, Millard pulled his phone out of his pocket and in a moment said, "Meet us on 17th between Race and Vine," then slipped the phone back into his pocket. He closed a hand over Mitchell's wrist where it draped over his shoulder.

"Just two guys out on a bender, right, Mitch?"

Mitchell nodded.

"Mortensen's coming to pick us up, then we'll get you back to Pocopson. She's going to be pretty happy with how that went, Mitchell."

Mitchell nodded and, despite the painful throbbing of his heartbeat in his head, he smiled.

10

L ouise stood by the bed where Mitchell lay, his arm thrown over his eyes. Millard stood behind her.

"Mitchell?" she said.

He moved his arm away from his face and looked up at her with bloodshot eyes.

"This will help," she said, handing him a pill and a glass of water.

"Thanks," he said dully. He tried to sit up, but groaned and fell back. Louise helped him sit and he took the glass with a shaking hand and swallowed the pill.

Louise set the glass on the bedside table. "Anything other than the headache?"

"Everything aches."

"It will be better by the morning. Try to get some sleep. George or I will check on you in a little bit."

He nodded, covering his eyes again.

Millard followed Louise out of the room, then downstairs to her study.

She crossed to the side table and poured herself a glass of

sherry from a decanter. She started for her desk, then stopped. "Anything for you?" she asked.

"No. Thanks."

She sank into the desk chair, then waved Millard into a chair on the other side of the desk. Instead, he clicked on the gas fireplace and stood with his back to it, enjoying the warmth on the back of his legs. They had kept the car windows open on the drive from Philadelphia back to Pocopson because Pieda kept complaining that he was burning up. The young man's legs had buckled when Millard helped him out of the car after they reached the house, and Millard had practically had to carry him up to his room.

"So, did you get what you wanted out of it?" he asked.

She shook her head. "I made a stupid mistake. I should never have suggested to him that he test his ability on someone he thought was dangerous. The whole point of the test was to see if he differs from Ballard in being able to create a cerebral hemorrhage when he's *not* angry or frightened. It's good to know he can do what he did, but will he be able to do it when we need him to get Brashear out of the picture?"

"Should we do another test?"

She sighed. "No. I don't want more people in the area dropping dead of unexplained strokes. I thought about taking him somewhere else for another test, but traveling with him would be complicated, and too risky." She took a sip of sherry. "I'll try to build a case against Brashear with him so at least he doesn't go into the situation feeling any sympathy for him. I suppose the worst that can happen is that *nothing* happens and we'll have to figure out another way to put a stop to the investigation."

"You could let me take care of Brashear and send Pieda to take care of Ballard and McNally."

She sighed again. "Maybe. We'll keep our options open."

Millard clicked off the gas fireplace. "From what I saw, the drug you gave him sure turned up the volume on whatever power he has. The homeless guy dropped like a sack."

She cocked her head at him. "Really?"

"Yeah. Like he had been hit with a battering ram."

"Interesting. I'd love to see the autopsy report. Maybe the dosage doesn't need to be that high." She swirled her sherry contemplatively and gazed into the flames dancing in the fireplace.

After a beat, Millard asked, "What did you give him?"

"A steroid compound."

"So what he's experiencing are withdrawal symptoms?"

"Yes."

"Why don't you just give him more of the drug? Or ease him off it gradually?"

"Giving him more of the drug would be like keeping a loaded gun in the house. You've heard of "roid rage,' right? And easing him off it ..." Her voice trailed off. In a moment, she continued. "If he thinks he has to rely on me to give him the antidote to make him feel better, it's leverage that might come in handy."

"The antidote is aspirin?"

"Yes. But he doesn't need to know that."

Millard shook his head, then asked, "How long will the symptoms last?"

"A few days, but the most severe symptoms—the joint and muscle pain, the headache, possibly nausea—will begin to lessen within twenty-four hours."

Millard sat down in a chair facing the desk. "Do you think he can read our minds? See what the plan is?"

She took a moment to answer. "Every indication is that he can't read the mind of someone who is actively putting up mental barriers against him."

"Maybe the steroids will make his mind-reading ability greater, like with the brain hemorrhage thing."

"That wasn't what I formulated it for, but it's experimental so I can't be absolutely sure of any unintended side effects. But in case it does have that effect, it's another argument for getting him off the drug fast. He doesn't need to know the whole plan, just the parts that he's involved in."

"How many times can you give him the drug?"

She pushed back from the desk. "It won't need to be frequent. He takes care of Brashear, you take care of Ballard and McNally. Or vice versa. That's it. We don't need to make this any messier than it already is."

She stood and walked to a William Harnett trompe l'oeil hanging on the wall. She swung the painting to the side and spun the dial on the safe behind it. She drew an envelope from the safe, closed and locked the safe door, and moved the painting back over it. She crossed to Millard and handed him the envelope. She returned to her desk and sank into the chair. "Keep an eye on him."

Millard stood, tucked the envelope into his inside jacket pocket, and left the study. Before heading upstairs, he made a detour to the kitchen. If Pieda had twenty-four hours of withdrawal ahead of him, it was going to be a long twenty-four hours for himself as well, and he wanted to be well supplied with caffeine.

11

Lizzy stayed close to home during the days following her encounter with the biker. She had come home to an anxious Uncle Owen—she hadn't noticed the texts he had been sending her since the storm had rolled in— and fortunately was able to hurry into the bathroom for a hot shower before he noticed the rips in her clothing and the scratches on her skin.

She didn't tell him what had happened, fearing that he would want to pack them up and move on again, probably even further from Philadelphia. Despite the encounter, she didn't want to run further than they already had.

In the following days she scanned the local news for any references to an off-road biker being accosted by a deranged teenage girl, and watched the street from the large windows in the living room for someone scouting the neighborhoods around the Sugarloaf trailhead, but saw nothing to alarm her.

Then she realized that there was a simpler solution to avoiding having the biker identify her than hiding out in the house.

It had been two months since she had cut and dyed her

long blond hair to a shaggy purple-black when she was in hiding from Gerard, Louise, and George Millard in Pennsylvania, and about an inch of her natural blond was showing at the roots. She actually kind of liked the effect, but its noteworthiness was its disadvantage as well as its appeal. She decided it was time for a change.

Lizzy had never been to a salon before—at least, not that she could remember. Her mother had been too nervous about what might happen if little Lizzy got a haircut she didn't like and got angry with the stylist, so Charlotte had just let Lizzy's hair grow long. After her mother died, it had never occurred to her father to do anything other than comb out her long blond hair and put it in a ponytail. When she had needed a new look in Pennsylvania, she had cut it herself, with a little help from Christine, the waitress who had befriended her.

But the change she was considering was not one she wanted to attempt on her own. She agonized over the websites of the Sedona salons and finally chose one that seemed reputable but not too upscale. She called to confirm what the cost of a haircut would be, looked up the appropriate percentage for a tip, and asked Uncle Owen for a loan of that amount. Uncle Owen had never refused her any money she asked for, but other than a small allowance, most of which she had saved, neither did he offer any without being asked. Lizzy suspected that it was his way of limiting the options she had for striking out on her own.

When Lizzy sat down in one of the salon chairs, the stylist asked, "What did you have in mind?"

Lizzy pulled up a photo on her phone and showed it to the stylist.

She raised her eyebrows. "Are you sure?" she asked.

"Yup."

The stylist grinned. "Good for you."

AN HOUR LATER, Lizzy clattered up the outside stairs of the house.

"Uncle Owen, don't look yet," she yelled from outside the door.

"Why? Did it not turn out like you wanted?" he called back.

"It's like I wanted, but I'm not done yet. Close your eyes."

"Okay, they're closed."

She peeked around the edge of the door. Uncle Owen sat at the kitchen table, his eyes closed, a fan of papers and an empty French press carafe in front of him.

She ran across the living room to the bathroom and closed the door behind her. "Okay, you can open them now. I'll be out in a little bit."

Another hour had passed when she called, "I'm coming out!"

"I'm ready!" he called back.

She opened the bathroom door and stepped out.

Her hair was cropped crew-cut close to her head and was now a rich copper red. A huge smile lit her face. "It's called Red Penny!" she said. "What do you think?"

Owen stared, then smiled. "It's gorgeous, Pumpkin."

"I could have dyed it orange, and then you really could have called me Pumpkin," she said, giggling. She pirouetted, then plopped down into one of the chairs at the table. She ran her hand up the back of her head, grinning. "It feels funny. Like animal fur." She glanced at Owen. "Why are you looking at me like that?" She noticed that his eyes were misty and leaned toward him. "Are you okay?" she asked, concerned.

He nodded. "Your new look is very fetching. But what's even better is that smile. I haven't seen that smile in months."

12

With her appearance changed, Lizzy was willing to venture out into Sedona again, but her encounter on the Sugarloaf Trail convinced her that, as Donna had predicted, yoga alone was not going to provide the solution to her issues.

"How about a therapist?" she asked Owen that evening.

"What would you talk with them about? If you don't mind me asking."

"I could just say I don't feel like I have enough self-control."

"You and every other teenager in the world."

"Yeah, but maybe they would have some tips for me."

"Possibly," said Owen, sounding skeptical. He shrugged. "As long as you have a cover story, I guess it couldn't hurt. Let me do a little research."

Research completed, he made an appointment with a therapist whose credentials passed muster, explaining that his goddaughter needed to talk with a professional about "teenage girl things."

Owen dropped her off the next day at an office complex where the therapist's office was. "I'll pick you up in an hour."

"Okay," said Lizzy, climbing out of the car.

"We can go to lunch at that airport place with the good burgers," said Owen, perking up.

By the time Owen returned an hour later, Lizzy had been waiting on the bench outside the office building for forty-five minutes.

"How did it go?" Owen asked cheerfully, then noticed Lizzy's scowl. "Uh-oh. Not helpful?"

"I need a burger," Lizzy grumbled.

When they had gotten settled in the restaurant, Owen asked, "So?"

"I told her I wanted to be more in control, that I needed to keep from getting angry at people because when I do, bad things happen. She asked what kind of bad things, and I said they get hurt. Then she asked if I meant their feelings got hurt, and I didn't know what to say, so I said yes." Lizzy took a sip of her prickly pear soda. "Then she gave me this big pep talk about how it's possible to be too concerned about other people's feelings, about how I seemed like such a 'polite and considerate young lady,' and how maybe I needed to get more comfortable with my effect on other people. Evidently I'm just being a 'normal teenage girl' to be worried about this, and if I were a normal teenage boy, I wouldn't care what effect I had on other people. I think she probably has a teenage boy. Anyhow, I was just about fed up with the whole situation so I told her I had changed my mind and didn't want to finish the session. I gave her the money and got up to leave and she got all huffy about it, so I said that I was getting more comfortable with my effect on other people. Then I left."

Owen laughed. "You did?"

Lizzy looked embarrassed. "Yeah."

He shook his head. "Well, she can hardly complain about you following her own advice."

Lizzy smiled. "Yeah, I guess so. Sorry I wasted your money for the session."

He waved his hand. "It's not wasted. I think the therapist idea is a good one. We just need to find a competent one." He took out his phone and tapped. "I know someone at the University of Arizona who can give us a good recommendation. I should have thought of that earlier."

"But it's always going to be the same problem, isn't it?" said Lizzy. "I'm not going to be able to tell them what the real problem is, so any advice they give me is going to be based on a lie."

Owen set aside his phone with a sigh. "Yes, that is a problem."

"Although maybe in a place like Sedona," she continued, "there would be people who would believe something that sounded pretty crazy."

"How much do you plan to tell them?" asked Owen, sounding alarmed.

"Not the whole story," said Lizzy, "but something a little closer to the truth. Enough so they could actually give me some good advice."

"There are a lot of charlatans out there," he said. "Especially around here—a lot of people preying on tourists. Just let me talk to my friend at Arizona and see what she says."

Their burgers arrived, and they watched the planes taking off from the Sedona Airport runway for a bit, Googling the planes' tail numbers to find out what kind they were. But Lizzy's mind was still stewing on her situation.

"Maybe I should be on some kind of medication."

"Don't think we didn't consider it," said Owen. "I don't know if you remember, but we tried a couple of drugs when you were little. They just made you sad or dopey, and I'm not sure a sad, dopey person is less dangerous than a happy, alert one. Maybe more so."

"Maybe I should try pot."

"What?" said Owen, glancing nervously at the occupants of the nearby tables. "I don't think that's wise—the chemical compound—"

Lizzy laughed. "Don't have a coronary. I was just kidding."

"Jeez, don't do that to me," said Owen. "I pictured that I was going to have to hit the mean streets of Sedona looking for a source."

Owen's phone pinged. He pulled it out of his pocket and glanced at it. "Andy," he said. He read the text. "Says he took our mom to Longwood Gardens."

"Oh, yeah? Did she like it?"

Owen tapped, waited for the response, then smiled. "Yeah, he says she liked it."

Owen tapped out another response, then set his phone aside. "There's a botanical garden in Phoenix," he said. "We should go down there. Maybe stay over a couple of days and check things out down there."

Owen pulled up a couple of photos from the garden and showed them to Lizzy, then put his napkin next to his plate and pushed back his chair. "If you'll excuse me for a moment." He levered himself up and made his ponderous way through the tables toward the restrooms.

Lizzy was slurping up the last of her soda—something that would have earned her a raised eyebrow from Owen if he were still at the table—when she heard the ping of his phone. She lifted his napkin, which had been covering it, and picked up the phone.

mom loved the orchids

Lizzy was keying in *hi it's lizzy* when another text came through.

she's doing better today

She hesitated, then deleted her message and put the phone back on the table where Owen had left it.

When he returned, he glanced at the message and, his face clouding, slipped the phone back into his pocket.

"I saw the message," said Lizzy.

"Oh?"

"I'm sorry, I was typing a message to him that it was me but he sent that message before I finished it. Is your mom okay?"

"Yup. Did you leave room for dessert?"

She knit her brows. "Uncle Owen."

"She's fine."

"But if she's 'doing better today,' she must have been doing worse yesterday."

He looked down at his plate for a long moment, then back at Lizzy. "She's showing some signs of dementia. And my dad's having a hard time dealing with it. She's been gradually getting hazier the last couple of years, but she took a turn for the worse this past fall."

"Right when you were having to deal with me."

"Well ... yes. These things do seem to happen in clumps."

"Things like your goddaughter killing someone and having to be hustled to a different part of the country," said Lizzy softly, her voice laced with tears.

Owen covered her hand with his, then glanced around, checking that no one had heard her. "You didn't know about my mother, and you couldn't have done anything about it even if you had known."

Lizzy extracted her hand to wipe her nose with her napkin. "Do you need to go home?"

"Andy's on top of things."

"But you probably want to be there for your mom and dad, right? I would if I were you."

"I'll give her a call this evening. We can FaceTime—with technology these days, it's practically like being there, right?"

She examined him for a moment, then said, "Yeah, that's a good idea." But she could see from his expression that he knew it wasn't the same.

13

Mitchell sat in one of the art deco chairs in the hotel room Louise had taken just off Independence Mall. She stood at the window, looking in the direction of the US Courthouse, her phone in her hand.

"I don't understand why we have to do it at a news conference," said Mitchell.

"We're doing it at a news conference," said Louise, "because it will give us a dozen in-person witnesses, and thousands of witnesses to the event on television, who can swear that no one did anything to Brashear that would cause his death." After a pause, she added, "If I had known he was going to make the investigation public this fast, I might have been able to come up with other options, but this is the one that presented itself."

Her phone buzzed. "Yes?" she answered. After a moment, she said, "All right," then dropped the phone into her handbag and removed the case containing the syringe and vial. "George says they're almost ready." She filled the syringe and looked expectantly at Mitchell.

He rose reluctantly from the chair. "Maybe I don't need the drug. Maybe I can take care of him without it."

"Mitchell, this is our best opportunity to put an end to the investigation before it goes too far. Once the process is underway, once there's any kind of momentum behind the investigation, it will be much harder for us to stop it. We can't afford to take chances."

"What if they don't drop it, even after he's dead? What if someone else picks it up?"

"We'll cross that bridge when—and if—we come to it."

He hesitated, looking at the syringe. "It's pretty unpleasant."

"I've adjusted the dosage based on the earlier test, and I've found something to make the aftereffects more manageable."

It wasn't only the aftereffects that he dreaded—the pain that set in after the effect peaked, and the lethargy and aches that took days to fade. Almost as bad was the descent into helplessness that required Millard to come to his aid, and the fact that Louise was witness to his helplessness. It wasn't how he wanted her to see him.

But it was true that without the drug he couldn't guarantee that he could have any effect on Brashear in the few minutes the plan called for Mitchell to be in his vicinity, other than the possibility of inflicting a minor headache. He pulled up the sleeve of his T-shirt.

Louise injected him. "Remember," she said, "we don't need an effect as dramatic as the one at Logan Square. Even if he's only incapacitated, it will likely meet our needs. But," she added, "dead would be better." She replaced the syringe and the vial in the case and dropped it into her purse. "Don't do anything until I'm inside the building. Afterwards, George will get you out of there and back to Pocopson."

"When will you get home?"

"I'm not sure." She glanced at her watch. "Mitchell, please get dressed, we don't have a lot of time."

Mitchell tucked in his T-shirt and put on the starched white shirt that was hanging in the closet. He moved to the mirror to knot a burgundy silk tie.

"I have every reason to believe that this investigation was driven largely by Russell Brashear's personal connections to one of Vivantem's clients," said Louise. "The attorney general's office has too many believable-sounding crimes to investigate to worry about Vivantem once Brashear is out of the way." As Mitchell made some final adjustments to his tie, Louise pulled his suit jacket out of the closet and held it up for him. He slipped his arms into the sleeves and turned toward her. She straightened the jacket lapels slightly and stepped back. "Russell Brashear may have a personal connection to a Vivantem client, but as you and I have discussed, he also had a personal vendetta against my husband. I'm counting on you to even the score."

A flush was beginning to suffuse Mitchell's body—not the boiling frenzy of his encounter at the Basilica, but a steady, glowing heat.

"I can do that," he said.

She nodded and stepped to the door.

"You're ready?" she asked.

"I'm ready," he replied. He crossed to the door, opened it, and stood aside. "After you, Louise."

14

Millard had staked out the site of the news conference early. The sun was bright and the weather warm for February, and Brashear was holding the event outside. Millard appreciated that as an unexpected bonus—not only had he not been looking forward to getting Pieda out of the courthouse after Brashear was taken care of, but he wasn't enthusiastic about having to go through security to get in. The more off-the-radar he could stay, the better he liked it.

The pleasant weather encouraged passersby to linger, and a small crowd had gathered even before Brashear appeared. They held coffee cups and chatted among themselves as they watched the news crews set up. Millard bought a coffee of his own and joined them.

There was a stir in the crowd as Pennsylvania Attorney General Russell Brashear appeared from the courthouse. The crowd might not have known who Brashear was, but it was clear not only from the small entourage hurrying to keep up with his long strides but also by his military stance and air of determination that he was the man in charge. He walked to a young Hispanic man in a suit who was directing the setup of the podium and microphones. Millard strolled toward them under the pretense of examining the broadcasting equipment.

"It'll be just a couple more minutes, sir," said the young man.

Brashear nodded. "Thank you, Marco."

Millard got his phone out and hit a speed dial. After a moment he said, "Looks like they're almost ready," then, "Okay," and dropped his phone back into his pocket.

"Nice we could do it outside," said Marco.

Brashear looked skyward, as if he hadn't previously noticed the fine weather.

"Yes. Nice day." His voice was gravelly. He smiled slightly. "Brianna has a field trip to the Franklin Institute today. Can you just imagine trying to herd a couple dozen seven-year-olds through that place?"

"No, sir, I can't," said Marco with a smile.

"If I take both my own kids out, I make sure Donella's with me so we can have a man-to-man defense."

Marco laughed. "How is your wife, sir?"

"She's one of the chaperones for today's outing—I'll let you know how she is after I see her tonight. Speaking of man-to-man defense—" And they were off on a discussion of the Sixers' latest indignity.

After a few minutes, Brashear glanced at his watch. "Let's get started," he said.

"Yes, sir." Marco checked in with the news crews, then stepped to the podium.

"Good afternoon, and thank you for joining us this afternoon. Attorney General Russell Brashear has called this news conference to announce an investigation that his office is launching. Attorney General?"

Marco stepped back and Brashear stepped up to the

microphones, resting his hands on the sides of the podium. "Ladies and gentlemen, as some of you are aware, my office has launched an investigation of the Vivantem fertility clinic. We planned to announce that investigation at the end of last year, but then Gerard Bonnay, the CEO of Vivantem, was killed in an apparent break-in at their Center City offices. At that time, we put the investigation on hold as a courtesy to Mr. Bonnay's wife, Vivantem's medical director and new CEO, Dr. Louise Mortensen. But now it is time to pick up that investigation again, and we have asked Dr. Mortensen to come to the courthouse later today to answer some questions." He flipped over a page of his notes, but didn't glance down. "When I first heard the accusations against Vivantem, I have to admit that I was skeptical. But as we looked into the accusations, my skepticism was challenged. The Vivantem clients who came to us were quite certain that they had been subjected to something beyond standard, approved fertility treatments. Our investigation has uncovered some troubling facts, facts that suggest that the claims made by some of Vivantem's clients are not as outlandish as they might seem on the surface. There is evidence that Vivantem may have manipulated the treatments of the women who came to them for help, and that these treatments are now producing disturbing symptoms in the children born to those women."

Millard had been watching for Mortensen and Pieda's arrival, so he was among the first of the crowd to notice when they appeared from around the corner of the building opposite and crossed Market Street, headed toward the courthouse. Mortensen, of course, looked cool as a cucumber, and Pieda appeared to be holding it together pretty well, too. It always helped to be walking down the street with a beautiful woman, whatever her age.

In a moment, others in the crowd had noticed them as

well, and a murmur arose. The man standing next to Millard said, "Hey, it's her!" Then he leaned toward a woman standing at his side. "Who's the guy with her?"

The woman shrugged. "Got me."

Mortensen and Pieda stopped near the podium, the crowd shuffling back to make room for them.

"Dr. Mortensen—a little early for your hearing, aren't you?" asked Brashear, clearly annoyed at the interruption.

"On the contrary, Attorney General, I believe it is you who are late." She nodded to Pieda and disappeared into the courthouse.

"Very theatrical," said Brashear, "but theatrics won't distract my office from—"

He winced slightly and put a hand to his head.

Millard's eyes were on Pieda, whose fists were clenched and whose eyes were fixed, unblinking, on the AG.

Brashear shook his head and continued, "—won't distract my office from the investigation into claims that were ignored for too long by my predecessors. Claims that, although, as I have said, may seem outlandish at first glance—"

He winced again, this time clamping his eyes shut and dropping his head.

"... on first glance ..."

He stepped back from the microphones just as Marco stepped forward and took his arm. "Are you all right, sir?"

"Yes, yes, I just—"

Then Brashear sagged, Marco grabbing him as he fell. Millard heard Brashear's groan—"Jesus Christ!"

The surge of Brashear's entourage and the small crowd toward the podium masked Pieda's advance on the stricken AG. He leaned over Brashear, the knuckles of his clenched hands now white. In a quarter of a minute, the attorney general lay unmoving.

Millard slipped through the crowd to where Pieda stood steadying himself on the side of the podium. Marco was loosening Brashear's tie and collar, and a young woman was trying to wave the crowd back with cries of "Give him some air!" Cell phones were appearing in the hands of the bystanders, and a woman beside Millard said into hers, "Send an ambulance to the federal courthouse—the attorney general just collapsed!"

Millard had been planning to grab Pieda's elbow to lead him away, but thought better of it—he didn't want to alarm or piss off the guy who had just done that to Brashear. Millard shifted position until he was in Pieda's line of sight, and didn't approach until he had caught his eye. By the time he got back to Pieda's side, the young man was swaying.

"Good job, Mitchell," he said. "I've got you now. Let's get out of here."

By that time, three men in uniform had arrived, evidently from the courthouse, and one was performing CPR on Brashear. The second was speaking into a radio. The third noticed Mitchell.

"He okay?" he asked Millard.

"Yeah, he'll be okay. Just the shock of seeing something like that," replied Millard.

The man nodded and turned back to Brashear.

"Can you walk?" Millard whispered to Pieda. "The less attention we attract, the better."

Pieda nodded, but stumbled on his first step. Evidently Mortensen hadn't adjusted the dosage very much.

"Damn," Millard muttered under his breath. "Okay," he said to Mitchell, "let's sit you down and I'll bring the car. That'll attract less attention than us stumbling around."

Millard maneuvered Mitchell over to a short flight of steps at the side of the courthouse and eased him down.

"You wait right here. If someone asks you what's wrong, just say you're upset, that you don't need any help. All right?"

Mitchell nodded.

"I'll be back fast, Mitchell. Hang tight."

He jogged the short distance to the parking lot, slipped into the car, and started the engine. He paused only long enough to tap out a text.

All taken care of

15

Owen was partway through a turkey and provolone sandwich and glass of milk when his phone buzzed and his brother's name appeared on the caller ID.

He hit Accept. "Hey, what's up?"

"Owen, I have Ruby on the call." Andy's voice was uncharacteristically tense.

Owen set aside his sandwich. "Hello, Ruby."

"Hello, Dr. McNally." The Ballards' former housekeeper was equally, although not uncharacteristically, terse.

"What's up?"

"I'll let your brother tell you," said Ruby.

"Is Lizzy there?" asked Andy.

"No, she's at yoga class." Owen glanced at his watch. "She's usually home by now. What's going on?" He pushed himself up from the table and went to the large front windows that overlooked the street.

"Did you see the news?" asked Andy.

"Andy, tell me what happened!"

"It's all over the Philly stations," said Andy. "Russell Brashear, the state attorney general, just collapsed as he was announcing an investigation into Vivantem. He was talking about claims by clients that Vivantem manipulated treatments, that there were disturbing symptoms in the children. They took Brashear to Jefferson, where he died. They're speculating it was a stroke."

"Jesus Christ," breathed Owen. He scanned the street, seeing no sign of Lizzy.

"Yeah. And Louise Mortensen was there. Hold on, I'm sending you a link to the video."

Owen tapped out a text to Lizzy—*where are you?*—and returned to the kitchen table. He put the phone on speaker, then clicked on the link.

"As soon as I saw it," Andy continued, "I called Ruby to make sure she was all right."

"I'm at my sister and brother-in-law's house now," said Ruby.

Owen watched the video: Louise Mortensen arriving at the courthouse with a young man—he caught only a glimpse of him as the camera zoomed in on Mortensen—who stayed outside at the news conference after Mortensen went into the building. After Brashear fell, the video caught the young man, from the back, leaning over the AG.

Owen tapped out another text to Lizzy—*lizzy where are you?*—then, with the sound muted, replayed the video.

"Maybe that guy caused it," said Andy. "Maybe this means that there are other Vivantem kids—or adults—out there with Lizzy's ability."

"Yeah, maybe," said Owen.

"Do you recognize him?"

"No, but the video doesn't show him that clearly," said Owen. "Plus, I hardly ran in the same circles as Gerard Bonnay and Louise Mortensen."

All three of them were silent while Owen finished watching the video.

When it was done, Owen said, "If Gerard Bonnay's widow has an ally who can cause strokes, and she's out there looking to get even with people who caused problems for her or her husband, then the two of you need to be careful."

"Yeah," replied Andy, "although I never met her, just Bonnay."

"But it's likely he would have told her about you helping us get Lizzy out of the hospital," said Owen.

"I suppose so. How about you, Ruby?" asked Andy. "Did you have much to do with Mortensen?"

"No, mainly just Mr. Bonnay," she replied. "And I don't have any reason to believe that they knew what I did to help you." She paused. "If Dr. Mortensen is on the warpath, Dr. McNally, then you and Lizzy have more to worry about than we do. Do you think she knows where you are?"

"I haven't seen anything, or anyone, suspicious."

"At least we know who we need to be watching out for," said Andy. "The guy in the video."

"Unless there are more we haven't seen yet," said Owen.

"Don't forget George Millard," said Ruby.

"Three of them, four of us," said Andy. "Odds are in our favor!" His usual cheer sounded forced.

Owen sighed. "I wish we weren't talking about odds at all."

At that moment, he heard the clatter of a bike being dumped in the driveway and then footsteps running up the outside stairs. The door banged open and Lizzy stood in the doorway.

"Did you hear?" he asked.

"Yes," she said, her color high with emotion. "They made another one of me."

~

THEY HAD ENDED the call with Andy and Ruby with promises of increased vigilance on all sides. Now Owen and Lizzy sat at the dining room table.

"I was worried about you," said Owen. "You usually get home from yoga class sooner."

"I was having tea with someone from class."

"Oh? Who was that?"

"Some guy named Eric."

"Eric?" Owen was evidently not effective at hiding his surprise at the name.

"Yes, Uncle Owen," said Lizzy, her voice veering toward anger. "An actual guy."

"I didn't mean it like that ..." he began, then sighed. "Just took me by surprise, I guess."

"We were going to go hiking at Cathedral Rock." Her voice was unsteady. "I guess we won't be doing that now."

Owen had a sudden, heart-breaking vision of what life might have been like it if hadn't been for Gerard Bonnay and Louise Mortensen: Patrick and Charlotte, flanking their daughter Lizzy and her date for the prom or homecoming or whatever dress-up dances kids went to these days, the proud parents beaming, the teenagers self-conscious and anxious to be on their way, himself snapping pictures. Lizzy would have been graduating from high school soon, would probably already know what college she would be going to. Her biggest concern might have been the well-being of a dog—now a venerable ten-year-old—that her parents would no doubt have surprised her with on her seventh birthday.

Her body wouldn't have been scarred by the bullets fired at her by the man she had ended up killing, and her mind wouldn't have been scarred by her guilt at the deaths she had, directly or indirectly, caused: her mother, Lucia Hazlitt, her father, Anton Rossi, Gerard Bonnay.

"Oh, sweetheart," he said, his hand going to hers where it lay on the table.

She pulled her hand back and stood up from the table. "I'm tired. I'm going to bed."

And without looking back at him, she disappeared into her room and closed the door behind her.

16

That night Lizzy lay awake, sweaty and uncomfortable in an uncharacteristically humid Arizona night, the windows open to the occasional sound of a car passing the house and the more frequent sound of the barks and howls of coyotes. When she finally fell into a fitful sleep, it was dogged by nightmares.

She was in a train car—she could tell it was a train by the screech of wheels on rails—but it was so narrow that she could have reached her hands out and touched each side. Her father was next to her, whispering frantically that they had to get out. He had her hand in his and was pulling her—she tried to follow but the floor of the car was soft and uneven and it was hard to keep her balance. Her feet got tangled in something and she tripped and fell. She was grateful for the softness of the floor, a softness of wool and fur.

Then she realized that what was beneath her hands was a coat and that the coat covered a body and that the aisle of the train car, which now stretched out of sight ahead of her and behind, was filled with bodies, each enveloped in the same mink-collared coat, and that what had tripped her was the leather handle of a Prada handbag—the handbag Lucia Hazlitt had been carrying on the train that was supposed to take Lizzy and her dad to New York City to see the Christmas sights. And she realized that the screech that was drilling itself into her ears wasn't the metal-on-metal of train wheels on track, but the keening wail building behind the clenched teeth of every one of those bodies she was desperately trying to climb over.

She woke with her breath whistling in her throat and tears filling her eyes.

Sleepless hours later, when the red numbers of the digital clock on her bedside table flipped to 5:00 am, Lizzy picked up her phone and tapped out a text: *Can I call you? Not an emergency.* With the two hour time difference, Lizzy guessed that Ruby DiMano was probably already puttering around her Overbrook apartment.

Yes came back the immediate response.

Lizzy hit the speed dial for Ruby.

"Is everything okay?" asked Ruby by way of a greeting.

"Yes," said Lizzy. "As much as it can be, I guess."

"Yes."

"I had a dream. I was on a train, and Lucia Hazlitt was there." She hesitated. "On the floor. Actually, there were a lot of bodies just like her on the floor, and they were all making the same noise she did when ... you know."

"Yes. I know."

"My dad was there, too. Trying to get me away. Just like in real life."

Neither of them spoke for a few moments, then Lizzy said, "I don't know what to do."

"You don't need to do anything."

Her hand went to the Zuni bear pendant. "I feel responsible."

"For what?"

"For what happened to Mr. Brashear."

"You're not responsible," said Ruby briskly. "You didn't have anything to do with the investigation he started, and you're not responsible for someone else trying to stop him. But if you lay low, maybe someone else in his office will finish up what he started and let everyone know what they're up to at Vivantem."

"But what if they look into the Vivantem client files and come after me?"

"That's why it's better for you to be in Arizona with Dr. McNally. Harder for them to get to you."

"Maybe you can come out here and stay with us."

"I can't. My brother-in-law is doing poorly and I need to stay here to help my sister."

"I'm sorry to hear about your brother-in-law."

"Thank you."

Lizzy kicked the sheet back where it had gotten wrapped around her foot. "I should never have gone after Mr. Bonnay."

"Lizzy, you and I hashed through all this. We both thought it was the only way you were going to get out from under his thumb. And we were both pretty sure he had your dad killed. But now you don't need to worry about Gerard Bonnay anymore. You just need to stay out of the way and let the authorities take care of Dr. Mortensen and Vivantem."

Lizzy rolled on her side and looked out the bedroom window at a bank of moonlit clouds hovering over the blackness of the mesas. "They're going to run tests on Mr. Brashear and find out that he had a stroke."

After a pause, Ruby replied. "Yes, I suspect they will."

"And they'll look back over records of other people who died of a stroke and find Lucia Hazlitt. And Anton Rossi." She thought back to the altercation with the lecherous Rossi in the library of Gerard and Louise's house. They had claimed that putting Lizzy in the same room as Rossi was a mix-up, and that the locked door had been her own mistake, but she was sure that they had chosen Rossi as the means of testing Lizzy's ability. And from the point of view of Gerard and Louise, she had passed that test with flying colors. Rossi's body, its brain riddled with bleeds, had turned up in the alley behind his Philadelphia row house the next morning.

"It's going to be tough for the authorities to tie Anton Rossi to Lucia Hazlitt," said Ruby. "And lots of people have strokes."

"Not when they're middle-aged and healthy."

Ruby said nothing.

"They all had strokes," continued Lizzy, "and you know what they had in common? They all had the bad luck to piss me off." She pulled a tissue from the box on the bedside table and wiped her nose.

"Lizzy, the situation with Lucia Hazlitt was bad luck—bad luck for her, bad luck for you—but if she hadn't been acting like a first-class b—" Ruby cleared her throat. "—jerk, she would have gone on her merry way getting on all those trashy news shows and complaining about how everyone had it in for whatever thug she was defending at the moment. You didn't mean to do what you did to her—we all know that. And as for Mr. Bonnay and Anton—well, in my opinion, they had it coming." She paused. "Lizzy, I know you feel guilty, but I'm just as guilty in all this as you are. Actually, I'm more guilty, because I was helping Gerard Bonnay."

"He didn't give you any choice."

"He didn't give you any choice, either. He didn't give you a choice, he didn't give your mother a choice, and he certainly didn't give your father a choice."

Lizzy hiccupped back a sob. Her father had gone to the Philadelphia police to keep them away from Lizzy after Lucia

Hazlitt's death, and had ended up dead himself—very likely at the hands of George Millard—just steps from the police station.

"Oh, Lizzy, I'm sorry," said Ruby, her voice as soft as it ever got. "I just wish you would realize that none of this is your fault."

Lizzy wiped her eyes again and tossed the sodden tissue in the direction of the wastepaper basket. "It's so frustrating to be here and know something's going on in Philadelphia and not be able to do anything about it."

"It would be worse to be in Philadelphia where it's all going on and not be able to do anything about it."

"*You're* in Philadelphia," said Lizzy.

"Yes, and I know I can't do anything about it. I'm just laying low and minding my own business."

"Well, what's happening there is my business," replied Lizzy, taking a deep breath. "I'm going to figure out what I need to do to be able to come back to Pennsylvania, and when I do, I *am* going to do something about it."

17

The medical examiner picked a microscopic piece of lint off his pant leg while he waited for his call to be answered.

"Chief Holland's office."

"Hello, Molly, this is Roger Stanislas—how are you doing?"

"Hey, Roger! I'm fine. You?"

"Quite well, thank you. Is the Chief available? I have some interesting news for him related to the Lucia Hazlitt and Russell Brashear deaths."

"Let me check, hold on one sec." In a moment, Molly was back. "He says to put you through."

Molly's voice was replaced by that of Philadelphia's Police Chief, Carl Holland.

"Stanislas," he boomed out, "what have you got for me? Molly said developments on Hazlitt and Brashear—I didn't know you were looking into those deaths."

"Not officially," said Stanislas, "but I got curious about them. Two relatively young people—and in this case, local celebrities—with no history of hypertension or other propensity for stroke dying like they did. I did some searches in our database and found another anomalous death."

"Who's that?"

"Homeless man. He was found a little over a week ago near the Basilica on Logan Square."

"And this homeless guy's death is somehow related to Lucia Hazlitt, every cop's least favorite lawyer, and Russell Brashear, top cop of PA?" the Chief asked, obviously dubious.

"Possibly. You recall the results of the autopsies of Ms. Hazlitt and AG Brashear, of course—significant cerebral hemorrhages that caused death within minutes."

"Yeah."

"The homeless man had also suffered a cerebral hemorrhage, but one so massive that I have no doubt he died almost instantly."

There was silence on the line.

"A homeless man suffering a normal stroke would hardly have merited mention," continued Stanislas, "but this is unlike any stroke I've ever seen. It's less like he had a stroke than that he got shot in the head without the inconvenience of entrance or exit wounds."

"What the hell," muttered Holland. "What could the three of them possibly have in common?"

"Brashear was about to launch an investigation into Vivantem about alleged unethical experimentation, Hazlitt was about to launch into a defense of Dollar Slash on drug charges. Maybe someone's decided to take the law into his or her own hands."

There was silence for a few seconds, then Holland said, "That makes no sense. If it was some pro-law vigilante, he might knock off Hazlitt, but not Brashear. If it was some anti-law extremist, he'd go for Brashear but leave Hazlitt alone."

"Just a thought," said Roger.

"Plus," continued Holland, "what's the tie-in to the home-less guy?"

"Maybe a trial run. They take out Hazlitt, then they plan to take out Brashear and want to practice first because it's going to be so public."

"The Amtrak Keystone is pretty public."

"But not captured by a whole gaggle of news crews."

Roger could hear a repeated thump thump over the line. Having had the pleasure of in-person meetings with the Chief in the past, he could picture the big man knocking the toe of his shoe against the metal filing cabinet next to his desk.

"Weren't we looking for someone as a person of interest in the Hazlitt case?"

Roger flipped over a page in the file in front of him. "Yes—Patrick Ballard and his daughter Elizabeth were seen fleeing 30th Street after Hazlitt's collapse. I know the detective who interviewed Ballard—Joe Booth—and gave him a call. Turns out that after Booth talked to him, Ballard ended up dead in an alley a block from the station."

"From a stroke?" asked Holland, his voice spiking.

"No. Two gunshots—one to the abdomen, one to the back of the neck. They figured it for a mugging."

"What about the daughter?"

"Elizabeth. Never caught up with her. That incident in Roxborough happened right after Patrick Ballard's death and all the manpower got diverted to that."

Roger heard the gust of an exhale from the Chief. "So what is this vigilante—protector of boutique fertility clinics and bane of rap stars—doing to stroke out the people he wants to get rid of?"

Roger shrugged. "Hard to say. It would have to be very targeted, since no one around the victims was reported to suffer any ill effects. That would point away from any kind of generalized virus or other infectious agent."

"Maybe they snuck them something in their food."

"I can't imagine what you could feed a person that would have the effects we're seeing. Especially the homeless man."

"Injection?"

"Possible, I suppose."

"Jesus, Stanislas—you're no help at all," growled Holland. He heaved a deep sigh. "I'll have someone do some digging, see if they can find any connection. And you let me know if you find any more bodies with exploded brains, will you?"

"Will do, Chief."

In the world of cell phones, one rarely had the opportunity to be on the receiving end of a loud hang-up. Roger suspected the Chief held onto his landline for just this purpose.

18

The lawyers had advised Louise to stay out of the public eye until the furor over Brashear's death subsided, and although it was clear that staying out of the public eye was no hardship for her, staying away from her lab was. So despite the lawyers' disapproval, she continued her daily commutes to and from the Vivantem facility in Center City, leaving through an entrance at the back of the property to avoid any reporters who might be staking out the front gate.

For a few days after the events at the federal courthouse, Mitchell was laid up at the Pocopson house. He didn't feel quite as awful as he had after the incident at the Basilica, but he felt awful enough—a throbbing headache that no amount of aspirin could cure, a dull pain in his legs and neck that made sitting in front of a fire in the library with a book the most appealing pastime. With Louise at the lab and Millard in Arizona to deal with Elizabeth Ballard and Owen McNally—and so no witnesses to his debilitated state—he gave himself over to Juana's care.

But once his symptoms began to ease up, Mitchell started

to find the solitude of the big house oppressive. Perusing a website of local events, one caught his eye: a whiskey tasting at a local restaurant. He broached the idea cautiously to Louise over dinner. Her mind was still as opaque to him as ever, but he didn't need to be a mind-reader to sense a flicker of relief at the idea of having the house to herself for an evening.

She loaned him an older but pristinely maintained Range Rover. She had offered the use of her Jaguar, but he declined. While saving for his dream car—an Audi A3—he had relied mainly on public transportation, and even though he was twenty-three, his driving experience was fairly limited. The bulky Range Rover seemed a safer bet than the Jag, at least for him. Once he brushed up on his driving skills, he hoped Louise would repeat the offer of the Jaguar, or possibly of Gerard Bonnay's Boxster, for his outings.

The event started out well. He was the only man wearing a suit, eliciting mental raised eyebrows from all the men whose thoughts he could sense, and approval from most of the women. The tasting was held in the bar of a Kennett Square restaurant, so once the participants were seated, his solo status was less apparent than if they had been sitting at tables. A line of six small glasses stood in front of each taster, and there was much joking and laughter among the guests about designated drivers.

Ten minutes after the tasting began, a group of three girls —he really couldn't think of them as women—made their entrance. They were celebrating the twenty-first birthday of one of the group, and with their over-loud talking and laughing, it was clear that they had already started the celebration. There weren't three seats together, and they exclaimed over the horror of having to sit apart from each other. The host rearranged the other participants so that there were three seats together—the three seats next to Mitchell.

The thoughts of two of the girls were jumbled messes, but the thoughts of the third—the birthday girl, the most drunk of the three, and the one in the seat next to him—wavered toward him and locked on. She examined him with frank, if bleary, interest. He did his best to block out her thoughts.

The bartender poured the whiskey while the host regaled the group with information about barrel-aging, the role of terroir, and the physics of snifters.

Mitchell didn't want to take any chances with Louise's Range Rover so he took a few tiny sips of each pour, leaving most of it in his glass. After a few minutes, the girl next to him leaned over.

"You're wasting it!" she said in a voice loud enough to cause several people on Mitchell's other side to glance over. Mitchell hoped it was clear he was not with her group.

"It's a whiskey *tasting*, not a whiskey *swilling*," he whispered back.

She shrieked with laughter, attracting the attention of the entire group. "'Not a whiskey swilling'!" she gasped. "You're funny!"

One of her less-drunk friends turned toward her. "Act like a grown-up, Kim—this isn't Chili's."

"It's my birthday," Kim retorted. "Don't be such a stick-in-the-mud."

The girl rolled her eyes and turned back to her other, somewhat less drunk, friend.

Kim turned to Mitchell. "It's my birthday."

"Happy birthday," said Mitchell mechanically.

Kim extended her hand. "I'm Kimberlee—" she said, and *with two Es* floated through Mitchell's mind. "—with two Es," she concluded.

"Pleased to meet you," whispered Mitchell, taking her hand.

She kept ahold of his hand. "What's your name?" she asked.

"Mitchell."

"Cool. That sounds so, like—" Evidently unable to decide what it sounded like, her voice trailed off.

Mitchell extracted his hand.

Kimberlee was quiet for a minute, her arm leaning against Mitchell's, watching the host with exaggerated gravity.

"Now take a sip of the next glass," said the host, "and you'll notice a much more peaty taste than with the first glass."

"Petey?" Kimberly asked.

"Peaty, as in 'like peat,'" said the host. "Peat is partly decomposed vegetable matter."

"Ew!" she cried, returning the glass in her hand to the bar top with a crash and slosh of whiskey. This time the eye rolls and head shakes extended all the way down the bar. Mitchell felt his ears burn with embarrassment.

Kimberlee reached over to the glasses in front of Mitchell. "I liked the first one. It didn't taste like dead vegetables. You didn't finish it, can I have the rest?" She tossed it back and smacked her lips.

"Excuse me," Mitchell whispered, sliding off the barstool.

"Where are you going?" she asked.

"I have to use the restroom."

"Kinda early to need to pee already."

Mitchell felt his ears turn redder, and slipped past the other tasters and through the dining room, his eyes on the floor.

In the men's room, he straightened his tie and smoothed his hair back. Was it worth it to stay? There were no empty seats at the bar, so he couldn't just switch to another seat—and even if he did, Kimberlee would no doubt make a scene about it. He couldn't slip out—he hadn't paid yet. Perhaps he would pay the maître d' and leave.

He stepped out of the men's room, right into the maître d' himself.

"I was just coming to see you," said Mitchell.

"And I was just coming to see you, sir."

"Listen, I can't stay," said Mitchell, getting out his wallet. "How much do I owe you for the event?"

The maître d' looked mollified. "That will be thirty-five dollars each."

Mitchell looked up. "Each?"

"For you and your girlfriend."

"She's not my girlfriend," said Mitchell, horrified.

"Okay. Your date," amended the maître d'. "So the total will be seventy dollars."

"She's not my girlfriend *or* my date. She's just some drunk girl who happened to sit next to me."

"That's not what she says," said the maître d'.

"She said she's my date?"

"She said she's your girlfriend." The maître d' leaned toward Mitchell. "I really think you need to take her home. I mean to *her* home. To sleep it off."

Just then, Kimberlee came around the corner, wobbling slightly on high heels. When she saw Mitchell she gave a coy giggle. "Sweetie, where in the world did you get off to?" she cried in a wavering soprano. Several diners turned toward Kimberlee, Mitchell, and the maître d'.

"Sir," whispered the maître d', "please just pay your bill and get her out of here."

"She's not my girlfriend," said Mitchell, trying to pitch his voice low enough to sound discreet but loud enough that the diners nearest to them would hear him.

"Okay, fine," said the maître d', exasperated, "please get your *date* out of here."

Kimberlee giggled, moved to Mitchell's side, and looped her arm through his. "Take me home, honey," she cooed.

An image leapt out at him from her mind: a nutcracker soldier straight out of the Christmas ballet, but with Mitchell's face above the clenched jaw.

He had to get her to shut up. He reached out with his mind and dropped that first stone of the peine forte et dure—the crushing death—he had described to Louise.

Kimberlee's scrunched up her nose for a moment, then amended her instruction. "Actually, we should finish our drinks, and *then* go home, Sweet Buns."

He dropped the second stone.

"Damn," she whined, "now I have a headache." She leaned into him more heavily.

"Sir," said the maître d', "please remove her."

Mitchell jerked his arm out of Kimberlee's hold, fumbled four twenties out of his wallet, and stuffed them into the man's jacket pocket. "Remove her yourself," he said. He brushed by Kimberlee, her laughter like salt to his wounded pride, and made his way through the dining room to the front door, hoping for a purposeful stride, but achieving only an embarrassed scuttle.

19

Mitchell drove the Range Rover carefully back to Pocopson, trying not to allow his anger at the girl to distract him from the task of maneuvering the large vehicle. He drove around to the back of the house and pulled the Rover into the detached garage where it was kept, the spaces in the attached garage being occupied by Louise's Jaguar, Gerard's Boxster, and the large black Mercedes they used when Millard was driving.

Mitchell parked the car, rolled closed the large barn-style doors that allowed the garage to pass for a stable, and let himself in the back door. Juana was pulling on her coat as he stepped into the kitchen.

"Good evening, Juana," he said.

"Buenas tardes, Señor Pieda."

"Is Dr. Mortensen home yet?"

"No, pero debería llegar pronto."

Since his knowledge of Spanish didn't extend beyond the niceties exchanged while Juana was serving dinners, he scanned Juana's thoughts to establish the general sense that

Louise had not yet returned from the lab. He nodded. "Gracias."

"De nada." Juana stepped outside and turned toward the back of the house where her car was parked.

Mitchell stood looking after her for a moment, unreasonably disappointed that Louise wasn't yet home. Perhaps he would get a glass of whiskey from Gerard's study and test out his newly acquired—although truncated—education on the topic.

At the bar in Gerard's study, he found a glass of the type that had been used at the tasting and poured himself a small portion. But when he took a sip, the liquid tasted bitter, and he returned to the kitchen and poured it down the drain.

He was still standing at the sink, gazing out at the inky darkness of the Pennsylvania night, when he saw the head-light beams from Louise's car sweep across the trees and bushes lining the gravel road that gave access to the back of the Pocopson property. The Jag passed the kitchen window and continued around to the side of the house, where the main garage was. A minute later he heard the muted rumble of the garage door, the clatter of hangers in the coat closet, then her steps heading toward her study. He let a few minutes pass, then followed her to the room.

She was seated at her desk, opening the letters that Juana had left on her blotter.

He knocked lightly on the door frame.

She looked up. "How was the wine tasting?"

"Whiskey."

"Pardon?"

"It was a whiskey tasting."

"Ah." Louise slit open another envelope and removed the contents.

After a few moments, Mitchell said, "The maître d' wasn't very professional."

"Oh?" Louise put the envelope in a wicker basket under her desk and the contents in a wooden tray on the desk.

Mitchell sat on one of the chairs in front of her desk. "There was a drunk girl there, and she told the maître d' that she was my girlfriend."

"Really? How awkward."

"Yes."

Louise opened the next envelope.

"She was being quite a nuisance," he said.

"I can imagine." Louise scowled at the contents of the second envelope and dropped both the envelope and the contents into the wicker basket.

"I thought I might just give her a little bit of the crush to keep her quiet."

Louise's eyes snapped up. "What?"

"I didn't do her any harm," he added quickly. He had gotten Louise's attention; he didn't want to incur her anger.

Louise set aside the letter opener. "You know you can't do that, don't you, Mitchell?"

"It was just to get her to shut up," he said, a slight whine that even he hated creeping into his voice. "She won't even have a headache by the time she gets home. *Staggers* home," he amended.

"It's important that you use your power judiciously, and only after we have a thorough plan in place."

"Yes, I know," he said irritably. "Next time I'll wait until you've given me permission to use it."

"Mitchell—" she began, then stopped and took a breath. "Glass of sherry?"

He didn't like sherry. He nodded. "Yes, that would be nice."

She stood and crossed to a side table and poured two

glasses, then sat down on the chair next to his. She passed him a glass.

"You're not my employee, Mitchell. We're partners."

He sipped his drink.

"We each bring something to the table. You bring your powers. And I"—she smiled ruefully—"bring many years of experience."

"And a plan."

"Yes. And a plan to turn the results of your powers into something beneficial for both of us."

They sat in silence for a minute, then Mitchell said, "I haven't seen anything in the news about the attorney general's investigation continuing. Seems like they lost interest."

"It sounds like it was a pet project of Russell Brashear," replied Louise, "and once he was gone—thanks to you—there wasn't anyone interested in carrying it forward."

"Lucky for us the story sounded unbelievable."

"Yes. Lucky."

He waited for more, but she was silent.

"So," he said finally, "what *is* the plan?"

"We need to find Ballard. And McNally. Then we can decide."

"Any progress?"

"George is looking for them in Sedona. He'll find them."

"I could help," he said. "It seems like it would be useful to have someone who can read minds involved."

Louise gave him a tired smile. "If we find someone whose thoughts might reveal where they are, we can reassess. But you've taken care of your part of the business, Mitchell. We need to let George take care of his."

He stood abruptly and saw a flicker of alarm cross her face. Did she think that his ability to use the crush without the benefit of the drug wasn't as limited as he had described? He made an effort to relax his posture, to soften the frown that had been forming on his face.

"I'm bored," he said, more mildly than he felt. "I've been here in Pocopson for almost two months. I need to do something."

"It's not so bad, is it?"

"I'm not saying it's been any sacrifice," he said. "It's been like a vacation. But I can't be on vacation forever. We have goals, and I want to work toward them."

She shook her head. "Gerard's death has put a bit of a damper on our original plans. We thought that with your mind-reading ability and his ..." Her voice trailed off, then she took a deep breath and continued. "Well, you know, with Gerard being who he was, there would be little that could stand in our way. In business. In politics." She looked at Mitchell sadly. "Now, I have to admit, my goals have become more focused on keeping Elizabeth Ballard and Owen McNally from ruining what is left of what Gerard and I built: the Vivantem clinic. My professional position. A quiet life here in Pocopson without the authorities breathing down our necks."

"But once that's taken care of," replied Mitchell, "isn't it possible that we can consider those original goals again? You can step into Gerard's role."

She laughed, an unaccustomed sound. "You flatter me, Mitchell, but my world is the scientific world—the world of the lab, not the world of the boardroom. And certainly not," she added with a shudder, "Washington and those halls of power."

He smiled. "I think you underestimate yourself, Louise."

"I never underestimate myself," she replied. After a moment, she added, "You, however ..."

His heart leapt. "What do you mean?"

She sat back in her chair and looked at him speculatively. "You're so young, Mitchell, but I can see in you some of the characteristics that made Gerard so successful in business, and could have made him so successful in politics. Intelligence. Drive. A sense of presence. A sense of decorum. Perhaps it's not out of the question that we may be able to pursue those goals again."

Mitchell's mind whirled at the possibilities of what Louise was suggesting, but he was saved from having to respond when Louise's cell phone whirred from her desk.

She stood, retrieved it, and glanced at the caller ID. "Yes?" she said by way of greeting, then, after a moment, "Hold on, Mitchell is here and I'd like him to hear this too. I'm putting you on speaker."

She returned to the chair and sat down. "Go ahead," she said toward the phone. "Start from the beginning."

"I found them," said Millard, the buzz of traffic filtering over the connection. "I figured that at this point even Owen McNally might have gotten tired of eating at restaurants all the time, so I took a photo I got from the Penn website and showed it around at the local grocery stores. Got lucky at the third one I went to—a place called Bashas' in West Sedona. They said McNally comes in almost every day, usually with a teenage girl, and sure enough, they showed up today."

"What if the person you talked to mentions to McNally that someone's looking for him?" Louise asked sharply.

"I don't think they will. I gave them a glimpse of a badge— no one ever asks to see it up close—and implied that the authorities would be none too pleased if the fat guy got wind of any interest in him."

"Very good," said Louise.

"He's driving an older SUV—too old to be a rental. If he's

bought a car, seems like they're planning on staying for a little while."

"His vehicle is still in the shed in back," interrupted Louise. "We need to get rid of that."

"Yeah, I'll work on that when I get back."

"All right."

"They're staying in a house nearby. I can't find any reference to it on the home rental sites, and I don't believe McNally owns it, so I figure it must belong to a friend."

"What are they doing there?"

"I just located them and the house a little while ago. I haven't had a chance to find out."

"Well, keep an eye on them and let me know what they're up to."

"Yeah," said Millard, in a voice that made it clear he didn't need to be told.

Louise addressed Millard but turned her eyes to Mitchell. "George, now that we know where McNally and Ballard are, I think it's working well to have you there to keep an eye on them, and for Mitchell to stay here with me for the time being."

"Sounds good to me," said Millard.

Mitchell nodded. "Yes, all right."

"Let me know what you find out, George," Louise said, and ended the call. She turned to Mitchell. "We'll wait to hear from George. We need to be patient, and we need to be careful. We've gotten away with Brashear's murder. We need to get away with two more."

20

"I'm going to yoga class," said Lizzy to Owen as she headed for the door.

"Again? Didn't you just go to yoga class yesterday?"

"Yes. But I like it a lot. I think I'm getting a lot out of it."

"Well, if you're going to have a teenage obsession, yoga is certainly a wholesome choice," he said agreeably.

Lizzy ran down the steps to the driveway and strapped her yoga mat to the back of her bike. She coasted to 89A, then pedaled east, toward Uptown Sedona, skimming past Namaste Yoga and Meditation, her professed destination.

Owen had contacted his colleague in Phoenix for therapist recommendations, and then got pulled into an all-consuming professional discussion about nature versus nurture. While the multiday debate raged, Lizzy returned to her own search for alternatives and found what she thought was a promising option. She showed her finding to Owen.

"That's interesting," he said. "But just give me another day or two, Pumpkin, and I'll find you a real therapist. Or," he said, glancing at the website, "a counselor with some sort of recognized certification."

As she approached Uptown Sedona, the view to her right
—the green and gold brush of the valley leading the eye to the
jagged red peaks in the distance—began to disappear behind
the stores and businesses catering to Sedona's visitors. They
strolled along tree-shaded sidewalks lined with Southwestern-
themed art galleries, clothing shops, jewelry stores, and
restaurants, or sunned themselves on the eastward-facing
balconies of hotels.

She approached the point just before the last stores gave
way again to desert scrub as 89A met up with Oak Creek and
began its increasingly green path up Oak Creek Canyon. She
pulled her bike to the side of the road in front of a building
whose stone facade and hacienda-style covered porch blended
pleasingly with its stunning red rock backdrop. The building
housed two businesses—a leather store on the left and, on the
right, the business whose website she had shown to Uncle
Owen: Philip Castillo, Psychic Counselor.

She chained her bike to a fence in back of the building,
then walked to the front. A sign behind the glass panes of the
door read *Walk Ins Welcome*. A small wooden box attached to
the wall held brochures. She pulled one out and read the
same information she had read on the website and shown to
Uncle Owen.

Take advantage of the positive energy of the Red Rocks of
Sedona to access your own limitless potential! Only your
self-doubt holds you back from achieving the goals you
aspire to, or from overcoming the barriers that are standing
in your way. Psychic Counselor Philip Castillo can help you
recognize and tap into your own power—the power to
achieve your dreams.

The photo on the brochure showed a man in his early thirties, with longish black hair combed back from dark eyes and a sun-weathered face. He looked directly at the camera, his mouth turned up in a slight smile.

She slipped the brochure into her knapsack. She wasn't going to wait around for Uncle Owen's professional debate to run its course. She was an adult—or almost. She was the one who had gotten them into this mess. It was only right that she should be the one to find a way to get them out of it.

She stepped into a waiting room furnished with a rustic bench and the half-circle pigskin chairs she had learned from Uncle Owen were called Equipale—"the Southwest's snub to people my size," as he described them. Complexly woven rugs hung on the walls, and kachina dolls stood on shelves in the corners of the room. A colorful striped curtain covered a door leading to the back. Native American flute music played softly on an old CD player.

She heard steps from the back room and the man from the brochure stepped through the curtained door.

"Miss Patrick?"

Elizabeth Patrick was the name she had used to sign up for her yoga class and for the unsuccessful visit with the therapist, the only other times she had had to provide a last name since leaving Pennsylvania.

"Yes. Please call me Elizabeth."

"Certainly, Elizabeth. I'm Philip."

He stepped to the door and turned the sign to display *Session in Progress - Please Stop Back Later*. He glanced out the door. "Did you come with anyone?"

"No. Just me."

He hesitated. "I usually lock the door so people don't come in while we're talking," he said. "Is that okay?"

"Sure," said Lizzy.

Philip flipped the lock, then held back the curtain leading to the back room.

It was windowless and darker than the sunlit front room. A woven rug softened the wooden floor, a low bookshelf along one wall was topped with Indian pottery. On the wall was a large painting on what looked like old paper or cloth. Its detail, an inked grid of red-bordered orange lines overlaid with human figures and undulating black shapes, was indistinct in the dim light. Two of the Equipale chairs faced each other across a narrow table. He gestured her into the one closer to the door and circled the table to the other chair.

"Can I get you something to drink? Tea? Water?"

"That's okay, I brought some water with me," she said, pulling a bottle out of her knapsack.

Philip sat in the facing chair. "I normally ask people to turn their cell phone off since it can be distracting if it rings during our session, but you can do whatever you find comfortable."

"That's no problem," she said. She pulled her phone out of her pocket and switched it off.

"So," said Philip, "what can I help you with?"

"I found you online. Psychic counseling sounds interesting. And useful."

"Do you have a psychic issue you're wrestling with?"

She laughed nervously. "Doesn't everyone?"

"Everyone should, but not everyone does. Or recognizes it."

Lizzy's hand drifted to the bear pendant at her throat.

"Blaming yourself for something?" he asked.

She started. "Why do you ask that?"

He gestured toward her necklace. "The Zuni bear."

She dropped her hand. "Isn't everyone?"

He laughed. Not the deep, harsh laugh she would have

expected from his speaking voice, but a light, happy sound. "Everyone should be," he said, "but not everyone does. Or recognizes it."

She smiled tentatively at him.

"I ..." She had planned to use the same "I want to be more in control" line she had used on the therapist, but was suddenly unwilling to risk a repeat of that conversation. "My dad died recently," she said, surprising herself.

"I'm very sorry to hear that," he replied, his eyes softening.

Lizzy wiped her nose with the back of her hand, and Philip moved a box of tissues from a shelf behind him to the table.

Lizzy pulled out a tissue and blotted her nose. "Thanks."

"How recently?" asked Philip.

"December fifth."

"It's never easy to lose a parent, but it's especially tough around the holidays."

Lizzy blew her nose. "It wasn't much of a holiday."

"No, I wouldn't think so."

He moved a wastepaper basket next to the table and she tossed the tissue into it.

"Are you here with your mom?" he asked.

Lizzy pulled another tissue from the box. "No. My mom's dead."

Philip knit his brows but remained silent.

"She died a long time ago. When I was seven." Her hand crept to the Zuni pendant again.

"Do you blame yourself for your mother's death?" he asked.

She smiled wanly at him and dropped her hand. "Now I know how you're doing that."

He smiled back at her. "I gave away my trick."

She sat back in the chair and sighed. She ran her hand up

the back of her shorn red hair. "My mom was sick. She had had a lot of little strokes, and ... I behaved in a way that made her situation a lot worse."

She expected to hear some variation of the response she had always heard from her father, Uncle Owen, and Ruby: that she had been a child, that she couldn't have known what effect she was having on her mother, that she couldn't blame herself for what had happened. But Philip merely said, "That would be a hard thing to live with."

They sat in silence for a few moments, then Philip asked, "And your father's death—do you feel responsible for that, too?"

She nodded slowly. "Yes. Not in the same way, but ... yes."

"It's a heavy burden for a young woman to bear."

They sat in silence again, then Philip asked, "You're not here in Sedona by yourself, are you?"

Lizzy shook her head. "No, I'm here with my uncle. Actually, he's my godfather, but I call him Uncle Owen."

"Do you get along with Uncle Owen?"

She smiled. "Oh, yeah. He's a great guy. And he would do anything for me. I love him a lot."

"Have you spoken with him about how you feel about your parents' deaths?"

"Yeah. He doesn't blame me for what happened to my parents, but it doesn't really help me feel better about it." She picked at a loose thread on the sleeve of her blouse. "Are your parents still around?"

Philip shook his head. "No. My mother also died when I was young, and my father disappeared a few years later."

"I'm sorry to hear about your parents." After a moment, she sat forward. "I didn't really mean to talk about my mom and dad. The reason I came is that ..." She took a deep breath. "I want to be more in control. So I don't hurt people the way I hurt my mom. I can't explain how. I can just say that being more in control will help." She pulled the brochure out of her knapsack. "'Only your self-doubt holds you back from achieving the goals you aspire to, or from overcoming the barriers that are standing in your way,'" she read, then looked up. "I want to set aside my self-doubt and overcome my barriers."

Philip laughed softly. "Then I guess you came to the right place. Why don't you tell me a little bit about yourself."

Lizzy told him.

Without naming any of the locations, she described her early years in a fashionable suburban town outside a large city. She described the need, although not the reason, for the move to a remote vacation cabin with her mother, and the circumstances, although not the cause, of her mother's death. She described the subsequent move with her father to a less fashionable town outside the same large city, and made a vague reference to the attempted Christmastime trip to one city that ended abruptly in another.

She made no reference at all to her kidnapping by Louise Mortensen and Gerard Bonnay, or to her rescue by Uncle Owen, Andy McNally, and Ruby DiMano. In the version she shared with Philip, her next stop after the aborted Christmas trip was an unidentified rural town, and from there through various interim destinations before arriving in Sedona. As she spoke, she realized she had never had to tell anyone about her life, because the few people in her small circle had been part of that life as she was living it.

She paused to decide where to go from there, then gave a start. "What time is it?"

Philip glanced at his watch. "Two-fifteen."

"I've gone over my time. I only brought enough money for half an hour."

"That's fine—I was interested in what you had to say."

She got the money out of her knapsack and handed it to Philip. "Can I come back for another session?"

"Of course."

"I'm not sure when I'll be able to get back."

"Just call me when you're ready."

She stood. "Thanks. That was helpful." She paused. "Although I didn't give you a chance to say much."

"Sometimes just talking helps. Sometimes hearing the words out loud can put things in a different perspective that enables you to see options you didn't see before. Plus, I'd like to think over what you told me anyway." He held the curtain back for her and followed her into the waiting room. "You're not from around here, are you?"

"No."

"Where do you come from?"

She hesitated. "Florida."

"Oh, yeah? Whereabouts?"

"The Keys."

He laughed. "Really? I didn't think anyone who was actually from the Keys ever left."

She smiled weakly. "I guess a lot don't."

"I love the Ferris wheel in Marathon."

"Yeah, it's a good one."

He opened the door for her and looked out at the few parking spaces—all empty—in front of the building.

"Did your uncle drop you off?"

"I have a bike, it's parked in back. I used to have to walk everywhere, but anymore I can ride."

She went to the back of the building, unlocked her bike, and started her ride back to West Sedona.

It had been a relief to talk to someone about her situation, even if she had to disguise the details. In fact, despite the fact that she had given Philip Castillo little opportunity to exercise his counseling skills, she felt more optimistic than she had in months. But she was pretty sure that Uncle Owen wouldn't be quite as enthusiastic as she was. As uncomfortable as lying to Owen made her, she would wait to tell him about her sessions with Philip until she could decide herself if they were what she was looking for.

21

Lizzy was making scrambled eggs for dinner. When she and Owen had settled into their borrowed house in Sedona, she had wanted to pull her weight—no pun intended, she added hastily, for Owen's benefit—and decided she would share the dinner preparation responsibilities.

She discovered she was woefully unprepared—her mother, her father, or Ruby, when she was working as the Ballards' housekeeper, had done the cooking when Lizzy was growing up—so Owen was giving her some cooking lessons. She had made a mess of a pork roast, and they had decided to go back to the basics.

She put a plate of eggs—two for her, four for Owen—at each place, next to plates of toast and bacon and a small bowl of jam. She brought a pitcher of orange juice from the fridge and filled the juice glasses. She had decorated the table with a centerpiece—a small potted cactus that usually lived on the patio—and had folded the napkins into fans based on a video she found online.

Owen sat down. "Doesn't this look nice," he said appreciatively.

He was regaling her with the details of a study that found a correlation between number of cortical neurons and yawn duration when Lizzy interrupted him.

"Uncle Owen, could I get a job?"

"I think you would need a social security card—or at least know your social security number—to do that. Do you know what your social security number is?"

She shook her head.

"We can look into that when we get home and can get to your house and find your card." He poured himself some orange juice. "What kind of job would you like to get?"

"Maybe I could help you out at Penn. Help you with research and stuff."

"Maybe, but those jobs usually go to grad students."

"I could get a job helping out at a yoga studio."

"Yes, that's a possibility. We can look into that when we get back to Pennsylvania."

They ate in silence for a minute, then Lizzy said, "Did I inherit any money from Dad?"

Owen took a sip of orange juice, then put the glass down. "Yes, you did. I didn't want to bring it up because I didn't know if you were ready to talk about that, but your dad left everything to you to have when you're eighteen, and I'm the trustee until then."

"Can I get some money ahead of time?"

He used a piece of toast to maneuver some egg onto his fork. "It would be tricky to take care of the paperwork long distance—the original of your dad's will is at your house in Parkesburg—but you aren't an extravagant person. I can probably give you whatever you need until we can get it."

"What if I wanted a car?"

His egg-filled fork stopped halfway to his mouth and he raised his eyebrows. "You want a car?"

"Why not? I'm old enough to drive, I might want a car of my own soon."

"You'd need a driver's license first."

"Okay, I'll get a driver's license."

Owen put his fork down. "Do you really want a car, or is this just a for-instance?"

She shrugged. "Just a for-instance, I guess."

He sat back, his chair giving a slight squeak of protest. "We're contending with a couple of issues, Pumpkin. One is that you're a little underdocumented. And it's not just the lack of a social security card. I don't know what records the authorities have on you since your mom started home schooling you when you were six. If you suddenly pop up on the official radar when you apply for a license, I don't know if that's going to cause problems."

Lizzy poked at her eggs with her fork. After a few moments, she asked, "What's happening with the house?"

"Your house?"

She nodded.

"I hired a service to take care of the yard."

"We could sell it."

He nodded. "Yes, we could do that. If we sold the house, you'd have plenty of money."

"Let's do that."

"I guess we could hire someone to pack it up—"

"Uncle Owen," she burst out, "let's just go home and pack it up ourselves—I'm just about tired of waiting here for something to happen!"

He sighed. "It *is* tricky trying to do all this long distance."

"We don't even need anyone to pack it up. Maybe you can sell the stuff that's in it too."

"Don't you want anything from the house?"

"No."

"Nothing?"

She thought back to the house in Parkesburg. It had been her home for a decade, but in some ways it had felt less like a home than a hideout, the place her father took her to keep her and her powers away from an unsuspecting world. She had never felt about it the way she had felt about her grandparents' cabin in the Poconos. That had been a hideout too, but she had been just a little kid, and it had seemed like a fun adventure with her mom—and her dad too, on the weekends. She remembered the walks they had taken, the games they had played, the crafts they had made. Her favorite had been a corn husk doll in a long corn husk dress with puffed corn husk sleeves, carrying a corn husk broom with a twig for a handle. That was on a shelf in her bedroom in the Parkesburg house.

"Well, maybe a couple of things," she said, almost reluctantly. After a moment, she added, "But most of it we could sell."

Owen nodded. "Okay. Let me make some phone calls and find out what we would need to do to put in on the market."

They ate in silence for a minute, then Lizzy said, "Could I have an advance?"

"Pardon?"

"An advance. On the house." She paused. "That's what it's called, right?"

Owen laughed. "Yes, that's what it's called. Depends on how much of an advance you want."

Lizzy did a quick calculation. "Four hundred dollars." At eighty dollars for a half hour, that would be five sessions with Philip Castillo.

Owen raised his eyebrows. "Four hundred?"

"I want to take extra yoga classes."

Owen pulled out his wallet and counted the bills. "I can give you one hundred now and the rest after I go to the ATM." He handed over five twenties.

"Thanks, Uncle Owen," she said. "I'll keep track."

He smiled at her. "I know you will, Pumpkin."

22

Lizzy's new hairstyle had reminded Owen that he was overdue for a haircut himself—his hair was now longer than Lizzy's—and he stopped at a barber shop after making the withdrawal at the ATM.

The receptionist said a barber would be available shortly, and while Owen waited he pulled the withdrawal slip out of his wallet. The account balance wasn't alarming; he had a comfortable income from William Penn University, he turned a small profit through his buying and selling of antique Craftsman furniture, and he was a silent partner in a business founded by some of his neurobiologist colleagues. The house they were staying in belonged to one of those colleagues, so they were enjoying room for free, and board was negligible, although hundreds spent on yoga classes might start to be a strain if Lizzy kept it up at this pace.

His phone buzzed: Andy.

He answered—"Hold on one sec"—and walked to the reception desk. "I'm just going to go outside for a minute to take a call."

The receptionist nodded. "No problem."

"Hey, what's up?" he said as he stepped into the sunny Sedona morning.

"Nothing exciting," said Andy. "Just had a minute before seeing a patient and thought I'd check in."

"How's Mom doing?"

There was a pause on the other end. "Not so good the last couple of days."

Owen rubbed the back of his neck. "I'm sorry to be making you deal with all this, Andy."

"No worries." Andy paused again. "Although she does keep asking for you."

"Damn." Owen stuffed his hand into his pocket. "I wish the FaceTime thing had worked."

"Seems like she can't quite get her brain around the fact that that's really you on the screen. I think it freaked her out more than helped."

"Yeah." Owen looked over the buildings on the opposite site of the street to the mesas beyond. "What I really wish is that I could just fly back for a day or two."

"No chance of that?"

"I can't leave Lizzy here by herself. You remember how well that worked when I left her in Smoketown. I'm afraid she'd get some harebrained idea and disappear again."

"I guess bringing her with you isn't a possibility? Considering what happened on the train, I can imagine she might not want to risk a replay of that at thirty-five thousand feet."

"It isn't just that, although that would be enough. The other problem is that she doesn't have any of the documentation she'd need to get through a TSA check."

"Good point, I hadn't thought of that." After a moment, Andy asked, "So, what are you guys going to do?"

Owen lowered himself onto a bench outside the barber shop. "I don't know. If it weren't for Mom, I wouldn't have much incentive to leave. Not only is it nice to have a continent between me and Louise Mortensen—I wish you and Ruby could say the same—but I have to say that Sedona in February is a nice alternative to Pennsylvania. I can do my research and writing here just as easily as in Philly. Easier, in fact, because there are fewer distractions."

"You have a class coming up in the fall, right?"

"Yeah. That's my nonnegotiable deadline—but that has felt so far away. I hadn't had much reason to think about coming back until Mom started getting worse."

"Setting aside the Mom situation for a minute, if you came back in the fall, what would you do about Mortensen and Millard?"

"I don't know, Andy," Owen said testily. "I thought I still had months to figure it out." He looked again at the withdrawal slip he still held in his hand. "The other complication is by that time, it will be only a few months until Lizzy turns eighteen. She'll get the money her dad left her, so she'll have the wherewithal to do what she wants. I hope she would listen to my advice, but she'll be an adult and can make her own choices."

"She'd be an adult with an oddly limited experience with the real world."

"Yes," said Owen, sighing again. "I'm well aware of that."

"What do you think she'll want to do?"

"She says she wants to sell the Parkesburg house."

"And live where?"

"With me, I hope." After a moment, Owen added wistfully, "It is nice having someone around."

He expected Andy to have a smart-ass response to that, but he just said, "Yeah." He sounded a bit wistful himself. "Anyhow, let me know if you see your way to a quick trip back—I know it would do Mom good to see you."

The receptionist popped her head out the door of the barber shop. "Owen, we're ready for you."

"I'll be right in," he said to her, then, to Andy, "I've got to go. Give Mom a kiss for me."

"Will do," said Andy. "You take care of yourself and Lizzy."

"I always try to," said Owen.

23

W hen Lizzy got to Philip's office for her second session, he was escorting a jubilant-looking middle-aged man out the door.

"He looks happy," said Lizzy, as the man walked away, humming softly.

"Yeah, that was a good session," said Philip, smiling.

Lizzy glanced at her phone. "Man, I just about made it on time."

Philip glanced at his watch. "You did make it on time."

"Yeah, just barely."

They stepped into the waiting room and Philip flipped the sign to *Session in Progress - Please Stop Back Later*, locked the door, and waved her toward the back room.

"Can I get you anything to drink?" he asked.

"No, thanks." She sat down at the table.

"Phone off?" asked Philip.

"Oh, right." Lizzy took her phone out of her pocket and switched it off.

Philip sat down opposite her. "I thought a lot about what you told me at our first meeting."

"Do you have any advice for me?" Lizzy asked.

"I don't think I can offer you good advice unless I know the whole story."

"What do you mean?" she asked, shifting in her seat.

"There is no Ferris wheel in Marathon."

"What?"

"I asked you if you liked the Ferris wheel in Marathon and you said it was a good one. But there is no Ferris wheel in Marathon."

"Maybe I got it confused with a different Ferris wheel."

"I don't think so."

"Do you do that to all your clients?" she asked angrily. "Try to trick them into agreeing to things that aren't true?"

"No, but I do enjoy trying to guess where people are from based on their accents or references they make or region-alisms they use, and you are definitely not from the Keys."

"Really? So where am I from?"

"Southeastern Pennsylvania. Philadelphia."

Her eyes widened.

"The way you say 'water' is typical of Southeastern Penn-sylvania. 'Water' is a marker word—you can really narrow down where a person comes from based on how they say it. And when you were here the first time, you said 'anymore' in a positive sense: 'Anymore I can ride my bike.' That's unusual. I looked it up and it's a Southeastern Pennsylvania regionalism. And when you showed up today you said 'just about' to mean 'just barely': 'I just about made it on time.' I'll bet if I looked that up, I'd find that that's a regionalism, too."

"But you said you thought I was from Philadelphia," she said, her voice tight. "What makes you think I'm from Phil-adelphia specifically?"

"Last night I spent some time on Southeastern Pennsyl-vania news websites looking for 'Elizabeth Patrick' and finally found an article on the *Philadelphia Chronicle* website about two people—Elizabeth Ballard and her father, Patrick Ballard —who the police wanted to talk to after a woman died on a train. Lucia Hazlitt. Evidently something of a local celebrity in Philly."

Lizzy stared at him.

"And then the next day there was a story about a Patrick Ballard being found dead in an alley. It was the same day you said your father died."

Lizzy grabbed her knapsack and stood. "I don't want to talk with someone who's going to try to connect me to people who are dying in Pennsylvania just because of the way I say 'water.'"

Philip remained sitting, his hands folded on the table. "And I started thinking," he continued, "that it was strange that a young woman would show up at the office of someone she doesn't know and seem completely comfortable turning her phone off and having the door locked behind her."

"I could have gotten out if I wanted to. I can get out now."

"I'm sure you can. You're not worried. You're not nervous. Mad, maybe, but not nervous about being here with me. Like you know you could handle the situation if I did something you didn't like."

"I could." She glared at him.

Philip nodded and gazed back at her. "When people in your life died—whether they were people close to you or people with no apparent connection beyond a coincidental crossing of paths —you moved on. From the mountains to a small town when your mother died, from one city to another at about the same time that this woman on the train in Philadelphia and your father died. You feel guilty about your mother and your father's deaths, and you're alarmed when I mention the death of the woman on the train."

"I'm not—" Lizzy began, then clamped her lips shut.

Philip leaned back. "The woman on the train died of a stroke, and you said your mother had had strokes as well, and that you made her situation worse. You're on the scene when seemingly healthy middle-aged people suffer fatal strokes, but here you are, walking around Sedona, and I feel fine, so it doesn't seem like something you're carrying, like a disease. Plus, your father died from gunshot wounds, and although you feel guilty about that, the guilt is different."

"You don't know what you're talking about," she said, her voice wobbly with barely-held-back tears.

"No, I don't. Not completely. But I'm not totally off track, am I." It was a statement, not a question.

"Why do you care?"

"Because I was truly interested in your story," he said, "and if you weren't going to tell me, I wanted to try to find out myself."

"But why?"

He leaned forward. "Because there is something special about you, Elizabeth. The 'psychic counselor' title is a little New Age—that's what people in Sedona want—but I do have the ability to sense things about people, and the advice I give people based on what I sense about them is good advice. I've changed people's lives for the better. I have a sense about you —a sense of power. I also sense you're afraid of this power— afraid of it because you believe you can't control it. Because that's why you originally came to me, right? 'I want to be more in control so I don't hurt people the way I hurt my mom'— that's what you said. That's what brought you to my office, what made you decide to find out what a psychic counselor could do for you."

Lizzy said nothing.

"Am I right about any of it? Because if not, I should hang up my shingle."

Seconds ticked by, and finally Lizzy said, "You just about figured it out."

"Does that mean I can keep my shingle up anymore, Elizabeth?"

"Yeah. And you can call me Lizzy."

LIZZY TOLD him about her power—that ability she referred to as the squeeze. About her mother's death. About hearing the news of her father's death as she sat, drugged, in Gerard Bonnay's Pocopson home. About her escape and her plans to avenge her father's death. About her last-minute change of heart as she stood in Gerard Bonnay's empty office, and about the confusion of his arrival, and the final betrayal of the gun he drew on her. Of Louise Mortensen's shouted instructions to Gerard to "Finish it!"—the "it" being Lizzy herself.

The only thing she didn't tell him was who Owen's accomplices were who had spirited her away from Gerard and Louise's control. She was willing to take a risk with herself— and, she realized belatedly, she had unintentionally involved Uncle Owen in that risk as well—but she saw no reason to share with Philip the role Andy McNally and Ruby DiMano had played.

When she was done, she felt a lightness that she hadn't felt in a long time. Not, she thought, since before her mother's death. He didn't comment, he didn't judge. He didn't try to convince her that she shouldn't feel the way she felt. He just listened and sometimes asked for clarification or acknowledged what she had said. And as she talked, she felt as if the constriction she had felt for most of her life—like the thorns that had held her down on the Sugarloaf Trail as the angry biker railed at her—were plucked free, one hooked barb at a time.

24

George Millard stepped into the Cowboy Club. Philip Castillo was already at the bar, chatting with the bartender who was pouring him a Knob Creek bourbon neat. Many of the other barstools were full, and the dining room was starting to fill up.

Millard slipped into a seat two stools down from Castillo. He didn't like sitting so close, but the room was buzzing, and it was the only way he'd hear anything if Castillo talked with the bartender or another patron.

Millard pulled out his phone. He missed the days when an open newspaper provided all the excuse you needed to sit and listen to a target—it not only gave him the appearance of being engrossed in something other than his actual focus, but also hid his face—but he was savvy enough to realize that these days a man with an open newspaper was an attention-getting sight.

He ordered a Corona. The bartender brought him the beer, then returned to Castillo. The conversation between the two of them wasn't worth the price of the beer—a lot of talk about sports and a little conversation about women, mainly the bartender's girlfriend. Millard had a hopeful moment when the bartender asked Castillo about his clients, but the answer he got was vague, which seemed to be what the bartender expected.

After Castillo had finished the bourbon, he ordered a burger and a beer and, defying convention, pulled a paperback from his jacket pocket. Millard angled his phone and snapped a picture over his elbow, then zoomed in to see the title: *The Monkey Wrench Gang*. Millard tapped the name into his phone and perused the Wikipedia entry.

The restaurant got louder, and the bartender no longer had time to chat with Castillo, but Millard had gotten enough. He paid his tab and stepped into the cool Arizona evening. He wandered up and down the street for half a block on either side of the restaurant, looking in windows of shops that were mostly closed, keeping an eye on the restaurant entrance.

Half an hour later, Castillo emerged and turned right. Millard followed. Castillo turned right off the main drag, and then right again onto a residential street. Earlier that day, Castillo had arrived at his office on foot, so Millard had spent some time researching where he might live that would be within walking distance. The apartment options were limited and the houses were pricey. If Castillo lived in Uptown Sedona, maybe psychic counseling paid better than Millard thought.

Castillo turned in at a driveway halfway down the street. Millard stopped short of the driveway and waited for lights to go on in the house, but none did. After a minute he strolled by the house and glanced up the driveway. From that vantage point, he could see lights from a structure behind the house, and Millard realized that Castillo had gone to a small, detached casita behind the main house, next to which a dark blue Ford Ranger stepside was parked.

A few minutes later, Millard heard the faint sounds of music—Rush's *Subdivisions*—coming from the casita. He walked up the driveway, keeping near the shadows cast by the red-tipped leaves of the hedge that separated it from the neighbor's yard, and knelt beside the pickup. He pulled a disc-shaped object from his pocket and reached into the wheel well, where it snapped on with a dull, metallic thunk.

Gotta love technology, he thought as he retreated down the driveway. One of those trackers on Castillo's truck and one on McNally's SUV made it possible for him to keep tabs on both of them without Mortensen having to send a second person out to Arizona. And who would she send? He couldn't see Pieda in the role.

With Castillo apparently in for the night, and with Millard being able to track his location if he were to go anywhere not within walking distance of the casita, Millard strolled back to the Cowboy Club. Castillo's burger had looked pretty tasty.

He got a table, not wanting the bartender to note his return, and placed his order. Ballard had met twice with this guy who styled himself a "psychic counselor." It seemed like a ploy to fleece tourists of their vacation dollars, but the question of whether the guy was a fraud was less important than whether Ballard thought she was getting anything out of his spiel. Castillo's brochure claimed he could tap into his client's powers to help them achieve their dreams. He knew what Ballard's power was. What was her dream?

The girl didn't fit anyone's picture of *revenge killer*, but Millard had cleaned up after the death of one of her victims—Anton Rossi—and was in the process of cleaning up after another—Gerard Bonnay. Millard didn't want to be within Ballard's striking distance when he took her out. And he wanted to do that soon, before she spent much more time with her new counselor, fraud or not.

25

Lizzy was lying on the couch in the living room reading *The Man Who Mistook His Wife for a Hat*, recommended by Uncle Owen. She had noticed that her home schooling assignments changed dramatically whenever a new adult took charge of the curriculum. She had been focusing over the last couple of weeks on Oliver Sacks and Daniel Pink, switching it up with the history of furniture design and, by her own choice, online Spanish courses.

Owen stood up from his de facto desk—the kitchen table —and stretched. "I'm making grilled cheese sandwiches for lunch, want one?"

Lizzy glanced at the time on her phone and jumped up. "No, I've got to go. I'm going to be late."

"Yoga?"

"Yup."

"On an empty stomach?"

"You can't do yoga if you have a big belly of food," she said. She grabbed her knapsack, ran down the steps to her bike, and pointed it toward Sedona.

It was Lizzy's third session with Philip in three days. The

advance from Owen wasn't going to last long at this rate, but she was finding the experience of sharing her story with someone who could be considered an impartial third party to be cathartic ... and, to be honest, somewhat thrilling.

She switched her phone off as she entered the waiting room. Philip emerged from the back room.

"I had an idea for something a little different today," he said. "If part of what we're supposed to be doing is figuring out how you can control yourself around other people, it's probably not so useful for us to be sitting in my office for all our sessions."

"Where would we go?"

"Anywhere there are people."

Lizzy looked uncomfortable.

"What's the matter? Worried that you'll fly into a rage if someone cuts in front of you in line at Starbucks?"

"No, not that so much. But Uncle Owen doesn't know I'm here."

"Why haven't you told him?"

"He's a scientist. He'd be skeptical."

"But he believes that you can do what you can, right? Is he skeptical about that?"

"I think he was at first, when I was little, but then evidence built up that even he couldn't ignore. But he's still a scientist first. He wants to find a scientific solution to the problem."

"We'll see if we can make some progress on the problem in our own unscientific way," he said with a wry smile, "and then you can decide if you want to bring him up to date." He thought for a moment. "Does he go shopping? Not grocery shopping, but 'ladies who lunch'-type shopping?"

"Not usually. He does like to go to lunch, but usually when I'm with him."

"Then I know just the place we can go. And there are lots

of nooks and crannies if he suddenly gets the shopping urge and we need to slip away from him."

They got in Philip's pickup truck and drove to a high-end shopping area further south on Oak Creek. Philip parked in one of the small, tree-shaded parking areas.

"Phone off?" he asked.

"Yup." She looked around. "What are we going to do?"

"Just wander around, look in shops, get ice cream. Whatever you want."

Lizzy climbed out of the truck. "There's not going to be a lot of actual shopping going on because I only brought enough money to pay you."

"Then the ice cream's on me."

OWEN NOTICED Lizzy's rolled-up yoga mat by the front door. He glanced at his watch. She'd only been gone a little while. She might not notice that she didn't have the mat until her yoga class started, and if she had to ride her bike all the way back to the house for it, she'd miss most of the class. If he left now, he might be able to get it to her before her class started.

He texted *yoga mat is here, i'll bring it over*

A few minutes later, he pulled into a parking space in front of Namaste Yoga and Meditation. He got the mat out of the back seat, went to the door of the yoga studio, and gave it a pull.

Locked.

He stepped back, checked the sign over the door, then gave the door another half-hearted tug.

He knew this was where Lizzy took lessons—he had driven her here before she got her bike. Was she going to another place now?

As he stood there, a brutally fit woman in a form-fitting top and harem pants rounded the corner of the building, sorting through her keys. She looked up and saw him.

"May I help you?" she asked.

"I thought my goddaughter had a class now. She forgot her mat so I brought it over."

"We don't have any classes until four o'clock. What's your goddaughter's name?"

"Elizabeth Bal—trick."

"Excuse me?"

Owen coughed delicately. "Patrick. Elizabeth Patrick."

"Oh, yes, Elizabeth—she's a sweetheart. When she comes, it's usually to the four o'clock class."

"She's become quite the convert," said Owen. "Yoga every day now."

"That's great to hear she's practicing outside of class as well."

"Um," said Owen, not quite knowing how to respond. "Anyway, I must have misunderstood where she was going today."

"I'll mention that you were looking for her if I see her this afternoon."

"Oh, no, that's okay—I don't want her to think I'm hovering." He laughed weakly.

She laughed too. "You could leave the mat with me if you'd like, but if she shows up without a mat, it's okay—we have extras she can use."

"If you have spares, I might as well take this one back home with me."

"That's fine," said the woman. "Namaste."

"Namaste to you," said Owen.

As he headed back to the car, an uneasy thought began

building in his mind. He got out his phone. There was no response from Lizzy to his earlier text.

He climbed into the car and hit her speed dial. The call rang directly to voicemail.

"Oh, Lizzy," he groaned, "what are you up to?"

Soon Lizzy was enjoying herself—looking in shop windows at the high-end wares, trying on a lapis ring in a jewelry store. They struck out on ice cream, but got two chais at a boho clothing store. They settled down on a low wall surrounding a lawn on which dozens of graceful metal sculptures rotated lazily in a light breeze.

Lizzy took a sip of her chai. "So, do you always take your clients shopping?"

"Hardly ever," said Philip breezily. He took a sip of tea. "A lot of my clients are tourists, and I only see them once or twice. Usually they just get intrigued with the idea of a psychic counselor and come in as a lark, but their money spends the same whether they're serious about it or not."

"Must be kind of a drag if they're just doing it as a goof," said Lizzy.

"It's not like they're obnoxious about it, and they generally seem to get something out of it, but I do sometimes feel like it's a toss-up between me or the Pink Jeep Tours." He took another sip of his tea. "Didn't seem like you had much trouble dealing with the people here."

She shrugged. "It's a beautiful day, most of the shoppers are probably on vacation, the people who work in the stores were friendly. There wasn't anything to upset me." She looked up at the hypnotic movement of the sculptures. "Dad and

Uncle Owen used to take me places on the weekends. Restaurants. Museums. Shopping—although not as fancy as this."

"But it sounds like you led a pretty circumscribed life."

"Yeah. After Mom and Dad realized what I could do, the only people I had much to do with other than them were Uncle Owen and our housekeeper, Ruby."

"No school?"

"I was home schooled."

"No friends your own age?"

Lizzy thought back to Christine, the young woman she had met when she was hiding out in Smoketown. The thought that that brief acquaintance was the only one she could call a friendship with someone near her own age was too pathetic to share with Philip.

"No, not really."

Philip leaned back against the wall and crossed one ankle over the other. "You know, your situation isn't all bad."

"What do you mean?"

"In a lot of ways, your life has been limited by what the people around you tried to do to control the situation. But in other ways, it's opened up opportunities for you. For example, most seventeen-year-olds wouldn't have the freedom to walk into the back room of a locked office with someone they didn't know—especially when that someone just asked them to turn off their cell phone. The biker you encountered on the trail turned out to be just a jerk, but if he had been a rapist, you could have defended yourself."

"Yeah ..." Lizzy said cautiously.

"You could walk the streets of Phoenix or Philadelphia in the middle of the night and unless you encountered someone with a weapon, you'd be fine." He turned and rested his forearms on the wall, looking out at the rotating sculptures. "I don't think you can fully appreciate how different that makes you, and how powerful that difference is. You might consider whether your ultimate goal is to create a situation where you never use your ability, which is what I gathered was your goal last time we met, or whether it's to create a situation where you use your ability only when you want to."

"I guess so," she said after a few moments. "I'll have to think about it."

Philip pushed himself up from the wall. "Let's go back to the office. There's something I want to show you."

From a balcony fifty yards away, Millard watched Castillo and Ballard talk and sip their drinks. When they were walking, the shopping village was a bitch to tail in—he had almost walked right into them in one of the courtyards when they had doubled back, evidently for their drinks. When they were stationary, though, the buildings provided plenty of second-floor vantage points from which to observe them.

He pulled out his phone and snapped a picture of them, texted it to Mortensen, then hit her speed dial.

"Yes?" she answered.

"I just sent you a picture of Ballard and that counselor she's seeing."

"I've got it," said Mortensen. "In what sense is she 'seeing' him?"

"Just professionally, as far as I can tell. This is their third meeting—twice in his office, once in this fancy shopping center."

"He's taking her out and, it appears, is having coffee with her, but you don't think it's gone beyond professional?" Millard began to bristle at the question, then realized that Mortensen was really asking.

"I don't think so. He's got to be almost twice her age—probably early thirties. I realize that doesn't mean much, but I only saw him touch her once, to get her attention to point out a bird in a tree. If I had to guess by the body language, I'd say that she has a little crush on him, but that it's all business on his side."

"Just as well," said Mortensen. "A romantic entanglement is an added complication we don't want to deal with. Castillo's more likely to shrug off an accident involving a client than a girlfriend. Does McNally go with her to see this counselor?"

"No. He might not know—being a medical doctor, maybe he wouldn't be so thrilled about his goddaughter going to see someone who looks like a New Age huckster."

"Do you have a plan for how to take care of them?"

"I'm still trying to figure out a good way to make it look like an accident. I've got the trackers on Castillo and McNally's vehicles, so none of them are going anywhere without me knowing about it. I think that as long as they're not showing signs of doing anything more proactive than taking yoga lessons and visiting psychics, we don't have to be in a big rush."

After a pause, Mortensen said, "I agree with not hurrying to action unnecessarily, but I don't want to wait long, especially if Ballard is striking up a friendship—romantic or otherwise—with a local."

"It won't take long—another day or two and I'll have a plan."

"No longer than that."

"Gotta go," he said. Ballard had hopped off the wall and she and Castillo were walking toward the parking lot. "They're leaving and I want to keep an eye on them."

"But with the tracker you can tell where they go without having to follow them," said Mortensen.

"It's not where they're going that interests me," said Millard. "It's what they do when they get there."

He ended the call, slipped the phone in his pocket, and jogged toward the parking lot.

PHILIP DROVE them back to the office. He locked the door behind them, leaving the *Closed* sign in the window, and led her to the back room.

He turned a knob on the light switch and a spotlight came up on the painting on the back wall, which had always been in shadow during Lizzy's previous visits. The grid of squares on the antique paper contained delicately inked characters, like an exotic periodic table. At the top corners were multiarmed men, the one on the left riding what looked like an antelope, the one on the right riding a multiheaded horse. On top of the large grid was a smaller grid, looking like the cross section of a tiny castle, each room of the castle occupied by one or two seated figures. She could now see that the forms stretching across the large grid were writhing black snakes.

"Do you know what that is?" he asked.

She shook her head.

"Did you ever play Chutes and Ladders when you were little?"

"I don't think so."

"It's a silly game, but it's based on an ancient game called Snakes and Ladders." He nodded toward the painting. "That game was meant to teach a morality lesson—that a person's virtues, the ladders, help them through their life journey, and their vices, the snakes, hinder them."

"That makes sense."

"The concept seems obvious, but the tricky part is what

one considers a virtue and what one considers a vice. You see your ability as a vice, but I believe it could be a virtue. If you're willing to use it to help people who can't help themselves, and to deal with people who are using their own powers for evil, then it's a ladder, not a snake."

Her eyes still fixed on the painting, she sank into one of the chairs. He sat down opposite her, and leaned toward her over the table.

"I want you to think about the people who crossed you. Your mother obviously doesn't fall into that category. She became a victim of your power because you and your parents didn't realize at first what was causing her strokes. The woman on the train was an unintended victim, and I would never argue that someone should die just because they're acting like a jerk."

Tears began to pool in the corners of Lizzy's eyes.

"But the people who truly meant to cause you pain— Anton Rossi and Gerard Bonnay—the world is better off without them."

"I guess I believe that," she said uncertainly, "but what am I supposed to do based on that?"

Philip leaned back. "Let's talk about that at our next session."

26

The next day, Philip stood under the hacienda-style porch in front of his office, the *Session in Progress - Please Stop Back Later* sign already turned out, and watched with some trepidation as Owen McNally climbed out of his SUV. The man was a mountain.

Lizzy had called Philip the previous evening, after their third session. She had returned home to a godfather who had discovered her deception and who was none too pleased about his goddaughter visiting a psychic counselor behind his back. He had demanded a meeting with Philip.

Philip hoped that Lizzy had been right when she said that McNally just wanted to talk to him. He was greeting McNally outside in case his intent was different than Lizzy believed—it would be easier for Philip to deal with a physical altercation outside than in the confines of the office.

But as he watched Owen McNally settle a Panama hat on his head, Philip's concerns lessened. He didn't look dangerous. Instead, he managed to look simultaneously resolute and apologetic.

As McNally stepped onto the porch, Philip put out his hand. "Dr. McNally, pleased to meet you. I'm Philip Castillo."

McNally did his best to glower as he shook Philip's hand. "Pleased to meet you," he growled.

Philip pushed the door open. "Please come in." He stepped aside—far aside—to let his visitor pass. "Have a seat." Philip gestured toward the bench in the waiting room.

McNally removed his hat and looked around the room. "You met with my goddaughter here?"

"Here, and at a shopping center nearby."

McNally looked hawkishly at Philip. "You met in your waiting room?"

Philip sighed inwardly. He had hoped McNally wouldn't press for the exact location of their sessions: a room that was sure to strike McNally not as a comfortable sanctuary for clients, but as a small, dark, windowless space away from prying eyes. "No, the times we met here, we met in my consulting room." He held back the curtain for McNally's inspection.

McNally stepped to the doorway, peered in, and grimaced. Lizzy had prepped Philip that not only might her godfather not appreciate the idea of her being in the back room with Philip, but that neither of the chairs there would accommodate him.

"Interesting," said McNally. He glanced back toward the bench that Philip had originally offered. "Perhaps we should talk out here. The furniture seems a bit more adequate." He lowered himself onto the bench.

"Can I get you something to drink?" asked Philip. "Coffee? Tea? Water?"

Owen pulled a water bottle out of his pocket and put it down on the bench next to him. "No, thanks. I brought some water."

Philip took a seat in one of the chairs.

"So," said McNally, "you are a 'psychic counselor.' 'Psychic' as in telepathy? Clairvoyance?"

"No. 'Psychic' as in 'of the soul or mind.'"

"Ah," said McNally. It was unclear whether or not he found this clarification reassuring. "And why did you find it necessary to keep your meetings with my goddaughter secret?"

"It wasn't my choice, it was Lizzy's choice."

"And why do you think she made that choice?"

"You should ask her that."

"I did."

"And what did she say?"

After a pause, McNally replied, "She said she didn't think I would approve."

"Did she tell you why she thought you wouldn't approve?"

"This is supposed to be my opportunity to ask you questions," said McNally sternly.

Philip nodded. "Certainly."

The pause was longer this time, then McNally said, "She thought I would be skeptical of your approach."

"And are you—" Philip stopped. "Sorry. I get used to asking my clients questions. It's a hard habit to break."

Owen waved away the apology. "I must admit I am skeptical of anyone labeling themselves 'psychic' in this area. Although your clarification of your use of the term is helpful." He cocked an eye at Philip. "Do your clients interpret 'psychic' differently than you describe?"

Philip sat back. "I did choose the term 'psychic counselor' with an eye to its different meanings. There are certainly people who come to Sedona looking for telepaths or clairvoyants, and the term is appealing to them."

"And do you disabuse them of their misconception?"

McNally was still managing, just barely, to maintain his scowl, but the tone of the conversation had changed. It was clear that inquiry, and not interrogation, was his natural approach.

Philip shrugged. "No. But I believe that there's a fine line between mind-reading and helping someone understand and work through the issues they're facing."

McNally considered. Finally he said, "Yes, I can see how that might be true." He glanced around the waiting room. "Did you have any sort of formal training for this type of work?"

"I studied at Williams."

"An accredited institution?"

"Oh, yes."

Owen looked expectantly at him, then evidently decided not to pursue that line of questioning. "So, what exactly has Lizzy told you?"

"Did you ask Lizzy that?"

"I did."

"And what did she say?"

For a moment Owen appeared ready to protest, then sighed. "She said she told you everything about herself—her ability, her situation. And I assume she must have told you something about me to explain why I'm here with her."

"She just told me that you helped her get away from Gerard Bonnay and Louise Mortensen, and then away from Philadelphia."

"Did she tell you about anyone else?"

"No."

"And you didn't ask her?"

"No."

Owen ran the brim of his hat through his hands. "I'm surprised she told you as much as she did."

"I think she only intended to tell me about herself, and that the part about you sort of slipped out."

Owen sighed. "She needs to be more careful."

Philip nodded, then said, "I think that having an impartial third party like myself to talk to would help her be more circumspect in her interactions with other people."

"I suppose so," said Owen.

"It seems like Sedona is good for her," Philip continued. "She told me about the yoga classes she's taking, and it sounds like she's enjoying that."

"Yes," said Owen. "Although she's not taking quite as many yoga classes as I had thought earlier," he added, a slight scowl returning to his face.

Philip crossed his legs. "Are you enjoying your time in Sedona?"

"Of course. In addition to the obvious incentive of staying out of the reach of Louise Mortensen and her associates—even if it is only a temporary solution—it was thirty-four degrees with freezing rain in Philly this morning."

"You're checking."

"Well, yes. Doesn't everyone? Check to see what's going on back home?"

"No, I don't think everyone does. A lot of people would be happy to put the cold temperatures and bad weather in their hometown out of their minds entirely while they're away."

Owen was silent.

"Missing family?"

Owen started. "Did Lizzy tell you about my family?"

"No, but you've known Lizzy since she was small. You're wearing a William Penn University ring. You say 'water' with the same slight Southeastern Pennsylvania accent that Lizzy has. You obviously have roots there. It makes sense that you would have family there."

Owen raised an eyebrow. "I can see why clients coming to you for clairvoyance wouldn't be disappointed."

Philip smiled.

After a moment, Owen said, "It's my mother. She's not well."

"I'm sorry to hear that. That must make it difficult for you to be out here."

"My brother's keeping an eye on her. And on my dad." Owen stared disconsolately at his hat.

"That can't be a comfortable situation for you."

"No."

"And I imagine you're not just missing family, but friends as well. I'm picturing you as someone with a large circle of friends, and as someone with favorite activities, favorite places, that you would like to get back to."

"Yes, that's true."

"How do you think Lizzy felt about hiding her visits to me from you?"

Owen raised his eyebrows at the apparent change in direction of the conversation. "Guilty."

"Why do you think that is?"

"She's a naturally open and honest person. It's probably a challenge for her to withhold information."

Philip uncrossed his legs and leaned forward, his elbows on his knees, his hands clasped loosely. "I hope you won't consider this an insult, because I don't mean it to be one, but you're very much like Lizzy—an open person. Easy to read." Owen began to look ruffled, and Philip held up his hand. "I only say that because for any person like that, living a life of subterfuge would be difficult. And I mean that not only in the sense of being difficult to do successfully—I imagine you, as well as Lizzy, are always having to be on the lookout that you don't say more to someone than you should—but also in the sense of being emotionally difficult to maintain over time."

Owen smiled wanly. "I'm really that much of an open book?"

Philip laughed. "Yup."

Owen shook his head. "I'll be more careful—although," he added, "I certainly didn't exercise much discretion in this conversation."

"You already know that discretion is important for Lizzy's safety," replied Philip, "and you know that the sooner the two of you can resolve this situation she's in, the better for both of you. I think the goal we all share is to create a situation where the two of you can go home without having to be fearful for your safety."

"Yes, that would certainly be the ideal outcome. I'm just having trouble seeing how to do it."

"If you give your approval to let my sessions with Lizzy continue, I think the three of us can make progress toward that outcome."

Owen gazed out the window then heaved a deep sigh. "She does seem enthusiastic about her sessions with you, and more optimistic than I've seen her in a long time. Yes, I give my approval for the session to continue. Although," he added ruefully, "history has shown that my approval or disapproval is not necessarily the deciding factor in Lizzy's decisions. She may be an open person, but she's got a will of steel."

Philip smiled. "She certainly does."

27

Millard sat in his rental car about half a block from Philip Castillo's office, a pair of binoculars held to his eyes. After a few moments, he put them aside, pressed a speed dial on his phone, and got Louise Mortensen's usual greeting.

"Yes?"

"McNally is at Castillo's office."

"With Ballard?"

"Alone."

"Damn." After a pause, she asked, "Did the meeting look friendly?"

"They shook hands before they went in the office, but neither of them looked super excited to be there. I'm guessing that Ballard was seeing Castillo on the sly, and McNally found out about it and came to see what the scoop was."

"If Ballard's godfather is now getting involved with this 'psychic counselor,'" said Mortensen, delivering the title with obvious contempt, "we've run out of time. We need to get Ballard and McNally out of the picture now. Have you come up with a plan?"

Millard tapped his fingers on the steering wheel. "If it was one or the other of them, and we didn't have Ballard's ability to consider, it would be easy. I could take Ballard out with a quick sideswipe of her bike if she would ever venture off the main roads. I can't just pull her into an alley and fake a mugging. That worked with dear old dad, but trying that on her seems like a suicide mission. I saw what she did to Anton Rossi."

Millard had helped to tidy up after the test that Bonnay and Mortensen had set for Ballard in Pocopson. They had locked her in the library with small-time mobster and big-time bully Anton Rossi, and when the inevitable happened, Ballard had reduced the bully to a corpse.

He continued. "McNally would be even easier: a fire at night, something blocking his path to the front door, a bedroom window too small for him to fit through."

"A fire could take care of both of them, if the situation were managed correctly."

"She's slender, and probably limber from all those yoga classes she goes to. Anything that would keep her in a burning building would likely be too overt to pass for an accident. Plus," he added, "fire is just generally unpredictable. I wouldn't want to count on it."

"Good lord," Mortensen muttered. "I'm getting tired of this. Just shoot them."

"To keep myself out of harm's way, I'd have to do it from a distance, and someone killed with a rifle shot is sure to raise questions, especially if I take out both of them that way."

She sighed. "The decision's yours, but make it quickly," she said, and cut the connection without waiting for his reply.

～

WHEN MCNALLY LEFT Castillo's office, Millard noted that the handshake looked more friendly, and the two men stood on the covered walkway chatting for a minute before McNally walked away with a wave. Whatever their conversation had been, it had certainly put the two of them in a better mood.

Millard followed McNally back to the house in West Sedona. McNally pulled into the driveway and Millard drove past, then pulled to the side fifty yards down the road. After a minute, Ballard appeared, ran down the steps, and climbed into the passenger seat. The SUV stayed in the driveway for another minute, then McNally backed out and pulled away. Millard followed from a distance, knowing that he wouldn't lose them with the tracker on the SUV.

Ballard and McNally stopped for lunch at a Mexican place, then headed out of town. Millard sighed. He had a pretty good idea where they were going.

As he had anticipated, Ballard and McNally drove to what was evidently her favorite hike: the Thread-the-Needle Trail.

As he drove, he thought back fondly to the previous day when he had followed Ballard and Castillo through the shopping village in Sedona. That had involved no climbing tougher than a flight of stairs, no pace faster than a stroll. Millard didn't have much fat on his frame, but his fitness came from a gym—a real gym, not one of those LA Fitness spandex palaces—and it was muscle built at the free-weight station. He had given up his daily run a decade before.

He was regretting it on this job. Ballard was a hiking maniac.

He had followed them to Thread-the-Needle for the first time a few days before. McNally had dropped her off and then sat in the SUV reading until she had come back.

The trail was a dozen miles outside of Sedona, and sparsely used. Even better from Millard's point of view, it was out of cell phone range, and Millard started to think that a hiking accident might be a viable option. He didn't think Ballard would recognize him if she encountered him on the trail: the only time she had seen him in person had been at Smoketown Airport, and she had mostly kept her eyes on the ground during that encounter. Plus, unlike that December in Pennsylvania, his face was now tan, his hair was short, he sported a beard and mustache, and he had replaced the winter overcoat with hiking gear. If he could catch her alone, it might be easy to pass her on a narrow path above a drop-off and give her a bump as he went by. If she survived the fall but was unconscious, he could hurry things along with a rock to the head.

The second time he followed them to Thread-the-Needle, McNally actually got out of the car and started down the trail with her. Millard shook his head. Maybe he wouldn't have to take care of McNally, maybe he'd just drop dead of a heart attack.

But the man was a machine. He wasn't fast—Ballard often took side trips then rejoined him a little further down the trail, which made following them tricky, especially since they hiked it as an out-and-back—but he was steady, like a locomotive.

As they got out of the car this day they were talking intently, probably about McNally's visit to Castillo, and as with their previous visit, McNally started down the trail with Ballard.

Also as before, McNally stopped about a mile in, and sat down on a rock with a view of the valley below. Ballard continued on, disappearing around a curve in the trail. As McNally peeled the foil wrapper off what looked like a granola bar, Millard turned back to the trailhead.

He knew why McNally stopped where he did. A few hundred yards further on, the trail led up to a tall, narrow spire of rock—the Needle, Millard guessed—through which hikers passed via a claustrophobia-inducing slit in the rock—which he guessed would make it the Eye. Ballard slipped through easily, but it was clear that McNally would never be able to fit his bulk through the opening.

A plan began to form in Millard's mind.

28

L ate the next night, Millard bumped down a rutted dirt road, his way lit not only by the headlights, but also by an arch of stars, brilliant in the desert darkness. He had driven south from Sedona, back toward Phoenix, and once out of the nighttime cool of the mountains, the air had become warm and still. A heat wave was coming, and the temperature tomorrow for this part of Arizona was forecast to be in the nineties.

He was a little concerned that he wouldn't be able to find the turn-off that had been hard enough to find in daylight earlier that day. Then he recognized the battered mailbox with *Wentz* painted on it in untidy black letters, and made the turn.

The ruts in the side road became deeper and the bumps more jolting until the road ended in a yard, little more than an area scraped clear of scrub, in front of a rust-pocked trailer.

Millard killed the headlights and the engine and retrieved a bottle, wrapped in a brown paper bag, from the passenger seat. As he approached the trailer, the front door opened.

The figure that stood outlined in the light from the trailer's interior was small—if Millard hadn't known it to be that of an adult man, he would have thought it was a child.

"Miller?" came a querulous voice.

"Yeah, it's me," replied Millard.

Wentz came unsteadily down the steps, pulling the trailer's door closed behind him. "Was starting to think you weren't coming back."

"I'm back," said Millard. He raised the bottle in its paper bag. "And I brought a friend."

The only light now was from the trailer windows and the stars, but Millard could see a grin cracking the old man's face. "What friend's that?" he asked.

"Our friend Jack."

Wentz cackled. "The best friend."

"Thought we could have a drink in the shed. Nice and cool out there."

The old man waved his hand in assent. "Let me get some glasses."

The glasses retrieved, Wentz led Millard out to the shed they had visited earlier in the day. From the front of his dirty plaid shirt he pulled a key on a string and inserted it unsteadily into the padlock on the door. He popped the lock, pushed the door open, and flicked on the light.

Millard had been in the old man's trailer that afternoon to discuss the deal, and it was a mess—unwashed dishes in the sink, the funk of spoiled food in the air. But the shed was pristine—the concrete floors swept clean, tools arranged neatly on a pegboard over a tidy workbench. The air was cool, the whir of the air conditioner creating a soothing background noise.

"So, you decided what you want?" the old man asked.

"Yes. The Western Diamondbacks. Both of them."

Wentz nodded. "Good-lookin' snake. Not flashy, but handsome, you know? And brave—they'll stand their ground when confronted." He looked at Millard cagily. "A hundred apiece, right?"

The old man had in fact quoted ninety apiece yesterday, and Millard knew he could get snakes cheaper if he was willing to do it on the books, but he wasn't in the mood to argue. Plus, it wasn't his money, and Mortensen wasn't going to quibble about twenty bucks on his off-the-books expense report.

"Yup, that's what I remember—a hundred apiece," he said. He counted out the bills from his wallet and handed them over.

Millard followed the old man down one of the aisles created by rows of chicken wire cages containing a variety of snakes and other reptiles. In the last cage on the left—really more a pen than a cage—were two enormous monitor lizards, looking like escaped extras from Jurassic Park.

The old man set the glasses aside. He got two white plastic buckets from a stack and retrieved two implements from a shelf—both about three feet long, one with a pincer-type contraption on the end, one with a hook. He opened the door of one of the cages containing what appeared to be a sleeping rattler. He gently closed the pincers over the snake's neck, slipped the hook under the snake's body about halfway down its length, and lifted it out.

It was four feet long and undulated slightly at the disturbance. Wentz lowered it carefully into one of the buckets, then quickly snapped the lid, into which air holes had been drilled, onto the top. He repeated the procedure at the next cage.

"Just fed 'em last week—a rat for each of them—so they should be good for another couple of weeks. Don't give 'em live ones—too likely they'll get bit—and make sure the frozen ones are all thawed out, otherwise they get indigestion."

"Sure. Warm, dead rats," said Millard. "We should have a toast."

The old man nodded, grinning, and motioned him to the back of the shed.

There was an ancient lawn chair and an upended milk crate on which sat a stack of magazines. The magazine on the top of the pile featured a close-up of a snake, its mouth agape, with the caption *Water Snakes: Special Edition!* Wentz moved the magazines from the crate to the floor and waved Millard graciously onto it. Another crate served as their table. The old man eased himself onto the lawn chair.

Millard opened the bottle of Jack Daniels and filled the glasses. He handed one to the old man.

"Cheers," said Millard, lifting his glass.

"Skoal," said Wentz, and tossed back the liquor. He smacked his lips and sat back in his chair. "Let me tell you about those Westerns."

As the story spun out, Millard kept the old man's glass full. He periodically held the bottle over his own glass, but didn't pour. Wentz didn't seem to notice.

Thirty minutes passed, then forty-five. The old man's stories began to wander, then his speech to slur. Finally he pinched the bridge of his nose.

"Had too much," he mumbled.

"Nonsense," said Millard. "Our friend Jack would never do you wrong." He refilled the glass again.

Wentz smiled and nodded, but the movement must have set off alarms again.

"Too much," he repeated vaguely.

He was silent for a full minute. His head began to sink forward, then jerked up.

"The snakes you came for ..." he said blearily.

"No hurry," said Millard. "I can come back for them tomorrow."

"Yeah ... tomorrow," said Wentz, and his head drooped forward again.

This time it did not jerk up, and in a moment, Millard heard a faint snorting snore. After another minute, he called the old man's name. There was no response.

Millard pushed himself off the milk crate and laid his hand on Wentz's shoulder. He didn't move. Millard shook him lightly, but the only response was another snort and a lolling of the head.

Millard poured the contents of his glass into Wentz's, then pocketed his own glass. After double-checking to make sure the lids on the buckets containing the snakes were secure, he put them in his car, then returned to the shed.

He snapped on a pair of vinyl gloves and, at a utility sink in the corner of the shed, rinsed and wiped out the bowls of water in the two snakes' cages and put them in a pile with others next to the sink. He removed the pieces of carpeting from the bottoms of the cages and hosed them off outside, shook them as dry as he could, and put them on top of a stack of others in the corner of the shed.

He went back to his car and got a pair of rubber-handled pliers out of the trunk. He went around to the back of the shed, where the air conditioning unit hummed softly in the darkness. He removed the cover from the disconnect switch and touched one jaw of the pliers to the red wire terminal and, turning his face away, the other to the white.

There was a flash and bang, and the AC fan clattered to a stop.

When he reentered the shed, it already felt warmer, although perhaps that was just his imagination. Perhaps it was also his imagination that the monitor lizards, which in the cool of the conditioned air had been still, seemed to be stirring.

He went to the old man and shook him again, but this time there was no response—it was like shaking a rag doll. He pressed his fingers to the man's neck and felt a pulse, strong and steady. He reached into the man's pocket and got out his wallet. He removed the two hundred dollars, then returned the wallet to Wentz's pocket.

Millard wiped down the Jack Daniels bottle, took the old man's limp hand and wrapped it around the neck of the bottle, then replaced the bottle on the milk crate table.

He stepped behind the old man's chair and gave him a sharp push. The chair tipped forward, and the old man went sprawling onto the ground. He stirred slightly at the disturbance, then settled in on the concrete with a soft snore.

Millard hoisted him back on the chair, and angled the chair slightly, toward one of the shed's support beams. He pushed again.

This time the old man's head cracked against the post as he went sprawling onto the floor. He let out a low moan, then was silent. Blood began to flow from his head.

Millard stepped to the monitor lizards' cage and opened the door. The lizards stirred and turned their dragon-like heads toward Millard, then began propelling themselves across the floor of their cage toward the open door.

Millard hurried to the door of the shed. He stepped through, then looked back. The creatures made their ponderous way toward the old man's body, their tongues flicking toward the growing pool of blood under his head.

Millard closed the door behind him, went to his car, and headed back to Sedona.

29

The sky was a cloudless azure, and a cool breeze blowing up the valley that ran below the Thread-the-Needle Trail counteracted the heat of the brilliant sun. Lizzy sang enthusiastically, if a bit off-key, as she walked—she had read that whistling or singing was a good way to warn wildlife of the approach of a human.

Uncle Owen had seemed a little tired on their way to the trail and Lizzy decided she'd turn around as soon as she got to the Needle so he didn't have to wait for her for too long on the rock they had dubbed the Pincushion. In fact, he had seemed tired and distracted for at least the last week, and since Lizzy had accidentally read the text from Andy, she understood at least part of the reason. She knew what it was to worry about a parent, and she could imagine the stress of doing that worrying long distance.

She also sensed that Uncle Owen was mulling over the conversation he had had with Philip. He had described the visit, concluding with, "I can see why you wanted to keep seeing him—he's an easy person to talk to." His comment had made her realize that he was not only worrying over his inability to be with his mother, but also missing the normal interactions with family and friends that she knew were an important part of his life. She and Uncle Owen were supporting each other as best they could, but she knew that there was no substitute she could provide for Owen sitting down with his brother, a six-pack of Yuengling, and a pizza to watch an Eagles game at their parents' home.

Even before she had read Andy's text at the airport restaurant, she had wanted to get back to Philadelphia to help protect Andy and Ruby, and to do whatever she could to resolve the situation with Louise Mortensen and George Millard. Now she had the added incentive of getting Uncle Owen back home.

As she approached the narrow opening, she heard the sounds of something scraping on the rocks from the far side. She stopped.

"Hello?" she called.

Silence.

She scanned the hillside above the Needle for falling rocks, but all was still. She considered turning around—if there was a rock slide, her special ability wouldn't do her much good against that—but then reconsidered. She was being melodramatic. She had walked all this way, she wasn't about to turn around a dozen yards from the Eye.

She could see the narrow strip of blue sky on the other side of the opening, a passage that always seemed a bit magical—like the wardrobe in the Narnia books or Alice's rabbit hole. Slipping through the Eye reminded her of the excitement of climbing into the forts she would create with a card table and blankets at the Poconos cabin. She would beg her mom to climb in with her, and her mom always had. Lizzy realized now how difficult it must have been for her mom, debilitated as she was at that point by her strokes.

She slipped her knapsack off her back and stepped through the Eye.

She registered an undulating movement on the path ahead of her and felt a clench of fear as she recognized what it was. The snake—a huge snake—was retreating down the path, and she had half a second to feel relief that it was slithering away from her when she felt a bolt of pain drill into her ankle.

She shrieked, just as she heard the telltale rattle at her feet.

The aggrieved snake struck again, this time burying its fangs in her hiking boot.

She tried to kick her leg out, to fling the snake away from her, but her leg felt rooted to the ground. She stumbled backward, hoping to get back through the Eye, but she misjudged and bounced off the rock and fell sideways, hard.

The snake detached itself from her boot, and she tried to snatch every part of her body out of its reach simultaneously, but the snake had evidently had enough and, turning, followed its partner down the path.

She gripped her thigh, as if she could hold back the pain that boiled up her leg. She clawed herself upright on the rock and staggered to the Eye.

"Uncle Owen! A rattlesnake bit me!"

OWEN SAT ON THE PINCUSHION, looking over the valley below. He had agreed to accompany Lizzy on that first hike as a favor to her but, much to his surprise, he had enjoyed it, and was not as bad at it as he had expected to be. An almost-daily trip to Thread-the-Needle had become a regular part of their routine.

Just the day before, he had climbed with some trepidation onto the scale that he had stowed in the linen closet when they had first settled into the Sedona house. Two ninety-seven. It was the first time he had weighed less than three hundred pounds since ... he couldn't remember when. He celebrated by having a salad for lunch. A few hours later, when it became apparent that the salad wouldn't tide him over until dinner, he had heated up a frozen pizza. But it was a start.

Finishing his granola bar and tucking the wrapper into his pocket, he rolled up his sleeves, exposing his pale forearms. During his time in the Keys and in Sedona, he had followed his usual practice of avoiding exposing his pale skin to direct sunlight, but perhaps he could develop a tan to go with his new, svelte frame.

Then he heard Lizzy scream.

He was on his feet and hurrying down the trail as the scream still echoed off the canyon walls. He heard her yell, and although he couldn't hear what she was yelling, it was clear she was in trouble.

"I'm coming, Pumpkin," he shouted back.

LIZZY'S LEG felt like it was burning from the inside out. She tried again to get back through the Eye, but the pain was worse when she moved, and she lowered herself to the ground. With trembling fingers she pulled up the leg of her hiking pants and pushed her hiking sock down to the top of her boot. The two puncture marks were just above her boot. Her leg was already swelling.

She pulled her phone out of her knapsack. No service. Choking back a sob, she pressed 911—what had she got to lose?—but was met with silence.

She heard Owen's yell—"Lizzy, I'm coming!"—and leaned back against the rock, trying to slow her breathing and the hammering of her heart. Half a minute later, she heard Owen's voice coming from the other side of the opening.

"Lizzy, can you hear me?" he gasped out.

"Yes," she said through gritted teeth. "I'm right on the other side of the Eye."

"What happened?"

She tried to shift so she could look through the Eye, triggering another shock of agony. "A rattlesnake bit me," she sobbed.

"Where?"

"On my leg."

She heard scuffling sounds, a grunt, and then Owen's voice again. "Damn it! I'm too fat to fit through. I'm going to see if I can go around."

Lizzy could picture the scene—a steep hill of unstable scree on the uphill side of the trail, a precipitous drop on the other.

"No, wait," she said, "let me try to get through again."

The thought of putting weight on her throbbing leg sent a wave of nausea through her, so she dragged herself back over to the Eye. She peered through, at Owen's big, concerned face on the other side. He reached out his hand—he could almost, but not quite, reach her.

She tried to heave herself up on one leg but fell back with a cry. "I can't do it."

"I'm coming around."

She heard scrabbling and heavy breathing, then the shush of sliding scree, and a thump and grunt.

"Damn!"

"Are you okay?"

"Yes, I'm fine. Just way too big to be useful." His voice was tight with frustration. "Where on your leg is the bite?"

"Right above my boot."

"Can you get your boot off? It will be better in case your leg swells."

She untied and loosened the laces and pulled at the boot, sending a fresh jolt of pain up her leg. Her vision distorted by tears, she removed the lace entirely and used her other foot to lever the boot off.

"Okay," she gasped. "It's off."

"I can't get a signal," said Owen from the other side of the Eye.

"Me either." What she wouldn't have done for the sight of a privacy fence or the pool house of a rich snowbird, like she might have seen on one of her Sedona walks.

"Damn!" There was a moment of silence, then he said, "Pumpkin, it's better if you stay still. I'm going to go back down the trail until I can get a signal and call 911. I may even have to drive a little way back towards town, but I'll be back with help."

"Okay."

"Can you sit up on a rock? It's going to be better if your body is higher than your leg."

"Okay." She pulled herself over to a rock. Under normal circumstances it would have been the perfect height to serve as a comfortable seat from which to enjoy the view of the valley below. In her current condition, it seemed an almost insurmountable height. She pulled herself up, then slumped back against the rock behind it, her breath rapid. "Okay, I'm sitting up."

"Good job, Pumpkin. Now, no cutting your leg, no trying to squeeze the venom out, that won't help. Do you understand?"

"No cutting. No squeezing."

"That's right. The best thing you can do—and I know this is easier said than done—is to try to stay calm. You're just as likely to shock your system by panicking as by being bitten."

"Okay, I'll try."

"Remember what you learned in yoga class. That's going to be a big help to you."

"Okay."

"I'll be back with help, Pumpkin."

"Okay. Uncle Owen?"

"Yes, Pumpkin."

"Hurry."

30

M illard listened to Ballard and McNally from beyond a bend in the trail. Things seemed to be progressing nicely. He had avoided the challenge of getting the buckets through the Eye by coming to the Needle from the other end of the trail. Getting both the snakes into one bucket had been nerve-racking, but it was easier to manage one snake-filled bucket than two. Plus, maybe they would rile each other up so that they would be conveniently irritated by the time Ballard stepped through the Eye. He had upended the bucket, lid still on, just next to the Eye, and then slid the lid out from under it. There had been a hair-raising moment when one of the snake's tails had wriggled out from the edge of the bucket, but he had poked it back under the bucket with a stick.

The bend in the path provided the perfect vantage point from which to listen to his plan play out, and a large rock provided a hiding place for the bucket and for the rope he had used to pull it off the snakes from a safe distance. If Ballard managed to get past the snakes without getting bitten and continued up the trail, Millard would appear to be just another hiker headed in the opposite direction.

She hadn't gotten past them. There had been a tense moment when first one and then the other snake had slithered down the path just a foot from where he stood, but they seemed intent on putting distance between themselves and the annoying human who had disturbed them, not in engaging in another confrontation. He was glad they had gotten through the encounter unharmed—he had begun to feel a sort of kinship with them, as if they were a trio of workmen out on an assignment.

Now McNally was gone, no doubt waddling as fast as his fat legs would carry him in search of a cell signal. Millard could hear Ballard's hitching gasps of breath. A minute ticked by and the gasps became further spaced and quieter. In another minute, he couldn't hear them at all.

Millard held his own breath, listening. All he could hear was the wind and, just barely, the distant hum of traffic on the freeway.

After another minute, he eased himself around the curve in the path.

She was sitting on a small boulder next to the Eye, her body sagging back against the base of the Needle. He watched her for some time but could see no movement.

His research hadn't suggested that death could occur from a snakebite in so short a time—at this point he would have expected her to be exhibiting difficulty breathing, perhaps even convulsions—but she was so still. Still as death. Maybe this plan had worked out even better than he had hoped.

He picked up a stone and tossed it down the path in her direction. It bounced and clattered down the hill. She made no movement.

He stepped out from behind the rock and took a step toward her, then another. There was no response. When he reached her, he stood over her, watching for any movement, even the rise and fall of her chest. Still nothing.

He leaned toward her, curious to see the bite marks at closer range.

She opened her eyes.

Millard managed to keep from jumping back. "Are you okay, miss?" he asked.

The muscles in her neck corded as she sat forward. "I got bitten by a rattlesnake," she said, her voice hoarse.

"Jesus." Millard looked around nervously. "Is it gone?"

"Yeah, there were two of them and they're both gone." She winced and licked her lips. "What direction did you come from?"

Millard jerked his thumb over his shoulder.

"I'm surprised you didn't see them," she mumbled, sitting forward unsteadily to examine her leg. Her ankle had swollen to the size of her calf, the bottom half of her leg a taut column of flesh. She groaned and slumped back onto the rock.

"We need to get you some help." Millard took his phone out and tutted at the No Service message he knew he would see there. "I can help you back to the trailhead. My car's there, I'll drive you to the ER."

"No, I shouldn't move. My godfather went to get help."

"And left you here?" Millard reached for her arm. "It's best if you're up and moving around."

"No!" she said sharply.

He stepped back. "Sure, not if you don't want to. How about a tourniquet? That would keep the poison from getting to your heart."

He was gratified to see that this seemed to light a flicker of incipient panic.

"He didn't say anything about a tourniquet." After a moment she shook her head. "I think it's best to leave it alone."

"Are you sure he knows what he's talking about? I read a lot about hiking safety and first aid, and they all say that you should apply a tourniquet."

Ballard clamped her lips over another groan and twisted on the rock, trying to look through the Eye in the direction McNally had disappeared.

"No," she said. "He'll be back soon." But her voice was uncertain. The sheen of tears was bright on her cheeks.

"Maybe cut it with a knife," Millard said, continuing to run through the list of actions that every article he had read had warned against. "Let the poison out that way."

"No!" yelled Ballard. "Go away! I don't want you here. I want Uncle Owen."

Millard took another step back. "Okay, okay, don't get upset, that's the worst thing you can do." He was going to push it further, see if he could fan the panic back to life, but decided he didn't want to risk having her alarm at her situation turn into anger at his meddling. "I'll just sit over here and keep you company until your uncle comes back."

"Okay, but stay quiet," she said through gritted teeth.

She lay back on the rock again and closed her eyes. Her breath rasped in and out a few times, and then began to even out. The muscles along her jaw relaxed, the lines around her eyes, which at first were squinted shut, began to smooth out. In a minute she was breathing deeply and slowly. She didn't even seem aware of his presence. If making her death look like an accident weren't so important, it seemingly would have been easy to take care of her now. But he remembered how alert those eyes had been when they popped open.

Millard recalled Gerard Bonnay's caution to his wife not to

underestimate Owen McNally. Millard was skeptical of that advice based on what he had seen of McNally, but Ballard was another matter. She might be a seventeen-year-old girl, but there was an old soul in those eyes. Underestimating Lizzy Ballard was not a trap he would let himself fall into.

31

Owen felt as if his lungs were going to tear and his heart hammer its way out of his ribcage.

He knew that running was beyond him, but he kept up a fast walk, occasionally breaking into a lumbering trot for a few steps. Every half minute or so he would slow to check his phone for a connection. Still nothing.

He was almost at the trailhead when a single bar of reception appeared. He dropped onto a rock and pressed in 911 with shaking fingers.

"911. What's your emergency?"

"My goddaughter was bitten by a rattlesnake," he gasped. "We're on Thread-the-Needle Trail and she had just stepped through—well, I guess it's the Needle—when she got bitten. She's still there. I had to leave her there to be able to call you."

"Which side of the Needle is she on?"

"The side further away from the trailhead."

"There are actually two trailheads. Can you describe which one you came from?"

Owen managed to provide enough detail that the dispatcher could identify Lizzy's location.

"She's only about half a mile from the other end of the trail," said the dispatcher. "We can get to her that way. Hold one moment please while I get an ambulance on its way to you." Owen didn't have to wait long before the dispatcher was back on the line with him. "They're on their way."

"I can drive around and meet them at the other trailhead," said Owen. ""How do I get there?"

"It will be faster for you just to walk back to the Needle."

"I can't get through it to the other side. I'm ... rather large."

"Gotcha. Don't try to force yourself through. Last year some guy got stuck in there and we had to use about a million packets of Surgilube to get him out. We don't want you getting stuck. Or worse."

"I agree," Owen said with a shudder.

"Hold on, let me check what they want you to do."

There was some indistinct conversation between the dispatcher and, Owen assumed, the EMTs en route to Lizzy's location.

"They said to go back to the Needle," said the dispatcher, "but stay on your side. Keep her company—and keep her calm—until they get there. Then you can meet up with them at the hospital. We'll probably lose our connection as you go back, but the EMTs should be there soon."

"Okay. Thank you."

The connection did drop almost as soon as Owen started back up the trail, his legs unsteady from the unaccustomed effort, and from anxiety.

As he approached the Needle, he caught a flicker of movement through the opening. He hoped that Lizzy wasn't moving around, and he found it hard to believe that the EMTs had gotten there so quickly. He hurried to the opening.

"Pumpkin, I'm back," he called. "An ambulance is coming. They can get you out from the other end of the trail."

"Okay," he heard her answer, her voice weak.

He saw the flicker of movement again. "Is someone over there with you?"

There was a long pause, then Lizzy answered, her voice quavery. "Some guy."

A male voice spoke. "I happened upon your goddaughter and thought I'd stay with her until help arrived."

"He wanted me to walk around," said Lizzy, "but you said to stay still."

"Yes, staying still is the right thing to do," Owen replied. He strained for a better view through the opening.

"Well, there are differing opinions on that," replied the male voice. He had disappeared completely from Owen's view, but it sounded like he was now standing near Lizzy.

"Come over here where I can see you," said Owen sharply.

In a moment, a face, bearded and tan, appeared on the other side of the opening. Owen compared it to Lizzy's description of George Millard.

"Who are you?" asked Owen.

"Jim."

Owen waited for more, but the man was silent.

"Can you come through to my side?" asked Owen.

"Sure, I *could*, but don't you think it's better if someone is over here with your goddaughter?"

"I think it's better for you to come over here so I can talk with you face-to-face. It sounds to me like she's doing fine without either of us. And the EMTs are on their way," he added.

"I think I hear them coming," said Jim.

Owen thought suddenly of the danger Lizzy might pose to the EMTs.

"Pumpkin, don't forget that these people are here to help you."

"I know, Uncle Owen."

"There you are!" he heard a hearty voice call in a Spanish accent. "The white knights have arrived!"

"Sir," a different voice said, evidently to Jim, "are you the young lady's father?"

"I'm her godfather," called Owen. "I'm her guardian."

One of the EMTs came to the Eye and glanced through. "Okay, sir. I'm Harold and my partner is Jose. We've also got some guys from the Verde Valley Fire Department over here. What's your goddaughter's name?"

"Lizzy."

"Okay, we'll let you and Lizzy know what we're doing." He disappeared in Lizzy's direction.

Harold narrated their actions—checking vital signs, providing oxygen, starting a saline IV—while Owen could hear Jose's soothing reassurances to Lizzy. After a few minutes, Jose said, "Harold's just going to let your godfather know where we're taking you. Is it okay if we give him your knapsack to keep for you?"

Owen heard a faint affirmative sound from Lizzy.

In a moment, Harold squeezed through the Eye to Owen's side. "We'll be taking her to Yavapai Regional Medical Center. Do you know where that is?"

"I don't, but I'm sure I can plug it into my GPS."

"Okay, we'll meet you over there—just go right to the emergency room when you get there." He held up Lizzy's knapsack. "Anything in here she would need on an emergency basis? Meds? Inhaler?"

"No."

"Can you hold onto it for her?"

"Sure." Owen took the knapsack. He tried to peer through the Eye. "How is she?" he asked softly.

"The doctors will be able to give you a better assessment when they get her to the hospital, but she's a trouper."

Owen lowered his voice further. "The man over there with her—I'd rather he didn't know where she's going."

"Won't be a problem," said Harold. "He left when we arrived." He clapped Owen on the shoulder. "We'll see you at the hospital." He disappeared back through the Eye.

Owen wasn't sure whether to be relieved or concerned that the man had left, but didn't have the mental bandwidth to consider it at the moment. He leaned as far into the opening as he could. "I'll meet you at the hospital, Pumpkin!" he called.

There was a pause, then Jose said, "She's giving you a thumbs-up!"

He heard shuffling sounds of what he assumed were the EMTs lifting the stretcher, then their steps on the path as they trooped away from the Needle.

Owen turned and headed down the trail as fast as his exhausted legs would carry him. As soon as he picked up a signal on his phone, he plugged *Yavapai Regional* into his GPS —twenty minutes away. He bet he could make it in fifteen.

32

The ER staff had given Owen a sheaf of forms to fill out, and he quickly decided that putting anything other than his and Lizzy's actual information on the forms would be asking for more trouble than they already had. Forms now completed, he sat in the waiting room, frantically scanning the search results for *rattlesnake bite and treatment* on his phone.

The search screen was replaced by an alert of an incoming call: *Andy*.

He thumbed the Accept button.

"Hey, bro, what's up in sunny Sedona?" asked Andy.

"Lizzy's in the ER. She got bitten by a rattlesnake."

"Holy shit—is she okay?"

"I'm waiting to hear."

There was silence for a moment, then Andy said, "It was an accident, right?"

"I don't know. She got bitten when she stepped through a narrow place in the trail. Maybe it was just a good place for a snake to catch some rays. If they even like that kind of thing." Owen typed *rattlesnake sunbathing* into his phone.

"Or maybe someone laid a trap for her," said Andy.

Owen sighed. "Maybe. There was a man there."

"What was he doing?"

"Claimed he had just happened upon her on the trail after she got bitten and while I was going for help. But Lizzy said he was telling her to do some questionable things, like walking around."

"Yeah, that wouldn't be a good idea," agreed Andy. "Did you get a chance to ask her if she thought it was Millard?"

"I haven't had a chance to talk with her yet. And she probably wasn't in much of a condition to do a careful examination in any case."

"I'll bet."

They sat in silence for a few moments, then Andy said, "Want me to come out there?"

"I appreciate the offer, but I don't think it's necessary."

"It would double the number of McNallys keeping an eye on her."

"But who knows how long you'd have to be here. If it was an accident, we might as well stay here—I suspect she'll need rest when she gets out, assuming—" He stopped and rubbed his eyes.

"Yeah," said Andy, his voice unaccustomedly serious.

Owen drew a deep breath. "And if it wasn't an accident, and she's in any condition to travel, we need to get out of here as soon as we can."

"Back here?"

"I don't know. I can't think straight at the moment."

"I can imagine."

Owen laughed humorlessly. "Maybe we should swap places. I can come back to Philly and cover for you and look after Mom and Dad, and you come out here and keep an eye on Lizzy. It seems like she ends up in the ER an awful lot while I'm on duty."

"That's not fair, bro—there's no way this is your fault. And her last trip to the ER was the only way to get her away from Bonnay and Mortensen."

"I suppose."

A ring tone emanated from Lizzy's backpack, which sat at Owen's feet. He found her phone in one of the outside pockets. The caller ID read *Philip*.

"Listen, I've got to take a call that's coming in on Lizzy's phone," he said to Andy. "I'll call you as soon as I know anything."

"Okay," said Andy. "Good luck."

Owen ended the call on his phone and answered the call on Lizzy's. "Hello, Philip. This is Owen McNally."

"Is Lizzy okay?" Philip asked, his voice worried. "She had a session scheduled for today."

"We were out on a hike at the Thread-the-Needle Trail and she got bitten by a rattlesnake right as she stepped through the Eye. I'm at the ER at Yavapai Regional, I'm waiting to hear how she's doing."

At that moment, a short, somewhat plump woman came through the doors from the ER treatment area into the waiting room. She looked at a tablet she was carrying, then glanced around the room, her gaze falling on Owen. "Dr. McNally?"

Owen jumped to his feet. "Yes, that's me." He spoke into the phone. "The doctor's here. I'll call you back once I know anything."

He just heard Philip's "But—" before he disconnected the call.

The woman put out her hand. "I'm Dr. Prowse, I'm treating Miss Ballard. If you'd like to follow me, I can give you an update."

He followed her through a set of swinging doors. She waved him into a small room containing a table and two chairs. "Please have a seat."

Owen sat, breathless with anxiety.

Dr. Prowse took the other chair. "I have good news for you," she said. "Your goddaughter is suffering some ill effects from the snakebite, and we'll be admitting her for a day or two to keep an eye on her, but I feel confident she will be fine."

Owen puffed out a bushel-sized breath of air. "Thank God."

"The bite was just above her hiking boot and through her hiking sock. I suspect the angle of the strike and the thickness of the sock may have kept her from getting a full, direct injection of venom."

He nodded. "That's good."

"Are you a medical doctor?" she asked.

"Yes. Not practicing—I teach neurobiology."

She looked back to the tablet. "The EMTs established a line and administered oxygen. She had some moderate respiratory distress and tachycardia but her vitals and SpO2 are back to normal. She has some ecchymosis around the bite and she had some pain and nausea. We administered antivenom and she responded well. We also gave her an anti-inflammatory and an antiemetic. She's stable right now." She glanced up at Owen. "I in no way want to understate the severity of any rattlesnake bite, but as these things go, she was lucky. Actually," she amended, "not so much lucky as mentally well-equipped to deal with the situation. The EMTs reported that she was able to calm herself—to keep her breathing and heart rate low—which certainly contributed to the favorable outcome."

"She's been taking a lot of yoga classes," said Owen.

"Yes, I imagine that would have been a great help to her.

Also, it's possible that the snake had recently struck and had not fully regenerated its venom. If she had been bitten by a domesticated snake, I would have guessed that the snake had recently been milked, but that's obviously not the case here. I don't believe she'll have any long-term ill effects, but it will be best for us to keep an eye on her here for a day or two."

"Yes, of course."

Dr. Prowse scrolled down through the information on the tablet.

"She has indications of recent wounds on her arm and back. Not from today, but fairly recent."

Owen hesitated. "She fell off her bike."

"Oh, yes?" Dr. Prowse looked at him expectantly.

"It was quite scary."

"Did you take her to the ER? Or to a doctor?"

"My brother is an emergency room doctor and he was with us. He treated her injuries."

The doctor examined him expressionlessly for a moment, then said, "They look like bullet wounds."

"Bullet wounds?" asked Owen, a little too loudly. "No, no. It was from the fall off her bike."

"Where did this fall take place?"

Owen did a quick calculation. A fall with injuries just to the arm and back seemed unlikely to happen in December in Pennsylvania, with anyone hardy enough to venture out for a bike ride likely to be bundled up against the cold. "In the Keys. We were vacationing there before we came to Sedona."

The doctor set the tablet aside.

"Are Miss Ballard's parents here in Sedona with you?"

"No. Her mother died when Lizzy—Elizabeth—was quite young, and her father died just a few months ago. That's why we're here in Sedona. He was killed in a mugging in Philadelphia, and as you can imagine, it was quite traumatic for her, and I decided it would be best for her to be away for a little while."

"Yes," said Dr. Prowse, her expression sober. "That is certainly a lot for a young woman to deal with—a parent's death and then an incident like this. I'm sure the yoga practice stood her in good stead." She rose from the table and Owen followed suit. "Where do you teach?" she asked.

"William Penn University in Philadelphia."

"William Penn? I was an undergrad there. Biology and chemistry."

They learned they had a few mutual acquaintances, and that they had both attended the same conference three years before.

Dr. Prowse glanced at her watch, then back to Owen. "I'll be checking in with your goddaughter, but she really just needs some rest and monitoring. You should be able to take her home by the day after tomorrow at the latest."

Owen followed her out of the small conference room and through the swinging doors to the waiting room.

"Someone will let you know as soon as you can see her," she said.

"Thank you."

She extended her hand and Owen shook it. She turned to go.

"Oh, Doctor," he said, and she turned back.

"How was Lizzy with the people who treated her? Was she, um ..."

Dr. Prowse raised her eyebrows questioningly.

"... polite?"

She smiled sympathetically. "'Polite' seems an odd word to apply to someone being treated in an emergency department, but she was very brave and cooperative."

"She's a pretty extraordinary young lady," said Owen. He

cleared his throat. "And everyone who treated her is feeling well?"

She looked at him, puzzled. "As far as I know."

Owen nodded. "Good to know."

Dr. Prowse shook her head—no doubt at the odd reactions people had in such crises—and disappeared back through the swinging doors.

33

That evening, Philip knocked lightly on the door of Lizzy's hospital room. Owen looked up from where he stood by her bed, holding a sheet of paper. Lizzy, evidently in the middle of some type of physical therapy under Owen's direction, fell back on her pillows with a look of relief.

"Hey, Philip," she said, her voice tired. "Come on in."

Philip stepped to the bed. Lizzy's leg was on top of the covers, a bruised discoloration running up her calf and ink lines from a felt tip marker showing where the EMTs had tracked the spread of the swelling.

"That's got to hurt," said Philip.

"Yeah. Some."

"Fortunately the swelling is already going down," said Owen. "The doctor says that Lizzy is doing as well as can be expected, considering what she's been through. She'll probably be discharged the day after tomorrow."

"That's great news," said Philip. "And I have something else that might make you feel better." He held out a small square of folded paper.

Lizzy unfolded the paper and drew out the Zuni bear pendant. "You found it! Where was it?"

"It was on the path, at the point where it narrows as you approach the Eye. I'm guessing that's where they loaded you into the ambulance."

"That sounds right. When did you get it?"

"I went over there after I heard from Owen what had happened."

Lizzy ran the necklace through her fingers. "It's on a new chain."

"I only found the pendant."

"You bought a new necklace?" She fastened it around her neck and stroked the pendant.

"I got the necklace in the gift store here. Used to have this on it." With a grin, he held out a Hello Kitty pendant.

She laughed. "Thank you. I feel better already."

"Not to rain on your parade," said Philip, tucking his hands into the pockets of his jeans, "but I found some other things near the Needle. There was a plastic pail and lid hidden behind a rock just a few yards from the Eye."

Owen's face tightened. "Like you might use to transport snakes."

"Exactly. There was also a length of rope tied to the pail, just long enough so that someone could pull the pail off from a safe distance."

"What did you do with the things you found?" asked Owen.

"I left them there. I figured it was best if whoever they belonged to thought they hadn't been found."

"So, it seems likely that it *was* George Millard at the trail," said Owen.

"Seems safe to assume that."

"The guy on the trail did keep suggesting things that didn't seem like good ideas," said Lizzy, "like putting on a tourniquet, or doing things that Uncle Owen had told me not to do, like trying to squeeze out the venom. I told him to be quiet, and he did stay quiet after that."

"Did you get angry with him?" asked Philip.

"I started to, until he stopped talking."

"Did you squeeze him?"

"Not intentionally." Lizzy considered. "No, I don't think I did, because at the time I thought he was just a clueless and annoying guy who was trying to be helpful."

"He certainly didn't seem like he was suffering any ill effects when I talked to him," said Owen.

"Might have been better if you had given him a little squeeze," said Philip, "but with him being squeeze-free, as far as we know, I think it would be a good idea for you guys to hit the road as soon as Lizzy's discharged."

Lizzy sat up. "But what about our sessions?"

"We can talk about that, but I don't think that's the highest priority at the moment." He turned to Owen. "And I don't think you should stay in your house tonight."

Owen nodded. "You're probably right." He ran his fingers through his hair. "I'll stay here in the hospital with Lizzy. If they kick me out, I can go to a hotel."

"That sounds like a good plan," said Philip.

Owen thought for a moment, then said, "Although I'll need to go to the house to pack up, and if I did that tonight, we'd be ready to go as soon as they discharge Lizzy."

"You shouldn't go by yourself," said Lizzy.

"I agree," said Philip. "And I'd like to stay here with Lizzy while you're gone. But I think I have someone who can help."

"I don't want to get anyone else involved in this," said Owen with alarm.

"My landlord is a retired Phoenix cop who moved to

Sedona and stays busy by flipping houses. I'm pretty sure he would like nothing better than to have an opportunity to play cop for an evening. I can tell him that the alarm at the house tripped and you want to check it out but don't want to walk into a possible burglary in progress alone."

Owen looked affronted. "Makes me seem a little bit wimpy."

"Not at all. Makes you seem smart."

Owen seemed to be marshaling other arguments against involving Philip's landlord, but Lizzy spoke up.

"I'd feel better if someone was with you."

Owen sighed. "All right."

Philip pulled out his phone and hit a speed dial. "Eddie, it's Philip—how're you doing? ... Yeah? ... Hey, I have a favor to ask." He gave the story about the tripped alarm. "Do you think you could meet up with my buddy there and check out the place with him? ... That's great, I really appreciate it. His name's Owen. He's tall and—" Philip glanced at Owen.

"Fat," supplied Owen.

"—sizable," said Philip. "Light hair. Fair skin." Philip relayed the address from Owen to Eddie, and ended the call. "He's heading over there now. If he's not at the house when you get there, you shouldn't have long to wait. He's a black guy with a shaved head, so no risk of confusing George Millard with him."

"Thanks," said Owen. "Although I still feel bad dragging your landlord out on what's probably an unnecessary errand."

Philip slipped his phone back into his pocket. "Once he heard what was up, he sounded more cheerful than I've heard him since he scared the crap out of some teenagers who were busting up jack-o'-lanterns on Halloween."

Owen put on his jacket and hat. "It shouldn't take me more than about an hour to get there, pack up, and get back here. If

I run into any problems, I'll let you know." He kissed Lizzy on top of the head. "Want me to pick anything up for you while I'm out?"

"No, but thanks."

"Magazines?"

"No, Uncle Owen, I'm fine. I have books on my phone."

"Okay, I'll be back in a jiff." He lumbered out of the room.

"Uncle Owen thinks magazines are the antidote for everything," said Lizzy.

Philip sat down on the guest chair next to Lizzy's bed. "Looks like you're probably going to be heading out of Sedona one way or the other. Getting bitten by a snake isn't the most fun way to go about it, but it's what you wanted to do, right?"

Her hand went to the Zuni pendant. "I wanted to go back to Pennsylvania and do something about Louise and George Millard, but now I feel like it's better to stay here for a little while so we can continue our sessions. Get me better prepared for ... whatever happens in Pennsylvania when I do go back."

Philip laced his fingers together and rested his elbows on his knees. "That's what I wanted to talk with you about, and why I didn't want to go back to the house with Owen. I need to tell you a little of my history, and explain why it has anything to do with your situation." He took a deep breath. "When I was nineteen, I went to jail for killing a man."

Lizzy looked at him, startled. "Really?"

"Really. I found him ... doing something not very nice to an animal. I was just going to teach him a lesson—take the animal away from him, rough him up a little—but he pulled a knife. And I pulled a knife. And it turned out that I was better with my knife than he was with his."

There was a long silence. Finally Lizzy said, "Wow."

"Yeah."

"Good thing Uncle Owen doesn't know."

Philip smiled. "Yeah."

"I'm surprised he didn't find out about that," she said. "He Googled you."

"I had a different name back then."

"Really?"

"Yup."

Lizzy considered. "But you were trying to rescue the animal. And then you were defending yourself. How could they send you to jail?"

"My lawyer was incompetent, the judge didn't place much value on the well-being of an animal, and the guy in question was the son of a big rancher in the area."

"That doesn't seem right."

"Yeah." Philip cleared his throat, then continued. "I went to the prison in Williams and was there for four years." He smiled again, but this time the smile didn't reach his eyes. "Those were not the best years of my life. Prison is not a great place to be if you're a relatively good-looking young man."

Lizzy stirred uncomfortably.

"You don't believe I was a relatively good-looking young man?" he asked, trying to lighten the mood.

"No, it's not that," she replied. "It's just that ..." Her voice trailed off.

"I know. I shouldn't make a joke out of it. It was no joke. If I ever got in trouble again, I'd leave the country before I'd go back to jail." He paused. "I'd consider killing myself before I'd go back to jail."

"It was that bad?"

"Yeah, it was that bad. On top of all the obvious disadvantages of being locked up twenty-four seven with a bunch of criminals who have no respect for their fellow man, being behind bars is just a soul-killing experience. Hell, I wasn't even in that long, and if I had been left to my own devices, I would have left more damaged than when I went in." He drew a deep breath. "Anyhow ... the whole experience did have a silver lining."

"It did?"

He nodded. "When I showed up at Williams, all I could talk about was how I was a victim of the system, a victim of my circumstances. No mom, no dad, no real home, no money. Then I met this guy named Oscar. He took a liking to me—and I mean that in a totally positive way. He was in for twenty years for first-degree murder, and he had done six years of it when I met him. He wasn't quite as pretty as I was," he smiled ruefully at Lizzy, "so he didn't have exactly the same problems I did, but being an old guy in the joint is no treat, either. There are a whole bunch of other ways they can make life shitty for you if you're an old guy. But he took care of me. I don't think it's too much to say he saved my life—literally and figuratively. He made me see that after I put in my time, I'd get out with my whole life ahead of me. He said if I wasted that, I should be ashamed of myself."

"Seems like you took his advice," said Lizzy.

"Yeah. Not only did he help me get through my time in prison, but he helped me see what I could do when I got out. He's the one who first saw that I had a talent for reading people, and got me thinking about making it into a profession. He said I had everything to live a good and happy life, and I just needed to recognize it and do something with it. He had this philosophy he called the Ruby Slippers. You know about the Ruby Slippers?"

"Sure. From *The Wizard of Oz*."

"So, what is the lesson of the Ruby Slippers?"

"That Dorothy can go back to Kansas."

"No." He said it so forcefully that she jumped. "Not just that. Think about it."

She considered, a little flustered. Finally, she said, "That Dorothy could have gone home any time she wanted to."

"That's right. That she didn't need to be helped any longer. That she'd always had the power to control her destiny, but had to learn it for herself."

"So you always had the power to make your life better," Lizzy said slowly, "like the ability to read people, and you just needed Oscar to help you see that."

"That's right." Philip held her gaze. "And I think the same is true for you."

"You mean I don't need to have any more sessions?"

"Truth be told, I think you probably didn't need *any* sessions. Much as I'd like to think otherwise, I don't think our sessions were what enabled you to keep yourself calm after being bitten by the rattlesnake—that was the yoga. And you didn't need sessions with me to keep from squeezing the man on the trail when he made you angry. The reason you didn't squeeze him is because you're a good person and you realized —or at least thought at the time, completely reasonably—that he was someone who was trying to help you. Don't get me wrong—I think our sessions were useful, but in a different way. I think they gave you someone to talk to who wasn't all wound up right along with you in the problems you were trying to solve. And who gave you some ideas for other ways you could think about your ability."

"Like a ladder and not a snake," said Lizzy.

"That's right."

Lizzy looked down at her hands, running the edge of the hospital blanket back and forth through her fingers. "So, you think I'm ... fixed?"

He smiled. "'Fixed' is not the word I'd use, because it implies you were broken before. But I think you have every-thing you need within yourself to solve your problems."

"Even when people are coming after me with poisonous snakes?" she asked, a bit angrily.

He sat back. "That's a different kind of problem, and anyone with that kind of problem can use all the help they can get. I'm thinking more of the problem you first came to see me about—the issue of self-control. I think only you will be able to decide how much self-control factors into your situation and, maybe more importantly, what you want to do with that control."

They sat in silence for half a minute. Finally Lizzy said, "In *The Wizard of Oz*, isn't there something about a person's own backyard?"

"'If I ever go looking for my heart's desire again,'" quoted Philip, "'I won't look any further than my own backyard. Because if it isn't there, I never really lost it to begin with.'"

"Maybe that's a message that Uncle Owen and I need to be getting back to Pennsylvania," she said, some excitement creeping into her voice.

"Maybe. But I wouldn't go overboard looking for too many secret messages in a Judy Garland movie."

She smiled. "Are you still in touch with Oscar?"

"He died."

Her smile faded.

"He ran afoul of one of the gangs at Williams," said Philip. "They wanted him to help them smuggle some drugs in, and he refused. They caught him in the cafeteria. Stabbed him in the stomach."

"It sounds like—" she began, then clamped her lips closed.

"Like your father," he said.

She nodded.

He leaned forward again. "I know what it's like to lose a father, Lizzy. I lost my biological father to drink, and I lost my true father—Oscar—to a bunch of bullies who thought that a hit of coke was worth an old man's life."

"Is the guy who killed Oscar still in jail?"

"Yes. Tobe Hanrick. He'll be there all his life."

"Still, he's alive. And George Millard, if that's who killed my dad, is still out there. It's not fair."

"Dorothy had her allies to help her learn the things she needed to learn to understand the meaning of the Ruby Slippers, and I hope I helped you with that. They also helped her take care of the Wicked Witch, and I think I can help with that, too. We haven't seen the last of each other, Lizzy Ballard."

34

Millard had planned to retrieve the pail, lid, and rope after the ambulance left with Ballard, but McNally had seemed suspicious and Millard had decided not to hang around when the EMTs arrived.

He had returned to the Needle a few hours later, but when he got there, there were a couple of earnest-looking student types examining the ground near the Eye and tapping on iPads.

"Hello, sir," one of them said. "A hiker was bitten by a rattlesnake here just a short time ago, so please be careful. Watch where you step, and don't reach your hand into anyplace a rattler might be resting—under rocks or in the brush, for example."

"Thanks for the warning," said Millard.

He thought he could hang around until they left, but they sat down on a rock and began a spirited debate about the evolutionary history of venom and he had returned to his car. He didn't fancy going back to the trail again after dark—too great a chance of a plan-wrecking slip or fall. He would collect the pail and rope in the morning. And with Ballard laid up and McNally no doubt thrown off-kilter, he would seize the opportunity to take care of McNally, leaving Ballard with one less ally when she got out of the hospital.

He weighed his options. Antifreeze in a carton of orange juice? He wasn't sure if the juice would disguise the taste, and he didn't fancy having to explain to Mortensen another target who was merely very sick but not dead. A sliced brake line on McNally's SUV? Not enough curvy, cliff-hugging roads between the hospital and their house to increase the odds of a fatal accident, and too much chance of attention-attracting collateral damage. The best option might be a straightforward scenario of an interrupted home burglary—clear the few valuables out of the house, then shoot McNally when he came through the door. Yes, that seemed like the most reliable plan.

Now the tracking app showed both McNally and Castillo's vehicles at the hospital, and Ballard would no doubt be spending at least one night there. Millard headed to the house off Coffee Pot Drive to set the trap for McNally.

Even though he had swapped out his rental car for a new one earlier in the day to reduce the chances of Ballard and McNally realizing they were being followed, he parked a block away from their house. As he walked back to the house, he glanced in any uncurtained windows he passed. He had always enjoyed the experience of watching people going about their normal routine, unaware of his passing presence.

The lock on McNally and Ballard's house was laughably easy to pick, and he relocked the door behind him. He checked the tracking app: neither car had moved from the hospital parking lot. While he waited for McNally's arrival, he conducted a search of the house, but it was strikingly unproductive. He did find a wad of cash—several hundred dollars—rolled in a sock in McNally's dresser drawer. Other than a laptop on the kitchen table, the cash was about the only thing of value that a burglar would be able to take with him. He tucked it into his pocket.

Not only were their belongings not of any resalable value, but they also didn't give up any secrets. It would have been too much to ask to find a pair of train tickets or a paper map with a route marked on it. But it didn't matter—pretty soon McNally wouldn't have to worry about hitting the road.

Millard checked the tracking app again and saw that McNally's SUV was on the move. He was gratified to see that Castillo's truck remained in the hospital parking lot. In a few minutes, he heard the approach of a vehicle. Millard watched the tracking app as the vehicle circled the block, then headlights swept the front of the house and the driver killed the engine. Hidden in the dark interior of the house, he glanced out the front window to see McNally hoist himself out of his SUV, talking on his phone. He unholstered his gun, fitted with a silencer, and stepped into a broom closet just off the kitchen. He couldn't shoot McNally while he was on the phone, and if he was still talking on the phone when he came in, Millard might learn something valuable before McNally died. He would still have Ballard to deal with, but he was looking forward to reporting to Mortensen that one of their problems had been taken care of.

35

Lizzy's phone buzzed. "Hi, Uncle Owen," she answered. "I'm putting you on speaker."

"Hi, Pumpkin—I just got to the house and everything looks okay."

"Is Philip's landlord there yet?"

"I don't see him, and a bald black man in this neighborhood would be hard to miss."

"Hold tight until he gets there," said Philip.

"I drove around the block and didn't see anything suspicious."

"I'm thinking that if it is George Millard," said Philip, "he probably wouldn't let you see him."

"I'm not totally clueless," said Owen. There was a pause, then he continued. "It looks fine. I'm going to go in and start packing. I'll stay on the phone with you and raise the alarm if anything happens."

"Owen," said Philip, "I didn't mean that *you* wouldn't see him, I meant it's likely *no one* would see him if Millard is the professional it sounds like he is."

"I'm going up the steps," said Owen.

"Uncle Owen, wait until Eddie gets there!"

"I'm opening the front door—still no sign of anything amiss," Owen narrated.

"Jesus, Owen, can't you just wait outside for a couple of minutes?" said Philip.

Owen continued his color commentary. "I'm going into my bedroom now and getting out the luggage. I'm going to put my phone on speaker and put it in my shirt pocket so I don't have to try to hold it and pack at the same time. Now I'm taking the clothes out of the dresser ... I'm putting the clothes in the suitcase."

Lizzy was staring at the phone as if hoping to catch a glimpse of Owen in its screen. Philip stood, glowering, his arms crossed.

"Wait a minute," said Owen.

"What's happening?" asked Lizzy, her voice rising with anxiety.

"I had some money in a sock in my drawer, and it's gone."

"Owen, just leave the house and wait outside until Eddie gets there," said Philip.

There was no response.

"Owen?" said Philip.

"I thought I heard something," Owen's lowered voice came over the phone.

"Uncle Owen, leave now!"

"Be quiet for a minute." Then they heard his whisper close to the phone. "There's someone in the living room."

Lizzy switched her wide-eyed stare to Philip. He opened his mouth—no doubt to repeat his advice to Owen to leave the house—but then they both jumped at a yell from the phone.

"Jesus Christ!" they heard, followed by the clatter of the phone hitting the floor.

"You Owen?" they heard a deep voice. "I'm Eddie."

FROM THE DARKNESS of the broom closet, Millard listened to McNally and the new arrival, Eddie, chat as McNally finished packing. Where were Ballard and McNally picking up all these helpers?

After Eddie identified himself as Castillo's landlord, he asked McNally about a tripped burglar alarm, which was news to Millard. Once Eddie had ascertained that there was not only no tripped burglar alarm, but no security system at all, and had vowed to find out what the hell Castillo was talking about, he regaled McNally with stories from his former life as a Phoenix cop.

Millard had picked the broom closet as his hiding place since it appeared not to have anything personal of McNally or Ballard's in it, and so might remain unvisited by the house's occupants—he wanted to pick his own timing for when he confronted McNally. There was a dicey moment when McNally voiced the need for some plastic grocery bags to pack the food into—Millard knew that a container filled with such bags was hanging from a nail near his elbow—but McNally located a supply in the cabinet under the sink.

Millard listened, stewing, as McNally and Eddie ferried bags and suitcases to the SUV, then listened to the sounds of McNally locking up.

After another minute, he eased open the door of the broom closet and stepped out. He pulled out his phone and watched as the tracker traced a path back toward the hospital.

He could hardly take out McNally there, but it was clear that they were vacating the house, which suggested that they would be leaving Sedona. When they did, he would be right behind them.

36

Early the next morning, Millard backed his car into a handicapped space from which he could see the hospital entrance. When Ballard and McNally left the hospital—today or tomorrow, he guessed—he would follow them, assisted by the tracker, and pick the best location to remove them from the picture. Unless Castillo was going to close up shop for a little getaway with his new buddies, they wouldn't have him looking after them once they left Sedona.

Millard had been waiting a little less than two hours when McNally appeared at the door—his bulk made him easy to pick out—pushing Ballard in a wheelchair. Two women flanked Ballard, one in a nurse's uniform, one in a doctor's coat. McNally and the doctor chatted for a few moments, then she shook his hand and Ballard's and disappeared back into the hospital. McNally trundled off toward the parking lot, leaving Ballard with the nurse. Millard started the car.

A few minutes later, McNally pulled up in front of the entrance, and Ballard climbed into the SUV. McNally pulled away as the nurse pushed the wheelchair back into the building.

Millard put the car in gear and took his foot off the brake. The car didn't roll the way he expected it to, so he tapped the gas. There was an immediate thump, a god-awful bang from the right rear, and the car ground to a stop.

He hammered the steering wheel. "Dammit!"

As McNally's SUV disappeared around the corner, Millard threw the car into park, got out, and circled to the back of the car.

A short length of two-by-four was stuck to the tire. Millard looked quickly around the parking lot and, seeing nothing suspicious, bent to examine the board more closely. The heads of four nails were visible in the wood.

It was clear what had happened—someone had driven four long nails through the wood, then propped the wood, nails up, in front of the tire. And whoever it was must have done it while Millard was sitting in the car. He stood and looked around again, his hand drifting toward the gun in its holster under his arm, but the only movement in the parking lot was a couple, the man's arms around the woman's shoulders, her hand holding a tissue to her nose, and an old codger sorting through keys at the door of a PT Cruiser.

It looked like one of Ballard and McNally's little helpers had paid him a visit while he waited in the car. And he had a pretty good idea who it was.

He pulled the phone from his pocket and pulled up the tracking app. McNally's SUV was tracking west, toward Jerome. The dot representing Castillo's truck hadn't moved since he had driven back to the casita from the hospital late the previous evening, although Millard had little faith that Castillo, as well as his truck, was there.

He took a deep breath. With the tracker on McNally's SUV, the flat tire was just an inconvenience. He'd catch up with them soon enough.

He banged open the trunk, continuing to scan the parking lot, and pulled out the spare tire.

37

O wen and Lizzy were only a few miles from the hospital when her phone rang.

"Hey," she answered. "I'm putting you on speaker so Uncle Owen can hear."

"He tried to follow you," said Philip.

Owen glanced nervously in the rear view mirror. "Do we need to take ... uh ... evasive action?"

"Nope," said Philip. "He's not going to be following anyone for a while."

"What happened?" asked Lizzy.

"Flat tire," Philip said, and laughed. "*Real* flat."

"I take it we have you to thank for that," said Owen.

"Yup."

"How did you know he was there?" asked Owen.

"Not having a tracking device of my own, I did it the old-fashioned way—I borrowed a friend's van and staked out the parking lot. He showed up early this morning."

"How early did you get there?" asked Lizzy.

"Earlier than he did."

"That can't have been fun."

"My friend's van is pretty plush."

"Did you get a look at him?" asked Lizzy.

"I'm looking at him now. He matches your description of the man you encountered on the trail."

"You're still at the hospital?" squawked Lizzy. "Is that safe?"

"Can't imagine why it wouldn't be," said Philip. "No reason for him to think I'm in this fancy van. And at the moment he seems pretty focused on getting the tire changed."

"Thanks for thinking of doing that," said Owen. "Wish I had thought of it myself," he added, chagrined.

"No problem. You have the tracker?"

Lizzy popped open the glove compartment and pulled out the disc-shaped device. "Yup. Good thing you thought to look for it."

"When I found the one on my truck last night, I figured he would for sure have put one on your SUV as well. It'll take a little while for him to change the tire—I'll give you a call when he leaves. Just stop at a rest area or a McDonald's and pop the tracker onto someone else's car."

"Won't that put them in danger?" asked Lizzy.

"Can't imagine it would. He seems like enough of a professional not to knock someone off just because he gets annoyed when he realizes we were on to him."

"What about the tracker you found on your truck?"

"I left it there. He might suspect that I had something to do with the flat tire, but he'd know for sure if I took the tracker off my truck. I'll leave it there unless I need to go somewhere I don't want George Millard following me to. Maybe if I need to give him the slip, I'll stick it on Eddie's truck." He laughed again. "Wouldn't that be a surprise for George."

Owen glanced at Lizzy, then back at the road. "Does this change our plans?" he asked of no one in particular.

"I'd recommend you go on to Phoenix," said Philip. "You

can stay there for a couple of days so Lizzy can rest up, then I think you might as well head back to Pennsylvania. If they've tracked you down out here, I don't see that being there is any more dangerous than being here, and there might be benefits to you being able to keep a closer eye on them yourself."

"That's what I think, too," said Lizzy. "But what about you?"

"Now that I know what Millard looks like," said Philip, "I can keep an eye out for him. But he knows you and Owen have left Sedona, even if he doesn't know exactly where you're headed. I can't imagine he's going to waste time hanging out here. Mortensen will probably call him back to Pennsylvania."

Owen sighed. "The part about resting up in Phoenix sounds good," he said. "We can take the part about heading back to Pennsylvania under consideration once we get settled."

"Don't spend too long figuring," said Philip. "I don't think a flat tire is going to be too much of a deterrent to your friend George."

38

W hen Lizzy and Owen arrived in Phoenix, they checked into a chain hotel next to a shopping center filled with chain stores—a configuration that, as far as Lizzy could see, was repeated with little variation throughout the suburbs encircling the city.

She had felt pretty good when they left the hospital, but by the time they got to their hotel rooms, her leg was throbbing in time to her heartbeat, and the meds that Dr. Prowse had prescribed barely took the edge off the pain. She snapped at Owen when he hovered about, trying to think of ways to make her more comfortable, and only narrowly avoided descending into whininess when he wasn't there to bring her a glass of water or adjust the pillows on which she rested her leg.

A heat wave arrived just as they did, and the rattling air conditioner couldn't keep up with the soaring temperatures. She spent the day flipping through channels on the television or starting and rejecting books on her phone, trying unsuccessfully to distract herself from the pain in her leg. She was still awake at midnight, both comforted and irritated by the sounds of Uncle Owen's snores from the next room, when another sound spiked her heart rate—the rattle of the handle of the door leading to the hallway.

She sat up.

The handle rattled again.

"Uncle Owen?" she whispered as loudly as she thought she could without having whoever was at the door hear her. The snoring continued unabated.

She swung her legs off the bed, triggering a jolt of pain from her ankle.

The handle rattled again, this time more forcefully, and she heard some indistinct muttering from the other side of the door.

She sat still, straining her ears.

"Damn card key ..." she heard. "Those morons at the desk ..." There was a long silence, then, "Oh. Damn," and the sound of footsteps retreating down the hallway.

She limped to the door and peered through the peephole. The hallway was deserted.

Just as she got back to the bed, she heard unsteady steps in the room above her, the flush of a toilet, more steps, and then silence.

She adjusted the stack of pillows she was using to prop up her leg and lay back down, waiting for her heartbeat to slow. Nerves and the ache in her leg kept her awake for the remainder of the night, without even the relief of being able to toss and turn.

FOR BREAKFAST, Owen brought her fruit, yogurt, and granola from the buffet in the hotel lobby. For lunch, he ventured out for provisions and returned with cheesesteaks.

"It will be a little taste of home," he said, unrolling them from their paper wrappings. He laid them out on paper plates and handed one to Lizzy. "Wiz wit!"

She picked it up reluctantly and took a bite. "That's disgusting," she said, and dropped it back onto the plate.

Owen had taken a bite of his as well. "Yeah, that's not good." He put it aside.

Much to her shame, Lizzy felt her throat tighten with impending tears. "I'm sick of this," she said. "I'm sick of living in crappy hotels where it's impossible to get a good night's sleep. I'm sick of not being able to do anything except lie here. And I'm sick of not being home." She kept her eyes steadfastly on her clenched hands, knowing that if she looked at Owen, the dam would burst.

"Oh, Pumpkin, I know. Is there anything I can do—"

"No," she interrupted him ungraciously.

He sighed. "It's too bad the yoga practice isn't helping."

There was a long silence, then Lizzy said in a voice that had lost the quaver of her earlier pronouncements, "I didn't think of that."

"Pardon me?"

She looked up, her expression a mixture of relief and embarrassment. "I didn't think about using the yoga."

Owen hopped up. "Tell you what—why don't you have a yoga whatever-it's-called and I'm going to go out again and see if I can find something decent to eat."

"Okay."

"Any requests?"

"Anything that isn't fake food from home."

"No scrapple?" he asked.

She smiled. "No, no scrapple."

Owen returned an hour later with Mexican to find Lizzy sleeping peacefully.

39

"You did *what*?"

Millard faced Louise Mortensen across her desk. He had rarely seen her furious, and when he had seen her furious in public, he had only been able to tell by a tightening of her lips and a whitening of her knuckles. But she evidently had no compunction about demonstrating her unhappiness more overtly in private.

"You wanted me to make it look like an accident."

"I wanted you to kill her!"

"I put two rattlers in her path—"

Louise cut him off with a slash of her hand and bent over the laptop on her desk. She hammered on the keyboard for a moment, then read from it: "'You are nine times more likely to die from being struck by lightning than to die of venomous snakebite.'"

"I put her out of commission."

"You didn't put her out of commission, you pissed her off! No, it's worse than that—you created a situation where it's easier for her to make the decision to go to the authorities."

"But if she goes to the authorities—"

"If she goes to the authorities," Louise interrupted, walking around the desk to where Millard stood, "she gets put in some posh research facility, which is better at least than having venomous—but not deadly—snakes thrown in her path."

Millard didn't need Mortensen telling him that he had screwed up. When he had finally gotten the spare tire on the car and, pushing it well past its recommended maximum speed of fifty miles per hour, caught up with the dot that was supposed to be McNally's SUV at a rest area, it had proven to be an eighteen-wheeler driven by a man even larger than McNally, and not nearly as benign looking. A sign on the back of the truck invited other motorists to *Tell me how I'm doing!!*

Millard's blood pressure rising, he had driven back to Sedona. The tracker he had put on Castillo's vehicle was evidently still in place—the truck was in the driveway of the casita, although Castillo's office appeared to be closed—but he wasn't going to assume that Castillo wasn't aware of it. He was none too pleased with his own performance—he didn't need Mortensen rubbing salt in the wound.

"What would you have liked me to do?" he said, his own voice rising.

"I would have liked for you to kill her and her obese godfather, and get us the hell out of this situation!"

Millard took a step toward Louise, but at that moment there was a knock on the door and, without waiting for an answer, Mitchell opened the door and stepped into the room. He stood in the doorway for a moment, his gaze flicking between Louise and Millard.

"Louise, are you all right?" he asked.

"What are you doing here?" she asked, redirecting her ire from Millard to Mitchell.

"I heard you arguing. I thought I could be of help."

"No, Mitchell, I have it under control. Please go to your—" Louise clamped her lips together. "Please excuse us. George and I need to discuss this privately."

Mitchell took another step into the room. "I'm part of this. I should be part of this discussion as well."

Louise opened then shut her mouth. She took a deep breath and pulled herself straighter, if that were possible. "Fine. Please close the door so Juana doesn't decide to join us as well." She circled to her desk chair and sat, then turned to Millard. "So. She was bitten by a rattlesnake."

"Yes."

"Where did you get the snakes?"

"From an old man."

"What old man?"

"An old man who sold snakes."

"So there's some snake-selling old man in Arizona who can tie you to the purchase of venomous snakes."

Millard was silent.

"George?"

"He can't tie me to anything."

"And how is that possible?"

Millard glanced at Mitchell. "He's dead."

"Dead."

"Yes."

"And how did that happen?"

"Fell and hit his head, maybe tripped on his way to check on the AC, which had just shorted out. Unfortunately a couple of monitor lizards got out of their cage, and—"

She held up her hand. "I don't want to know."

"There's nothing to tie me to it," said Millard. "And nothing to tie his death to Ballard getting bitten."

"Rattlesnakes disappear from a dead man's possession and

next thing you know, some hiker from Philadelphia has been bitten."

"There's nothing to tie them together," said Millard, enunciating each word with fuming precision.

Louise glanced at Mitchell, then back to Millard. She folded her hands on the polished surface of the desk.

"I want Ballard dead," she said. "I want McNally dead. And I don't want any collateral damage."

"I've got it."

She shot to her feet, sending her wheeled desk chair careening back into the wall. "Do you? Because that's what I said I wanted when I sent you out to Arizona the first time. And that's not what I got."

"You didn't say 'no collateral damage,'" said Millard.

"What the hell—?"

Millard took a step toward the desk, but suddenly Mitchell was between them.

"Leave her alone!" said Mitchell, his voice pitched high with emotion.

Millard drew his arm back to backhand Mitchell, when he felt a twinge of pain behind his forehead. He stepped back, his hand going to his temple. "Goddamn you—"

"Stop it!" snapped Louise. "Both of you—stop it!"

A fraught silence descended on the room, the only sound the breathing of the three people in it.

Finally, Louise said, "George, are you all right?"

Millard glowered at Mitchell. "Yeah."

Louise turned to Mitchell. "Mitchell, please go away. You're making the situation worse."

Mitchell, face white with anger, appeared ready to respond. Then he nodded tightly and, without looking at Millard, stalked out of the room, banging the door closed behind him.

Louise turned to Millard. "*Are* you all right?"

Millard nodded. The pain was already starting to fade. "Just a kid chucking stones," he said. "Good thing he wasn't on the drug you gave him for the homeless guy and Brashear. You?"

"I'm not the one who was making him angry."

"I don't like pussyfooting around that freak."

"Don't call him a freak. And you'd do well to resign yourself to some pussyfooting when you interact with him." She considered him for a moment. "We could check you at the lab tomorrow."

"No. I'm fine."

Louise looked at him, expressionless, for another moment, then gave a short nod. She walked slowly to the window and looked out over the bucolic landscape, which was slipping into dusk. Across the small valley that separated Mortensen's property from the neighbors, Millard could see a woman in English riding gear taking a horse over jumps. A half minute ticked by. A minute.

Finally, Louise spoke, monotone. "I want them both dead."

"Okay."

"No other casualties."

"How about Castillo?"

"No. Let's not make this any more complicated than it already is."

"All right."

"I'm holding your payment until Ballard and McNally are out of the picture."

Millard hesitated for a fraction of a second. "Okay."

"Go back to Arizona and take care of it."

Millard put his hands in his pockets and nodded toward the door to the hallway. "What about him?"

Louise turned from the window and returned to her desk.

She wheeled the chair back to the desk and sat down. "What about him?"

Millard held up a finger, crossed to the door, opened it, and stepped into the hallway. He looked up and down, then stepped back into the room, closing the door behind him. "Just don't want any eavesdroppers," he said. "Are *you* going to keep pussyfooting around him?"

"He's a young man who is only now fully coming into his powers. He's bound to be confused. We owe it to him—and to ourselves—to treat him with consideration." She swiveled in her chair to look out the window again. "He's exactly what Gerard and I were trying to create: a telepath. His ability to have an actual physical effect on the brains of other people was an unexpected side effect, but one that we can obviously use to advance our goals. I thought Ballard was the best we had been able to achieve, but I was wrong. Mitchell is the ultimate manifestation of what we wanted to create."

"He's going to start thinking he's running the show."

"I disagree. As long as we treat him fairly, and our goals align with his, I believe he'll be willing to support our plan."

"And exactly what *is* our plan? Long-term."

Louise sighed. "Let's take care of Ballard and McNally and then regroup."

"We had higher goals when we started out than just getting rid of a lab rat gone rogue and her keeper."

Louise narrowed her eyes. "George, may I remind you that this is not about *your* goals. The goals that I am continuing to pursue are the goals that *Gerard* and I formed many years ago. You've been extremely helpful in our pursuit of those goals, but as far as I can tell, your goal is to get paid. Handsomely paid, I might add."

The blood drained from Millard's face.

Louise stood. "I've been satisfied with your services up

until now, but I am not happy with how this Ballard situation has played out."

He nodded again, his mouth a tight line.

She waved her hand in dismissal.

Millard walked stiffly to the door, then turned back to her. "The Ballard girl—she's maturing."

"What do you mean?"

"I made her pretty mad on the trail, after she had been bitten, and got away with no ill effects. That suggests a level of control."

"Or perhaps she's lost the power," said Louise.

"Maybe. But the way she calmed herself when she had been bitten—almost like she was putting herself into a trance. She's learning. Maybe from Castillo."

Louise fixed him with a hard gaze. "No collateral damage unless it's absolutely necessary. Is that clear?"

He paused for a beat, thinking back to the humiliation of the flattened tire in the hospital parking lot and the swapped tracker. "Yeah," he said grudgingly. "It's clear."

"And don't take too long with Ballard and McNally. I've run out of patience."

Millard nodded, not bothering to answer, and closed the door behind him.

40

Mitchell stood in the hallway after being sent out by Louise, his cheeks still flushed with anger at Millard. *If Millard had laid a hand on Louise—*

But he recognized that even with the full power of his anger behind the crush, the effect on Millard without the benefit of the steroid drug had been insignificant—greater and quicker than with Mitchell's late boss, Brett Ludlow, but nowhere near what he knew Elizabeth Ballard could do. And he hadn't been able to read Louise or Millard's thoughts—Louise's because they were masked by the usual opacity, Millard's because he always had his mental defenses up around him. Mitchell had been powerless.

He stood in the hallway, hearing the uneven buzz of conversation beyond the door but unable to pick out any words.

He did a quick calculation of what room would be directly above Louise's study. His bedroom was over the kitchen, and through the air vent in the floor he could sometimes hear the faint sound of Juana singing as she cooked dinner. Perhaps there was a similar dynamic in play over Louise's study.

He jogged up the steps and went to the room he estimated to be in the right location. It was the bedroom in which, he had learned, Louise and Gerard Bonnay had kept Elizabeth Ballard—a pretty room with cheerful yellow walls and bleached hardwood floors. The air vent was near the bed, and he bent over it. He could hear voices, but they were too low to distinguish words. He lay on the floor, pressed his ear to the vent, and heard Louise's voice.

"He's a young man who is only now fully coming into his powers. He's bound to be confused. We owe it to him—and to ourselves—to treat him with consideration."

His smile broadened as he listened to Louise praise him, then berate Millard: "I've been satisfied with your services up until now, but I am not happy with how this Ballard situation has played out."

It was clear that she was dismissing Millard. Mitchell pushed himself off the floor and went to the hallway. He turned toward his room, then changed direction. He was damned if he was going to run away from the hired help.

He ran lightly down the upstairs hallway, and took the back stairs, which came out near the kitchen. When Millard stepped into the kitchen, Mitchell was taking a beer out of the refrigerator.

Millard pulled up when he saw Mitchell.

Mitchell raised the bottle to Millard. "Beer?"

"No. Thanks."

Mitchell got the opener out of one of the drawers and popped the top off the bottle. "Sorry about before," he said, nodding in the direction of Louise's study.

"No problem."

"You okay?"

There was a dangerous pause. "I said no problem."

"Glad to hear it." Mitchell raised his bottle to Millard again, this time in a toast. "To goals."

He took a swig of the beer and, with Millard's glare boring into his back, left the kitchen, humming.

41

The next morning Lizzy was feeling better. Her leg was less swollen and she had an easier time walking. She was also desperate to get out of the hotel room. They managed to find a non-chain restaurant for breakfast and shared a platter of bagels, lox, cream cheese, sliced red onions, and capers.

When they were done, Owen flagged down the server for their check while Lizzy drained the last of her fresh-squeezed orange juice from her glass.

"Can we do something other than going back to the hotel?" she asked. "I have cabin fever."

Owen patted his mouth with his napkin. "I've been thinking about that. I think it would be a good idea to get on the road."

She looked resigned. "It's not really what I had in mind, but—okay. Where are we going to go?"

"Back to Philly."

"Really?" asked Lizzy cautiously.

"You want to go back to Pennsylvania, right?"

"Yes, but I've been saying that for weeks. I thought you were worried about going back."

"Philadelphia's a big city, and like Philip said, we can likely hide as effectively from Louise Mortensen and George Millard there as anywhere. Easier, because it's our home turf."

"And you can see your mom," said Lizzy, her voice excited.

"Yes, that's another benefit."

Lizzy looked at Owen and tried to dial back her enthusiasm. "But that's not the main reason ...?"

Owen ran his hand over his head. "Pumpkin, I started thinking about where else we could go—places even further away from Philly than we are now—and then I started imagining what it would be like. To show up in San Diego or San Francisco or Seattle and not know anyone. I realized that if it hadn't been for Philip—if you hadn't found Philip—we'd have been in a world of trouble. He's the one who thought to go back to the Needle and found the bucket, the one who found the tracking devices on the cars, the one who kept George Millard from following us. And the chances of finding another Philip in San Diego or San Francisco or Seattle are pretty much nil. We can't stay in Sedona and let him babysit us. If we were in Philly, we'd have more resources to call on. I'm not talking about getting Andy or Ruby involved again, but there are other resources I could call on if we were home—medical colleagues, university colleagues, even legal resources." He ran his hand over his head again. "If I'm on my home turf, I'll feel less helpless than I do here. And I can't afford to be helpless in our situation."

Lizzy nodded. "Neither of us can."

Owen smiled. "'Helpless' is not a word I would ever think to associate with you."

The server dropped the check at the table, and Owen counted out some bills and put them under the salt shaker.

"What do you think about going back home, Pumpkin?"

"That's what I've been wanting to do all along. Living out here like we're on some sort of multimonth vacation while Andy and Ruby are looking over their shoulders doesn't seem right."

"Should we start today?" he asked.

"Might as well," she said, her voice excited again.

Owen pushed himself to his feet and stepped to Lizzy's chair to give her a hand up. "You know one thing I'm looking forward to?"

She pulled herself up and tested her weight on her injured leg. "What's that?"

"Not having to live out of a suitcase."

She nodded. "Yeah, I can agree with that."

"What are you looking forward to?" he asked.

She considered as she slung her knapsack over her shoulder. "Sleeping in my own bed."

Owen followed Lizzy out to the car and helped her into the passenger seat. When he got settled in the driver's seat, he asked, somewhat tentatively, "Where's your own bed?"

"What?"

"If we're going to sell the Parkesburg house, where would you consider 'your own bed'?"

She smiled. "Lansdowne?"

Lansdowne was where Owen's home was. He smiled back. "That sounds good to me, Pumpkin." He was still smiling when they got back to the hotel to pack.

42

Mitchell didn't see Louise again until late the next evening. He had spent the day wandering the house restlessly, too wound up to sit down to a book or a movie in the theater in the basement, too distracted to look for occupation elsewhere.

They ate dinner together. Mitchell was gratified to realize that Millard had never eaten dinner in the dining room with Louise, at least during the time Mitchell had been staying in Pocopson.

As they were finishing the meal, Mitchell said, "It would be nice to sit by the fire in the library for a while."

Louise opened her mouth to respond, and Mitchell could tell that her first reaction was to decline, but then she seemed to reconsider. "Yes," she said, "it would be a nice evening for that. But can we sit in my study instead?"

"Of course."

When they reached the room, Louise went to a tray of a few bottles and crystal glasses on a side table. "I'm having a sherry. Would you like something?"

"I'll have a sherry also."

Louise smiled politely. "You don't have to have sherry, Mitchell. Would you like something different?"

"No, I'd like sherry."

"All right." She poured two glasses and gave one to him.

He raised his glass. "To goals."

After an almost imperceptible pause, she raised her own glass. "To goals."

Mitchell clicked on the gas fireplace and they each took one of the wing chairs facing it. Louise looked into the flames for a moment, sipping her drink, then said, "Would you mind if I looked through some papers? I have a meeting with some colleagues from Switzerland tomorrow, and I'm hoping to make it an early night tonight."

"Certainly."

Louise went to the leather bag that sat on her desk and drew out a manila folder. She returned to her chair, took another sip of sherry, and opened the folder in her lap.

"What's the meeting about?" asked Mitchell.

"They have some interesting insights into the genetic basis for infertility, and some really groundbreaking ideas about how that could be reversed in some women."

"Is it ..." Mitchell's voice trailed off, and Louise looked up at him expectantly. "Is it about creating more children with ... special talents?"

"No. Just your everyday babies."

"And you care about that?"

Louise looked surprised. "Of course."

"Why? When you have done so much more?"

She considered the question, then said, "Many of the women who come to Vivantem have been to a number of other doctors, have tried a number of other approaches. Often Vivantem succeeds in achieving a successful pregnancy where others have been unable to. I consider that a source of great professional pride."

"Do you ever stay in touch with the children?"

"No. Gerard did sometimes." She took another sip of sherry and stared into the dancing flames.

"But you are in touch with some of them," he said, smiling tentatively.

"Yes," she said vaguely, then roused herself as she took his meaning. "Yes, I am." She smiled at him. "Only the most extraordinary ones."

He mentally reached out to probe her thoughts, but they were, as always, inaccessible to him.

He asked her about the work of her Swiss colleagues, and Louise launched into an explanation, becoming more animated as she spoke. Although it was clear that she was simplifying for his benefit, he lost the thread of the conversation pretty quickly, but he enjoyed it nonetheless.

In fact, there was little not to like about the evening. Here he was, sitting in an impressive home in front of a fire, sipping after-dinner drinks with a beautiful woman. The home wasn't his—that would have made the scene perfect—but the more he was able to help Louise toward her goals, the more he would become a true partner in all those goals entailed.

And in a way his inability to read Louise's thoughts was a relief, especially when compared to dealing with the distasteful, low-brow mental gyrations of girls like the one at the whiskey tasting. This evening with Louise was how normal people got to know each other—not by an illicit probing of thoughts, but through conversation, through shared interests and shared efforts.

"I'm going to have a little more sherry," said Louise, standing. "Would you like a top-off?"

"Yes, thank you." He handed her his glass.

Louise crossed the room to the side table. Mitchell stood and followed her. He could hear the gurgle of sherry as she poured, the clink of the crystal stopper dropping into the mouth of the decanter.

As she picked up the glasses, he reached out and lightly laid a hand on each of her hips. She gasped and whirled around, as if he had grabbed her.

He stepped back. "I'm sorry, I didn't mean to startle you."

Some of the sherry had sloshed onto the cuffs of her blouse, a blood-brown stain on the beige silk. She turned to set the glasses down, their bases clattering briefly on the tabletop. "I need to clean this up," she said, her voice unsteady. She crossed to the door quickly and turned in the direction of the kitchen.

Mitchell went to the window, his hands stuffed into his pockets, his face red. Perhaps he had underestimated the value of being able to see Louise's thoughts.

She was back in a few minutes, a white linen napkin gripped in her hands. She stayed by the door.

"Mitchell, I'm sorry if I gave you the wrong impression about my intent," she said, a little more loudly than the distance required. "Not only am I ridiculously old for you—to say I'm old enough to be your mother would be a gross under-statement—but Gerard has only been gone a few months. If I misinterpreted your intent, I apologize," she continued. "This is a stressful time. My nerves are on a bit of a hair trigger."

Mitchell shrugged. "It's no problem, Louise. I think you're a beautiful woman, and you look much younger than you are, but of course I understand that you're still in mourning for Gerard. My mistake."

Louise took a step into the room, folded the napkin, and placed it on a table. "I would have thought—" she began, then stopped. "Does your ability to read minds—" She stopped again. "Have you sensed something from me that led you to ..." Her voice trailed off.

"You're a hard woman to read, Louise," he replied. "Maybe other people have told you that, but I can confirm that it's true." He gave her a strained smile.

"Yes, I have heard that before." She paused. "How about George? Can you read George's thoughts?"

"I can't read George because he's actively blocking me. It's difficult unless someone wants me to do it, or they're unaware that I'm trying."

"How about Juana?"

"Yes, I can see her thoughts very plainly."

"The fact that she speaks a different language isn't a problem?"

"When I perceive her thoughts, I'm picking up images and concepts, not words."

"Can you give me an example?"

"Sure. She's concerned about her son. He's been planning to go to DVCC in the fall, but he's fallen in with a group of guys she thinks are going to get him in trouble. He's always said he wanted to live in California, and she's wondering if she should move them there, and wonders what the residency requirements are for going to a state school there. She also really likes her new car. A Ford Taurus. Yesterday she was thinking—"

Louise held up her hand with a smile that this time was more pleased than polite. "That's enough. Very impressive, Mitchell."

She resumed her seat in front of the fire and gestured him into the other one. She looked into the flames for a moment, then turned to him.

"Mitchell, I'd like you to go to Sedona. We need to locate Elizabeth Ballard and Owen McNally—George can give you the background. I think it will be difficult for George to find out where they've gone, but they made an acquaintance while they were there—a man named Philip Castillo—and perhaps you could find out from him."

Mitchell sat forward. "I'd be happy to do that."

"I don't know how much this man knows about Ballard and McNally's background, but if he does know about the Vivantem connection, he may have seen the video from the news conference. You were on camera so briefly that it would be hard for someone to identify you based on that, but it can't hurt to change your appearance a bit. But even if he does recognize you and lets them know you're in Sedona, I can't see that it will make much difference—they already know, or must suspect, that we're looking for them."

He nodded, "Yes, that all makes sense." He paused. "Do you care what happens to Castillo?"

She turned back to the fire. Half a minute ticked by. Then she turned again to Mitchell. "I would much prefer that he not even know that we are trying to get the information from him, but if he does know, and if that knowledge puts us in jeopardy, then you and George can do whatever you need to do to make sure that the situation doesn't blow up."

Mitchell nodded solemnly.

"In case you do need to use ... the crush, I can show you how to inject yourself. I'll package the syringe and vial so it looks like insulin, in case there are any questions from airport security. I'll also give you something to give to Castillo to lower his defenses. It would help you get past any mental barriers he puts up if he's trying to withhold information from you." She brightened. "We can try it out on George."

Mitchell nodded again, trying to suppress a gleeful smile.

She stood, and he stood as well.

"I'd like you to go out there as soon as possible. Castillo

runs a sort of consulting business, so it should be easy to arrange to talk with him, posing as a client."

"I'm glad to finally be doing something useful," said Mitchell.

"I'm lucky to have you here to help me," said Louise.

The praise sounded a bit awkward, but he flushed with pride.

She held out her hand. "Thank you, Mitchell."

He took her hand. "It's my pleasure, Louise."

43

The next morning, Millard, Louise, and Mitchell stood in Louise's study, three points on an equilateral triangle. On a table in the center of the room was a small paper cup containing a white pill.

"What is it?" Millard asked warily.

"A variant of flunitrazepam."

"Flunitrazepam? Why have I heard of that?"

"You may have heard it referred to as Rohypnol."

"The date rape drug?" asked Millard, his eyebrows arching.

"Well ... yes."

Millard shook his head. "Fantastic."

"It's also used as a muscle relaxant and to reduce anxiety."

"Well, that will be handy," said George caustically. He glared at both of them. "You better not make me do anything foolish."

"I'm not accustomed to making my test subjects do anything foolish," replied Louise tartly. She crossed to the liquor bottles on the side table. "What did you say he drank?"

"Knob Creek bourbon," said Millard.

She scanned the bottles. "I don't have that. Maybe in Gerard's study—"

Millard headed for the door. "I doubt he's going to have Knob Creek, but I'll check."

He was back in a moment with a bottle of Blanton's. "This is the closest I could find, although it seems like a shame to spoil it."

"The drug should be tasteless and odorless, but I want to put it in something as close to what he's likely to drink as possible so you can confirm that's the case." She took the bottle from George and poured some of the bourbon into a heavy crystal tumbler. She held the glass out to him. "Do you want to taste it before I put the drug in, as a point of comparison?"

"Sure." He took a sip and handed the glass back to Louise, then pulled his phone out of his pocket. "Let me just turn the ringer off in case I get a call while I'm out ... so to speak."

Louise dropped the pill from the paper cup into the glass, swirled the liquid for a few moments, then handed the glass to George. "Drink up."

AN HOUR LATER, Millard stood in the pantry-cum-security center, feeling a little lightheaded but otherwise fine. Neither Louise nor Mitchell showed up on any of the monitors, which probably meant that she had gone to her Center City lab and that he was upstairs, where there were no cameras installed.

He tapped some commands into the computer that controlled the security system, and brought up the video recording he had made of the little test with the date rape drug. He was damned if he was going to let someone drug him without checking on what they did while he was out.

The system didn't record sound, but he had turned on the voice recorder on his cell phone right before he had taken the pill and was able to roughly sync the audio and the video.

After he had tossed back the glass of bourbon—he had been able to confirm for Louise that the drug didn't affect the taste—Louise had him sit down. She stood next to him, watching him with interest. Mitchell sat on the corner of the desk, swinging his leg. God, the guy was annoying.

It was shocking how quickly the drug took effect: one second he was looking understandably irritated and the next his face had cleared of any emotion and his eyes held only a frightening blankness.

Louise took his pulse, then bent down to look directly into his face.

"George?" she said, then again, louder, "George, can you hear me?"

He nodded.

Louise straightened. "Okay, Mitchell, go ahead."

Mitchell pulled up a chair so he was facing Millard. "George, what's your birthday? Don't say it out loud, just think it." A moment passed. "September seventh."

"That's right," said Louise.

"How old are you?" asked Mitchell. A pause. "Forty-nine."

"Yes," said Louise.

"What's your social security number?"

"Just the last four digits," interjected Louise.

"The last four digits," Mitchell amended. A moment later, he said, "Three three eight six."

"Yes." Louise smiled.

"What's the most embarrassing thing that ever happened to you?"

Louise stepped forward. "George, don't think about that,"

she said loudly. "Think about the last time you ... went grocery shopping."

Mitchell was grinning, but his grin faded when he saw Louise's expression.

"That's enough, Mitchell, I think we got what we need."

"I did get this quick image of a circus and—"

"I'm not interested," she interrupted him. "And we agreed on the questions to be asked. I don't appreciate when the people I'm working with go off-script."

Mitchell colored and Millard, watching on the security monitor, grinned.

The rest of the recording was uneventful. Louise, evidently satisfied with the results—if not with the approach—of what he realized had been just as much a test of Mitchell as of the drug, suggested that Millard lie down on the couch. She guided him there with a light hand on his elbow, then covered him with a mohair blanket with the practical efficiency of a medical professional tending to a patient. Then she led Mitchell out of the room, turned off the light, and closed the door.

He fast-forwarded the video. He had slept, still and unmolested, until he eventually rose a little unsteadily, and disappeared from the frame.

He deleted the recording, stepped out of the pantry, and started a pot of coffee brewing. He was glad he had thought to record the session. In addition to the obvious benefit of being able to see what had happened, it reminded him why he enjoyed working with Louise Mortensen. She could be a cold bitch sometimes, but that had its benefits—she was never clingy, never weepy, never a damsel in distress. Yes, she was the one to hitch his wagon to—even when Gerard Bonnay had been alive, Millard had believed that. He knew that the big picture stuff would never be his thing, but if she had the brains and the backbone, he could supply the muscle. And, as she said, she paid handsomely for him to do it. That life of leisure in his own fishing camp in Dillon felt closer than ever.

When the coffee had brewed, he poured himself a mug and took a careful sip. He could even laugh off Pieda's gag with the unauthorized question—Millard had to remember he was dealing with a boy, not a man, and react accordingly. And if Mitchell kept pulling stunts like that—well, Louise might get tired of Mitchell Pieda even before Millard himself did.

44

Before they had fled from Philadelphia to the Florida Keys after Lizzy killed Gerard Bonnay, Lizzy had barely been out of Pennsylvania, but with the pain of the gunshot wounds Bonnay had inflicted on her, and the emotional trauma of that encounter, she had hardly enjoyed that trip.

Now, despite some lingering pain from the snakebite, she was an enthusiastic traveler—her interest in the country through which they drove began to overcome her stress over their situation and her anxiousness to get back to Pennsylvania. Concerned that long periods of inactivity would slow Lizzy's recovery from the snakebite, Owen had sketched out a plan that wouldn't keep her cooped up in the car for more than five or six hours a day, and made frequent stops for her to get out and stretch her legs.

On the second day of the trip, between Grants, New Mexico, where they had spent the first night, and Amarillo, their target for the second night, Lizzy was wandering around a rest area gift shop while Owen got coffee. She was examining an item when he appeared at her side.

"Whatcha got there?" he asked.

She handed it to him. It was a map of the United States, with fifty state-themed stickers with which to mark a visit to that state.

"That looks fun," he said.

"It's supposed to be for little kids."

"I'm a kid at heart."

She smiled. "Me too. Can we get it?"

They purchased the map, and Lizzy spent the first few minutes of the next leg of their trip happily sticking stickers onto the states where she and Owen had made stops over the last few months.

On the fourth day of the trip, as they passed from Oklahoma to Missouri near Joplin, she pointed to the GPS.

"Look, we're only a couple of miles from Kansas."

Owen turned off Interstate 44 onto 400 and they drove as far as the exotically named Bagdad Road, then turned onto Apricot Drive and Coyote Drive to return to the main road. Lizzy stuck a sticker on Kansas, then consulted a booklet that had come with the map. "The state amphibian of Kansas is the Barred Tiger Salamander."

"What's the sticker?"

She glanced at the map. "A tornado."

"Ouch," said Owen, and they laughed.

THAT EVENING, after a dinner of barbecue, Owen pulled into a Walmart.

"I need to pick something up. Need any supplies?" he asked.

"Maybe some warner clothes." It was growing progressively colder as they drove east and north.

When they got into the store, Owen said, "Why don't you get a cart and I'll meet you in the clothes section in a minute."

Lizzy had picked out a puffy chartreuse jacket when Owen appeared and put a flat, square box into the cart.

"What did you get?" she asked.

"A scale," he said, blushing.

"No kidding!" she said. "Well ... good for you."

They paid for their purchases and returned to the SUV.

As they drove back to their hotel, Lizzy said, "Sorry, I didn't mean to sound so surprised about the scale."

"Oh, no problem," said Owen. After a pause, he added, "Probably surprised I didn't need two of them." He laughed weakly.

"No, that's not true," she said. "You know, now that I think about it, you have been eating less. Like at dinner tonight."

"I ate twice as much as you did."

"Sure, but less than you would normally eat. Uncle Owen, are you on—gasp!—a *diet*?"

"Yup, I guess I am." They drove in companionable silence to the hotel, where Owen parked, then turned to Lizzy.

"Pumpkin, I felt so bad that I couldn't help you when you got bitten. All I could do was stand on the other side of those rocks and shout over at you because I was too fat to do anything else."

"That's not true, you were a big help. No pun intended. You told me what do to and what not to do—"

He was shaking his head. "No. It wasn't enough. You got through that despite me, not because of me. You had to do it all on your own because I'm too—"

He broke off and turned his gaze to the front of the SUV, his hands gripping the steering wheel.

Lizzy reached out and patted his arm. "I don't agree with you. You did help me." After a moment, she went on. "But losing some weight is probably a good thing anyway. I'll bet you're feeling better, right?"

He nodded. "Yes, I am. And I liked the hiking—or at least the walking. Maybe I'll work up to real hiking once everything has settled down."

"Maybe yoga," said Lizzy.

"Now, that's just crazy talk," he said. He was silent for a moment, then continued. "But walking and hiking for me must be what I imagine yoga is like for you. The walking made me feel like I could hike, and if I could hike, maybe I could do yoga, and if I could do yoga ... well, heaven knows what would be possible!" He laughed somewhat sheepishly.

Lizzy grinned at him. "Imagine how impressed Andy will be when you show up all skinny!"

Owen laughed. "I'm never going to be skinny, but it would be fun to surprise him."

They passed into Pennsylvania on the sixth day, just after Owen insisted that they get out of the car in the narrow finger of West Virginia that they passed through so there could be no question about their claim to that state. But by this time Lizzy's interest in the map and in the sights had waned, replaced with anxiety about what was to come.

45
───────

M itchell waited in the warmth of the Sedona
sunshine for only a few minutes before the door,
bearing a sign reading *Session in Progress - Please
Stop Back Later*, swung open. A young couple stepped out,
arms linked.

"I told you it would be fun," said the woman.

"Yeah, not bad," said the man. He pulled a piece of paper
out of his pocket. "So, what's next on the agenda?"

Mitchell heard a soft clatter on the glass of the door as the
sign was flipped to *Walk Ins Welcome*.

Mitchell opened the door and stepped into the waiting
room, hooking his sunglasses over the neck of his University
of Arizona T-shirt. He was wearing cargo shorts, flip-flops, and
a two day growth of beard, and since he hadn't had a haircut
in over two months, he was looking considerably less tailored
than he had the day of the Brashear news conference. It was a
far cry from his usual pulled-together look, but he wasn't
entirely unhappy with the effect.

Philip Castillo turned back from where he had been about

to step through the curtain to the back room. "May I help you?"

"Yes. I'd like to have a reading. Or whatever it's called."

"Eighty dollars for a half hour, a hundred and fifty for an hour."

"I think half an hour will be enough time."

"I have time now," Castillo said.

"Great," said Mitchell.

Castillo held out his hand. "Philip Castillo."

Mitchell grasped the hand. "Mitch Foot."

"Pleased to meet you, Mr. Foot. Come on back."

Castillo held the curtain aside and Mitchell passed into the back room. Castillo waved him into a seat at the table.

"I like to take payment before the session. Hope you don't mind," Castillo said.

"No problem." Mitchell extracted cash from his wallet and handed it over.

Castillo put the bills in his wallet. "Something to drink?" he asked. "Coffee? Tea? Water?"

"I'll take water. Thanks."

Castillo opened a mini fridge hidden behind a woven cloth and handed Mitchell a bottle, then sat down opposite him.

"Could you turn your cell phone off? I find it can be a distraction, even when it's on vibrate."

"Sure." Mitchell switched his phone off.

"What can I help you with?"

"I'm looking for my girlfriend. I think she might have come to Sedona, and I thought you could help me find her."

Castillo sat back. "I might have to give you a refund—that's not really the kind of thing I do."

"What kind of thing do you do?"

"Help people with issues they're struggling with—internal issues. Help them sort through them."

"Sounds like therapy."

"Yes, I suppose it is like therapy."

"Is that what the couple who was in here before me was here for?"

Castillo smiled thinly. "I don't discuss one client with another client. It *is* like therapy in that way."

Mitchell sat back and looked around the room. "I don't mind still having the session. Maybe if I talk about my girlfriend, we'll come up with some ideas about how I can find her."

"Sure," said Castillo.

"She's a little younger than me—seventeen."

Mitchell opened his mind to Castillo and scanned his thoughts. There was a flicker of something there, but very faint.

"How old are you?" asked Castillo.

"How old do you think?"

Castillo considered for a moment. "Twenty-two."

"I'm twenty-three."

Castillo nodded noncommittally.

"My girlfriend—she's tall for a girl ... athletic-looking," Mitchell continued.

There was a flicker of something in Castillo's mind.

"Likes to hike," said Mitchell.

This time the reaction was less a flicker and more a flash, quickly extinguished. Behind it was a rising wall of suspicion.

"I'm not a fortune-teller," said Castillo. "I'm not going to be able to help you just on the basis of a physical description of your girlfriend and her hobbies."

Castillo's mental defenses were going up, and Mitchell could tell he wasn't going to be able to glean Elizabeth

Ballard's location, or even whether Castillo knew where she was, without the help of Louise's drug. The best he could do was to divert the suspicion solidifying in Castillo's mind.

"She was pregnant," said Mitchell. "I told her I would marry her, but she said she didn't want to get married, then she disappeared. I'm afraid she's thinking of getting an abortion. I don't want her to do that. I want her to have the baby. I want to marry her and be a dad."

Castillo's suspicion smoothed and dissipated. "Instead of trying to guess where she is," he said, "maybe we should talk about why she doesn't want you to find her."

46

Philip sat in the Cowboy Club, a shot of bourbon in front of him. It had been a good day at the office—one regular, another local who held promise of becoming a regular, the couple who was methodically checking Sedona activities off their vacation to-do list, the college boy with the pregnant girlfriend, and an elderly hippie who wanted to discuss the local vortices. In addition, he had heard from Lizzy and Owen that they had arrived in Philadelphia without mishap. They no doubt had more challenges before them, but at least he had been able to arrange for them to get away from Sedona without George Millard on their tail.

Philip usually stopped by the Cowboy Club a couple of times a week after closing up the office. It might be a tourist trap, but Philip had started coming to the Club over a decade before, when he turned twenty-one, drawn by the stories his grandfather had told of meeting movie stars there in the sixties. His grandfather had run some errands for Robert Mitchum, and had once sat in a booth next to John Wayne. Plus, the tourist angle was a benefit from a business point of view—Philip picked up a number of his clients at the Club.

Tonight he wasn't sure if he was picking up a client, or something else. The woman who sat beside him had caused every male head in the place to turn when she entered—startling blue eyes, a body that belonged on a beach, long blond hair, and long tan legs shown to best advantage under her short skirt. She had taken a seat two down from Phillip, and two up from a pair of frat boy types. She ordered a beer from Zach, feigning unawareness of the stir she had created. She took a sip of the beer, then pulled a book—an actual book—out of her bag, and began to read.

The frat boys lost no time making their move. With much whispering and nudging, they shifted down so they were sitting on the two stools nearest to her. She continued reading.

"Hey there, beautiful," said the one closest to her. "Funny place to pick to read a book."

The two of them guffawed and grinned expectantly at her.

She turned a polite gaze their way. "I'm waiting for someone."

"Whoever it is shouldn't keep you waiting too long, beautiful."

"I'm sure he won't."

"Can we buy you a drink?"

She nodded toward her beer. "I just got one. Thanks."

"We don't mind waiting for you to finish that one," one of them said, to more guffawing.

She looked away from them with a sigh and her eyes met Philip's.

"Honey!" she exclaimed. "I didn't see you sitting there. If you had been a snake ..." She turned to the two frat boys. "Sorry, I realize the person I was waiting for was right here all along." She picked up her beer and shifted to the seat next to Philip, then turned her back on the annoyed pair. "I'm sorry," she whispered. "If you could just pretend like you know me until they leave."

Philip lifted his glass of bourbon. "No problem."

She clinked her beer glass against his. "Thanks."

That had been three hours before, and the frat boys had long since left, throwing dirty looks at Philip.

He and the woman—her name was Lorna—each picked up a shot glass, raised them in salute, and tossed the drinks back. The newly empty glasses joined the others in front of them: three in front of Lorna, including the still-full glass of beer, and five in front of Philip.

Lorna, her face prettily flushed, laughed. "My goodness, Philip, you're a bad influence." She glanced around the bar, which was now buzzing with evening patrons. "I need to use the restroom. I'll be right back."

She slid off the stool, her dress momentarily hiking up to expose a tantalizing flash of hip, and headed for the restroom, steadying herself surreptitiously on the top of the half wall that separated the bar from the dining room.

Zach appeared in front of Philip. "Hey, how come you get all the pretty ones?" he asked.

Philip shrugged hazily.

"Want me to clear these away?" Zach asked, indicating the empty shot glasses.

"Better leave them here so I can remember how many I've had."

Zach nodded. "Good luck," he said, and disappeared to answer the call of another patron.

Philip picked up the book that Lorna had been reading: *Desert Solitaire.* It was Lorna's second reading of it; Philip had read it three times. Lorna had quizzed Philip on where the author's introduction had been written, and when he got it wrong—the correct answer was Nelson's Marine Bar in Hoboken, New Jersey—she had told him he had to do a shot of bourbon. The game had escalated, with Lorna getting more of the answers right than Philip. Philip blamed the fact that his last reading of the book had been over five years ago. On the last question, they had found they were both wrong, and both drank.

Lorna returned from the restroom and climbed gamely back onto the stool. "Whew. I better take a break from the game," she said.

"Sounds good to me," said Philip.

They discussed the book a bit more—this time without a shot riding on the result—then Lorna asked, "Do you live in Sedona?"

"Yup."

"I hope you don't think I'm being too forward, but could we go to your place? I'm visiting here with my sister, and she has a guy in our hotel room, and I'm tired of sitting in a bar."

"Sure," said Philip, and he flagged down Zach to pay the bill. As he took Lorna's elbow to help her off the barstool, Zach wiggled his eyebrows and gave him a thumbs-up. Philip tried to look disapproving.

They stepped outside into the cool evening air.

"Are you okay to drive?" she asked.

"Actually, I don't have to. I don't live far."

"Excellent," said Lorna with a smile, and hooked her arm under his.

BY THE TIME they got to the casita, he was starting to feel a little more clearheaded, but it wasn't to last.

"I wouldn't mind another drink," said Lorna. "Do you have any bourbon here?"

They dispensed with the *Desert Solitaire* game, but she downed her first drink as she perused the books and CDs on his shelves. She asked for a refill and he felt obliged to join her. Nearing the end of his seventh drink of the evening, he walked over to where she was examining the jewel case of Incubus's *Morning View* and slipped his arms around her waist. She turned with a smile and, with the CD in one hand and her glass in the other, kissed him.

After a minute, she pulled back with a breathless laugh.

"Can you excuse me for a minute, Philip? I'll be right back. I promise."

"Sure thing."

He showed her where the bathroom was, then went to the kitchen to get a glass of water, hoping to dilute the bourbon a bit. He wished he had made the bed that morning.

When he got back to the living room, Lorna was there, sitting on the couch with her legs pulled up under her.

"You look very pretty, Lorna," he said.

"Thank you, Philip," she replied, and laughed. "Listen to us. So formal."

He smiled. "Now you'll have to excuse me for a minute. I'll be right back. Promise."

"I'll be here," she said.

When he got back, she had the bottle of Knob Creek out and was topping off their drinks. She stood as he approached the couch and handed him one of the glasses. "To a lovely evening that I think may be about to get even lovelier," she said, and tossed back the drink.

With an internal groan, Philip tossed back his own drink.

Afterwards, that was the last thing he remembered.

47

M itchell and Millard sat in a rental car on the dark Sedona street, neither one attempting to fill the silence with conversation. Since they had flown out to Phoenix two days before, Mitchell had spent most of the time following Millard around or waiting in the hotel room while Millard hired the prostitute to bring to Sedona—he obviously didn't believe that Mitchell would be able to find out Elizabeth Ballard's location without the help of the fluni-trazepam. Sure enough, they had had to resort to Lorna's wiles.

Millard's phone buzzed and he pulled it out. "Hello. ... He's out? ... Okay, we'll be there in a minute." He slipped the phone back into his pocket. "Let's go."

They climbed out of the car, which was parked just down the street from Castillo's casita.

Millard pulled his collar up around his face and gestured for Pieda to do the same, then led the way to the driveway. Lights were on in the main house, but Mitchell didn't see any movement from inside. They went to the front door of the casita and knocked lightly. Lorna opened it and stepped aside to let them in.

"Where is he?" Millard asked.

"In the bedroom."

Millard raised his eyebrows.

"Nothing happened. But it didn't work as fast as you said it would."

"How fast?"

"Maybe five minutes."

Millard nodded, then led the way to the bedroom, followed by Lorna and Mitchell.

Philip slouched in an easy chair next to the bed, his boots on the floor next to him. Millard approached the chair and bent down. Castillo's eyes didn't move.

"He was okay for a couple of minutes after he had the drink I put the pill into," said Lorna, "then he just kind of ... turned off."

Millard straightened and gestured Lorna to follow him to the kitchen. Mitchell followed as well. Millard handed Lorna an envelope.

She counted the bills. "You're a hundred short."

"We said seven hundred."

"It's extra for the time to read the book."

Millard rolled his eyes and got two fifties out of his wallet and handed them over.

She tucked them into her purse. "I should charge you extra for having to throw up the bourbon. I hate throwing up. For that matter, I hate bourbon. Why couldn't he have been a tequila drinker?" She slung the purse strap over her shoulder and looked toward the bedroom. "What does that pill do?"

"Nothing you need to worry about," replied Millard. He took her arm and escorted her to the door. "Back to Phoenix with you."

She glanced once more toward the bedroom, appeared about to say something, then shrugged and stepped outside. Millard locked the door behind her, then returned to the bedroom, Mitchell still trailing him.

"You want to ask him the questions, or do you want me to?" asked Millard.

"I will," said Mitchell. He looked around the room. "Can I get a chair?"

"Sure. There are chairs in the kitchen."

Mitchell waited a moment, looking expectantly at Millard. Millard gazed back placidly. With a scowl, Mitchell left the room and returned with a kitchen chair. He put it down in front of Philip and sat.

"Philip, can you hear me?" he asked.

He sensed an affirmative response.

"That's good. I have some questions for you. Do you know Elizabeth Ballard?"

He sensed a slight resistance, but Louise's drug seemed to be doing its work. Again an affirmative response.

"I see you do," he said, for Millard's benefit. "Were you helping Elizabeth and Dr. McNally?"

Philip stirred slightly. Affirmative.

"I see you were. Are you the person who disabled George's car?"

Mitchell this time got a clear image—a foot holding down a short length of wood, a hammer coming down on a nail.

"Very clever, Philip," he said, fighting the urge to glance back at Millard. "So you helped them get away from Sedona. Where did they go next?"

The picture went fuzzy. An image almost swam into view, just a bright light, then faded.

"Where did they go next?" repeated Mitchell. "Where did they go when they left Sedona?"

The bright light again, but this time, in vague outline, an aerial view of a sprawling city.

After a few moments, Millard said, "Well?"

"It's not clear," he whispered. "I think Phoenix." In a slightly louder voice, he asked, "Did they go to Phoenix, Philip?"

This time a highway exit sign snapped into view, then was gone again before Mitchell could read it. Then a bird—a stylized rendering of a red bird's head. A cardinal. The Arizona Cardinals, based in Phoenix.

"Yes, I think they're in Phoenix," Mitchell whispered. Then, louder, "Are they in Phoenix now, Philip?"

The cardinal faded away, replaced by a jumble of images. Objects, scenes, thoughts popped in and out of view too quickly for Mitchell to absorb.

The silence stretched out to almost half a minute.

Finally, Millard said, "Are you getting anything?"

Mitchell turned to Millard. "It's not like watching a TV show. Just give me a minute. Can't you wait in the other room?"

"No."

"Then at least stop interrupting," said Mitchell, and turned back to Philip. "Philip, are they still in Phoenix?" A few moments went by. He changed tack. "Were they planning on going somewhere after Phoenix?"

An affirmative response.

"Where will they go, or where have they gone, after Phoenix?"

The images were getting hazier, whether as a result of the drug's decreasing effect or Philip's increasing resistance Mitchell couldn't tell. He gazed at Philip, his brow knit. He had to get this answer for Louise.

"Philip, if the Cardinals were playing an away game in the

city where Elizabeth and Dr. McNally are going, who would they be playing?"

This time the image popped up much like the television show he had just told Millard it wasn't: another stylized bird's head, this time an eagle. Philadelphia Eagles.

Mitchell smiled. "They're going back to Philadelphia?"

A grudging affirmative.

"Are they flying?"

"I don't think flying would be an option for Ballard," said Millard.

"Are they driving?" Mitchell asked Philip.

This time the response was a clear affirmative.

"They're driving to Philadelphia," he whispered to Millard. Then louder, to Philip, "And what are they going to do? What's the plan?"

There was a long pause. Finally, Millard said, "What?"

"I see ..." Mitchell hesitated. "Someone standing in a cafeteria line. With an old man."

Millard snorted. "I think your reception has gotten a little messed up, Mitch." He pulled out his phone and hit a speed dial. After a moment, he spoke. "Yeah. They're on their way back to Philly."

48

P hilip moved his head and immediately regretted it. He eased his eyes open. He thanked God that the blinds were closed, but even the sliver of light seeping into the room stabbed through his corneas like a knife. He carefully levered himself forward in his chair until he could see the bedside clock. Ten fifteen. He eased back and closed his eyes. He had expected to be hung over after eight shots of bourbon, but he hadn't expected to be this hung over.

What he had expected, he realized, was a woman in the bed.

Then another oddity registered and he cranked his eyes open again. His wallet was on the bedside table next to the clock. Philip always put his wallet in the drawer, never on top. He groaned and pushed himself out of the chair, knowing already what he would—or wouldn't—find.

He shuffled carefully over to the table and picked up the wallet. It was empty—cash, credit cards, driver's license, even his Bashas' loyalty card ... gone. He opened a little pocket inside the wallet, looked in, and gave a sigh of relief. It wasn't as bad as it could have been. But it was bad enough. He lowered himself onto the edge of the bed and dropped his face into his hands with a groan.

He sat like that until the pounding in his head that his exertions had triggered quieted to timpani level, trying to think over the din. Finally, he pushed himself upright, limped to the bathroom, and washed down four aspirin. Then he made his way to the kitchen and started a pot of extra-strong coffee.

With the coffee brewing, he patted his shirt pocket where he normally carried his phone, and groaned again when he found it empty. He returned to the bedroom and searched half-heartedly for the phone on the floor and in the cushions of the chair he had been sitting in. Nothing.

By the time he had finished his search, the coffee had brewed. He pulled on his boots, tucked in his shirt, and filled a travel mug with coffee.

He crossed the driveway to the main house and knocked on the door as loudly as he could bring himself to do, which wasn't very loud. No answer. He swore silently, then, sipping as he went, made his slow way to the office. Even though it was only a five minute walk, he was tempted to drive, since every step was like a blow to the inside of his skull, but he didn't fancy taking to the road without a license in his pocket, especially in his current condition. Tourists tended to step unconcerned into the four-lane state road that ran through the center of town, as if they were walking through Disneyland, and a squashed pedestrian and a charge of driving under the influence would be a bitch of a way to end up back in prison.

When he reached the office he kept the *Closed* sign in the window and locked the door behind him against any drop-ins. He didn't recall having any appointments that morning—in fact, he had congratulated himself on his luck on that front when Lorna suggested they go to his place. He went to the back room, to a seldom-used landline phone on a small desk in the corner, when he realized that he had no idea how to get in touch with Owen or Lizzy—their numbers were just entries in his cell phone's contact list. He swore and flopped into one of the Equipale chairs, regretting immediately not having eased himself into it.

He was considering the likelihood that someone at William Penn University would give him Owen's cell number when he realized with weak excitement that he had another option.

He went to the answering machine attached to the landline, hit the replay button, and tracked back through the stored messages until he found the one he was looking for.

"Hello," came the now-familiar voice. "My name's Elizabeth Patrick and I'd like to make an appointment with you. Could you call me?" Then Lizzy gave her phone number.

Philip silently thanked the reliability of analog technology and dialed the number.

He got it wrong the first time and had to hang up on a woman who felt it necessary to share with him in an agonizingly loud voice her opinion of telemarketers. Providentially, he dialed right the second time.

"Hey, Philip, what's up?" Lizzy asked cheerfully, reigniting the hammering in Philip's head.

"Hi, Lizzy. Can I talk with Owen?"

"Uh, sure. One sec." She lowered the phone from her mouth and said, "Uncle Owen, it's Philip and he wants to talk with you."

After a few seconds, Owen came on the line. "Hello, Philip —what's up?"

"I haven't any idea, but I don't think it's good. I, uh, met a woman at a bar yesterday ..."

"Oh?"

"We got into a drinking game ..."

"Aren't you a little old for that?" He heard Lizzy say something in the background. "I'll explain later," said Owen, evidently to her.

"Yes, I am. At least it was a literary-based drinking game."

Philip heard a door open and close on Owen's end of the call.

"Not beer pong?" asked Owen pointedly.

"No, not beer pong." The thought made Philip's stomach flip. "Anyhow, I woke up this morning and my wallet and phone were gone."

"Jeez, that sucks," said Owen. Then, with some concern, he asked, "Was there anything in your wallet or on your phone that would tie you to Lizzy?"

"Her phone number is in my contact list under Elizabeth Patrick, so just in case they find a way to hack into the phone, tell her not to pick up any calls that look like they're coming from my cell phone. Other than that, I can't think of anything on the phone or in the wallet related to Lizzy."

"That's good."

"But it does seem a little coincidental that this happened so soon after you and Lizzy left, and after I booby-trapped George Millard's car." He drew a deep breath. "I was pretty drunk. If someone questioned me while I was that out of it, there's a possibility I might have said something about Lizzy."

"Is there any evidence that they tried to force information out of you? All your fingernails accounted for?"

"Other than my head, everything seems to be in working order."

Owen was silent for a moment, then said, "Would this woman have had a chance to put something into your drink? *One* of your drinks," he added.

Philip thought back to his trip to the bathroom and the

glass of bourbon Lorna had handed him when he got back. "Yes, it's possible."

"There are psychoactive drugs that can lower one's defenses—scopolamine, flunitrazepam, amobarbital. If this woman was working for Louise Mortensen, it's possible she could have put something in your drink and then questioned you."

Philip pressed the bridge of his nose with his thumb and forefinger. "Yeah. Maybe."

"And if she does work for Mortensen, maybe she's another Vivantem baby, like the guy in the video with Louise Mortensen," added Owen, suddenly worried. "You did say your head hurt."

Philip's stomach did another flip. "True. I just thought it was a normal—although monstrous—hangover, but I'll get it checked out. "

"You should get to the ER right away," said Owen.

"Will do," said Philip. "At least they didn't take my car keys."

"Don't drive yourself," said Owen. "Take a cab. Or use one of those ride share cars."

"No wallet. No credit cards," said Philip.

"Do you have someone who can drive you?"

Philip sighed. "Yeah, I should be able to round someone up. Actually," he continued, "if I can track down Eddie, I can ask him if he's seen anything odd going on around my place."

"Do that now," said Owen.

Philip ended the call with Owen and placed a call to Eddie. He was hanging drywall when Philip reached him, but was at Philip's office within ten minutes.

"I appreciate you coming to the rescue again," said Philip as they headed for the hospital.

"No problem," said Eddie. "Although I am curious as to

why you sent me to check out a tripped security alarm in a house without a security system."

"Miscommunication. Sorry about that."

Eddie waved his hand. "No problem. A little excitement in an otherwise humdrum life. Speaking of a humdrum life," he continued, "or, in your case, its opposite—you had quite a busy time last night."

"What do you mean?"

"People coming and going all evening."

Philip turned in the seat to look at Eddie, wincing at the pain caused by the movement. "Who was coming and going?"

"You tell me. You show up with a beautiful blonde, pretty soon two guys show up, the blonde leaves, then the guys leave."

"Two guys showed up?"

"You didn't know that?"

"No," said Philip. "I think the beautiful blonde slipped something in my drink."

"Going to take advantage of you?" asked Eddie with a laugh.

Philip ignored him. "What did the guys look like?"

"Hard to tell, they had the collars of their coats turned up. White guys, one older—maybe in his late forties—one younger—maybe in his early twenties."

"How long were they in the house?"

"You seriously didn't know they were there?" asked Eddie, shooting him a look. "I thought maybe they were a husband or boyfriend of the beautiful blonde and a buddy, coming to teach you a lesson. I listened for noise just in case you needed the cavalry to ride in, but didn't hear anything."

"How long were they there?" Philip repeated.

"About fifteen minutes."

"Fifteen minutes?" said Philip, eyebrows climbing.

"Guys arrived at ten fifteen, beautiful blonde left about five minutes later, guys left around ten thirty."

"Jesus, Eddie," said Philip, "you're creeping me out."

Eddie shrugged. "You spend a career doing stakeouts, old habits die hard."

Philip gazed out the window for a minute, then asked, "Can I borrow your phone for a sec?"

Eddie unlocked his phone and handed it over.

Philip tapped, then held the phone up to Eddie. He had pulled up the video of the Brashear news conference, with the video stopped at the brief moment when Louise Mortensen's unidentified escort had been in the frame.

"Was it that guy?"

Eddie glanced over. "Could be, but I can't be sure. Like I said, he had most of his face covered up."

Philip gazed at the image. He had seen it before, when Lizzy had played the video for him, but now the face looked familiar for some other reason. Then he made the connection—yesterday's client, Mitch Foot. Foot had looked younger than the guy in the video, but maybe that was only because of how he had been dressed. And now that he thought about it, Foot had said "water" the same way Lizzy and Owen did.

Eddie pulled up to the entrance to the ER. "I'll park and meet you inside."

Philip opened the door. "No need, Eddie—I really appreciate it, but I can take it from here."

"Hey, you'll need a ride home when you're done. I don't have anyone else on my dance card today."

After a moment, Philip nodded. "It would be a big help. Thanks, Eddie."

Two hours later, Philip had gotten a clean bill of cerebral health, another dose of aspirin, and a lecture about the evils of alcohol. A few hours after that, he had cancelled his credit cards and been ferried by Eddie to get a new driver's license and pick up a prepaid cell phone.

By the time he got home that night, his head was throbbing again, but he had no doubt as to its source: a day spent dealing with irritable medical staff, credit card fraud departments, and the DMV would be enough to give anyone a headache.

49

W hen they reached the Philadelphia area, Owen checked them into a Hampton Inn in King of Prussia. They had gotten on the road earlier than usual that morning, and Lizzy suspected that the reason was Owen's impatience to see his parents. After Owen carried the luggage to their rooms, he began arranging pillows on the bed for her to prop her leg on.

"I can do that," said Lizzy, taking a pillow from him. "You should go see your mom and dad now."

He stood back and looked critically at the construction. "They should have more pillows—now you don't have enough for behind your back. I'm going down to the desk and get some more."

"This is fine—if you make me too comfortable, I won't want to move, and I think I should try to walk around a little after having spent so much time in the car."

"Are you hungry? I could run out and pick up some food for you."

"There's cheese and crackers and fruit in the cooler."

"Will that be enough? It seems a little light for a meal ..."

"It's plenty! Now go on and see your mom."

"If you're sure."

"Yes, I'm sure."

Owen nodded and shrugged into his coat.

"Say hi to Andy for me," she said.

"Actually, I probably won't see Andy today. When he found out we were almost home, he left for a meeting with some colleagues in Louisiana." Owen shook his head. "I didn't realize he had been putting that off because I wasn't around to take care of things." He glanced around the room. "I'll leave my laptop in case you want to stream a movie." He looked at her anxiously. "You sure you'll be okay?"

She pointed imperiously at the door. "Go. Now."

Owen gave her a thumbs-up and hurried out the door. Lizzy heard his heavy tread receding down the hall.

Lizzy read for a while and ate a banana when she got hungry, then took a walk around the hotel parking lot. The exercise actually made her leg feel better, and she walked the short distance to the huge King of Prussia Mall. Once she got there, though, she found the crowds and the sensory stimulus overwhelming and returned to the hotel. Then she signed on to Owen's laptop to do some research into an idea that had been coalescing in her mind during the drive from Sedona.

Owen showed up around dinnertime with a Wawa bag.

"How is your mom doing?" Lizzy asked as he unpacked the bag—hoagies, milk, and an assortment of fruit—and set the food out on the table.

"I think she was glad to see me. We had a nice talk when I first got there, but she got hazier later. At one point she thought I was Andy." He gave a weak laugh. "Wait until he hears that—it'll kill him." He examined the food. "I'm getting really tired of restaurants and take-out food," he said. "I can't wait until we're settled somewhere and we can cook."

"What are you going to cook first?" asked Lizzy.

"Excellent question," he said, sitting back and taking a bite of an apple. He considered while he chewed. "A big pot of soup. Maybe vegetable beef soup. Grass-fed beef. And we could go to the market in Lancaster and get vegetables." He picked up steam. "And you know what would be perfect with that?"

"What?" asked Lizzy through a mouthful of hoagie.

"Homemade bread. I love the way the house smells when bread is baking. And a big salad, with Italian dressing. And then for dessert we could have espresso and biscotti."

"I don't like biscotti," said Lizzy. "It's like trying to chew a brick."

"Cappuccino and spritz cookies," he amended.

"And then a long walk."

Owen laughed. "Yes, a very long walk."

Lizzy set aside the hoagie. "I've been thinking about what to do," she said.

"Yes?"

"I was thinking I could turn myself in."

"To Louise Mortensen?" asked Owen, aghast.

"No, Uncle Owen, not to her," she said, a hint of a verbal eye-roll in her voice. "To someone who can stop her. Her and the guy she was with at the courthouse. Then they can put Louise and George Millard in jail and put me and that guy somewhere safe."

"Who's 'they'?"

"I don't know—the government, I guess."

Owen stirred uncomfortably. "It's not what your parents wanted for you."

"They kept me at home and look what happened," she said, her voice rising. "Or if they were going to keep me at home, then they should have kept me there all the time. If

Dad had kept me in Parkesburg, none of this would have happened."

"You wanted to go to New York so much—"

"He was the dad, he should have said no!" she yelled.

"I know, I know," he said.

They sat in silence for a minute, Lizzy tearing her paper napkin into thin strips.

"Maybe it wouldn't be that bad," she said eventually.

Owen said nothing.

"They wouldn't gain anything by treating me badly. In fact, they couldn't treat me badly, because I'd squeeze them if they did."

"I—" he began, then his voice caught, and he cleared his throat. "Maybe."

They sat in silence for another minute, then Lizzy set the napkin aside.

"How about Penn?"

"Penn?"

"William Penn University. Maybe I could turn myself in to them. Not just to them, but to your department. You said that you'd have more resources you could tap into in Philly. Maybe that's one of them."

"What about Louise and Millard and the guy in the video?"

"I don't know," she said, clearly exasperated at his lack of enthusiasm. "Maybe the university could notify the police. But if they were protecting me, I'd be safe, and Louise and Mr. Millard would have no reason to bother you or Andy or Ruby anymore."

After a moment he said, somewhat reluctantly, "The idea of turning yourself in to a university isn't totally outlandish—I've thought about it myself—but I don't know that Penn would be the place to do it. Any organization that was protecting you would no doubt come under considerable pressure from other interested parties, like the government. To withstand that pressure, you'd need to have as an ally someone who was in a position of authority at that organization *and* who displayed some intestinal fortitude. Or you would need someone who would be willing to try to keep you a secret within the university, which would be difficult if not impossible. I don't think my boss fits any of those criteria."

"Maybe keeping it a secret wouldn't be so important," she said, warming to the idea. "If enough people knew what I could do, it would be a sort of protection, wouldn't it? Like if someone can create a nuclear bomb, they're probably more safe if a lot of people know they can do it than if just a few people know."

"I guess so," replied Owen warily.

Lizzy's excitement was building. "You could go to the person who runs your department, and describe a what-if scenario to him. 'What if we knew of a person with this ability? What would we do with them?' And see what he says."

"He's going to say I'm crazy. Or at least think it."

"That might be better—if he thinks you're just discussing some crazy scenario that could never actually happen, you might get more information from him."

"Oh, Pumpkin, I don't think—"

"Please, Uncle Owen, can't you just try? What can it hurt?"

He heaved a sigh and, after a moment, nodded. "Okay. I'll give it a try."

50

The next morning, Owen stepped into the William Penn Neurobiology Department office. "Hi, Gina," he said, "I'm back!"

The young woman at the desk looked up from her monitor. "Dr. McNally! I didn't expect you back yet—how are you doing?"

She circled the desk to give him a hug, then stood back and examined him.

"You look great—Sedona must have agreed with you."

"I took up hiking," said Owen, sheepish but pleased.

"I can tell," she said with a smile. "I know lots of good hiking trails in this area, I can give you some recommendations."

Owen had never in his life expected to be discussing hiking trails with an attractive young woman. He blushed. "That would be great, thanks."

Gina returned to her seat and began rummaging under the desk. "I have a stack of journals I was getting ready to send to you. Can't you get this stuff online these days?"

"Some of it, but paper's more fun," he replied. "Is Ambrose in?"

"As luck would have it, he is," she said, plopping the journals on the desk.

"Does he have a minute?"

"For you, Dr. McNally? Absolutely."

She crossed to a closed door and rapped on it smartly. "Dr. Steck?" she called through the door. "Dr. McNally's back and he'd like to speak with you."

A muffled response came from behind the door.

"Sounds good, sir," said Gina, with a shrug at Owen. "I'll send him in."

She threw the door open and stood aside. "Good luck," she whispered as Owen stepped into the office.

Ambrose Steck rose from behind his desk to his inconsiderable height and extended a pudgy hand.

"Owen, what a pleasant surprise! Welcome back."

Owen shook the hand, finding it damp and limp, as always.

"Thanks, Ambrose. Good to be back."

"Please, have a seat," said Steck, waving toward one of the chairs facing his desk. He flopped back into his own chair. "So, I understand you were on a little break?"

"Yes, enjoying warmer climes."

"Gina was so secretive about where you were—where did you go?"

Owen couldn't imagine it could matter whether or not Steck knew where he had been. "A couple of weeks in the Florida Keys, about two months in Arizona."

"Both lovely places, I'm sure—and so appealing at this time of year."

"They were very nice."

"All ready for your classes in the fall?"

"Yes, I'll be ready. Listen, Ambrose, I had a question for you ..."

"Yes?" asked the little man, suddenly looking wary.

"What's the most unusual neurobiological or psychological case you've ever encountered?"

"Personally?"

"Yes."

Steck leaned back in his chair and interlaced his fingers over the mound of his stomach. "As a graduate student, I did some work with a couple who displayed characteristics of telepathy. They had responded to an ad for participants in a study of decision-making between couples in established relationships—it was related to a study I was assisting with in the Psychology Department—but it soon became apparent that their decisions were based on something beyond just familiarity with each other. We began applying standard tests for telepathy—Brugmans, Rhine—then started coming up with tests of our own. The couple aced them all. A fascinating area of study, really—there was an interesting article not long ago in *Frontiers in Human Neuroscience*—"

Owen cleared his throat loudly and, in the resulting pause in Steck's story, interjected, "Have you ever had the private sector, or the government, express interest in one of your subjects? For example, the telepathic couple?"

"Well, certainly various government agencies have used the findings of studies with which I was involved—"

"Not just the findings, but the people themselves."

Steck knit his brow. "What do you mean?"

"For example—just as a theoretical case—let's say there was someone who was displaying unusual mental abilities. Telepathy or telekinesis or, say, the ability to cause strokes in other people just through the power of their minds. That would certainly be of interest to the private sector or government, wouldn't it?"

Steck examined Owen with narrowed eyes. "You have quite a bee in your bonnet about this topic, Owen."

Owen tried to settle back in the inadequate chair. "I'm thinking of writing an article on the moral obligation of educational institutions to protect their research subjects from exploitation."

"Sounds to me like a topic more appropriate to Ethics and Health Policy."

"But of interest to any institute of higher learning involved in research, wouldn't you say?"

Steck steepled his pudgy fingers and examined Owen. After a moment, he sighed. "I would expect any member of my department to keep the identity of his or her research subjects confidential, of course. As long as a subject's ability did not pose a danger to the researchers, or to the general public, I would assume no obligation to alert the authorities to its existence. I would put telepathy in that category. Probably also telekinesis. However, if the subject posed a danger to society, as in your example of the person with the ability to cause strokes, then of course we would have an obligation to protect the well-being of the community."

"What would that entail?"

Steck shrugged. "FBI ... Homeland Security. I must say I have never been in a position to have to give it much thought."

"No. But it is an interesting question. Might an academic institution not have a responsibility to protect its subjects from exploitation by private for-profit or government organizations?"

"Dr. McNally," said Steck, unsteepling his fingers, "you have been a member of this department for a good many years, and a member of the academic community for many more. You surely can't imagine a scenario where we would become the defender of a research subject with an extraordinary and dangerous ability." He sat forward. "What would you suggest—our own version of a witness protection program? Perhaps we could barricade ourselves in the faculty club, deploying sharpened mortarboards like throwing stars as the SWAT teams descended." He raised his eyebrows expectantly at Owen, clearly amused by the picture he had painted.

"No, of course not," Owen replied testily. "I was thinking more of a legal defense than a paramilitary one."

Steck sat back. "It will make an interesting article," he said, "but perhaps one best published under a pseudonym."

51

Millard jogged up the steps to the floor housing the Penn Neurobiology Department office. His pursuit of Lizzy Ballard on the hiking trails of Sedona had convinced him of the need for some more aerobic activity, so he had bypassed the elevator. They hadn't yet located Ballard and McNally, and he figured he had nothing to lose by trying the package-for-McNally approach again.

He had checked out McNally's house in Lansdowne, outside and in, and there was no sign that anyone had been there since McNally and company's abrupt departure in December. Ditto with the Ballard house in Parkesburg. If they had driven from Arizona—and if Pennsylvania was in fact their destination—then they should be back by now, depending on how many scenic side trips they took.

He pushed open the door to the department office and was irritated to see the same girl at the desk.

"Hi," she said. "Another package for Dr. McNally?"

"You've got quite a memory," he said with a smile. People with good memories were the bane of his existence.

"You're in luck," she said. "Dr. McNally's back."

"He is? That's great news. Is he around?"

"He was here a little while ago. You just missed him by half an hour or so."

"Do you expect him to be in again soon?"

"I'm not sure, but he collected the journals I hadn't mailed to him yet and didn't leave instructions for me to mail any more of them, so I figure he's back for good. If you want to leave your phone number or email address, I can let you know when he'll be having office hours."

Millard was running through the options in his head—he'd start with the closest faculty parking area to see if McNally's SUV was there, and then continue scouting the campus if it wasn't. He wanted to find McNally as soon as possible, but in the worst case he would stake out the office, waiting for his next visit.

"That's okay, I'll catch up with him one way or the other," said Millard. "I'm looking forward to running into him again."

He closed the door behind him and broke into a jog toward the stairway.

52

After his visit with Ambrose Steck, Owen's next stop was the library to return a woefully overdue book. The walk through the campus reminded him why he didn't pine after travel the way some of his colleagues did. The central campus of William Penn University had always represented his dream of college life—had when he first admired it as a prospective student, still did as he enjoyed it as a faculty member. The hundred-year-old stone and brick buildings exuded a sense of timeless permanence. In the aftermath of an early warm spell the previous week, some of the dogwoods and forsythia lining the wide walkways had started to flower. In response to the uptick in temperatures, the students had predictably broken out shorts and flip-flops, and hadn't returned to warmer clothes despite the now more seasonally appropriate temperatures. The people hurrying to a class or talking and laughing in small groups also gave him a sense of confidence that he wouldn't disappear into a dark alley.

He had a nice chat with the young man at the returns desk at the library, searched for and checked out a book he needed to prepare for his fall class, and had started back toward his car when he remembered that he needed to pick up a paper from his office. He got on the elevator before it occurred to him that he should probably add stair climbing to his new exercise regimen. He'd at least take the stairs down.

He retrieved the paper from his office and added it to the briefcase of journals he was carrying. He had started for the stairs when Gina emerged from the department office.

"Jeez, Dr. McNally, you and the guy who's looking for you keep just missing each other—it's like *Noises Off*. He was in the office not five minutes ago."

"Who was that?"

"I don't know his name, but he was in about a month ago to drop off a package for you."

"What was it?"

"I don't know, I just put the forwarding address on it and sent it out."

Owen recalled an envelope he had received in Sedona with Gina's forwarding label attached to it that contained only a copy of *Psychology Today*, definitely not a magazine on his subscription list.

"What do you do with the envelopes after you put the forwarding address on them?"

"The mail girl picks them up. Why? Was there a problem?"

Owen was starting to picture how George Millard might have discovered that he and Lizzy were in Sedona.

"No, no problem. What did he look like?"

"Average. Average height. Average build. Dark hair." She considered for a moment. "Tanner than you would expect someone to be in March, but he must have had a beard and mustache when he got the tan, because his skin wasn't as tan around his mouth and on his chin."

"Did he leave anything this time?"

"No. He had another envelope, but he didn't leave it. Said he'd catch up with you."

"Thanks, Gina."

"Sure thing, Dr. McNally."

Gina continued down the hall, leaving Owen standing by the door to the stairway, his heart thumping. He guessed that Jim of Thread-the-Needle Trail had come visiting to Pennsylvania.

Owen trotted from office to office and window to window, checking every possible view, and finally spotted his target. He was standing in what from the ground would be an inconspicuous spot overlooking the faculty parking lot. He was wearing jeans, a blue windbreaker, and a black cap. When he turned his head slightly, Owen could see on the front the white and orange of a Flyers logo, which had always looked to him like a fried egg.

Owen also noticed, much to his irritation, that his Arizona SUV had a ticket under the windshield wiper, since his properly tagged Pennsylvania SUV was no doubt still somewhere on the Pocopson property of Louise Mortensen and the late Gerard Bonnay.

He removed his phone from his pocket, zoomed in the camera as far as he could, and snapped a photo.

He gazed at the image. It was fuzzy, and had caught the man only in profile. Without the beard and mustache, he couldn't positively identify him as the man from the trail—even with a beard and mustache, he hadn't seen enough of the man through the Eye to make an informed assessment. Owen looked out the window again. The man glanced at his watch, then scanned the area around the parking lot.

Owen had told Lizzy he wanted to come back to Philadelphia in part because he would have access to more resources, but at the moment his best resource was Ambrose

Steck. It was not a comforting thought. Maybe, he thought bitterly, he could just ask Gina to escort him to his car.

A minute, then two, ticked by as he watched the man watch his car. He tapped his phone on his open hand, considering and eliminating options until only one was left. He sighed and hit a speed dial.

"Philip Castillo, Psychic Counselor. Can I help you?"

Owen sighed. "I hope so."

AFTER OWEN ENDED the call with Philip, he dialed Lizzy's number.

"Hey, Uncle Owen," she answered.

"Hey, Pumpkin."

"How's it going?"

"I talked with my department head."

"Yeah?"

"Yeah. He wasn't very helpful."

"Really?" Her disappointment was clear.

"Really. He basically said that it would be his responsibility to turn anyone who posed a threat over to the authorities."

There was a pause.

"Maybe his boss ...?"

"Maybe, but we have another problem. It looks like Jim from Thread-the-Needle Trail is here."

He heard her quick intake of breath.

"I'm sending you a picture I took of him," he continued. "It's not very clear, but can you take a look? If it is the guy from the trail, he's shaved off his beard and mustache, so it might be easier for you to tell if it's George Millard."

"Got it," she said in a moment. "It's pretty fuzzy. And the hat makes it hard to see his face."

"I know. I'm pretty far away from him."

"What's he doing?"

"He's watching my car."

"Watching your car?" she said, her voice rising. "Uncle Owen, you have to call the police!"

"What could I tell the police, Pumpkin? That I want someone arrested for watching my car? And I'd no doubt have to file some sort of complaint, and that might make it easier for Millard and Mortensen to find me. No, I don't think we can call the police yet."

"What are we going to do?"

"The more I think about it, the more I think that the idea of getting the protection of some large, powerful organization isn't a bad way to go. Penn was a bust, but I know people at Harvard and MIT—at the NIH, for that matter—who might have more influence, or at least be willing to try. Are you still thinking that's the right plan?"

"Yeah, I think so," said Lizzy.

"Okay. As soon as we get things under control, I'll start getting in touch with those people who might be able to help us. I think that discussion will be better done in person than via email or phone."

"What are we going to do in the meantime?

"I called Philip and he's coming out here. He'll keep an eye on you."

"Philip?" He couldn't tell whether this news had lessened or fueled her panic.

"Yes. I'm sure we're being overcautious, but better safe than sorry. I want you to pack up our stuff and go to a different hotel. Or motel. Or bed-and-breakfast. But wherever it is, don't tell me where, because I don't want to know."

"Why not?"

"Just in case they catch up with me ..." Owen didn't finish the thought.

"Uncle Owen—" Lizzy's voice was reedy with panic.

"I'll be okay, Pumpkin. It will be in my favor that I don't know where you are."

"How am I going to get to a new place?"

"Take a cab."

"I don't have any money—"

"There's money in my suitcase."

"But what if you aren't back before that money runs out?"

He could tell she was crying now, and that her concern wasn't about the money running out, but about his time running out.

"If you need more money, or need anything, call Andy." He gave her his brother's number.

"How about you?" she asked.

"Maybe I can line up someone to keep an eye on me until we get this thing worked out."

"Andy?"

"I'm thinking more of a professional."

"Yes, that's a good idea," she agreed. "Especially if you think they might try to force information out of you like ... like in some movie interrogation scene." Her voice was starting to spin up again.

"Don't worry about me, Pumpkin. Until I get that lined up, I'm going to go somewhere where there will be lots of other people, so nothing bad will happen to me. And Philip will be here soon. Give him a call and let him know what your new location is. And I'll get away from George Millard as soon as I can. I'll 'shake his tail,'" he added, in a bid to elicit a laugh from Lizzy.

She obliged, but without much enthusiasm.

"Sound like a plan?" he asked.

"Yes," she said, her voice exhausted. "Be careful, Uncle Owen."

"You know I will, Pumpkin."

He ended the call, then returned to his office. He removed the journals and paper from his briefcase and replaced them with four of his heaviest reference manuals. It was the best he could do for self-defense.

Owen eased the door of his office open and peered into the hallway. He would have felt better if Gina had been on her way down the hall on some errand for Steck, but it was empty.

He hurried down the hall to the window from which he had been able to see the parking lot, and the presumed George Millard, but a large van had parked in a position that blocked his view. He started for the elevator, then changed direction to the stairway. At least he wouldn't get trapped alone in a tiny cube with whoever was watching his car.

When he reached the first floor, he switched his usual route to a less-used side door. He peeked out and saw nothing but passing students. He descended the steps and started down the walk. It would take him toward the parking lot, but he would be coming up behind the position he had seen Millard in. Maybe Millard had given up, and Owen could just drive away.

He was about to round the corner of the building when he jumped at the sound of a male voice and running feet on the walk behind him.

"Hey! Dr. McNally!"

He turned, drawing back the arm holding the briefcase, only to be confronted by Randy, a student from his research seminar the previous year. He groaned inwardly as he let his arm fall to his side. Randy was a bit of a groupie.

"Dr. McNally, I didn't realize you were back in town!"

"Yes, just got back." Owen glanced around, trying to see if Randy's call had attracted any unwanted attention. "Now I'm trying to get caught up on all those things I should have been doing while I was away." He looked meaningfully at his watch.

Randy laughed. "I can imagine—you were away for a long time! Where are you off to now? Want me to carry your briefcase for you?"

Owen almost succumbed to the urge to have the company even of Randy as some protection against George Millard, but he battled it down. He didn't want to risk getting anyone else involved in the dangerous game they were playing with Millard and Louise Mortensen.

"No, thanks. I appreciate it, but I have an appointment to see someone in just a few minutes and I really need the time to get my thoughts in order. I hope you don't mind."

Randy tried unsuccessfully to hide his disappointment. "Sure, Dr. McNally, I understand." He stood smiling at Owen. "Hey, I'm signed up for your Systems and Behavioral Neuroscience class in the fall!"

"That's great," said Owen, with as much enthusiasm as he could muster. "I'll look forward to talking with you then."

Randy continued smiling at him. Evidently he wasn't going to be the first to walk away.

"See you later!" Owen said jovially, and turned away. He took a few steps and looked back. Randy was still smiling gamely after him.

Owen no longer wanted to go toward the parking lot, just in case Randy's greeting had alerted Millard to his presence. He didn't want to walk back in the direction he had come for fear he wouldn't be able to disentangle himself from a second encounter with Randy. And he had an idea of where he could go. He stepped off the walkway to cross the lawn.

"See you later, Dr. McNally!" Randy called after him.

Owen waved his hand in acknowledgement but didn't turn around.

As soon as he was out of Randy's sight, he changed direction toward his new destination. As he did, he caught a glimpse of a cap with the concentric white and orange circles —the Flyers' fried egg.

Owen stopped in his tracks. The wearer of the hat was behind a small group of students, and Owen shifted back and forth, trying to get a better look. The group shifted as well, stymieing his efforts. Then the students called farewells and the group broke apart, but the man and the hat were gone.

Owen turned and began walking again, his heart hammering and his legs trembling. The image that filled his mind was one he had never seen in life, but had imagined many times in his mind—his friend Patrick Ballard, lying on the frozen, filthy ground of a Philadelphia alley, his life draining away from two bullet holes from George Millard's gun.

In a few minutes, Owen reached his destination—the one place he could think of that was open twenty-four hours a day, always busy, and unlikely to kick him out.

He crossed the ER waiting room to the admission desk and pressed his hand to his chest.

"Excuse me, Miss, I think I'm having a heart attack."

53

"He's *where*?" Mortensen's voice vibrated with irritation across the connection.

"The Penn ER. It looked like he was having a heart attack."

"And how in the world could you tell that?"

"I followed him and watched him from outside. He put his hand on his chest and then someone ran out with a wheelchair and wheeled him into the treatment area."

"Does the man think that emergency departments are his own personal sanctuary?" she said with disgust.

"Maybe he really was having a heart attack. He's been under a lot of stress—"

"He's not having a heart attack—it would be far too great a coincidence. He must have realized you were following him and figured this was a way for him to hide out in safety. And as far as he knows, if we can't get to him, we can't get to Ballard."

"I'll keep searching the campus—"

"No," she interrupted him, "I do give McNally enough credit to think that if he was going to risk showing up at the university, he would have hidden Ballard away somewhere else while he ran his errand." She took a deep breath. "That's not our only problem. I just heard from the AG's office. They haven't dropped the investigation. Someone else there thought there was sufficient merit to pick it up."

"Damn," said Millard under his breath.

"Yes. On top of dealing with McNally and Ballard, we have to speed up getting the rest of the records scanned and destroyed." She was silent for a moment, and Millard could hear fingers tapping on a hard surface. "Whether he's faking or actually having an attack, he's likely to be admitted. We'll find a way to give McNally the flunitrazepam, and then get Mitchell into his room to find out where Ballard is."

"Once we get the information from him, want Pieda to give McNally the crush?"

"No. No more strokes. There have been too many strokes already. Plus," she added, "I want to avoid giving Mitchell more of the steroid drug if we can help it. It's undoubtedly unpleasant for him, and he might balk." She was silent again for a moment, then said, "Meet me at the lab. I'll have something else for you as well. I am done dealing with Owen McNally. Once you get Ballard's location from him, administer the drug I'll give to you. If he's telling the doctors he's having a heart attack, we'll make his story come true."

54

Owen had been admitted and called Lizzy to let her know where he was. She reported that Philip would be leaving Phoenix for Philadelphia on the red-eye that night.

Now it was evening, and Owen sat in a chair in his hospital room, perusing the websites of firms offering bodyguard services, when a voice interrupted his research.

"Well, I'll be, all those doughnuts finally caught up with you."

Andy McNally stood in the doorway.

"What are you doing here?" asked Owen in alarm. "I thought you were in Louisiana."

"I just got back this afternoon. Then I got a call from one of the docs in the ER whose sister I dated a few years ago," said Andy, stepping into the room. "She said she noticed the family resemblance—I said, 'What? A resemblance? Say it ain't so!'—and then saw the last name and called me up." He sat down on the bed. "I looked at your chart. It appears you have suffered the first completely symptom-free myocardial infarction in medical history."

Owen glanced toward the door. "I didn't really have a heart attack," he whispered.

"No kidding," said Andy, deadpan. "So, what's up?"

Casting nervous glances toward the door, Owen said, "I was at the Neurobiology office talking to Ambrose Steck, and afterwards I saw this guy watching my car in the parking lot. I think it was George Millard. I couldn't think of how else to get away from him, so I went to the ER."

"So how long are you planning to enjoy fraudulent room and board at the expense of our fine insurance system?" asked Andy.

Owen blushed. "Only for a day or two—"

Andy shook his head. "It's just professional courtesy that they haven't kicked you out already. Look, they barely even have you hooked up to any monitors." Andy leaned forward. "Why didn't you just call me, bro?"

"The whole point," said Owen, exasperated, "was not to get you or Ruby reinvolved in this whole fiasco!"

"Ruby, sure. But you and me, we're the Dynamic Duo. I, of course, am Batman to your Robin. Or maybe Robin Hood to your Friar Tuck—"

"Andy, I appreciate it, I really do—despite the insults—but I think we're close to finding a way to resolve this whole thing."

"How's that?"

"That's what I was talking to Steck about. Lizzy wants to turn herself in to the authorities—"

"*What*?"

"Listen, I think it might be for the best—"

"It's not for the best. Aren't you the one who used the phrase 'lab rat' at one time?"

Owen sighed. "Yes, I did, but we're running out of options.

I wouldn't have approached Steck on my own—Lizzy asked me to. It's all coming to a head. We're pretty sure that it was George Millard who we ran into on the trail in Arizona, and who probably put the snakes in her path. I don't think we're a match for them on our own. We need help—some official help —and I can use the time in here to figure out how to get that."

"Where's Lizzy now?"

"She moved out of where we had been staying. I told her not to tell me where, just in case Mortensen or Millard caught up with me. Philip Castillo, the guy I told you about in Sedona, is coming out here to keep an eye on her."

"How much do you know about him?"

"Not a lot. I couldn't find much background on him online, but he seemed to be a big help to Lizzy, and she really trusts him."

"She's just a kid."

"Yeah, but she's an insightful kid." Owen paused. "I talked with him myself," he continued, looking a bit embarrassed. "Meant to give him the third degree and ended up unloading about the situation with Mom and Dad, the difficulties of being away from home. I can say from personal experience that he's easy to talk with."

"Yeah, but con men can be easy to talk with—"

"I know, but I feel like he's trustworthy."

Andy opened his mouth, but Owen held up a hand.

"I know, I know—not very scientific. But that's my assessment. I trust him enough to ask him to come out here and keep an eye on Lizzy."

Andy ran his fingers through his hair. "Christ, what a mess."

Owen levered himself out of the chair and went to stand by the window. It provided a view of the parking garage across the street and, if the viewer's angle was just right, the towers of Center City. "I've run out of ideas, little brother."

"Owen."

Andy never called him by his actual name. Owen turned from the window.

"Have you ... lost weight? Do you have what others would consider normal skin color but for you constitutes ... a tan?"

Owen looked down at himself. "Uh, I guess so ..."

"You keep it up, pretty soon you'll be so handsome that there *will* be a family resemblance."

Early the next morning, Millard, dressed in an orderly's uniform, stepped out of the elevator on the fourth floor of William Penn University Hospital, sauntered down the corridor, and glanced into Owen McNally's room. The same visitor was in the room as had been there when Millard had cased the room the night before, a man who even the least astute observer would have identified as McNally's younger, thinner, and better-looking brother, Andrew McNally. Millard kept walking to the end of the corridor, glancing into rooms as if looking for someone, then returned to the elevator. This family was evidently determined to make the life of Louise Mortensen and her associates as difficult as possible. Millard was looking forward to eliminating that annoyance in short order.

When he reappeared from the elevator a short time later, his uniform was covered by a long coat and scarf. He sat down in a visitor waiting area near the elevator lobby. A few minutes later, the elevator chimed open and the large metal cart carrying the patients' breakfast trays trundled out. Millard pulled out his phone and pressed in a number.

"Dr. Andrew McNally's answering service."

"Hello, this is Dr. Jarvis Pruitt," said Millard. "I'm working with a patient at CHOP—a seven-year-old girl awaiting a lung transplant—and I urgently need Dr. McNally's advice. Can you ask him to meet me at the CHOP ICU as soon as possible?"

Mortensen had been able to ascertain that Andrew McNally's clinical advisor in medical school had been Jarvis Pruitt, and that McNally had in fact consulted with him on several cases at Children's Hospital of Philadelphia. The woman on the phone took down the information without question and rang off. A minute later, a concerned-looking Andrew McNally stepped out of Owen McNally's room and walked quickly to the stairway, almost bumping into the actual orderly who was delivering trays from the cart to the patient rooms.

"Sorry about that," said McNally.

The man shook his head, slid out two more trays, and headed down the hall as McNally disappeared into a stairwell.

Millard dropped his coat and scarf on one of the visitor area chairs and stepped to the temporarily unattended cart. Each tray in its slide-out rack was labeled with a room number. He slid Owen McNally's tray out. Pulling a syringe from his pocket, he uncapped it with his teeth, stabbed the needle through the foil covering of a plastic orange juice container, depressed the plunger, and had just recapped the syringe and slid it into his pocket when the orderly returned.

"What's up?" the man asked.

"I'm looking for breakfast for 487," said Millard. "She's kicking up a fuss."

The man looked at the tray in Millard's hand. "That's for 477," he said. He slid out the tray under the empty slot that had held McNally's and handed it to Millard. "That's the one for 487."

"Thanks, man," replied Millard, passing McNally's tray to the orderly. Then he hurried down the hall, glancing back to see the orderly step into McNally's room with the tray. Millard stepped into 487 and dropped the tray unceremoniously on the table next to the bed in which a white-haired woman snored. Then he walked quickly to the service stairs.

A FEW MINUTES LATER, with trays continuing to be delivered to the other rooms, Millard led Mitchell Pieda, also dressed in an orderly's uniform, to McNally's room.

Millard eased his head around the doorway. McNally sat facing the window. His tray, with the empty orange juice container on it, was on the table beside him. His arm hung over the side of the chair, still gripping a fork, but the piece of food that had been speared on it when the drug kicked in was lying on the floor. It looked like a piece of fruit cocktail.

Millard rapped lightly on the open door, ready to jump back should McNally turn around, but there was no movement. He stepped into the doorway.

"Dr. McNally?"

No reaction.

He gestured to Pieda to follow him into the room.

McNally was in the same state that Castillo—and, for that matter, Millard himself—had been in under the influence of Louise's concoction: unresponsive, his eyes fixed on the floor in front of him. Millard swished the privacy curtain closed and said to Mitchell, "Hurry up, we don't have long before the brother realizes it was a fake call."

Mitchell squatted down in front of McNally.

"Dr. McNally, can you hear me?" Pause. "That's good. I need you to answer a question for me. Where is Elizabeth Ballard?" After a moment, Mitchell looked up at Millard.

"He doesn't know."

"Bullshit. Ask him again."

Pieda pressed his lips together, then turned back to McNally. "Dr. McNally, I want you to think about the place you left Lizzy." Almost immediately he said, "Hampton Inn in King of Prussia."

"There we go, just needed a little persistence," said Millard, drawing a second syringe out of his pocket. He filled it and stepped to McNally's side. "Want to scoot over a little, Mitchell? Give me some room?"

Pieda was still squatted down in front of McNally, examining his face. He ignored Millard.

"Dr. McNally, is she still there now?" After a moment, Mitchell said, "She's not there anymore."

"Damn!" Millard stepped back. "Why not?"

"Why isn't Elizabeth Ballard at the Hampton Inn, Dr. McNally?" After another moment, he said, "He sent her away."

"Dammit!" Millard stood staring at McNally's inert form for a moment, until the clatter of the cart, returning to collect the trays, roused him.

"Fine, we'll find her some other way. Move over, Pieda."

He felt a slight twinge behind his left eye, which he tried to ignore.

"Why bother killing him?" whispered Pieda. "He won't remember we were here. You should know that better than me."

"I'm sick of dealing with him," said Millard. *And sick of dealing with you, too*, he added silently. "I got my orders from Mortensen and I'm carrying them out."

He jabbed the needle into Owen McNally's arm and depressed the plunger.

56

At ten o'clock in the morning, after a few scant hours of sleep at the Motel 6 to which she had relocated, Lizzy jumped to her feet at a knock on the door and pressed her eye to the peephole. Philip stood in the hallway. She threw the door open and gave him a hug.

"I'm so glad you're here!" She stepped aside to let him in. "Where are your bags?"

"Just one bag. It's in the car."

"I'm going to call Uncle Owen and let him know you're here—I haven't talked to him since last night. He went to the emergency room yesterday and told them he was having a heart attack, and they checked him into the hospital," she said, her words spilling over each other with pent-up excitement.

She speed-dialed Owen and listened through a few rings. She was expecting the call to go to voicemail when a voice answered.

"Hi, Lizzy, it's Andy."

"Hey, Andy—are you with Uncle Owen?"

"In a manner of speaking, yes. I'm at William Penn Hospital. He had a heart attack."

"No, he was just faking," she said. "He was being followed by George Millard—at least that's who we think it was—and he thought of going to the ER to hide out. He told them he was having a heart attack so they'd admit him."

"I know, Lizzy. But this is the real thing." Lizzy heard a whoosh of expelled breath. "I was here with him at the hospital, but they lured me away with a fake phone call. They told me I was supposed to meet someone about an emergency surgery at CHOP. But when I got there, the person who the call was supposed to be from wasn't there. Hell, he's not even in the country—he's on a cruise in the Mediterranean. I tried calling the nurse's station on Owen's floor but couldn't get through. I ran back to Penn and found the crash team working on Owen."

Her voice jumped an octave. "He really had a heart attack?"

"Yeah. I tease Owen about his weight, but honestly, he has the constitution of an ox. I don't believe he had a heart attack unless he had some help. At first I thought someone might have gone to his room disguised as a nurse and given him an injection—maybe potassium chloride or digoxin—but I doubt Owen would have let anyone inject him with anything, and it didn't look like there had been a struggle. Maybe they gave him a sedative—slipped something into his breakfast. I'm going to see if they have any security tapes they can pull—maybe we'll see someone we recognize."

Lizzy dropped onto the bed, her face white. "Why didn't you call me when it happened?"

"I don't have your cell number, and I didn't know the passcode for Owen's phone to get it. How are you doing? Where are you, for that matter?"

"I'm fine," she said, not sounding fine. "I'm not supposed to tell anyone where I am."

"Even me?"

"Especially you. Uncle Owen didn't want to get you involved again, and I agree with him."

"Lizzy, Owen's my brother, I need to be involved. I want to make sure you're okay."

"Philip's with me. He came all the way out here from Arizona to help me when Uncle Owen called him."

"If Owen trusts him," said Andy, "I guess that's okay."

"*I* trust him," Lizzy shot back.

"Of course, sweetheart, I didn't mean to suggest—"

"And don't call me sweetheart! Everyone's always treating me like a baby. People treat me like a baby and try to look out for me, and look what happens!"

"Lizzy, you need to calm down—" said Philip in a soothing voice.

"No, I won't calm down," said Lizzy, crying now. "First Mom, then Dad, now Uncle Owen. I'm going to do something about it, and I'm not going to let anyone else get hurt in the process."

And she stabbed off the connection.

57

It was an hour after the conversation with Andy. Lizzy's near hysteria at the news of Owen's heart attack had gradually given way to an air of grim determination. She was standing near the window, her hands jammed into her pockets.

"Are you sure about this?" asked Philip.

"Yes, I'm sure," she said.

"This isn't going to be easy."

"I know that!" cried Lizzy. "How come everyone—"

Philip held up his hand. "I'm sorry, I shouldn't have said that."

Lizzy glared at him.

"So," said Philip, "what's your plan?"

"Well, we have to find them first."

"It sounds like we could catch Dr. Mortensen at her offices downtown—"

"No, I don't want to go there."

"Why not?"

"I just don't." She crossed her arms.

"'I just don't' isn't a good plan."

She stared at him, stony-faced, for a moment, then looked away. "It's where ... Gerard ..."

"It's where you killed Gerard Bonnay."

She nodded.

"You're talking about doing the same thing to someone else."

"What's that supposed to mean?" she asked, her voice rising again.

"Lizzy, I just want you to think about what you're planning to do. I'm asking you these questions because I want you to be absolutely sure about the path you're choosing."

"I don't know what else to do," she said, her voice trembling, "at least about George Millard. Laying low doesn't work. Uncle Owen tried to talk to his boss about me turning myself in to the university, and that backfired. Uncle Owen wasn't even safe from them in the hospital, and he's not the only one who's gotten involved in all this. You. Andy. Ruby. You're probably all in danger because of me."

"Owen's brother Andy?"

Lizzy sighed. "Yes. He helped get me away from Gerard and Louise."

"Who's Ruby?"

"The other person who helped. I shouldn't have said anything."

Philip was silent.

"Don't you think I'm doing the right thing?" she asked.

"I think you're doing the only thing that's going to get you out of this mess, and the only thing that's going to stop these people from going after your friends and family. On top of that, I think you're right to want to even the score."

She nodded, not looking at him.

He waited, but when he got no further response, he slapped his thighs and stood up. "We need to get prepared.

You have your own built-in weapon, but I don't have that advantage. I'm going to remedy that situation."

Lizzy stood and reached for her coat.

"You're staying here," said Philip.

"Why?" asked Lizzy. "Don't you think it's better if we stay together? Plus, I'm curious to see a gun store."

"I'm not going to a gun store."

"Where are you going?"

"Nowhere you need to know about."

"You're getting an illegal gun?" she asked, shocked.

"I'm a convicted felon," said Philip. "Illegal is my only option."

IT WAS dusk by the time he returned, having texted Lizzy every fifteen minutes per her instructions: *Still okay ... Still okay.*

"How did it go?" she asked.

"Other than being called Tonto, it went fine," he said peevishly.

He upended a large plastic shopping bag over the bed.

"What's all that?" asked Lizzy, moving to the bed and sorting through it.

"The spoils from the more legit part of my shopping trip. Some dark clothes for you—because I don't want to case Mortensen's house with you dressed in that neon jacket." He handed her a black jacket. "Plus, this one has a lot of pockets, which is handy—better than carrying a knapsack."

"What am I going to be carrying?"

He handed her two other items from the pile. "Duct tape and zip ties."

"We're going to be tying people up?" she asked, alarmed.

"Best to be prepared for any eventuality." He picked up a small cardboard box. "Plus, a knife for me."

Lizzy blanched. "Are you going to ... you know, like you did before?"

Philip opened the box and tipped out a small pocket knife. "It's not really that kind of knife."

Lizzy looked over the items on the bed. "Seems like you've done this before."

"I led a dissolute youth."

"Where's the gun?"

He sat at the desk and from another bag pulled a cloth-wrapped item and a small black, red, and white box labeled *American Eagle*. He removed the cloth and set the gun on the desk.

"What is it?" asked Lizzy.

"Glock 19. The Honda Civic of handguns."

He popped the magazine out of the grip and began loading bullets. "Let's review where we stand. There are three threats out there. There's this George Millard guy, who sounds like he's the one who killed your dad, tried to kill you with the rattlesnakes, and maybe gave Owen something that caused the heart attack. There's Louise Mortensen, who sounds like she started the whole business with her husband. And there's the guy in the video who likely killed the attorney general. And," he added, "who I think showed up at my office for a session."

Lizzy's voice spiked again. "The guy from the video came to your office?"

"I think so. He said his name was Mitch Foot."

"What did he talk about?"

"I think he talked about you."

Lizzy gave a start. "Me?"

"I think so. He said he was looking for his girlfriend. He

started describing someone who sounded like you. I was suspicious at first, but then the story changed to describe someone obviously not like you, and I thought I was just over-reacting. Now I think he could have been seeing if he could get a reaction out of me, and then changed his story to throw me off once he had assessed my reaction." He snapped the magazine in and out of the grip, then set it aside and sighted down the gun's barrel. "It's like a game of cat and mouse. Actually," he amended, "it's like a game of chess: the queen, the knight, and the pawn."

"Who's the knight and who's the pawn?" asked Lizzy.

"I guess we'll find out."

Lizzy gazed out the window for a full minute, then turned back to Philip. "I think Millard is the knight. Maybe once we take care of him, Louise and Mitch will go away."

"That's not how the game works. The queen doesn't retire from the board because one lesser piece has been captured."

Lizzy waved her hand impatiently. "Okay, maybe it doesn't work out exactly like a chess game. But I think Mitch is a pawn of both of them. Louise might even be forcing him to do her dirty work."

"Didn't look like it on the video."

"You can't tell what's going on in that video," she said angrily. "The camera was bumping around, you could only see the guy with her for a second. Maybe if we take care of George Millard and Louise, he'll run away."

"But he's still out there with the same power you have and, unlike you, not much compunction about using it as far as I can see. He walked up to a man he had probably never met, and squeezed his brain until he died."

"Isn't that what I'm planning on doing to George Millard?" she shot back. "Walking up to a man I never met and squeezing his brain until he dies?"

"But you've got right on your side. Looks to me like he's just got might on his."

Lizzy sat down on the bed and rested her elbows on her knees and her face in her hands. Finally she raised her head.

"I think I can kill George Millard because of what he's done to my dad and to Uncle Owen. I might even be able to kill Louise Mortensen, although for some reason that would be harder, even though I believe she's behind all this. I guess because it seemed like she was being nice to me when I was in Pocopson. But I can't kill the guy in the video. I just can't. He may be working for the bad guys now, but if he really is like me, he didn't ask to be the way he is. He really is a pawn."

"Okay. Let's start with Millard, and then reconsider our options."

She nodded, not meeting his gaze.

"You're still not sure, are you?" he asked.

"I'm sure," she said, sounding not entirely sure.

He set the gun aside. "Lizzy, look at me."

She looked up.

"Do you know why I'm here?"

"Because Uncle Owen asked you to come."

"Sure, but I could have said no."

"I know you could have—I don't want you to think I don't realize how much you're helping us—"

He waved his hand. "I'm not fishing for compliments about my selflessness. But I think it's important for you to understand why I'm here."

She hesitated. "Okay."

"I have two reasons for wanting to help you. One is that I don't like the idea of you turning yourself in to the authorities. I don't want to see you in prison any more than I wanted to be there myself."

"But it wouldn't be prison." She hesitated. "Would it?"

"It might not be a jail, but it would be a prison. And your wardens wouldn't be some anonymous guys who don't know you from Adam. They would be people who would want something from you, and could make your life pretty unpleasant if you didn't give it to them." He paused, then continued. "You're a different person from the person I was when I went to prison, even though you're not much younger than I was. You're optimistic where I was pessimistic. You're big-hearted where I was cold-hearted. But I think you would suffer in that kind of world just as much as I did. When Owen told me you were thinking of turning yourself in to the authorities ... well, I didn't want to see that happen, especially because for you it would be a life sentence. And you might not be lucky enough to find someone to save you from despair like I did."

She gripped her fingers together in her lap.

"Another reason I'm helping you is that I don't like seeing bullies take advantage of good people—and you're good people. Owen's good people, too. Neither of you deserves this, and your parents didn't deserve what happened to them either."

She looked down at her hands.

He leaned forward. "Lizzy, I would have done anything to have your ability when I ran into that rancher's son doing what he was doing. You remember what I said about Snakes and Ladders?"

She nodded.

"I killed him, and as far as I'm concerned, that was a ladder and not a snake—a virtue and not a vice. I have never for a minute regretted what I did to him. I regretted going to jail— and although that ended up having a silver lining, I would have much preferred to have found my mentor somewhere other than in prison. If I could have squeezed that bastard and walked away with no one knowing that I had done it—well, I would have done it and never looked back."

Lizzy looked at Philip, her eyes wide.

Philip sat back. "Unfortunately, I don't have your ability." He smiled tightly. "Or maybe I should say 'fortunately,' because who knows what trouble I might get into if I did." His smile faded. "But I have a weapon that's just as effective"—he raised the Glock—"and I don't have any compunction about using it on a bastard like George Millard."

58

I t was the evening of the day Millard had injected Owen McNally, and against all odds the man had survived. Louise was at her computer, evidently trying to get information on McNally's condition, and probably assessing how the dose of potassium chloride hadn't killed him. To say that Louise Mortensen was displeased was to put it mildly. At least she had the grace not to try to pin that screw up on Millard.

The unexpected complication of McNally's survival and the uncertainty about what Ballard and her other allies might be up to had put everyone in the Pocopson house on edge, and Louise was insistent that Millard complete the scanning of her research documentation and the destruction of the paper copies quickly.

His work at the scanner had been complicated over the last few days by the arrival of workmen installing new window coverings throughout the first floor of the house. They had removed the blinds and valances and light silk curtains that had hung at the windows and replaced them with heavy floor-to-ceiling drapes. Even the small window in the alcove off

Louise's study, where he was doing the scanning, had been covered.

"I'm not interested in having people be able to wander by the house and look in," Louise snapped when he asked her about it.

At first it had seemed like overkill to Millard, but he had to admit that the new curtains would disappoint any prying eyes. He circled the house the night after the installation started and, in the rooms with the new drapes, it was impossible to tell even whether or not a light was on, much less what activity that light might be illuminating. The material was unusually heavy, with a strange, almost oily feel. Maybe some new form of blackout material.

Millard straightened from the scanner, twisted to ease the kink in his back, and looked to his right at his output for the day: two copier paper boxes worth. At the end of the day he'd give Mortensen a thumb drive with that day's scans on it, then in the morning would shred the scanned papers and take the remains out to an old oil drum at the back of the property and burn them. He had already processed at least a dozen boxes. He looked to his left at the papers still to be scanned: five boxes remained. He should have gotten a higher end machine, and then maybe he wouldn't have had to spend quite so much time playing secretary.

He heard the faint sound of a knock coming from Louise's study, and then Pieda's voice.

"Louise, I need to go out for a little while."

"I don't think it's a good idea for you to be going out," she replied. "It's best that we all stay in the house until we're sure everything is under control."

"It's not like I'm going to a party," said Mitchell irritably. "I got a call from my aunt. I need to run out to her house in Jenkintown and help her with something. I'll be back by midnight."

Millard stepped out of the alcove and leaned against the wall, enjoying the look of annoyed surprise from Pieda.

"George," said Louise, "Mitchell was just saying he needs to go out, but I think it's best if we all stay here, especially since we don't know where Ballard is."

"Seems wise," he said.

Mitchell's color rose. "My aunt needs me."

"What does she need you for?" asked Louise.

Mitchell stuffed his hands into his pockets. "Her ex-boyfriend showed up. He moved a bunch of his stuff into her house when they were dating, then left most of it there when they broke up, but he comes back every now and then to get something. She's making him wait outside until I get there."

"To protect her? Seems like something better suited to George, although I can't really spare George at the moment."

Mitchell bristled. "I can take care of this myself."

Louise looked speculatively at him. "Why does your aunt need you at the house while her former boyfriend is there?" she asked again.

"Because," said Mitchell, "I can tell her whether he's really there for the reason he's claiming."

"Ah," said Louise. "I understand." She gazed at Pieda a moment longer, then stood from the desk, crossed to the small table where the liquor was kept, and poured herself a glass of sherry. She turned back to the room.

So, your aunt knows about your ability to read minds?"

"Yes. My mother—her sister—told her."

"Who else knows?"

"No one."

"No one?"

"No one knows for sure. I used it to do tricks when I was little, until my mother told me to stop."

Louise sighed. "I suppose you can't very well ignore a request for help from a family member."

Pieda was silent.

She nodded as if he had said something. "All right. But please keep an eye out for Ballard. Or Owen McNally's brother." She sighed again. "I wish George could go with you."

"I don't need George to babysit me," he blurted.

"No, of course not," Louise said irritably. She put her glass down on the table. "I'll give you a dose of the steroid compound to take with you just in case you run into someone. Do you think you could inject yourself if the need arose?"

"Sure. If I had to," said Mitchell sulkily.

"You might as well have it with you," she said. "It can't hurt."

Millard could tell from Pieda's expression that he knew that it would, in fact, hurt, but Pieda kept his mouth shut.

59

Lizzy and Philip left for Pocopson after dark, wanting the cover of night in case they passed Louise Mortensen, George Millard, or even the mysterious Mitch Foot on the roads of southern Chester County.

The previous year, Lizzy had spent nine days as the involuntary guest of Louise and Gerard Bonnay, until Owen devised a ploy to land her in the emergency room, from which he, Andy, and Ruby DiMano had spirited her away. Lizzy's trips to and from Pocopson had been made under less than ideal circumstances, but she felt sure that she would recognize the lamp-topped stone pillars and decorative metal gate that guarded the entrance, and Pocopson wasn't such a big area.

As they drove, Lizzy called Andy for an update on Owen. She put him on speaker.

"He's not much better," said Andy, "but also not worse, which is probably the best we can hope for at this point."

"Does your mom know what happened?" asked Lizzy.

They heard Andy's sigh across the connection. "We tried to explain to her. At first she was confused, then she totally went off the deep end—screaming and crying. We—" His voice broke and he cleared his throat. "We had to give her a sedative."

Lizzy dropped her head, then said, "I'm so sorry, Andy."

"Not your fault, kiddo."

"Was there any security footage to look at?" Philip asked.

"Yes, they pulled some from a camera covering the hallway of the floor Owen was on. There are two guys who are dressed like orderlies, but the hospital can't identify them as employees. One looks like your description of George Millard, and the other one could be the guy from the Russell Brashear news conference video."

Lizzy felt Philip glance over at her. "Good information to have," he said.

Andy continued. "The cart with the breakfast trays had just showed up, and the video shows the one we can assume is Millard doing something to one of them. With the angle of the camera, you can't see what he's doing, but the tray would have included a foil-covered cup of orange juice and there wasn't one on Owen's tray when we got there. Our guess is that Millard injected something through the foil—the hole would have been tiny, and easy to miss—and then took it with him when he left."

"Jesus," said Philip.

"So where are you guys?" asked Andy. "Or aren't you allowed to say?"

"Just taking a drive," said Lizzy. "I'll check back again with you soon."

They found the drive to the house a few minutes later, then located a seemingly little-used road that ran along what appeared to be the back of the property. Philip parked the car on the shoulder.

"So are we just scouting tonight?" asked Lizzy.

"Probably. I'm usually not one to rush into things, but on the other hand, we have them off-balance now—I've got to believe they didn't expect Owen to survive, they don't know where you are, and unless they had someone in Sedona trailing me ever since you left, which seems unlikely, they probably don't know I'm here."

"What happened to the tracker on your pickup?"

He laughed. "Safely affixed to Eddie's truck."

She smiled.

"For tonight, let's just try to find out if they're all staying in the house. It will be convenient if we end up locating them all together, although it would be more challenging to deal with them all at once. Also, if Millard and Foot are holed up with Mortensen, it suggests that they're hunkering down, that they expect something to happen. We'll get the lay of the land and then decide on next steps."

They got out of the car, checked their bulging jacket pockets for their supplies, and started up the small hill in the direction of the house. The moon was almost full, and with the branches still bare of leaves, it was easy to make their way across the wooded hill. The March evening was cool but not frigid. They topped the rise and the house came into view. Lights bordered the driveway, and a sconce burned cheerfully near the back door, but except for a dim glow coming from what looked like a mud room beyond the back door, the house itself was completely dark.

"Is that it?" asked Philip.

"I only ever saw it from the front, but I think so." She scanned the grounds around the house. "Yes, this is it. I recognize things I could see from the window of the bedroom I stayed in."

"Okay, let's see if we can get a little closer."

Lizzy nodded.

Philip ran, bent low, from the cover of one tree or bush to another, headed for an outbuilding near the house.

Lizzy ran after him.

60

I f Millard never saw another piece of paper, it would be too soon. He dropped one more box on the "done" pile, then stepped out of the alcove. Louise was still at her desk.

"I'm making coffee—want any?" he asked.

"No. Thank you. I'm hoping to turn in soon."

Millard went to the kitchen. While he waited for the coffee to brew, he washed, dried, and put away the plate, glass, and utensils he had used for his dinner. Louise had given Juana a week off with pay when Mitchell reported that she was getting flustered by, and curious about, the unaccustomed activity—the installation of the drapes, the scanning, shredding, and burning of the papers—as well as by the general sense of stress among the house's other occupants. Just as well—Juana made a mean espresso, but she didn't brew the regular coffee as strong as he liked.

As the last drops of coffee drained into the carafe, the motion sensor alarm in the pantry chimed.

Millard filled his coffee cup, then went to investigate. He scanned the bank of monitors arrayed on the shelves on one side of the pantry, expecting to see the deer that had tripped the alarm every night for the past week.

Instead he saw two forms emerge from behind a carefully groomed yew bush, scuttle across the yard, and disappear behind one of the outbuildings. The images weren't distinct, but based on the size of the people and the way they moved, he was fairly certain who was prowling the grounds of Louise Mortensen's home: Elizabeth Ballard and Philip Castillo.

He put his coffee cup down, pulled out his phone, and tapped out a text.

We have company.

A minute later, Louise stood next to Millard in the pantry.

"Where are they?" she asked.

Millard pointed to one of the monitors. "Behind the detached garage."

"What in the world are they doing?" she asked, her voice tight.

"Just surveilling the place at the moment," said Millard, "but I'm guessing they have more in mind than just keeping an eye on us."

"Damn. Why did this have to happen when Mitchell was out?"

"Just our lucky day, I guess."

She crossed her arms and stared at the monitor. "With the attorney general's office reopening the investigation, we can't risk Ballard or Castillo falling into the hands of the authorities. And we certainly can't let anyone know they came here. Take care of them. I'm going to the safe room."

It gave Millard a moment of bitter amusement that Mortensen never called the room that before tonight had only served as Gerard Bonnay's wine cellar the "panic room."

"How much latitude do I have?" he asked.

"As much latitude as you need. Just make sure to clean up any mess," she snapped.

"You know," he said, "this is a bit beyond normal job duties. I assume I can rely on you to pay accordingly."

"Yes. Fine," she said, heading for the door.

"How much?"

She turned. "Pardon?"

"How much will you pay me to take care of them?"

Her eyes narrowed. "This hardly seems like the appropriate time to be negotiating a bonus."

"My feeling exactly. I'd say a hundred thousand would make it worth my while." That life of leisure at his Montana fishing cabin might be closer than he had thought.

She looked at him for a long moment, then said, "Fine." She turned and left the room, the heels of her shoes ringing on the parquet floor of the corridor.

"What if Mitchell shows up?" he called after her.

"Send him down to the safe room," she called back. "Or not. Your call."

61

It took Mitchell a little over an hour to get from Pocopson to his aunt's home in Jenkintown. He had a panicky moment when he realized that the GPS had put him on the entrance ramp to the Pennsylvania Turnpike—he had quit his job when he had joined forces with Louise and Gerard, and had been relying on funds from Louise. He had no idea how much, or little, money he had in his wallet for tolls.

That concern was put to rest when he realized that the Range Rover was equipped with an E-ZPass transponder, but then his attention switched to the gas gauge, which showed less than a quarter of a tank. He hoped he wouldn't need to call Louise to have her or, even worse, George Millard come to his rescue if the tank ran dry.

He had lived with his aunt since his mother had died when he was fifteen—his father having died six years earlier while serving a sentence for wire fraud—until he had moved into the Pocopson house. His aunt thought he was sharing an apartment with a buddy from work—although "buddy" was not a term that sprang easily to Mitchell's lips—unaware that he hadn't been to work in almost three months.

When he arrived at his aunt's house, the ex-boyfriend was stewing in the car. He couldn't know the real reason his former girlfriend always wanted her nephew around before she would let him into the house they had shared, but he evidently thought it was worth the inconvenience since the result was usually that he gained admittance. Mitchell had advised his aunt to send him away only once, when he claimed he was there to pick up a miter saw from the basement when his desired prize was in fact a small stash of commemorative coins belonging to his aunt. Those now resided in her safe deposit box.

This time the ex-boyfriend claimed—truthfully, as far as Mitchell could tell—that he was there for, of all things, a VCR. Mitchell and his aunt watched him as he carried it away, grumbling but evidently satisfied with the outcome.

As Mitchell began the drive back to Pocopson, his eye on the slowly dropping fuel level, he thought back over the last three months. He was more confused than ever about where he stood with Louise. She treated him alternately like a visitor who had overstayed his welcome and like the man who might step into her late husband's shoes. She praised him for his ability and achievements—all the more gratifying when compared to her dressing down of Millard—but also treated him like a child with a curfew, a man who couldn't be expected to protect his own family.

If he was going to make any progress toward becoming a true partner with Louise, he needed to have a serious conversation with her about their plans. Perhaps tonight was the best time to have that conversation. With Owen McNally still alive, at least as of the last intelligence Louise had been able to glean, and Elizabeth Ballard's whereabouts unknown, it was important that they present a unified front against any threats. Perhaps he could convince her that she no longer needed

George Millard's strong-arm services. Perhaps he could pave
the way for that conversation with a special bottle of wine
from Gerard's cellar.

When he reached the house, he pulled off the road and
onto the drive, hitting a button on the Rover's visor to open
and close the metal gates at the entrance, then drove to the
detached garage behind the house where the Rover was kept.
Leaving the engine running and the lights on, he stepped out
to open the garage door. He unlatched the padlock that
secured the big barn-style doors and, as they rumbled open, a
burst of light exploded behind his eyes, and the world went
black.

62

"There's a car coming," said Philip.

Lizzy scrambled to the corner of the building next to Philip and peered around. A Range Rover had just turned the corner of the house, the line of lights bordering the drive casting a glow into the vehicle's interior.

"That could be the guy from the video," whispered Lizzy.

"It could definitely be the guy who came to my office," Philip whispered back.

They jumped back behind the corner of the garage as the vehicle's headlights swept past their hiding place.

"Now what?" asked Lizzy.

"Well, he's not top on our hit list, right?" said Philip.

Lizzy winced.

"He's not who we're here for," he amended. "We just need to get him out of the way. I'll take care of him."

"How?"

Philip pulled out the Glock. They heard the sounds of the car door opening, and steps on the gravel just a dozen feet away.

Lizzy pointed to the gun and waved her hands in negation,

but relaxed when Philip turned the weapon so he was holding the barrel. He put his finger to his lips and she nodded. He stepped around the corner of the garage.

Lizzy heard the rumble of the door sliding open, then the cringe-inducing sound of the gun handle hitting bone and the thump of a body hitting the ground.

She peeked around the corner and in the car's headlights saw Philip standing over a crumpled shape. He slipped the gun into the waistband of his jeans, then hoisted the man's shoulders up and began to drag him away from the pool of light. Lizzy darted out and grabbed the man's feet. They hustled him behind the detached garage and laid him on the ground.

"One down," she whispered.

"Fasten his ankles and wrists with the ties and put tape over his mouth."

Lizzy pulled the items from her jacket pockets and bent to her task as Philip looked around the edge of the garage.

"Do you think anybody saw anything?" asked Lizzy.

He turned back to her. "Nothing to indicate anybody's home—still all dark. But if there is someone in the house, leaving the car running and its lights on for more than another minute or two is definitely going to attract their attention. I'm going to pull the car into the garage."

"What if someone's looking?"

"I'm about the same height as he is, and we both have dark hair."

"Yours is a lot longer, though."

He shrugged. "This far from the house, if I stay out of the headlights, I think I can pass a casual glance. If Mortensen or Millard sees someone they think is this guy pulling the car into the garage, it will probably take them a while to wonder why he hasn't come in the house, and we can take off if someone comes out to check on him."

Lizzy nodded and returned to her task. She heard the soft thunk of the vehicle's door closing, then the crunch of tires on gravel.

In a moment, Philip was back. "I left the garage door open," he said. "If they saw the car arrive and look out, maybe they'll think he's just sitting in the car waiting for a song on the radio to finish." He squatted down next to Lizzy. "Why don't you watch the house and I'll search his pockets."

Lizzy nodded and took up the observation post at the corner of the building.

Philip patted the man's pockets and pulled out a wallet. He flipped it open and cupped his hand around a penlight he pulled from his pocket, then read, "Mitchell Robert Pieda of Jenkintown, Pennsylvania." He flipped the wallet closed. "Also known as Mitch Foot." He rolled his eyes. "Cute." He did a quick calculation against the birth date. "Twenty-three years old." He slipped the wallet into his jacket pocket, and continued patting down Mitchell. After a moment, he said, "Interesting."

Lizzy turned toward him. He was holding a small oblong object, like a pencil case.

"What?" she asked.

"A syringe and vial. Maybe he's diabetic?"

Philip started to slip it into his own pocket, but Lizzy said, "If it's medicine, maybe it should stay with him."

He sighed and replaced the items in Mitchell's jacket pocket. He moved Mitchell's arms so that they were resting on his hips, wrists together, then tightened the ties around his wrists and ankles. "Let's roll him face down. It'll be hard for him to move if he's lying on his arms. Plus, if he starts to regain consciousness, I can sneak up on him and give him another rap on the head before he knows what's going on. Zip ties aren't going to protect us from the squeeze."

They rolled Mitchell down a slight depression near the garage, into the darker shadows next to the foundation.

"Maybe we can hand him over to the government," whispered Lizzy.

"Maybe. Let's keep our options open."

Lizzy peered into a garage window above where Pieda lay. "I wonder if there's something in there we can cover him up with ..."

"Being chilly is going to be the least of his problems," replied Philip.

63

On the monitors, Millard watched Castillo and Ballard carry Pieda behind the garage. He couldn't tell how hard Castillo had hit Pieda—he hadn't looked like he had held back. If Pieda wasn't dead, and if he got away from Castillo and Ballard, Millard would decide what to do with him then. In the meantime, he'd figure Pieda had been sidelined.

He clicked on an intercom that connected the pantry with the safe room.

"They got Pieda."

"I saw." The safe room had its own set of monitors. The tinniness of the speaker's sound didn't mask the tightness in her voice.

"Good idea with those new drapes," he said. "I doubt they can tell whether anyone's in the house or not."

"Yes, that is one of their advantages," she replied. "What do you think their plan is? Do you think they'll come in together or separately? And if separately, in what order?"

"That probably depends on how chivalrous, and how persuasive, Castillo is. I'm guessing he isn't the type to let

Ballard lead the charge, or maybe even come into the house at all."

"Or Ballard could convince him that she has a weapon much more powerful than the gun he used to club down Mitchell."

Did he hear a hint of regret in her voice? Millard gave it a brief moment of consideration, then decided it was only a trick of the speaker.

"Unless they get a lot more stealthy than they have been up until now," he said, "I'll see them when they come out from behind the garage."

"If you take care of them in the house, you'll have to keep it clean in case someone from the attorney general's office feels the need to come here."

"I'll get him somewhere the AG won't be likely to visit."

"You have a plan?"

"Oh, yeah," said Millard. "I have a plan."

64

P hilip pulled out the keyring he had taken from the car and sorted through the keys as Lizzy kept watch on the house. "One for the Rover, one likely for the padlock on the garage door, and two door keys." He looked toward the house. "One must be for the door to the garage and one must be for the house. Probably to the back door, since that's closest to the detached garage."

"What now?" asked Lizzy.

"No movement from the house?"

"I would have said," she replied, offended.

Philip sat back on his haunches. "I don't think we can pass up the opportunity that having a house key presents. I'll go in and check things out. We don't want to assume that they don't know we're here—a place like this probably has a pretty sophisticated security system—but we do have the advantage of having one of them out of commission, at least for the moment. Now we need to find out if anyone's home."

"I should go," she said.

"It's better if you stay with Pieda. If he starts to regain

consciousness, you giving him a little squeeze is likely to do less damage than me giving him another rap on the head."

"I don't know if I can give him just a little squeeze."

"I don't know if I can give him just a little rap on the head."

He could sense her wavering, then she shook her head. "No, I don't want you doing my dirty work."

"Lizzy," he said, trying to keep his voice light, "anyone who is as concerned as you are that a man who killed a government official in cold blood might get chilly is unlikely to be successful as a murderous vigilante."

She looked toward the house, then down at her hands. "I can do it."

He leaned toward her. "Lizzy, you might be able to do it someday, but not tonight. I can see it in your eyes, I can hear it in your voice. The easiest way to send this whole thing to hell in a handbasket is for you to go in there thinking you're ready to give George Millard the squeeze and find out you're not. That's not only going to be bad—maybe fatal—for you, but it's going to put me in a difficult position."

In the light of the nearly full moon, he could see tears glistening in her eyes.

"You don't need to be upset about it," he said, "but you do need to be realistic about it. I have no doubt Millard is going to have a gun, and one second of indecision on your part means that our plan falls apart."

"But it's my problem to take care of."

They were both silent for a half a minute, looking across the lawn to the equally silent house.

Finally, Philip drew a deep breath. "Lizzy, I have a favor to ask you, when this is all done."

"What's that?"

"I want you to take care of the man who killed Oscar."

After a beat she asked, "What do you mean?"

He leaned toward her. "I told you I would have been happy to have had your ability to use on the rancher's son, but I would have killed—and I mean that quite literally—to have had it and been standing next to Oscar in that cafeteria line when those bastards came to make an example of him."

Lizzy watched him, her eyes wide.

"Oscar isn't the only man Tobe Hanrick has killed in prison—or out of it, for that matter," he continued. "His gang protects him, and sometimes they do the dirty work for him, so the authorities have never been able to pin anything on him. He deserves the death penalty, and the state isn't going to oblige. I'd do it myself and deal with the consequences, but I don't have any way of getting to him. I'm asking you to kill him."

"How would I get to him?" she asked, horrified.

"You could visit him in prison."

"I don't even know him."

"He's not likely to turn down a visit from a pretty young lady. And there would be a glass partition between you— you'd never have to physically interact with him."

She stared at him. "But ... I don't even know him," she repeated.

"But you know what he's done. If you trust me, that is."

"Yes, I trust you, but ..."

He watched her, his eyes steady on hers, but she was silent.

"I think if I told you more about the kind of person he is, you would be convinced that he doesn't deserve to live. I'll tell you later, but now is not the time."

She wrapped her arms around herself as if she were suddenly cold. "I don't know if I could do it."

He nodded. "I can understand that. So I won't ask you to promise me you'll do it. But I will ask you to promise me you'll think about it. I've been trying to come up with a way to do it myself and I haven't been able to. But I know exactly how to take care of George Millard. If you'll promise me just to think about doing that for me, then I'm happy to take care of George Millard for you."

Her head fell forward and her shoulders slumped, as if she were trying to curl in upon herself. The seconds ticked by, Philip straining his ears for any sound from the house—a door opening, footsteps on the driveway. Finally he heard her voice, barely audible. "How did I get to this point?"

"How? Because Louise Mortensen and her husband decided that their goals were more important than your happiness and your parents' or Owen's lives."

Finally she looked up, and her eyes were dry, her mouth pressed in a thin line. "Yes," she said. "You're right."

"You'll let me go into the house?"

"Yes. And I promise I'll think about Tobe Hanrick."

65

Philip pulled out the Glock. "If I open the back door and an alarm goes off, we'll run. I'm pretty confident that we could get to the car and away before anyone could catch up with us. We will have blown our plan, but that's why there's a Plan B."

"What's Plan B?" asked Lizzy.

"TBD," he said with a grin.

"And what if the alarm doesn't go off?"

"I'll take a look around." He checked the gun's magazine. "Don't text me."

"What if it's an emergency?"

"I can't imagine a situation where the information I could get in a text would trump the distraction of having my phone buzzing away in my pocket, even if I could take the time to read it."

Lizzy described the layout of the house to Philip, although she couldn't provide much more detail than he could have guessed.

"I know I spent over a week there before Uncle Owen

rescued me," she said miserably, "but I was drugged up most of the time. I'm sorry I can't remember more."

"Don't worry," replied Philip. He checked his pocket for Pieda's keyring. "Remember," he said, "give him a squeeze if he starts to wake up."

She nodded.

He took a step toward the corner of the building, then turned back to her.

"Are you good at memorizing numbers?"

"What?"

"Can you memorize a phone number without writing it down?"

"I think so," she said, confused.

"Okay, I want you to memorize this number." He gave her the ten digits, then repeated them. "Can you say it back to me?"

She did.

"Do it again."

She repeated the number.

"If things *do* go to hell in a handbasket and you need a new identity—you know, a fake driver's license, social security card —call that number and tell them Philip Casal asked them to help you."

"Casal?"

"What was the number again?"

She said it a third time.

"Don't forget. And don't write it down."

Philip stepped to the corner of the detached garage and peered around it. He could see no change in the seemingly dormant appearance of the house. He jogged toward the back door.

He kept low to limit his profile, and kept to the shadows of trees and shrubs where possible to limit his visibility. When he got to the house, he flattened himself against the wall next to the back door, then eased himself over to look through the door's glass panes. The mudroom just inside was empty. He tried the knob—locked. He got out the keyring, unlocked the door with the first key he tried, and cracked it open.

No alarm.

He stepped into the mudroom, then into the kitchen, leading with the Glock. It was deserted. Dimmed under-cabinet lighting provided faint illumination. He could smell the aroma of freshly brewed coffee. He looked around for the coffee maker, intending to see if any warmth in the coffee or carafe indicated that it had been brewed recently, but didn't see one.

He crossed the kitchen to a short hallway that led to the dining room. Here the room was dimly lit by a display light over a large oil painting depicting a scene that could well have been the view a hundred years ago from the hill on which the house stood. But he realized why he and Lizzy had not seen any lights from outside—the windows were completely covered by heavy drapes.

He passed cautiously from room to room, each one looking ready for an *Architectural Digest* photo shoot: not a chair out of place, not a stray magazine or electric bill on a counter. And each room was illuminated by some faint light, which was screened from the outside by drapes of the same heavy material. If Mortensen and Millard were in the house and knew he and Lizzy were outside, why would they have left lights on as a convenience to an intruder?

Since he hadn't wanted to handle the gun wearing gloves, he pulled his sleeve down over his fingers to open the few closed doors. They revealed a coat closet, a powder room, stairs to a darkened basement.

He finished his circuit of the first floor back in the kitchen.

He noticed a door he had overlooked when he entered, and cracked it open. Inside was a pantry. The shelves on one side were stocked with standard pantry fare: canned food, jars of spices, spare serving pieces. The shelves on the other side held darkened monitors. No doubt the security system.

He clicked the power buttons on a few of them, but they remained dark. Perhaps Mortensen and Millard were not only not in the house at the moment, but not planning on coming back. Had they fled, sensing the authorities closing in, and shut down the security system when they left? Did they know that Pieda would be returning to the house and didn't want him to have access to the monitors? Did it indicate a rift among them?

He climbed the stairs to the second floor, testing each step for a squeak before putting his full weight on it, although this didn't strike him as the type of house that would be prone to anything as mundane as squeaky floors. Unlike the first floor, the upstairs windows weren't dressed with the heavy drapes, and here the illumination was provided by the moonlight seeping in from the uncovered windows. Other than that, the rooms upstairs were like the ones downstairs: silent and devoid of even that movement of air that suggests a human presence.

If the house was as deserted as it seemed, it would be foolish to pass up the opportunity to find more evidence of what Mortensen and Gerard Bonnay had been up to. He descended the stairs to the first floor and made his way to the room that he assumed to be Mortensen's home office. Just in case the house was not as deserted as it seemed, he locked the door behind him.

He went first to the desk, which held only a dimly glowing desk lamp and an empty wooden inbox. He tried the desk drawers. The top drawer slid open to reveal neatly arranged pens, paper clips, tape, and rubber bands. The larger side drawer was locked.

Philip noticed a doorway leading off the study and crossed to it. Behind it was a small alcove, and even this space contained a window that was covered by the heavy drapes. The light from the study provided little illumination here. He got out his penlight and clicked it on. The alcove contained a table on top of which was what looked like a computer printer, and copier paper boxes sat on the floor to the left and right of the table. Holding the penlight between his teeth and the Glock in his right hand, he pulled a sheet out of one of the boxes.

It looked like a medical record—a computer printout, but heavily annotated by hand. Phrases popped out at him: *adverse reaction ... non-viable fetus.* He put that sheet back on the pile and picked up another one: *signs of telepathic ability accompanied by slight mental retardation.* He glanced through a few more of the sheets, many containing equally chilling commentary.

He had already developed an aversion to Louise Mortensen and George Millard based on what they had done to Lizzy; this evidence of the pain they had caused so many others cemented his loathing.

If he knew for sure the house was deserted, he would have taken one of the boxes of papers with him, but a sample would have to do. He picked up the first sheet, folded it roughly, and tucked it into his inside jacket pocket, then returned to the desk in the main room.

He had hoped that the locked side drawer would be equipped with the standard flimsy hardware found on most office furniture—a mechanism intended to thwart curious family members or a nosy maid—which could be easily jimmied with his pocket knife, but the lock was substantial.

He wished lock picking had been a skill he had learned in his dissolute youth.

He decided that he wasn't particularly concerned about Mortensen or Millard knowing someone had broken into the desk—not only were they not likely to report this break-in, but he figured that one way or the other, Millard wasn't going to be around long enough for it to matter.

He briefly considered firing the Glock at the lock assembly, but didn't want to risk getting caught by a ricochet. He scanned the room for other options and spotted a possibility.

On one of the bookshelves was a display of marble spheres of various sizes. He hefted the largest one. It was about the size of a small grapefruit and had to weigh fifteen pounds. He carried it back to the desk and crouched in front of the drawer, shining the penlight on the lock. He was pleased to see that although the lock itself was substantial, it had been retrofitted into wood that by his estimation was at least a hundred years old. He didn't fancy bashing his way through the drawer front itself, but he might not have to.

He returned to the display and picked up one of the smaller marble spheres, this one about the size of a baseball —big enough to keep his hand out of harm's way, but small enough to concentrate the force of a blow on an area the size of the lock. Returning to the desk, he put down the Glock, positioned the smaller sphere over the lock, drew back the larger sphere, and, hoping he didn't misjudge his trajectory, swung the larger sphere into it. With a dull thunk that barely reflected the tremendous jolt that traveled up his arm, he felt the lock give a fraction of an inch. After listening for a full minute for any attention that his activity might have triggered, he drew back the larger sphere again and brought it down on the smaller one. The wood around the lock splintered as the lock was driven into the drawer. After another minute of listening, he brought the larger sphere down for a third time.

The lock had now sunk far enough into the drawer front that the smaller sphere no longer concentrated the force of the blow on the lock mechanism. Philip went back to the book-shelf and retrieved the smallest sphere, this one no bigger than a cherry tomato. Back at the desk, he used the tape from the top drawer to secure the sphere over the lock. He swung the larger sphere one more time. The wood gave a last splin-tering crack and the drawer rolled open as the wood holding the interior mechanism gave way.

The drawer held a rack from which files hung. Philip pulled out one labeled *Gerard - Cards* and flipped it open. Inside the folder was a fat stack of greeting cards in envelopes, the flaps neatly slit open. He flipped through them quickly. On each envelope was written *For Louise* in what looked like a masculine hand, and in the upper right corner, in a different hand, a date. The earliest was dated two dozen years before. He returned the file to the drawer.

Behind it were other *Gerard* folders: *Gerard - Media*, *Gerard - Awards & Recognition*. It looked like the woman who was willing to cause a child to be born with slight mental retarda-tion—or worse—in pursuit of her scientific goals had a senti-mental streak when it came to her husband.

The next file was labeled *Alvarez* and contained employ-ment documents. Evidently Mortensen's housekeeper.

He glanced through several more files—Louise's will, her birth certificate, the deed to the house—then came to several files labeled only with numbers.

648-854-777. He flipped the file open. It was a medical record for Antonia Pieda and Antonia's baby, Mitchell Robert. The file was large, but stapled to the front of the folder was a handwritten page—evidently a summary of the contents of the file. He pulled off the summary sheet, folded it, and tucked it into his inside jacket pocket.

There were several other files in the drawer with numbered labels. The next two contained names he didn't recognize, but the third one—*185-701-411*—did. Vivantem patient Charlotte Ballard and her baby, Elizabeth Marie. He pulled off the summary sheet and put it with the others in his inside pocket and zipped the pocket shut.

The last file in the drawer was labeled *Millard*. It held several sheets of yellow legal-sized paper containing columns of handwritten notes: dates followed by two-letter codes and locations: *KK Palo Alto, AC Baltimore*. The first date was fifteen years earlier. Some of the entries were in the same handwriting as the *For Louise* inscriptions on the greeting cards—Gerard Bonnay's, he assumed—and some in the same handwriting as the dates on the envelopes—probably Mortensen's. Philip scanned the list. A final column on each line contained what looked like a dollar amount. Assuming it indicated payments made by Bonnay and Mortensen to George Millard, the man was likely a millionaire with a tax-free income.

An entry on the last sheet read *12/5 PB Philadelphia* in Louise Mortensen's hand. The last entry read *3/6 PC Sedona*. His jaw tightened. He glanced at the last column—George Millard had made more for his few days in Sedona harassing Philip than Philip made in a month. He wondered ruefully if Millard had paid Lorna out of that money, or if Louise had reimbursed him for that expense.

As he scanned the other entries on the sheet, he became aware that something had changed in the house. He grabbed the gun from the desk and brought it up. There was a faint sound that hadn't been there before.

He stuffed the legal sheet into his outside jacket pocket, then walked carefully to the closed door to the hallway and pressed his ear against it. After a few moments, the hum resolved itself into voices—one male and one female, if he had to guess—coming from within the house but at a distance.

He unlocked the door, opened it slowly, and peered into the hallway. The sound of the voices came to him slightly more clearly, but not clearly enough for him to hear what they were saying. He stepped into the hallway and turned his head back and forth to identify the direction from which the voices were coming. Toward the back of the house. He crept down the hallway.

The door to the basement stood ajar. Philip was certain it had been closed when he made his pass through the first floor, and that he had reclosed it after checking it. He stepped to the side of the door and listened. The voices were clearly coming from the lower level—a male voice, the tone pitched up in a question, the female voice responding, then the man laughing politely.

Was it possible that Mortensen and Millard were in the basement, and were unaware that he was in the house? It was hard to imagine that they could have missed the noise from Louise's office, but if they wanted to take him by surprise, wouldn't they have been careful enough to close the basement door behind them?

He eased the door open and stepped into the stairwell, then closed it silently behind him so he wouldn't be backlit by the dim light from the hallway. A light in the basement was on —he had no doubt it had been dark when he had checked earlier. He descended step by careful step, straining to hear what the voices were saying.

The male voice: "... incredible ..."

The female voice spoke what sounded like an acknowlededgement of a compliment.

Philip reached the bottom of the steps. A carpeted hallway led away from the stairs and a dim light spilled from the second doorway, fading and brightening slightly as if something or someone was moving between the door and the light source.

The voices became clearer as he neared the door, the Glock drawn.

"... hard to overstate the impact ..." said the man.

He stood next to the door, his back to the wall. If it really was Mortensen and Millard, he'd shoot Millard first, then hold Mortensen at gunpoint unless she had a weapon. What he did after that would depend on how cooperative she was.

If it wasn't Mortensen and Millard, there was a man and a woman who were in for quite a surprise.

"It must have taken great commitment—" said the male voice.

He spun into the room, the gun held in front of him.

"—to pursue your theory in the face of your colleagues' skepticism," finished the man, who was seated at the front of the room, a clipboard on his lap.

"Ah, if only you knew," replied Louise Mortensen.

66

Lizzy's senses were strained to harp-string tautness, her eyes searching for any sign of light or movement from the house, her ears tuned to any sound from Mitchell Pieda. She cupped her hand around her phone and hit the power button to display the time: nine eighteen. Philip had been inside for almost fifteen minutes. She wished she had thought to ask him how long he expected to be in the house. She itched to send him a text and longed for him to send one to her: *Still okay.*

Another minute ticked by, and she could no longer contain her impatience, or her concern. She stepped out from behind the detached garage and trotted toward the house.

Lizzy stepped cautiously through the door by which Philip had entered the house and tiptoed across the mudroom and into the kitchen. When Louise Mortensen and Gerard Bonnay had held her hostage in the house the previous year, she had never been in the kitchen—meals had always been brought to her in the bedroom where she had spent most of the time in a drugged stupor.

There was a closed door across the kitchen from the

mudroom—she had a vague idea that it might lead to the basement. She tiptoed across the kitchen and pressed her ear against the door. She didn't hear anything, but she was also beginning to doubt her memory that it led to the basement. Perhaps it was just a closet, which would be a handy place to hide while she decided what to do next.

She stood to one side of the door, trying to keep an eye on both of the hallway entrances that led off the kitchen, and opened the door slowly. The room beyond was dark, lit only by the dim light from the kitchen. She stepped in and realized that it was a pantry, food on one side and rows of computer monitors on the other. She pressed the power button on one of the monitors with no effect. She tried several more with the same result.

Without thinking, she patted the wall to the side of the door and flipped on the pantry's light switch to see what was wrong, then, her heart thundering at the stupidity of her mistake, quickly flipped it off, but not before she had noticed that the monitors' power cords had been pulled out of the power strip attached to the back of the shelf.

She stood in the darkness, straining her ears for any sound that would indicate that she had given away her location, but could hear nothing. As her heartbeat slowed and her night vision slowly returned, she realized that she might have an easier and safer way of finding out where Philip was than sneaking from room to room.

Mainly by touch, she plugged the monitors back into the power strip. The first ones showed not the interior views she had expected, but exterior views. One, she noticed with a stomach-churning realization, displayed the detached garage behind which she and Philip had "hidden," and behind which Mitchell Pieda's trussed body lay.

Her fear mounting, she began plugging in and powering

up the monitors on the bottom shelf. One by one, the rooms of the first floor of the house appeared on the screens—dining room, living room, the library that she recognized as the site of her altercation with Anton Rossi. Each was illuminated by some dim light source; each was deserted.

She clicked on the last monitor, which displayed a room unfamiliar to her, but it was not the room itself that made her breath catch, but the view of Philip standing at a desk, the Glock in one hand, a sheet of paper in the other. As she watched, his already tense posture changed to an even higher level of alert. She had heard it, too—a sound coming from somewhere within the house. He walked to a door, listened, and then stepped through.

She frantically scanned the other monitors and picked him up as he stepped into a hallway. She cast her mind back through her limited mental map of the house. The hallway down which Philip was walking must be the main hallway through the center of the house. He was only a few dozen feet from her.

She stepped out of the pantry and hurried as quickly as stealth would allow to the doorway from the kitchen to the hallway. She reached it just in time to see a door—*that* must be the door to the basement—close. The hallway was deserted again.

Should she follow him? Unless she could alert him to her presence in the house, he might shoot her as she came through the door—he would be expecting her to be waiting for him outside. With Philip's instruction not to text him, she couldn't think of a way to let him know she was in the house without also alerting anyone else who might be there. She hurried back to the pantry.

She scanned the monitors again and spotted Philip on the lower level. The plushly carpeted hallway gave access to several doors, one of which—the door to the movie room, she was sure—was open. The doorway was lit by a flickering light. Philip made his way slowly down the hall toward the door, his back pressed to the wall.

Her heart pounding, she looked for the monitor showing the movie room, but couldn't find it. In desperation, she turned on the light again and saw that most of the monitors had switches on them with neatly hand-lettered labels. She finally located the right one—*Theater*—and flipped the switch.

She saw a stage at the front of the room, on which two people sat: Louise Mortensen, legs crossed, fingers interlaced in her lap, and a portly man holding a clipboard. A banner reading *Vivantem: For Life* hung behind them. After a disorienting moment, she realized that it was not a stage, but a video of a stage playing on the room's huge display wall.

At that moment, Philip whirled through the open door into the movie room, sweeping the room with the Glock.

In the flickering light, Lizzy saw the open door behind Philip move and George Millard step out.

"Philip—he's behind you!" she screamed.

Philip must have heard her. She couldn't imagine that he could hear what she was saying through the thick walls of the house, but it was enough to make him turn, just as George Millard raised his gun.

Philip was only feet away from Millard, and rather than bringing his own gun up to fire, he used the momentum of his turn to swing the Glock in an arc, connecting with Millard's gun just as it leveled at his chest.

A flash burst out from the monitor.

"Philip, I'm coming!" Lizzy cried, and shot out of the pantry.

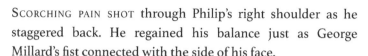

SCORCHING PAIN SHOT through Philip's right shoulder as he staggered back. He regained his balance just as George Millard's fist connected with the side of his face.

He dropped to a crouch, partially to avoid another blow, partially because his swimming head couldn't keep him upright. He was miraculously still holding the gun, but his arm hung useless at his side. He grasped his right wrist with his left hand and wrenched the gun up, sending another bolt of pain shooting through his shoulder. He pulled the trigger.

He heard a cry from Millard. The shot must have hit him, but Philip didn't fool himself that it was enough to stop him— the shot had gone too low. The bullet had probably hit him in the leg. Philip scrambled backward, behind one of the large theater chairs, readying himself for another attack. As his mind cleared, he realized the foolishness of his position—the only effect of being behind the chair was that he couldn't see what Millard was doing.

"How did you deal with the resistance you faced to your revolutionary approach to fertility treatments?" asked the portly man with the clipboard from the screen.

Philip could hear Millard swearing, his voice near the ground, and realized that he was searching for the gun that must have flown out of his hand when Philip hit him.

"One must have the courage of one's convictions when one faces opposition," replied Louise Mortensen.

Philip was the one with the gun—he couldn't afford to be on the defensive. He had to take care of Millard before Millard located his gun.

He dragged his right hand over the arm of the chair with his left and fired in the direction of Millard's voice. Philip heard the bullet ping on metal and the image on the screen disappeared, plunging the room into near darkness. Not only the sound from the video, but also Millard's swearing, fell silent.

Philip tried to push himself up and his hand squished into a sticky dampness in the carpet that he knew must be his own blood. His vision darkened, lit only by the bright white pain of his wound. He grabbed the arm of the chair and pulled himself up, right into the barrel of George Millard's gun.

67

As Lizzy ran to the door through which Philip had disappeared, she heard a second gunshot.

She wrenched the door open and ran down the steps, but tripped on the last one and went sprawling on the carpeted floor of the hallway. As she scrambled up, she heard another shot. She ran down the hall and careened around the door.

Despite her headlong flight and fall, neither man appeared to have heard her approach. George Millard might have been distracted by the spreading red stain on the thigh of his pants. Philip Castillo was no doubt distracted by the gun pointed at his face.

"No!" she screamed, and as Millard turned toward her voice, she released the coiled energy of her rage, and in the back of her mind she heard the whirring rattle of the snake as it struck her at the Needle.

Millard's gun discharged and she heard a bullet whine past her ear. Then, with an expression of aggrieved disbelief, George Millard dropped to the ground.

Lizzy ran to where Philip had collapsed and dropped to

her knees at his side. "Are you okay?" she asked, then gasped. "Oh my God!" Philip's right shoulder was dark with blood, like a gaudy epaulette. "What can I do?"

"Is Millard dead?" he rasped.

"Yes."

"You better check."

"I don't have to check," she said, her voice tight. "He's dead."

Philip hesitated, then nodded. "Okay. We've got to get out of here. I don't fancy hanging around to see if Louise Mortensen shows up."

"Me either."

"First get Millard's gun, then we'll each have one."

"I don't need the gun."

He seemed about to argue, then capitulated. "Okay. Let's go. Can you help me up?"

She got his left arm hooked around her shoulder and helped him stagger to his feet. "Where are we going?" she asked.

"Back to the car."

"Can you make it that far?"

"I sure hope so," he said through gritted teeth.

They started toward the door when the light in the hallway went out.

"What happened?" Lizzy yelped.

"Mortensen must still be around, she must have shut down the power."

"But how?" Lizzy's voice was spiraling up in panic.

"She must have shut down the main circuit breaker. Listen, I'll explain the ins and outs of electrical systems when we're out of here."

"Should I get out my phone? I have a flashlight app."

"Let's not waste the time," said Philip. "We're almost at the door, and it's a straight shot down the hallway and up the stairs."

She didn't move.

"Isn't all that electrical stuff usually in the basement?" she asked.

"Yes, Lizzy, it is. It's quite possible that Louise is down here with us. So if you sense anyone out there, make sure to give them a big squeeze."

After a slight hesitation, Lizzy said, "Okay."

At the door of the hallway, Philip stopped. "Actually, we should check the hallway first," he whispered. "Can you shine the light from your phone into the hallway?"

Lizzy propped Philip against the wall next to the door and got out her phone.

"Stay inside the room, just put your hand out," he said.

"Okay."

"Okay. Shine it toward the right. Go."

Lizzy popped the phone out the doorway, and Philip, gripping his right wrist with his left hand, looked out and then jumped back.

"Okay. Now to the left. Go."

He looked in that direction, then back to the right.

"Okay, it looks clear at the moment." He leaned back against the doorframe. "Just give me a sec."

Lizzy watched him, her eyes wide with concern. "Are you okay?"

"Yeah." He pushed himself away from the doorframe and swayed.

She caught his arm to steady him.

"Thanks. You might as well keep your phone out to light the way."

Lizzy looped Philip's left arm over her shoulders and they started down the hallway.

"I know you have to be a contortionist, but try to keep an eye out behind us," said Philip.

"Okay."

When they got to the stairs, Lizzy hoisted Philip from step to step, his breath whistling in and out in painful gasps, hers not much less labored. When they reached the top, Lizzy grasped the doorknob and tried to turn it.

"It's locked," she said, her voice jumping an octave.

"Dammit!" Philip swore through gritted teeth.

Lizzy slipped out from under his arm, almost sending him tumbling back down the steps, and began banging her shoulder against the door.

"Calm down," came Philip's voice, sharp, from the dark.

Lizzy turned toward him. "We have to get out!"

"Let's just think this through. If she locked the door, she's probably not waiting on the other side for us to eventually burst through so she can shoot us. I'm guessing it means she knows what happened to Millard, and she's trying to give herself time to get away. Let's not do anything rash."

Lizzy considered taking another run at the door, then took a deep breath. "Okay."

Philip slid down the wall until he was sitting on the top step. His face was pasty, a slick of sweat on his forehead. They were silent for a few moments, the only sound the hoarse rasp of his breath.

"Want me to try to wrap up your shoulder?" Lizzy asked, her voice unsteady.

He shook his head. "No. I'll be okay. I just need to rest for a minute. Sit down for a sec."

She sat.

"Are you okay?" he asked.

She nodded, but her lower lip trembled.

"You're not upset by what you did, are you?"

She shook her head unconvincingly.

"He would have killed you—and me too, for that matter—if you hadn't squeezed him."

She nodded again, but didn't meet his eyes.

Philip tried to move his right arm, then stopped with a grimace. "Lizzy, there's a piece of paper in my jacket pocket—can you get it out?"

She reached carefully into his pocket and pulled out a crumpled sheet of legal paper.

"Take a look at it," he said, wiping the sweat off his forehead with his good hand.

Lizzy shone the light from her phone onto the sheet. After a few seconds, her face went still. "What is this?" she asked, her voice stony.

"I found it in Louise Mortensen's desk. In a file labeled *Millard.*"

She pointed with a trembling finger to the entry *12/5 PB Philadelphia.* "That's the day my dad died."

"I know."

"PB. That's Patrick Ballard, isn't it. They killed him in Philadelphia."

"That's what I think it means." He leaned toward her. "We always thought that George Millard killed your dad," he said, his voice thready, "and that Louise Mortensen or her husband had him do it, but that paper proves it. I wanted you to see it."

"Are these all people he killed?"

"I don't think so. I think it's a list of all the jobs he did for them." He pointed to the last entry. "Does that look like someone you know?"

"PC Sedona. That's you."

Philip nodded.

Lizzy folded the paper and tucked it into her own jacket pocket.

They sat in silence for a moment, then Lizzy said, "How *are* we going to get out of here? Are we going to have to call 911?"

Philip was silent for several seconds, and Lizzy was about to repeat the question when he spoke. "We could," he said, his voice weak, "but we'd have an awful lot of questions to answer when the police showed up, including why I'm shooting up a mansion with an unregistered gun, and how yet another corpse shows up with a massive stroke."

"Yeah," said Lizzy. After a moment, she said, "Should we call someone else?"

"Like who?"

"Andy?"

"Do you want to call Andy? Get him involved?"

"Not really. But I'm worried about you. You don't look good."

He gave her a sickly grin. "Don't worry about me, I'm tougher than nails." He took a deep breath and winced. "Let's see what we can do before we call in the cavalry. Can you look around and see if there's another way out of here? If you can get out, you probably just need to flip the lock on the other side of the door to let me out."

"Okay," she said, and stood.

"Lizzy."

"Yes?"

"I doubt Mortensen is still in the house, but be careful."

She nodded and hurried down the stairs.

Lizzy carefully opened the first door and shone her phone's flashlight into the room. It was a windowless utility room and, she noticed with a jolt to her stomach, contained the electrical panel. She opened its metal door and shone the light inside. She found the switch labeled *Main*, which was set to *Off*, and flipped it to *On*. The dim light that had illuminated the hallway when she had first made her way down the stairs came on.

"Lizzy?" she heard Philip's faint call.

She ran to the bottom of the stairs. "That was me."

He nodded and let his head fall back against the wall of the stairwell.

Lizzy returned to her search.

The second door led to the movie room. She recalled it as also being windowless, and she wasn't enthusiastic about reentering the room in which George Millard's body lay to confirm that fact. She would return to the movie room if she wasn't able to find an alternative.

She opened the third door and flipped on a light inside the door. It was a storage area, neatly stacked boxes and furniture creating a central aisle, at the end of which, directly under the ceiling, was a tiny window.

Lizzy ran to the window. She expected to see a moonlit sky but saw nothing but blackness. Even as slender as she was, it was hard to imagine fitting through it. There was still one door at the end of the hall to check—maybe it would provide a more appealing exit.

She ran out of the storage room and to the last door. It didn't look like any house door Lizzy had ever seen—it looked like metal, and hung in a metal frame. There was a handle next to a keypad. She tugged at the handle with little hope. The door didn't budge.

She ran back down the hall, then pulled up at the door to the movie room. Taking a deep breath, she stepped inside. She shone the flashlight around the room, keeping the beam off the crumpled shape on the floor, but it was, as she had remembered, windowless.

She backed out of the room and ran back up the stairs to Philip. He was slumped forward.

She bent over him. "Philip?"

He roused himself and looked up. His face was gray, his eyes squinted in pain.

"Find a way out?" he asked, his voice a whisper.

"Philip, you look really bad," she said. The stain on his jacket had spread down the sleeve to his elbow. "Are you sure we shouldn't call 911?"

"No. I'll be fine." His face was wet with sweat. "Remember what I said about prison? I really can't see a way that calling 911 wouldn't end up with me back in jail. And you somewhere maybe not much better. Like a lion in a circus."

Lizzy bent closer to him, thinking she had misheard him. "What?"

"Like a lion in a circus," he said, his voice barely audible. "In the wild, she could kill a man in seconds, but in the circus they pull her teeth, they cut off her claws, they make her perform tricks. Don't let them do that to you, Lizzy."

Lizzy's face blanched. "I won't."

Philip tried to pull himself more upright, and failed. "Did you find a way out?"

"Maybe, but through this door would be better. I'm going to try again."

Lizzy braced herself on the stair and banged her shoulder into the door.

"Lizzy, it's not going to work," he said, his voice weak. "You're too light to break the door down with your shoulder. Kicking it might work if you had a place to stand, but on the stairs you don't. If you found another way out, you should try it."

"It's ... tight."

"Try it anyway," he whispered. "We're running out of time."

68

Reaching the window was not her biggest challenge. There was an old mahogany dining table directly under the window, and once she wrestled one of the table's matching chairs on top of it, she could reach the window. Opening the window was not her biggest challenge. It swung up from a hinge at the top, with no bars blocking the way or, as far as she could tell, trip wires to sound an alarm. Evidently whoever had installed the security system hadn't thought it necessary to protect this window from someone coming in from the outside. It was hard to imagine anyone but a child fitting through it—not only was the window itself small, but from what she could see, it opened into an equally small but deep window well.

She put her phone in the pocket of her jacket, grasped the edges of the window and pulled herself up, but at that point her arms were useless to pull herself further, and her feet scrabbled against the wall with no purchase. She could have piled more items on top of the table to provide a higher platform, but that wasn't the only problem. The back of the window well was only about a foot and a half from the window opening, and the well, she could now see, was several feet deep. No amount of yoga stretching would have enabled her to bend her spine backwards enough to fit through.

She extracted herself from the opening and turned around so she was facing toward the room, with her back toward the outside wall. She grasped the window frame again and pulled herself up. Her feet dangled uselessly, but now she had more leverage with her arms. She squirmed her head and upper torso through the window, then was brought up short. She felt a tug and realized that the back of her jacket must have caught on the window latch.

She lowered herself back onto the chair, took off her coat, balled it up, and tossed it up toward the top of the window well. She realized almost before it disappeared over the edge that her phone was in its pocket.

"Crap!"

She took a deep breath. There was no need to panic—Philip still had his phone.

She jumped off the table and was partway across the room before she realized that running back to Philip was going to be no help. He had enough to deal with without having to help her deal with her screw ups.

She climbed back up on the table and chair and hoisted herself up again. She tried once more to pull herself through, but again something was holding her back. She realized the back of her shirt was now caught. She worked one hand beneath her back, trying to dislodge the snag—her other arm shaking under the strain of holding her body in place—and, when that didn't work, tried to rip the fabric, but there was no way she could do it with just one hand.

Her heartbeat pounding in her ears, both from exertion and building panic, she lowered herself onto the chair and pulled off her shirt. Mentally checking that she wasn't about to throw another resource out of reach, she tossed it up to the lip of the well to join the jacket.

She pulled herself up once again, her arm muscles spasming. Inch by inch, she dragged her torso through the opening, her shoulder blades scraping along the concrete back of the window well, the metal edge of the window frame scoring her lower back. She shivered as the cold nighttime air swirled around her. Finally, she got most of her torso through the window, the weight of her hanging legs digging the frame painfully into her tailbone.

And then her forward progress stopped. The further she wormed her way into the window well, the less leverage she had to pull herself up with her arms. And there was nothing to push against with her legs. She twisted, trying to find a position that would enable her to push herself forward with at least one arm, but there wasn't room. Maybe she would have to pile more things on top of the table to provide more leverage. She took a breath, steeling herself for the pain of scraping her shoulders and spine back across the concrete and metal, and pulled against the window frame to drop back into the room.

Nothing.

Her heartbeat accelerating further, she pulled again. She realized that the window latch had caught the back of her pants. She scrabbled frantically, now being able to use both hands since she obviously wasn't in any immediate danger of falling back into the room, but she was too tightly wedged into the space to reach behind her.

Then she heard the sharp crack of an explosion coming from somewhere above her.

A gunshot?

She began to thrash, the concrete wall scraping skin from her shoulder blades, the metal frame cutting into her back.

She tried to take a deep breath—*breathe in the good energy*—but it just jammed her ribs more firmly against the edges of her prison.

But her mounting claustrophobia wasn't the only thing that fanned her panic back to life.

She could smell smoke.

The house was on fire.

69

L izzy twisted in the coffin-tight confines of the window well, trying to see into the basement storage room through the small spaces on either side of her hips. She couldn't see any light from a fire, or feel any heat on her legs, but perhaps something was smoldering. Then she wrenched her head to the side to look up, and saw the source of the smoke.

The window directly above her was emitting a flickering light and smoke was wafting out and up the side of the house.

She heard the cracking sound again, then felt a stabbing pain in her cheek. She reached up, thinking for a moment that an insect had stung her, but her hand came away wet and sticky.

When she looked up again, the amount of smoke coming from the window had doubled. Then she realized that the cracking noises were the window panes shattering in the heat of the fire.

Maybe one of the neighbors had seen the flames—maybe there was a fire truck already in the drive, maybe firemen were right now circling the house, ready to aid any victims. She took a great gulp of air, ready to scream.

Once again her ribs pressed against the window frame, and a coherent thought drifted above the churn of her panic.

She took another deep breath just as she had in yoga class —*breathe in the good energy*—and this time breathed it all out —*breathe out the bad.*

The pressure reduced infinitesimally, and she squeezed her fingers behind her and found where her pants were snagged on the latch. She took another breath, jamming her fingers painfully into the window frame, then exhaled again. She was able to twist her body just enough to free the fabric from the latch.

She breathed in again, then out, her chest contracting with the effort, and pushed against the window frame. Her body scraped up a painful inch, then jammed in place again.

Another crack sounded above her, another shower of glass shards struck her head and bare shoulders.

Breathe in the good. She took another slow, deep breath, and breathed out again, trying to empty her lungs completely. Again the grip of the frame lessened almost imperceptibly, and again she pushed. Another inch.

Three more times she breathed in and out, three more times dragged her bleeding back across the concrete. Each time, she reached up, groping for the top of the window well. She dared not look up for fear that it would be further away than she estimated and that the sight would snuff out her last remaining resolve, but she could tell from the sound, and from the flickering light now making its way down into the window well, that the fire was building. She reached up once to wipe her eyes, smearing blood and tears together.

She reached up again, and this time her fingers found the

top of the well. She scrabbled at it, unable to get a hold, then, without bothering to blow her breath out, gave one terror-fueled push against the frame. She hooked her fingers over the edge of the well and finally hauled herself onto the blessed cold of the lawn and into the welcome expansiveness of the night.

Flames lit the windows of a room directly over the window well. In fact, she could see flames in the first-floor windows of the rooms all along this side of the house. She grabbed her shirt and jacket off the ground and pulled them on over her bleeding back, then sprinted for the back door.

The fire had not reached the kitchen, but as she stepped into the hallway leading to the basement door, the waves of heat momentarily rocked her back. A Persian rug in the foyer at the end of the hall smoldered, and a flame sprang up at its edge as Lizzy watched.

Shielding her face with her arm, she made her way down the hall to the basement door and disengaged the lock with laughable ease. She swung the door open, and Philip flopped onto the parquet floor.

She crouched next to him. "Philip!" she yelled over the roar of the fire.

He didn't respond.

She tried to feel for a pulse at his neck, but could feel only the pounding of her own heartbeat in her fingers.

He was still sitting on the top step, only his upper body on the hallway floor. She grabbed his uninjured arm and pulled. She might as well have been pulling against a block of concrete. Her stomach flopping, she grabbed his injured arm as well, and pulled again. Her feet slipped and she fell back at the exact instant that an unidentifiable boom echoed from the front of the house. She tamped down a hysterical giggle.

Dropping Philip's arms, she grabbed the waistband of his pants and heaved him up onto the floor of the hallway.

She grabbed his arms again and pulled him down the hall toward the kitchen. At that moment the basement door, which until then had been shielding them from the brunt of the heat, banged back against the wall, sucked back by the draft created by the growing fire. Lizzy felt the skin on her face shrivel against the heat.

When she got to the kitchen, her breath coming in fast gasps, she slammed the door against the fire. She ran to the refrigerator and pulled open the freezer door. Inside, among tidily wrapped cuts of meat and a small container of frozen yogurt, was a large bottle of clear liquid. She grabbed the bottle, wrenched out the stopper, then ran back to Philip and emptied it over his head.

He let out a sputtering squawk. "What the hell—"

She tossed the bottle aside and was only dimly aware of it shattering on the kitchen floor.

"Philip, you have to get up."

She grabbed both his arms and pulled him into a sitting position.

"Goddamn it!" he croaked. "Watch my arm!"

"Your arm's the least of your problems," she retorted. "Get up!"

She slung his good arm over her shoulder, wincing as it pressed the cloth of her shirt into her raw back, and hauled him to his feet. "Come on—up you go!"

He staggered, then regained his balance. They passed through the mudroom, then made their unsteady way down the outside stairs. Lizzy was dimly aware of flames licking at the branches of a large maple tree next to the house. As they crossed the lawn, headed for a marble bench, Philip stumbled and almost fell, but the night air seemed to revive him, and he recovered his footing and made it to the bench. Lizzy lowered him onto it, then stood doubled over, her hands on her knees, her sides heaving.

Philip was having trouble catching his breath as well. After half a minute, he said, "What happened?"

"I think Louise set the house on fire."

"Did you call 911?" he asked, his voice barely more than a whisper.

"No." She fell onto the bench next to him. "Do you want me to call them now?"

He shook his head and Lizzy had to bend to hear his words. "No. Not yet."

"If you think you can get to the car and drive a little distance," she said, "we could call an ambulance and maybe no one would make the connection. You wouldn't even have to drive as far as the hospital, just get far enough away that people don't assume you were involved with the fire."

Philip raised his head, still panting from exertion, the light from the growing fire flickering in his eyes. "I think I can make it to the car. You sure woke me up." He licked his lips. "What did you pour on me?"

"Vodka."

He let out a weak laugh. "Vodka? Where did you get it?"

"From the freezer."

"Well, that would explain why it was so friggin' cold. Why in the world did you think of looking in the freezer for vodka?"

"Dad used to make some kind of drink for him and Uncle Owen and he kept the vodka in the freezer."

"What if there hadn't been vodka in the freezer?"

"I figured I'd find something in the fridge. Maybe orange juice," she said, a smile hovering on her lips.

"I like the vodka better," he said.

She began to smile, then her eyes, directed over his shoulder, widened in alarm.

"What?" he asked, turning to follow her gaze.

"The garage is on fire."

70

I gnoring Philip's strangled calls for her to stop, Lizzy ran for the garage. The flames had spread from the maple to the cedar shakes on its roof, and fingers of fire crept down the sides of the building.

She peeked around the corner to where she and Philip had rolled Mitchell Pieda's unconscious body.

He had regained consciousness: Lizzy could see him struggling next to the foundation. However, the slight dip in the ground made it impossible for him to roll away from the building, and the fact that he was lying on his zip-tied hands prevented him from using them to lever himself up from the ground. She watched him for a few moments longer, then called out softly.

"Mitchell."

Through the duct tape on his mouth, he made a sound that she thought might have been *Louise!*

"Mitchell, I'm going to come and move you away from the building, okay?"

He made another sound, this time with a rising inflection: *Louise?*

"I'm not Louise, but I'm a friend of yours and I'm going to help you, okay?"

He made a frantic affirmative sound.

She stepped out from behind the building and walked carefully toward him, as if walking through a minefield.

Did he believe she was a friend? If he didn't, could he squeeze her even if he wasn't looking at her? She cast her mind back through her own experiences and couldn't think of a time when she had squeezed someone without looking at them.

"Mitchell," she said, making her voice as soothing as possible, "I'm going to grab your legs and pull you away from the building to where you'll be safe."

He said something that might have been *Untie me!*

"I can't untie you right now, but you'll be safe."

She grabbed his feet and hauled him on his stomach up the small slope, away from the building. As soon as he got on the flat ground, he used his momentum to roll himself over, pulling his legs from Lizzy's grip.

As he was still rolling, she ran back behind the edge of the detached garage, the heat from the fire singeing the back of her neck, then looked carefully around the corner. He continued rolling until he was about fifty feet from the garage, then struggled to a sitting position and pulled the tape from his mouth.

"You're Elizabeth Ballard," he said loudly.

She was silent.

"Louise set the fire. She set the fire to cover her tracks, and she left me tied up behind the garage to burn."

Lizzy felt it was important to keep him calm. "Maybe she didn't know you were there."

"Oh, she knew I was there," he replied bitterly. "I've been in that safe room in the basement they use as the wine cellar.

There are monitors everywhere—you can see the grounds as well as the inside of the house. One of them points right at the detached garage—I remember it. I'll bet she was there, watching Castillo knock me out, watching the whole thing." His voice started to spin up. "Waiting for the fire to get to the car and explode the fuel tank. That would have been a fun way to go—burning to death with my hands tied." He bent his knees and began pulling at the ties on his ankles with his bound hands, then paused and looked toward where Lizzy stood. "That guy from Sedona—Philip Castillo—shot Millard."

Lizzy said nothing.

"Castillo injured Millard, but you killed him. You ... 'squeezed' him. That's interesting that you think of it as the squeeze," he rattled on. "I always thought of it as the crush."

Lizzy stepped tentatively out from behind the corner of the building.

"You and Castillo are going to try to get to your car," continued Mitchell.

"How do you know all this?"

"Because where you got the squeeze, I got the ability to read minds."

The heat from the fire was mounting, and she took a few steps away from the building, and toward Mitchell Pieda. "But you can squeeze people too. Or crush them."

"Not all the time. Just when Louise gave me some steroid drug she created."

"Is that what the glass container in your pocket is? With the needle?"

His tied hands went toward his jacket pocket. After a moment he said, "Yes."

"Why were you carrying it in your pocket tonight? Were you supposed to crush someone tonight?"

"No. It was just in case I ran into trouble."

"What kind of trouble were you planning to run into?" she asked, her voice turning hard.

"It was just in case," he repeated, his voice becoming a bit shrill. "Owen McNally had survived, you were probably in the area, no one knew where Castillo was. I had to go out to help my aunt. Louise didn't want me to, but she finally agreed as long as I had a way to defend myself."

"You helped George Millard hurt Uncle Owen."

"No, I was only there to read his mind. I didn't do anything to hurt him."

She was silent.

"I'm like you," he said, pleading now. "I didn't ask to be this way—I didn't ask to be able to do what I can do. Please take me with you. I just want to get out of here before the police get here."

"Why?"

"Why?" he said angrily. "Because they're going to put me in jail for killing the attorney general of Pennsylvania, and without more of the drug I won't have any squeeze to protect me. All I'll be able to do is see what my fellow prisoners are planning to do to me before they do it."

She hesitated. "Hold on, I need to talk with Philip."

As she jogged painfully back to the marble bench, she heard the distant wail of a fire engine. There was no longer anyone sitting on the bench, but in the moonlight she could see an unmoving lump on the ground nearby. She skidded to a kneeling position next to it.

"Philip!" She patted his cheek lightly, then harder. There was no response, but she could hear the labored whistle of his breath even over the crescendoing roar of the fire and the sirens. The gun was still gripped in his hand.

The fire engine had turned off the road and was now

making its way up the drive. Its wail had been joined by the distant whooping siren of a police car.

Philip stirred slightly and muttered something unintelligible as she pried his fingers from the grip of the gun.

"It's Lizzy, I'm going to get you out of here."

She examined the weapon in the light of the fire. She flipped the switch on what she thought might be the safety, but when she went to slip it into the pocket of her jacket, she realized she wasn't sure enough of what she had done to feel comfortable that she wouldn't accidentally shoot herself. She fumbled at the various levers until the magazine ejected, then pointed the gun at the ground and pulled the trigger several times to make sure there wasn't a bullet still in the gun. She put the gun in one pocket and the magazine in another.

She bent to him again and shook his uninjured shoulder. "Philip? Philip!"

There was no response.

She patted his pockets until she found the pocket knife and ran back to the detached garage. She could hear the crackle of radio calls on the other side of the house, and strobes of blue and red danced in the branches of the trees.

Mitchell had managed to move himself further back from the now blazing garage. She stopped a few dozen feet from where he sat, although she wasn't at all sure that the distance was sufficient to protect her from him if he was lying about the limits of his ability or, she realized belatedly, if he had been able to inject himself with the steroid while she was with Philip.

"Philip passed out," she yelled over the growing cacophony. "I don't want the police to get him—"

"He doesn't want to go to jail," he said. "*Back* to jail," he amended.

"Stop doing that!" yelled Lizzy.

"I can't help it," he replied.

She took a deep breath. "Fine. Then I guess you know that I've got to get him to a hospital, and I can't drive. I'm going to cut the ties on your arms and legs if you'll help me do that, or at least get him away from here. Once you do that, you can go wherever you want to. If you can really read minds, then you can tell if I'm telling you the truth."

There was a pause. "Yes, you're telling me the truth."

"But you can't use the crush anymore."

"No, I won't," he said quickly. "I just want to be out of this whole mess."

Lizzy approached Mitchell cautiously, although at the moment he didn't look very dangerous. Philip had said Mitchell was twenty-three based on his driver's license, but with the flames from the house and garage illuminating the fear on his face, he looked younger—not much more than Lizzy's seventeen years.

Another vehicle—probably a police car—had joined the fire truck on the other side of the house, and Lizzy could hear radio chatter and shouts. Another approaching siren joined the auditory fray.

She crouched by Mitchell's feet and sawed at the tie around his ankles. She could tell by his flinch that she had cut him, but he didn't make a noise. When the zip tie sprang free, she turned to cut the tie off his wrists.

He was holding his arms out, the tie holding his hands in a position like a supplicant's.

"Sorry about your ankle. I'll be more careful with your wrists," she said.

"I know you will," he said.

She cut the tie without drawing blood. Mitchell stood and staggered a bit, then gained his equilibrium.

"Is your head okay?" she asked.

He probed his scalp gingerly. "Yeah, it's okay."

"Will you be able to drive?"

"I think so."

"Okay, let's go."

She had turned back to where she had left Philip when an explosion tore through the night. She dropped to the ground, covering her head with her arms. When she looked up, the fire was burning more furiously at the side of the house, and the radio chatter had taken on a more excited tone.

"What's that?" she yelled, with no fear of being heard by the growing army of first responders on the other side of the house.

"The cars in the garage," Mitchell yelled back. That theory was supported by another explosion a few seconds later. A twisted piece of metal that looked like it might have been a rear view mirror landed on the ground a dozen feet away.

"One more," yelled Mitchell, and sure enough, less than half a minute later a third explosion tore through the night. He scrambled to his feet. "That should be all of them," he said. "What a waste."

She hauled herself up and went to Philip's still unmoving form, her pace now not much more than a limping walk. When they reached him, she said, "You take his—"

"I know," said Mitchell.

He hoisted Philip under his arms and Lizzy grabbed his legs, much as she had done with Mitchell not an hour ago. She started to tell Mitchell which way the car was, but he had already turned in that direction.

71

M itchell walked backwards, holding Philip Castillo under the arms as Lizzy staggered under the weight of his legs. Just as they reached the wooded area that bordered the lawn, he saw a pair of fire-fighters rounding the corner of the house. They found the back door open and rushed in.

He tried probing Lizzy's thoughts again. Earlier, she had been easy to read—as easy as anyone he had ever met. It was as if her earlier panic had left her mind unprotected. But as she concentrated on the task of getting Castillo to the car, the clarity of her thoughts faded a bit. What he could still sense was the pain she was fighting through: sharp pain in her back and shoulders—that was from squeezing out of a window in the basement—and a throbbing pain in her ankle—that was from the snakebite. And layered over all that, the sting of desperation and bone-deep ache of exhaustion.

As they made their way through the wood, a fourth explo-sion—no doubt the Range Rover—rang out, but Lizzy barely flinched.

They were about a hundred yards from the house when

she caught her foot on a branch and went down with a cry. He lowered Castillo's body to the ground and bent over her.

"Are you okay?" he asked, although he didn't really have to ask. Her mind was open to him once again, and he was jolted by the blue-black despair of her thoughts, so much like his mother's in the final weeks of her life as the cancer had claimed her.

Lizzy nodded miserably and tried to stand, but fell back.

"Can you make it as far as the car?" he asked.

A part of her mind answered in the negative, but she was having none of it. "I don't have any choice, do I?" she said angrily, and pushed herself to her feet.

"I think we're not too far from the road," he said.

She steadied herself on a tree. "The car is a little further down."

Mitchell looked back toward the house, now illuminated in a light show of flashers.

"Why don't I get the car and move it as close as I can."

She looked at him without speaking, her uncertainty clear in her mind and in her eyes.

"I'll come back for you. I promise," he said.

"Why?"

"What?" He hadn't seen that coming.

"Why would you come back?" she asked.

He hesitated. "It doesn't do me any good if the police find you in the woods and start asking you questions about what you were doing there and who was in the house."

Lizzy sagged against the tree trunk. "I wish I could read minds," she mumbled. Then she bent over Philip's unconscious form, dug through his pockets, and pulled out a car key with a rental tag hanging from it. She handed it to Mitchell. His fingers closed over it but she didn't let go. "Promise?" she asked.

"Promise."

She released the keys with a look of resignation.

The road was about fifty yards away. When he reached it, he grabbed a dead branch from the ground and dragged it onto the shoulder to mark where he had come out of the woods, then jogged down the road to where the car was parked.

He started up the engine, then felt his heartbeat accelerate as he became aware that the thrumming he was hearing was not only the result of the blow to his head. He lowered the window and looked up—a chopper was hovering over the house. He stared at it for a moment, slack-jawed—were the police looking for them already? Then he realized that the chopper bore the markings of one of the Philadelphia news stations on its side.

Without turning on the headlights, he coasted down the road and was able to pick out the dead branch in the moon-light. When he got out of the car, he realized that he wasn't sure what angle to take as he entered the woods, then he saw a flicker of light in the trees. He made his way toward the light and found Lizzy stooped over Castillo. She slipped the phone, with which she had signaled Mitchell, into her pocket.

The rest seemed to have revived her, and it took them only a few minutes to get Castillo to the car.

They propped him up in the back seat, then Lizzy climbed in back with him, cradling his head in her lap. Mitchell got in the driver's seat, started the car, and turned on the headlights.

Just then, a light illuminated the interior.

Mitchell glanced into the rearview mirror. "Someone's coming," he said.

"What if they stop?" Lizzy asked, her voice tremulous.

"If they stop, we'll tell them our friend is drunk and we think he's going to throw up—that should move them along."

He glanced back at Lizzy and Philip. "Do we have something to cover the blood up with?"

But there was no time—the car, an SUV, was pulling even with them. It slowed slightly, then accelerated again. As it sped away, the lights from the rental car's headlights illuminated its back.

"That's Uncle Owen's car!" Lizzy exclaimed.

"What?"

"Not the car he has now—the one he used to have, before we left Pennsylvania. That's his license plate: NUROBIO."

Mitchell knit his brow. "They had it hidden in a shed on the property," he said. "That must be Louise."

"At least she's heading in the right direction," said Lizzy. "Away."

Mitchell nodded. "Let's not worry about her right now," he said, his voice tight. "Listen, I was thinking while we were getting him to the car—we should find a restaurant or bar. We'll pull around back and roll him out. Then you can run into the restaurant and yell that there's a guy who's been shot, like you just happened to see him there. Then you run away. They'll call 911 and an ambulance will come. It will look like he got shot there—nothing to tie him to Louise or the fire. And nothing to tie either of us to him."

"As long as he doesn't have this," said Lizzy.

Mitchell turned around to see Lizzy holding up his wallet. He reached for it, but she moved it out of his reach.

"Trade you for the squeeze medicine," she said.

"What?"

"The squeeze medicine. Crush medicine. Whatever you call it—the stuff Louise Mortensen gave you to be able to give strokes."

Mitchell hesitated a moment, then reached into his jacket pocket and pulled out the case holding the vial and syringe.

He handed it to Lizzy. She unzipped the case, glanced at the contents, then zipped it back up and slipped it into her pocket. She passed him his wallet.

"Thanks," he said.

"Sure. I don't know what *I'd* do with it."

He put the wallet in his pocket, then continued. "After you let the people in the restaurant or bar know that he's in the parking lot, you can slip away in the confusion and we can meet up and get away from there." He gestured toward her face. "You have blood on your cheek." He dug in his pocket and passed a clean handkerchief back to her.

She pressed it to her cheek and winced, then examined the streak of red staining the cotton.

"I think there's a water bottle up there, can you hand it to me?"

He passed the bottle back to her and she wet the cloth and rubbed her cheek gingerly.

"So, what do you think of my plan?" he asked, although he knew already.

"Yeah, it sounds good," she said, her fatigue clear in her voice as well as her thoughts. "Let's do that."

72

Mitchell took a circuitous route that brought them to Route 1 near Longwood Gardens. When he got to the intersection, he asked, "Which way?"

"Right, I guess," said Lizzy. "That will take us toward Kennett Square." As Mitchell made the turn, she added, "My dad and I used to live not that far from here, in Parkesburg. I think there's a Wawa somewhere along here. That would be a good place—it'll be open, and we know there will be people there who can call an ambulance."

"Too many people," said Mitchell. "And probably security cameras everywhere. We need someplace that isn't a big chain."

They scanned the businesses lining the road looking for candidate locations, their slow speed less of an issue than it would have been during the daytime when the four-lane road would have been buzzing with traffic. Lizzy periodically tried to assess Philip's condition in the light of the oncoming cars' headlights.

After a few minutes, Mitchell pointed. "There, that's perfect."

He pulled off the road into the parking lot of a restaurant with a sign in front reading *Dos Sombreros*. He slowly circled the building.

"Hurry up," said Lizzy tensely.

"I don't see any cameras. This looks good." He coasted to a stop. "Ready?"

"Yes."

They stepped out of the car.

"You've got blood on your pants," he said, pointing toward her leg.

She looked down. In the dim light, she saw a smear of blood on the side of her pants where Philip's shoulder had rested.

"Maybe I should go in to the restaurant," he said.

"No, I'll go. I'm not planning to stick around long enough for anyone to ask me about it." She looked at him. "Plus, you have some blood on the arm of your coat."

He brushed ineffectually at it.

"Come on," she said, "let's get him out."

Mitchell pulled Philip out of the car, largely complying with Lizzy's hissed instructions to be careful.

Lizzy arranged Philip so he looked a bit more comfortable, then stepped back. "Is the idea that he was supposed to have been mugged?"

"I guess so," said Mitchell.

"Maybe we should take his wallet."

"Good idea."

Lizzy retrieved Philip's wallet and put it in another of her rapidly filling jacket pockets.

"Anything else we should take?" he asked.

Lizzy patted her pockets. "No, I have the duct tape and the zip ties."

"He gave you something else, didn't he?"

"It's none of your business," she said, realizing even as she said it that evidently everything she thought was, in fact, Mitchell Pieda's business.

He looked at her for a long moment, then shrugged. He looked up and down the nearly deserted highway. "I'll pick you up down there," he said, pointing to an intersection about a hundred yards from the restaurant.

"Okay."

Mitchell got in the car and drove slowly away. Lizzy didn't even watch long enough to see if he turned at the road he had pointed out—if he was planning to leave her behind, there wasn't much she could do about it now. Mind-reading ... she would give her right arm to swap abilities with Mitchell Pieda.

She checked Philip as best she could in the dark. His breathing was loud and rough. She tried to imagine what she must look like—she thought she had gotten most of the blood off her face, and hoped that the cut from the falling glass hadn't opened up again. At least her hair was too short to get messed up.

Casting one more concerned glance toward Philip, she jogged toward the restaurant entrance. The interior was cheerful with Mexican decor: piñatas hung from the ceiling, and the backs of the chairs and booths were etched with brightly colored landscapes. Despite the late hour, several of the tables were occupied: a young man and woman, probably on a date; a slightly older man and woman with two small children; a group of three teenagers.

She wrenched the door open and stepped inside.

"There's a guy in the parking lot, and it looks like he's been shot!"

THE ENTIRE RESTAURANT emptied into the parking lot, the cook leading the way. Lizzy led them to the crumpled form on the pavement. The crowd gathered around Philip, the cook kneeling next to him.

";¿Quién es?"

"I'll go get help," Lizzy said from the back of the crowd.

"No, le voy a marcar a la policía."

She remembered enough of her online Spanish classes that she knew what he had said: "No, I'm going to call the police." She had a heart-stopping moment of déjà vu: her dad trying to get her out of that train car where everything had started to fall apart—"We'll go get a doctor!"—and the conductor's shout—"No, I'll call 911."

"I'll go get help," she said again, and turned and ran.

She heard a few shouts from the crowd, but no footsteps pursuing her. When she reached the highway, she kept to the shadows of trees and bushes, just in case anyone changed their mind and decided to come after her. She turned at the intersection that Mitchell had indicated and slowed to a fast walk, trying to press a stitch out of her side with a balled fist. The road climbed away from the highway, and she had slowed to a trudge by the time she crested the hill. She could hear the wail of an approaching ambulance.

She looked down the road where it continued down the other side of the hill. Lights shone from a few houses, and somewhere nearby a dog gave a single sharp bark. There was no car parked by the side of the road.

She sank down onto the curb and began to cry.

She looked up when she heard the sound of an approaching car, too exhausted to scurry into the bushes by the road. The car glided to a halt in front of her and the driver's window whirred down.

"I was parked in a driveway a couple of houses down," said Mitchell.

She pushed herself to her feet and, wiping tears from her eyes, climbed in.

73

Lizzy gave Mitchell directions to William Penn University Hospital. As Mitchell drove—he drove the way she would expect an old man to drive, although she admittedly didn't have a lot of experience riding in cars with old men—she tapped on her phone. As they neared Essington, she said, "I need to make a stop first."

"Getting rid of the gun?"

"Stop doing that," she said angrily.

"Sorry."

"Do you need me to tell you the directions?" she asked peevishly.

"Yeah. Just to be on the safe side."

A few minutes later, he turned into the parking lot of a hotel on the banks of the Delaware River. A tarp-wrapped tiki bar overlooked piers extending over the water.

She pulled the gun out of her pocket and wiped it vigorously with the edge of her jacket. Pulling the sleeve of her jacket over her hand, she tossed it into the back seat, then got the magazine out of another pocket and wiped it down. When she was done, she glanced at Mitchell.

"Can you see what the plan is?"

He hesitated. "Not in any detail."

"You take the gun and I'll take the magazine. We go to the end of the dock and throw them in the water. I want you to throw the gun because you can probably throw it further than I can."

He nodded. "And you tossed it in the back seat so I couldn't easily get to it and put the magazine in it and have a weapon."

"Yeah."

"I think you'd be able to incapacitate me before I could do that."

"Probably. But I'd rather not have to." She opened the car door. "Don't forget to cover your hand up when you pick up the gun so you don't leave fingerprints." She climbed out of the car.

Mitchell got the gun out of the back seat and followed Lizzy to the end of the pier.

She glanced around, although the darkness beyond the dim lights on the pier would have hidden any observers. "Can you tell if anybody's out there?" she asked.

He glanced around. "No."

"I mean, could you, like, pick up their brain waves?"

"Oh." He shook his head. "No."

She sighed. "That would be handy if you could."

"Sorry."

She shrugged. "Okay, throw it out there."

Mitchell flung the gun as far as he could, although he could tell that Lizzy was disappointed it didn't go further. She drew back her arm to throw the magazine, but winced.

"Want me to throw that too?" he asked.

She nodded, and he took the magazine from her and threw it after the gun.

As they approached the car, Mitchell pushed the button to pop the trunk.

"Thanks," said Lizzy sulkily, and retrieved Philip's duffel from the back.

They climbed into the car and Mitchell pulled away. After a minute, he said, "Going to see what's in it?"

"No. It's probably just a change of underwear and a toothbrush. But whatever it is, I don't want you to know." She hugged the duffel protectively.

It was after midnight when he pulled to a stop near the hospital entrance.

Lizzy turned to him. "What are you going to do now?"

"I thought I'd leave the car somewhere near the restaurant."

"What if there's blood in the back seat?" she asked with a start. "We want them to think he was shot in the parking lot, not in the car."

"I checked while I was waiting for you," he said. "It looks like all the blood went on your pants."

"Okay." She was silent for a moment. "What are you going to do after you drop the car off?"

"I don't think I should tell you that."

She nodded and pushed the car door open.

"What are *you* going to do?" he asked.

She turned back to him. "I thought you wouldn't need to ask that."

"Of course I don't really need to, I just thought ..."

She waited, not patient, simply too tired to push herself out of the car.

"I can't see it now," Mitchell admitted.

She regarded him, then said, "I'm going to check on Uncle Owen. Then I'll find out where they took Philip and check on him. After that, I don't know." They were both silent for a long moment. The cold air from the open car door soothed the sting of the cut on her cheek. Finally, Lizzy asked, "Are you going to tell people about me?"

"No." He shook his head. "Are you going to tell people about me?"

"No." She climbed stiffly out of the car, still hugging the duffel bag in one arm, then bent to look back in. "Thanks for helping with Philip."

"Thanks for letting me go."

She swung the door shut, then watched as Mitchell pulled carefully into traffic and turned at the next street.

She held the duffel bag at her side so that it covered the bloodstains on her pants, then stepped into the hospital's lobby and crossed to the information desk. The security guard manning the desk looked up and, by the widening of his eyes, she could tell she hadn't cleaned herself up as much as she had hoped.

"I'm here to see Owen McNally. I'm his goddaughter," she said. Then, to explain her late appearance, added, "I just got in from out of town."

"Owen McNally," repeated the guard, turning to his computer and tapping the keyboard. "ICU, room six-twelve." He turned back to her. "It's past visiting hours, but if you tell them you had to travel to get here, they might let you see him. Elevators are down the hall, on your left. Take them to six and someone at the nurses station can direct you to the room." He hesitated. "Miss, are you okay? Your cheek's bleeding."

She touched her fingers to her cheek, then wiped them on her pants, over the stains of Philip's blood. She laughed shakily. "I fell outside. Tripped on a curb." She looked away from his concerned eyes. "Thanks for your help."

She tried to break into a jog toward the elevators, but was too tired to manage more than an unsteady walk. The wait at the elevator seemed interminable. When it arrived she entered, then stood dully for several seconds before she realized she hadn't pushed a button for the floor.

The doors slid open at the sixth floor. The nurse's station was unstaffed, but she could hear voices coming from down the corridor to her left. She turned right and walked down the hall, reading the room numbers and glancing into the rooms.

She had almost reached the end of the hall when a man stepped out of one of the rooms. Andy McNally.

His face, haggard for the first time that Lizzy had known him, split with a wide grin. "Aren't you a sight for sore eyes."

He opened his arms and she ran into them.

OWEN LAY ON THE BED, eyes closed, face drawn, monitors beeping quietly around him. He looked, Lizzy thought with a jolt, frail—a word she would never have expected to associate with her godfather.

"Is he okay?" she whispered.

"Yes, I think he's going to be okay. I guess in the scheme of things, it's lucky that they decided to give him a heart attack rather than having that kid from the Brashear video give him a stroke."

"I found out some things tonight," she said. "I'll tell you and Uncle Owen later." She gazed at her godfather from the foot of the bed.

"You better let him know you're okay," said Andy.

"Can I?"

"He wouldn't forgive you if you didn't."

She went to the side of the bed and leaned toward him.

"Uncle Owen?" she whispered. "It's Lizzy."

Owen stirred, then opened his eyes with an effort. They

moved around the room, unfocused, then came to rest on Lizzy.

"Lizzy?" His voice was a painful rasp. "Lizzy!"

"Here I am, Uncle Owen," she said, taking his hand. "How are you?"

"I'm fine now. How are you?"

"I have lots to tell you when you're feeling better. But for now you better just rest up. I'll sit here with you." She sank into a chair that Andy had moved up to the bed.

"Okay, Pumpkin. Just a quick nap, then you tell me ..." His eyes closed again and his breathing smoothed out into sleep.

Fifteen minutes later, Andy had gotten the highlights of the story out of Lizzy, and ten minutes after that, Lizzy and Owen were both snoring away, Lizzy slumped in the chair, covered with a blanket Andy had gotten from the nurse, her hand still gripped in Owen's.

74

Mitchell drove carefully back toward Kennett Square, nerves jangling with the expectation of seeing the flashing lights of a police car appear in the rearview mirror, but he arrived at Dos Sombreros without incident.

As he approached the restaurant, he saw that the back parking lot where they had left Philip, as well as part of a small wooded area just behind the parking lot, was cordoned off with yellow crime scene tape. Two portable pole-mounted lights, now unlit, stood just outside the tape. A police cruiser was parked in front of the restaurant, its headlights on.

Mitchell drove past the restaurant, his heart thumping, and pulled over when he was out of the cruiser's line of sight. He had planned to park as close to the restaurant as possible without actually being in the parking lot, ideally in a location where someone walking from the car to the restaurant would pass through the area where they had left Philip. That wasn't possible with the police still watching the area. He pulled into the parking lot of a darkened insurance office and shut off the ignition. It was the best he could do—if Philip Castillo recovered, he could figure out how to explain how he had gotten from there to the back parking lot of Dos Sombreros.

Mitchell got out and locked the doors, then considered what to do with the keys. Finally he shrugged and pocketed them. He'd drop them in a Dumpster somewhere, and the cops would likely think that whoever had shot Castillo and taken his wallet had taken the keys as well.

He glanced at his watch: almost one thirty. He didn't want to order a ride share originating anywhere in the vicinity of the supposed site of a shooting, and even if he did, where would he go? He supposed he'd have to make his way to his aunt's house in Jenkintown eventually. He'd tell her things hadn't worked out with the roommate from work, but it would be harder to use that story if he showed up at her house in the middle of the night, especially with bloodstains on his jacket. A jacket that was better suited for a classy party in Chester County horse country than to a nighttime walk in March.

He shoved his hands into his pockets and began walking toward the town center. The first car that passed slowed, as if it was going to stop to pick him up—that was a result of dressing decently. He waved the car away, and turned away from the road.

He sat down on a low brick wall outside a beauty salon and tapped on his phone for a few minutes, his shoulders hunched against the cold. A result popped up that seemed promising. There was a twenty-four hour urgent care center not far from where he was—he'd take a page from Dr. McNally's playbook and use it as a refuge. He did have a lump on his head that would be the perfect excuse—he'd tell them that he'd slipped and fallen. He considered the blood on the sleeve of his jacket, then removed the jacket and, trying to put the jacket's price tag out of his mind, rubbed the sleeve on the ground. He examined the results—the dirt masked the bloodstain, and it looked like the kind of stain that would result from a fall.

He started for the urgent care center, realizing immediately that his shoes as well as his jacket were ill-suited to his current needs. By the time he got to the urgent care center, he might be able to use serious blisters as a secondary excuse for his visit, although the cut on his ankle that Lizzy Ballard had made when she sliced the ties would be hard to explain.

He turned the collar of his jacket up against the night breeze and jammed his hands deeper into his pockets. He had seen enough of her thoughts to know that she concurred with his belief that Louise had left him to burn behind the garage. Louise might have talked a good game about Mitchell stepping into Gerard's shoes, might have called him the ultimate manifestation of what she wanted to create, but when her back was against the wall, she had been all too willing to sacrifice him to the flames, or at least to the authorities. And they would no doubt have quickly identified him as Louise's escort to the federal courthouse, and as the person bending over Russell Brashear as he died.

His right shoe was already rubbing a raw spot on his heel.

He was glad Owen McNally had survived. He would have been happy to leave him unconscious in the hospital room once they had learned all they could from him, to wake up confused but unharmed when the Rohypnol drug wore off. And he would be happy if Philip Castillo recovered. He didn't seem like a bad guy.

But he was nothing but glad that George Millard was out of the picture. If Lizzy Ballard could pack the same punch that Mitchell had been able to under the influence of Louise's drug, then he guessed that George Millard's end had been quicker and more painless than he deserved.

He bent down to loosen the tie of his shoe, hoping that might lessen the rubbing.

So he had finally met the infamous Elizabeth Ballard. She was just a girl, albeit a pretty one, especially if she would grow out that red crew cut. And she was tough. And powerful, based on what he had learned about her from Louise. And straightforward, based on what he himself had seen of her mind when it was open to him. And ... he searched for the right word, then realized what it was. Kind. She was kind. Even to him, whom she had every right to consider her enemy. She had known what he had done, who he had worked for, and she had let him go.

And, he thought with sudden surprise, she hadn't squeezed him.

75

The next morning, with Lizzy still sound asleep, Andy was bringing Owen up to date on Lizzy's story of the night before when Owen's breakfast arrived. He eyed the food with distaste as the nurse eyed his visitors with some misgivings.

"This is the ICU," she said to Andy. "He shouldn't be wearing himself out with visitors."

"He's not wearing himself out," said Andy. "Look how much more cheerful he looks."

Owen gave the nurse a somewhat ghastly but nonetheless heartfelt smile.

"You do look better," she said reluctantly. She turned to Andy. "But, Dr. McNally, I'm counting on you to make sure he doesn't overexert himself."

"He's the king of underexertion," said Andy.

The nurse glared at him.

"But I'll make sure he doesn't turn over a new leaf right yet."

She rolled her eyes and stalked out of the room, leaving

Owen poking disconsolately at a bowl of jello. "Could you get me an egg sandwich from the Sleeping Owl?" he asked.

"I could, but I won't. Pretend for a moment that you're a medical doctor, and consider the consequences of indulging in a cholesterol binge at the moment."

Owen pushed the bowl away and looked down at Lizzy's sleeping form. "How could I have gotten her into this situation?"

"You didn't get her into it, she got herself into it. She and this Castillo guy."

"But I could have—"

"No, you couldn't have. You did everything you could to help her. She decided to go to Pocopson, and she knew the risks."

Owen was silent for a minute, patting Lizzy's hair. He pointed to the blanket that had fallen away from her shoulders. "Can you pull that up?" he asked.

Andy adjusted the blanket.

Owen leaned his head back on the pillows. "So George Millard is dead. If what Mitchell Pieda told Lizzy was true—that he can only squeeze people in a major way when he's on the drug that Louise Mortensen gave him—then we don't need to worry too much about him right now. Lizzy took the drug from him, and it doesn't seem likely he'll be getting more from Mortensen—it sounds like being left to burn to death behind the garage means he's not likely to be teaming up with her again anytime soon. It does seem likely that she escaped somewhere, and if she was planning to come here and finish me off, she would have gotten here before Lizzy, right?"

"Maybe," said Andy, sounding unconvinced.

"So what now?"

"I can check on Castillo, see what his condition is."

"Where would they have taken him?"

"Chester County ... Brandywine ... Mercy ... maybe even Christiana. I'll find out."

"When Lizzy wakes up, she's going to want to go to see him."

Andy ran his fingers through his hair. "Yeah, I know. I'm not sure what to do about that. Of course it would be best if we could keep our distance from Castillo. Him not having a wallet isn't going to stop them from figuring out who he is, especially since he has a prison record. They're going to know he's from Arizona and wonder why he's out here. If we knew he was going to keep his connection to Lizzy secret—assuming he recovers—then it would take some digging to connect Lizzy, or you, with him. But I don't think we can assume that."

"He doesn't seem like the kind of person who would spill his guts to the authorities," said Owen.

"Maybe not intentionally, but you know that people are confused when they regain consciousness after a trauma like that. He could easily say something before he has his wits about him. And if he dies, the police are going to be digging for details about why he was out here. Either way, it looks less suspicious if we've acknowledged the connection than if the police find out on their own. We could say that you had taken Lizzy to Sedona to recover from her father's death, she had gone to Castillo for counseling and benefited from it, you guys came back here thinking she was better, she had a relapse, and you asked Castillo to come out here for more counseling."

"Why was he in Kennett Square at Dos Sombreros?"

Andy shrugged. "Had a hankering for good Mexican."

Owen considered. "It's a little thin, but not totally unrealistic. I'm sure Lizzy would be happier with that approach than having us just abandon him—regardless of the outcome." He looked down at her again. "She's going to want to go to whatever hospital they took him to one way or the other."

"Maybe, but I'm not sure enough that Louise Mortensen has hit the road to leave you here alone."

Owen smiled weakly. "An insoluble dilemma."

Andy suddenly grinned. "Not necessarily."

WHEN LIZZY FINALLY WOKE, she was blinded for a moment by the bright morning sun pouring in the window. When she had blinked away the dazzle, she saw three sets of eyes examining her with concern.

"Ruby!" Lizzy tried to jump up, but every part of her body protested. She limped to the woman who stood at the end of the bed.

When Lizzy was four, Gerard Bonnay had arranged for Ruby DiMano to get a job as the Ballards' housekeeper so she could report back to him on Lizzy's behavior and Charlotte Ballard's gradually deteriorating condition. Ruby had been with the Ballards through Charlotte's death from a stroke and until Patrick's death at George Millard's hands. Patrick's death had been the turning point for Ruby. She had secretly withdrawn from her unwilling alliance with Bonnay and assisted Owen and Andy McNally in getting Lizzy away from Bonnay and Mortensen.

She folded Lizzy in her bony arms, then held her out at arm's length. "Your hair is very short."

Lizzy ran her hand across her head. "Yeah."

"And very red."

Lizzy smiled. "Yeah."

"It's fetching," said Ruby.

Lizzy laughed. "You think so?"

Ruby smiled. "I do."

"What time is it?" asked Lizzy.

Andy glanced at his watch. "About ten o'clock."

Lizzy gave a start. "Ten o'clock? We have to find Philip!"

"I found him," said Andy. "He's at Mercy. I'll take you there."

"Is he okay?"

"He's hanging in there. I couldn't get much detail over the phone. It'll be easier to get information in person."

Lizzy turned to Ruby. "Why are you here? Not that I don't love seeing you, but I didn't want to get you involved again."

"She's just here on babysitting duty," said Andy. "So Owen won't get lonely when you and I go to visit this Castillo character."

"And I brought you some fresh clothes," said Ruby, holding up a bag.

"Thanks," Lizzy said gratefully.

She went into the bathroom, bringing Philip's duffel bag to put her old clothes in, and pulled the new clothes out of the bag. There was a pair of jeans decorated with a pattern of tiny rhinestones on the back pockets, a fuzzy pink sweater, socks with a pink and orange floral pattern, a pair of pink sneakers, and a puffy pink jacket. She also found underwear, a prim cotton nightgown, a toothbrush and toothpaste, deodorant, and a comb and brush. She smiled—evidently no one had told Ruby that, with her new hairstyle, she hadn't had to comb her hair for a month.

She brushed her teeth, then removed her clothes. When she tried to take her shirt off, though, she found with a stomach-turning jolt that it was stuck to her back. She would have to soak the shirt off later—once she could find a bathtub, and the time for a long, hot bath.

She pulled the pink sweater over her shirt and donned the rest of the new clothes. The pink sneakers were too small, so she put her boots back on. She removed the contents of her jacket pockets, including Philip's wallet, and put everything into the duffel bag.

She stepped out of the bathroom, carrying the parka, just in time to hear Andy tell an irritated-looking nurse, "Just a couple more minutes, I swear."

"That's what you said an hour ago, Dr. McNally."

"Oh, so now I'm 'Dr. McNally'?"

"That's what you said an hour ago, *Andy.*"

Andy saw Lizzy and heaved a sigh of relief. "Okay, we're almost ready to go. Except that Miss DiMano"—he indicated Ruby—"is going to stay with my brother."

The nurse grimaced. "Andy—!"

"Robin!" he parroted back, then leaned toward her. "I'll buy you dinner."

She rolled her eyes. "As long as *you're* gone in five minutes, I'll try to exercise some latitude." She turned and marched away.

"Dr. McNally, it looks like you've lost your touch," said Ruby.

"Nonsense," said Andy. "She's just playing hard to get." He turned to Lizzy. "Look at you, all gussied up!"

"I love the clothes. Thank you, Ruby," said Lizzy, crossing to Ruby, who blushed with pleasure.

Lizzy couldn't contain a wince when Ruby hugged her, and Ruby stepped back. "Are you okay?" she asked.

"Yeah, just sore, I guess," replied Lizzy, then turned to Andy. "Can we go now?"

"The sooner the better," he replied. "Before I get in more trouble."

76

The emergency room at Mercy Hospital, where the ambulance had taken Philip, was the same place that Owen, Andy, and Ruby had arranged Lizzy's escape from Gerard Bonnay and Louise Mortensen three months earlier. However, it was unfamiliar to Lizzy, who had been in no condition—either arriving or departing—to notice her surroundings.

When Andy pulled into a space in the parking lot of the hospital, Lizzy had the door open almost before the car came to a stop.

"Hold on there, Wonder Woman."

Lizzy turned to him, impatient. "What?"

"I should go in by myself. I know a couple of the people in the ER from back in December, and I can probably find out more if I talk to them one-on-one."

Lizzy scowled at him, then sighed. "I guess you're right. Let me know as soon as you find out anything, okay?"

Andy had been gone only a few minutes when she got a text.

Lost a lot of blood and is in ICU now. Will see if I can find out more.

Lizzy texted back: *Can I see him?*

Not yet.

A few minutes later, Andy emerged from the hospital and gave her a thumbs-up. He crossed the parking lot and dropped into the driver's seat.

"I don't have a lot more to tell you—he was in rough shape when he arrived, but they got him patched up and they seem pretty confident that he'll recover."

Lizzy slumped back in her seat and felt tears of relief spring to her eyes. "That's good. That's really good." She sat forward. "Will I be able to see him when he's out of ICU?"

"Yes."

"When will that be?"

"Probably not for a day or two."

Lizzy chewed her lip. "Maybe someone should stay with him, like Ruby is staying with Uncle Owen."

"I think he'll be fine as long as he's in the ICU. The police are obviously going to be interested in him, which has its drawbacks, but also its benefits in that they'll be keeping a close eye on him. When he gets out of ICU, we can ask Ruby to keep him company until he's discharged."

A small smile smoothed the lines on Lizzy's forehead. "I'd like to be around to see how that goes."

"Want to get back to Owen?"

"Yes, please."

"First we need to stop for—" Andy glanced at his watch. "—a very late breakfast. That sound okay?"

"Yeah, it does—I'm starving."

At Lizzy's request, Andy drove to Jimmy John's while Lizzy sent Ruby a text message about Philip's condition. Any route from Mercy to anywhere east inevitably took a traveler via

Route 1 through Kennett Square, and as they passed Dos Sombreros, Lizzy saw two police cars in the back parking lot, with an officer taking down the crime scene tape.

"That seems like a good sign," she said to Andy.

"Let's hope so," he replied.

After a meal at Jimmy's—several frankfurters for Andy and a breakfast sandwich for Lizzy—they stopped in King of Prussia to pick up Owen and Lizzy's luggage and check Lizzy out of the Motel 6, then returned to Penn U Hospital. They found Owen sleeping and Ruby perusing the news sites on her phone.

"Looks like that fire did quite a number on the house," she whispered. She showed Lizzy and Andy a video of an aerial view of the remains of the Pocopson house.

As Ruby and Andy watched the video, Lizzy lowered herself into a chair and felt her eyes drifting shut.

"You need a better place to have a rest than the guest chair of a hospital room," whispered Ruby.

"Why don't we get you a room at the William Penn Hotel?" said Andy. "It's close by, and you can stay there until Owen's discharged."

"That sounds good," said Lizzy, her voice revealing more weariness than she intended.

"Want to go there now?" asked Andy.

"I think I'll sit with Uncle Owen for a little bit."

"I could go reserve the room so it's ready when you are," he said.

"I'll go with you," said Ruby. "I wouldn't mind stretching my legs."

Andy turned to Lizzy. "Do you mind being here alone?"

"No."

Ruby spoke up. "I think that having Lizzy standing guard will be the best protection the two of them can have."

"True," he said. He crooked his arm. "Miss DiMano?"

Ruby blushed and hooked her hand over his elbow.

They left the room, and Lizzy smiled at the thought of the odd couple they would make at the reservation desk. She pulled the chair nearer to Owen's bed, got out her phone, and pulled up the video Ruby had shown them.

Most of the upper structure of the Pocopson house had burned away—only the kitchen was still intact—exposing the basement rooms like a structural cutaway. She leaned back in the chair. She could imagine how it had happened: Louise in the room behind the metal door at the end of the basement hallway, Millard setting a trap for Philip in the movie room using a video of Louise at a conference; Louise leaving the safe room after Millard was dead and turning off the power at the panel in the utility room while Lizzy tended to Philip in the movie room, then climbing the stairs and locking the door behind her. Then she must have set the fire—there was no other explanation. From there she had made her way to the shed where Mitchell had said Uncle Owen's SUV was hidden. Maybe she had looked back and seen the flames spread from the house to the maple tree to the detached garage, behind which, if Mitchell were to be believed, she knew he lay.

And where was Louise Mortensen now? Far away, she hoped—the queen retiring from the game now that her knight and pawn had been removed from the board.

But had they both been removed? They no longer had to fear George Millard—her stomach flipped at the memory of that moment in the basement when she had struck him down—but what about Mitchell Pieda? Had she been right to let him go? Not that she had much choice—she couldn't imagine how else she could have gotten Philip away from Pocopson without his help. But was Mitchell no longer a threat? Wasn't there a move in chess where the pawn could be transformed into the most powerful piece on the board?

She thought of the phone number Philip had given her, and repeated it again to cement it in her mind. Philip had said she could call the number if she needed a new identity. Would she need to use it? She would ask him when he was out of the ICU.

She thought of the vial and syringe she had taken from Mitchell. She unzipped Philip's duffel to examine them more closely, then noticed Philip's wallet. She pulled it out, turned it in her hand, then opened it a bit guiltily. It contained a driver's license, a bank debit card, and a healthy supply of cash. She was about to close it when she noticed a small interior pocket. She opened it and pulled out a photo.

It showed two men—one younger, one old. The younger man was Philip Castillo, one arm slung around the old man's shoulders, the other giving a thumbs-up. The old man, grinning widely, had his arm around Philip's waist and was holding a hand-lettered sign: *3 Months To Go!* The *3* was smudged, as if other numbers had been written in that space and erased. The bit of background suggested an institutional setting. Lizzy flipped the photo over. A date had been handwritten on the back—the picture had been taken in December.

Lizzy leaned her head back on the chair. This had to be Oscar. Oscar, who was in prison for twenty years for murder. Whose friend, Philip Castillo, had evidently visited once a month with an updated sign, counting down to what could only be Oscar's release date. A release date that would have been this month. And sometime between *3 Months To Go!* and the end of his sentence, Tobe Hanrick had knifed Oscar in the cafeteria line. She felt tears burn her eyes. No wonder Philip wanted revenge.

She thought of George Millard, her own Tobe Hanrick, and the list of assignments that Gerard Bonnay and Louise Mortensen had sent him on. What if rather than running away from him when he had caught up with her in Smoketown, she had squeezed him? It was likely that neither Uncle Owen or Philip would have ended up in the hospital, fighting for their lives. What if she had squeezed Gerard Bonnay not after her father was dead, but before? What if someone with her ability had squeezed Louise Mortensen before she had made that first, horrifying modification to the fertility treatments to which she had subjected her unknowing patients— the treatments that resulted in freaks like her and Mitchell Pieda. And no doubt others.

How much suffering and how many deaths of innocent people could have been avoided if Gerard Bonnay and Louise Mortensen had been killed before they started down the path that had led to here?

How much suffering and how many deaths of innocent people like Oscar could be avoided if Tobe Hanrick were killed before he went further down the path that he would take?

Owen stirred and she sat forward.

He opened his eyes, saw her, and smiled. "Pumpkin. How are you doing?"

"I'm fine. We checked on Philip. He's in the ICU at Mercy Hospital but it sounds like he's going to be okay."

"I'm glad to hear that." Owen fumbled at the controls on the side of the bed.

"What do you want?" asked Lizzy.

"I want to make this thing go up so it's easier to talk."

Lizzy stood and operated the control and the top of the bed whirred up. She looked him over carefully. "You look better," she said.

He made a small hrumphing noise.

"No, it's true—you have a little bit more color in your face, and you look a little more rested."

"I could hardly help but look a little more rested—I haven't been doing anything other than napping."

Lizzy extracted a pillow from behind his head, fluffed it up, and repositioned it. "That's exactly what you're supposed to be doing."

"Now you have two invalids on your hands," he said apologetically.

"You're not an invalid, and Andy and Ruby are here to help."

He patted her hand where it rested on the metal gate of the bed. "You're a sweet girl, Pumpkin."

She pulled the chair closer to the bed and sat down.

After a moment, Owen asked, "What now? I'm still not thinking straight. Do we have a plan?"

"Let's wait for you and Philip to get better, then we'll decide."

"Back to Sedona?" he asked, a tired smile on his lips.

"Not for me," said Lizzy. "I'm not running away anymore. If Louise Mortensen is looking for me, she knows where to find me."

EPILOGUE

A middle-aged man, his tie knotted in a jacked-up half Windsor that hung loose from his neck, his eyes bleary from lack of sleep, sipped coffee from a large Wawa cup and gazed morosely across the gutted remains of the Pocopson home. The sun had come up about an hour before and was only now starting to take the chill out of the early morning air.

A younger man slogged toward him across a lawn made mucky by the water the fire companies had poured on the building.

"Hey, Brady, what have you got?" asked the older man when the younger one reached him.

"Body of a male on the basement level. Driver's license says George Millard. Not badly burned—maybe died of smoke inhalation, although it looks like Mr. Millard took a bullet to the thigh before he died. And it looks like he was prepared to try to defend himself because he was wearing a shoulder holster and holding a Sig Sauer." He flipped a page in his notebook. "We found an open window in the basement, with furniture piled up like someone got out that way. And there are some stains on the walls of the window well that could be blood—we're checking that out."

"Someone forced their way *out* of the house?"

"Looks that way."

They looked up as a news helicopter banked toward the house, then maneuvered for a position that would give them the best shot of the damage.

The older man sighed. "How about the cause of the fire?"

"Gotta be arson. The fire chief says that there's not just one origination point—fires started in a number of rooms, all about the same time. It appears that the fire started near the outside walls and worked its way in. We're guessing someone put a match to the drapes, but not just any old drapes. The bits that are left look like they are impregnated with an accelerant."

"What the hell—?"

"Looks like whoever did the decorating wanted the option to be able to torch the place on demand."

"Jesus." The older man shook his head. "Who are the owners?"

"Gerard Bonnay and Louise Mortensen. Husband and wife, ran the Vivantem fertility clinic in Center City. Bonnay died back in December, Mortensen is under investigation by the AG's office. We haven't been able to locate her yet."

The older man sighed again and wiped a hand down his face.

"Anything else?"

"Broken vodka bottle in the kitchen."

"What?"

Brady shrugged.

They stood in silence, watching the fire investigators, dressed in protective gear, clamber over the remains of the building.

After a moment, the older man said, "Busy night last night. I heard there was a shooting in Kennett Square."

"Yeah, some guy mugged behind Dos Sombreros. Took a bullet in the shoulder. He's at Mercy."

"How's he doing?"

"Still unconscious, but they say he should make it."

"Local?"

"Don't know. No wallet, no ID. Folks at the hospital think he might be a doctor. He had some medical-type documents in his pocket."

"And they can't tell who he is based on the documents?"

Brady shrugged again. "No doctors' names listed on them. Also, he has a tattoo that's not like what I would expect a doc to have. A big castle on his arm, with initials worked into it: OR. Not referring to any organization we're aware of. Maybe a girlfriend."

"Run the tattoo through the system, see if there are any hits on it."

"We're on it."

The older man took a sip of his cold coffee, grimaced, and tossed out the dregs. "Let's get the mugging cleared up ASAP. We're going to be spending a lot of time figuring out what Louise Mortensen and George Millard were up to."

END OF BOOK 2

NEXT IN THE LIZZY BALLARD THRILLER SERIES ...

Book 3: *The Iron Ring*

She has a promise to fulfill ... but she never anticipated the evil that awaited her at the end of her journey. Will keeping her word cost her everything?

Lizzy Ballard is headed to the Red Rock Country of Arizona on a mission of vengeance ... and although she doesn't know it yet, the Vivantem forces are no longer her biggest problem.

She and her allies have attracted the attention of a reclusive billionaire, a man who is determined to enlist them to his own cause ... willingly or unwillingly. Even Lizzy's enemies at Vivantem seem to be no match for his power.

With the lines of communication cut, Lizzy struggles to understand exactly who the enemy is. And when Lizzy faces the killer, even her special ability can't protect her.

Will Lizzy grab the iron ring, or be left on the field of battle?

Find out in the third installment of the Lizzy Ballard Thrillers Trilogy, *The Iron Ring*!

Join Matty Dalrymple's occasional email newsletter (mattydalrymple.com > About & Contact) and receive an Ann Kinnear Suspense Short and notifications of book launches and author events!

ALSO BY MATTY DALRYMPLE

The Lizzy Ballard Thrillers

Rock Paper Scissors (Book 1)

Snakes and Ladders (Book 2)

The Iron Ring (Book 3)

The Lizzy Ballard Thrillers Ebook Box Set

The Ann Kinnear Suspense Novels

The Sense of Death (Book 1)

The Sense of Reckoning (Book 2)

The Falcon and the Owl (Book 3)

A Furnace for Your Foe (Book 4)

The Ann Kinnear Suspense Novels Ebook Box Set - Books 1-3

The Ann Kinnear Suspense Shorts

All Deaths Endure

Close These Eyes

May Violets Spring

Sea of Troubles

Write in Water

Non-Fiction

Taking the Short Tack: Creating Income and Connecting with Readers Using Short Fiction (with Mark Leslie Lefebvre)

The Indy Author's Guide to Podcasting for Authors: Creating Connections, Community, and Income

ABOUT THE AUTHOR

Matty Dalrymple is the author of the Ann Kinnear Suspense Novels *The Sense of Death*, *The Sense of Reckoning*, *The Falcon and the Owl* and *A Furnace for Your Foe*; the Ann Kinnear Suspense Shorts, including *Close These Eyes* and *Sea of Troubles*; and the Lizzy Ballard Thrillers *Rock Paper Scissors, Snakes and Ladders*, and *The Iron Ring*. Matty and her husband, Wade Walton, live in Chester County, Pennsylvania, and enjoy vacationing on Mt. Desert Island, Maine, and in Sedona, Arizona, locations that serve as settings for Matty's stories.

Matty is a member of Mystery Writers of America, Sisters in Crime, and the Brandywine Valley Writers Group.

Go to www.mattydalrymple.com > About & Contact for more information and to sign up for Matty's occasional email newsletter.

facebook.com/matty.dalrymple

twitter.com/mattydalrymple

instagram.com/matty.dalrymple

ACKNOWLEDGMENTS

Thanks to all the people who shared their expertise on various aspects of the story: Nancy Gable, Jane Gorman, Donna Yates Kling, Jen Lawrence, Vance Martin, and Jeffrey Walton.

Special thanks to Austin Conley of the Delaware Museum of Natural History; Sergeant Aaron Dick of the Coconino County Sheriff's Office; David L. Fried, MD, FACP; Ken Fritz, FF/EMT-P; Linda R. Liotti D.O. (a.k.a. author Linda Rawlins); and Sergeant Rodger Ollis of the Coatesville Police Department.

Thanks to editor Marta Tanrikulu for taking this craft on its shakedown cruise.

Thanks to Mary Dalrymple for her multiple reads of the evolving book and her unflagging enthusiasm about my authorial endeavors.

And, as always, thanks to my partner in crime, Wade Walton, for his tireless support and encouragement.

Any deviations from strict accuracy—intentional or unintentional—are solely the responsibility of the author.

ISBN-13: 978-0-9862675-3-6 (Paperback edition)

ISBN: 978-0-9862675-7-4 (Large print edition)